AURORA'S END

Shauna

AURORA'S END

AURORA CYCLE_03

AMIE KAUFMAN & JAY KRISTOFF

EMBER

Text copyright © 2021 by LaRoux Industries Pty Ltd. and Neverafter Pty Ltd.
Cover art copyright © 2021 by Charlie Bowater

All rights reserved. Published in the United States by Ember, an imprint of Random House Children's Books, a division of Penguin Random House LLC, New York. Originally published in hardcover in the United States by Alfred A. Knopf, an imprint of Random House Children's Books, a division of Penguin Random House LLC, New York, in 2021.

Ember and the E colophon are registered trademarks of Penguin Random House LLC.

Visit us on the Web! GetUnderlined.com

Educators and librarians, for a variety of teaching tools, visit us at RHTeachersLibrarians.com

Library of Congress Cataloging-in-Publication Data is available upon request.
ISBN 978-1-5247-2088-9 (trade) — ISBN 978-1-5247-2089-6 (lib. bdg.) —
ISBN 978-1-5247-2090-2 (ebook) — ISBN 978-1-5247-2091-9 (pbk.)

Printed in the United States of America
10 9 8 7 6 5 4 3 2 1
First Ember Edition 2022

For the members of our squads
we'd be lost without:

Amanda,

Brendan,

and now Pip.

STUFF YOU SHOULD KNOW

▶ **SERIES: AURORA CYCLE**

▼ **CAST**

AURORA JIE-LIN O'MALLEY—THE GIRL OUT OF TIME. CENTURIES AGO, HER COLONY SHIP, THE *HADFIELD*, WAS BOUND FOR OCTAVIA III. WE NOW KNOW IT'S A GOOD THING SHE DIDN'T MAKE IT THERE BECAUSE VERY BAD, VERY . . . BOTANICAL THINGS HAPPENED TO THE COLONISTS WHO DID. UNFORTUNATELY, THIS INCLUDES HER DAD.

MORE ABOUT HIM IN A MOMENT.

AFTER JOINING FORCES WITH SQUAD 312 OF THE AURORA LEGION, AURI STARTED HAVING PROPHETIC DREAMS, EXHIBITING TELEKINETIC POWERS, AND GENERALLY TRANSFORMING INTO A SMALL BUT DETERMINED SUPERHERO. SHE LEARNED HER POWERS HAD BEEN GIFTED TO HER BY THE ESHVAREN, A MYSTERIOUS RACE WHO DEFEATED THE RA'HAAM EONS AGO.

KNOWING THEIR ANCIENT FOE WAS ONLY SLUMBERING, THE ESHVAREN LEFT BEHIND A WEAPON, AND A WAY FOR THE TRIGGER OF THAT WEAPON TO UNDERTAKE TRAINING IN ITS USE.

INSIDE THE ECHO, A PSYCHIC TRAINING SPACE, AURI MASTERED HER POWERS—AND PRACTICED SOME OTHER THINGS WITH HER BOYFRIEND, KAL. SHE EMERGED, READY TO TAKE DOWN THE RA'HAAM, ONLY TO DISCOVER THAT SOMEONE ELSE HAD ALREADY STOLEN THE WEAPON.

ALSO TRAINED AS A TRIGGER, THE SYLDRATHI WARLORD KNOWN AS THE STARSLAYER HAD USED THE WEAPON TO DESTROY HIS OWN PLANET'S SUN, AND WAS NOW THREATENING EARTH WITH IT. OH, AND TURNS OUT HE'S KAL'S DAD. *THAT* WAS A CONVERSATION THAT DID NOT END WELL.

LAST SEEN: ABOARD THE WEAPON, A CRYSTAL SHIP, FIGHTING THE STARSLAYER FOR CONTROL OF ITS PLANET-SHATTERING, UNDERWEAR-SOILING POWER.

TYLER JERICHO JONES—THE LEADER TURNED FUGITIVE. WHEN TYLER JOINED THE AURORA LEGION, HE NEVER IMAGINED HIS SQUAD WOULD BE FULL OF THE ACADEMY'S BOTTOM-OF-THE-BARREL CHOICES. THEN AGAIN, HE NEVER IMAGINED HE'D END UP ON THE RUN FROM HALF THE GALAXY, ROBBING BANKS AND RANSACKING SHIPWRECKS, LET ALONE TEAMING UP WITH THE MEANEST SYLDRATHI WARRIOR HE'S EVER LAID EYES ON.

DID I MENTION SHE'S KAL'S SISTER, SAEDII? THAT BOY HAS A *LOT* OF SKELETONS IN HIS CLOSET.

ANYWAY, TYLER USED HIS TACTICAL BRILLIANCE AND UNPARALLELED DIMPLES TO LEAD HIS SQUAD'S ESCAPE FROM OCTAVIA TO EMERALD CITY, WHERE THEY HEISTED A FAT STACK OF CASH, A BOX OF MYSTERIOUS GIFTS LEFT LONG BEFORE ANY OF THESE SHENANIGANS BEGAN, AND THE KEYS TO A VERY, VERY FANCY NEW SHIP.

IN THE MIDDLE OF STEALING THE *HADFIELD*'S BLACK BOX, THE GANG WAS TAKEN PRISONER BY THE AFOREMENTIONED SYLDRATHI WARRIOR, SAEDII. ONE DRAKKAN PIT FIGHT LATER, TY FOUND HIMSELF CAPTURED BY THE GLOBAL INTELLIGENCE AGENCY (AKA THE GIA) ALONGSIDE HIS NEW SYLDRATHI ENEMY.

HE LEARNED MANY THINGS, INCLUDING WHAT SHE LOOKS LIKE IN HER UNDERWEAR, AND THAT HE AND SCARLETT ARE NOT HUMAN, AS THEY THOUGHT, BUT THAT THEIR MOTHER WAS A SYLDRATHI WAYWALKER.

LAST SEEN: ON THE RUN WITH HIS NEW FRENEMY, SAEDII.

KALIIS IDRABAN GILWRAETH—THE MISUNDERSTOOD WARRIOR. FROM THE HIGHS OF FINDING A NEW FAMILY IN SQUAD 312 AND FINDING LOVE WITH PSYCHIC WEAPON AURORA TO THE LOWS OF HIS UNMASKING AS THE SON

OF THE STARSLAYER AND HIS EXPULSION FROM THE SQUAD, KAL HAS HAD QUITE A TIME RECENTLY.

CAST OUT FOR OMITTING THE TEENSY DETAIL THAT HE WAS THE SON OF THEIR ARCHENEMY, HE RETURNED TO THE FAMILY FOLD. BUT, *TWIST!* HE REMAINED LOYAL TO AURORA, AND FOUGHT BESIDE HER WHEN SHE ARRIVED TO TAKE ON HIS FATHER.

LAST SEEN: UNDER PSYCHIC ASSAULT ABOARD THE ESHVAREN WEAPON.

SCARLETT ISOBEL JONES—THE FABULOUS ONE, INSTALLER OF MY PERSONALITY PROGRAM, LIGHT OF MY LIFE. SHE ALSO KNOWS WHERE MY OFF SWITCH IS.

THE WORDS "IF SHE ONLY APPLIED HERSELF" APPEARED MORE ON SCAR'S ACADEMY REPORTS THAN ON ANY OTHER CADET'S IN HISTORY, BUT HER UNCANNY EMPATHY (OR NOT-SO-UNCANNY, IF YOU KNOW HER MOTHER WAS A SYLDRATHI WAYWALKER, WHICH SCAR DOES NOT) AND ABSOLUTE LOYALTY TO HER TWIN BROTHER, TYLER, SAW HER CAREENING ACROSS THE GALAXY WITH SQUAD 312, NEVER ONCE CHIPPING A NAIL.

DURING THEIR TIME ON THE RUN, THE SQUAD DISCOVERED A COLLECTION OF GIFTS AT THE DOMINION REPOSITORY, LEFT FOR THEM MANY YEARS BEFORE THEY'D EVEN JOINED THE AURORA LEGION. SCAR SCORED THE BEST ONE—A NECKLACE INSET WITH A CLUSTER OF DIAMONDS. THEY ARE, AS EVERYONE KNOWS, A GIRL'S BEST FRIEND.

AFTER TYLER WAS TAKEN PRISONER BY THE GIA, SCARLETT AND THE OTHERS PUSHED ON TO HELP AURORA RETAKE THE WEAPON FROM THE STARSLAYER, SAVE EARTH, AND GET ON WITH THE JOB OF KILLING THE RA'HAAM BEFORE IT WAKES UP AND EATS THE GALAXY. NO BIG.

Last seen: About to make out (!!!) with Finian (!!!), but thwarted at the last moment by his realization that the diamonds on her necklace aren't diamonds at all but Eshvaren crystal (!!!).

Oh yeah, and then everything exploded.

Finian de Karran de Seel—The one who really does grow on you, once you get to know him. Resident Betraskan mechanical genius, Finian's proven his loyalty to Squad 312 over and over.

He might have softened his abrasive exterior, but you can pry his smart-assery from his cold, dead hands. Which you might yet get to do, given that the last thing he, Scarlett, and Zila saw at the end of our last volume was a blinding flash of light in the middle of a giant space battle to defend Earth from a very cranky Starslayer.

Last seen: Interrupting his own lifelong dream of kissing (!!!) Scarlett Jones (!!!) with his necklace realization. This boy needs to get out of his own way, seriously.

Zila Madran—The one with the earrings. And the brain the size of a planet.

Although Zila's squad thought for quite some time that she was a straight-up sociopath—and in their defense, she did show a very unhealthy affection for her disruptor's Stun setting—we've since learned that as a child she saw her parents killed as they tried to protect her, and that she's been alone in the galaxy ever since.

Pulling off some considerable badassery, including rescuing

Squad 312 from imprisonment on Saedii's ship, she's upped her game from theoretical to practical, and slowly but surely, the ice seems to be melting.

Last seen: Getting blown into her component molecules, along with Scarlett and Finian, during the battle to save Earth.

Catherine Brannock—The fallen comrade. Best friend to Tyler and Scarlett, and the pilot for Squad 312, Cat "Zero" Brannock was an ace without equal.

She was consumed by the Ra'haam as the squad fled Octavia, but that wasn't the last we saw of her. Now she's a part of the Ra'haam, and it's been using her knowledge to pursue Aurora, Tyler, and the rest of the squad. It's not above using her familiar face, either. When Tyler was taken prisoner, she interrogated him as part of the GIA.

Last seen: Firing a bunch of missiles at Tyler's favorite face.

Caersan, Archon of the Unbroken—Every family's got one, and he's Kal's. It's helpful to know Syldrathi politics here.

So the Syldrathi are split up into cabals, yes? The Warbreed are the warriors (the hint's in the name, really), and when the Syldrathi signed a peace accord with the Terrans and Betraskans, the warriors, well . . . they'd have preferred to keep fighting.

A pack of them dubbed themselves the Unbroken and started a Syldrathi civil war. They were led by Caersan, Archon of the Unbroken, aka the Starslayer. He earned the name by stealing the Eshvaren Weapon that Auri was training to use, and blowing

UP HIS OWN PLANET'S SUN IN AN EPIC POWER MOVE THAT CONVINCED EVERYBODY ELSE TO STAY *RIGHT* OUT OF HIS WAY WHILE HE MADE WAR ON HIS OWN PEOPLE.

HIS SON, KAL, WANTED NOTHING TO DO WITH HIM AND SPLIT TO JOIN THE AURORA LEGION INCOGNITO. WE'VE SEEN HOW WELL THAT WORKED OUT FOR HIM.

HIS DAUGHTER, SAEDII, REMAINED LOYAL, AND WHEN SHE AND TYLER WERE TAKEN PRISONER BY THE GIA, HE MADE IT QUITE CLEAR THAT HE WAS PREPARED TO BLOW UP EARTH TO GET HER BACK.

LAST SEEN: PSYCHIC-WRESTLING AURI FOR CONTROL OF SAID WEAPON.

SAEDII GILWRAETH—THE SCARY SISTER. WHILE KAL AND HIS MOTHER LEFT CAERSAN AT A YOUNG AGE, KAL'S SISTER CHOSE TO STICK WITH HER FATHER. SHE NOW SERVES AS ONE OF HIS TEMPLARS, COMMANDING A HUGE AND TERRIFYING BATTLESHIP, AND A SIGNIFICANT PART OF HIS FLEET.

SHE'S BEAUTIFUL, SHE'S DEADLY, AND SHE'S GOT A NECKLACE OF FORMER SUITORS' THUMBS AROUND HER NECK, SO YOU SHOULD REALLY THINK TWICE BEFORE YOU TRY HITTING ON HER.

AFTER A COUPLE OF THE UNBROKEN PICKED UP KAL'S NAME DURING A BAR FIGHT BACK ON SEMPITERNITY, SHE TRACKED THE GANG FROM EMERALD CITY TO THE WRECK OF THE *HADFIELD*, WHERE SHE TOOK THEM PRISONER. AFTER THAT CAME THAT WHOLE THING WITH THE DRAKKAN PIT FIGHT, AND SHE AND TYLER WERE TAKEN PRISONER BY THE GLOBAL INTELLIGENCE AGENCY. THE GIA, CORRUPTED BY THE RA'HAAM, WAS TRYING TO START AN INTERPLANETARY INCIDENT TO DEFLECT ATTENTION FROM ITS QUICKLY RIPENING NURSERY PLANETS. IT'S ALL REALLY QUITE COMPLICATED.

She grudgingly admits Tyler turned out to be semi-useful during their escape.

Last seen: Making a break for it with Tyler Jones.

The Eshvaren—The mysterious aliens. Eons ago, the Eshvaren fought the Ra'haam to stop it from taking over all life in the galaxy, and they won.

Well, almost.

The Ra'haam was actually driven into hiding, waiting approximately a bazillion years to regain its strength.

Knowing they wouldn't be around by the time Round 2 kicked off, the Eshvaren seeded the galaxy with hundreds of species—all bipedal, carbon-based, and capable of communicating with each other, a previously unexplained event that prompted the formation of the United Faith. Scholars will next turn their minds, no doubt, to the question of who made the makers.

Known for their beautiful crystal artifacts, their flexible relationship with time, and their general mysteriousness, the Eshvaren created the Echo, where Aurora transformed herself from stressed-out time traveler to a brain warrior with a singular purpose.

The Eshvaren told Auri she could only summon the power she needed if she freed herself from all the ties that bound her to her old life. But Aurora realized in the end that those ties were the reason she was willing to fight.

Last seen: Being extinct for eons.

THE RA'HAAM—THE RELENTLESS AND SINGLE-MINDED (LITERALLY) ENEMY.

THE RA'HAAM HAS BEEN TRYING TO TAKE OVER THE MILKY WAY SINCE TIME IMMEMORIAL, AND AFTER ITS LAST GREAT DEFEAT AT THE HANDS OF THE ESHVAREN, IT RETREATED TO TWENTY-TWO OBSCURE NURSERY PLANETS, WHERE ITS LAST SURVIVING SEEDS COULD SLOWLY GROW BACK TO HEALTH BENEATH THE SURFACE. NOBODY WAS COUNTING ON THOSE PESKY TERRANS COLONIZING THE PLANET OCTAVIA, WHICH WOKE THE RA'HAAM FROM ITS SLUMBER EARLY. IT TOOK OVER THE BODIES OF THE COLONISTS—INCLUDING, ALAS, AURORA'S FATHER—AND USED THEM TO INFILTRATE TERRAN SOCIETY.

A COUPLE OF CENTURIES AFTER THEY WERE ORIGINALLY INFECTED, THE OCTAVIA COLONISTS HAVE WORKED THEIR WAY INTO POWER, NOW CONTROLLING THE GLOBAL INTELLIGENCE AGENCY, EARTH'S SUPER-SCARY BLACK-OPS AND PLANETARY SECURITY OUTFIT.

THEY ARE LED BY PRINCEPS, WHO IN MIND IS SIMPLY ANOTHER PART OF THE RA'HAAM, BUT IN BODY IS AURORA'S DAD.

THESE INDIVIDUAL AGENTS CANNOT GENERATE THE SPORES NEEDED TO INFECT OTHERS—THEY ARE ONLY GUARDING AGAINST FURTHER INTERFERENCE WITH THE NURSERY PLANETS, WHERE THE RA'HAAM HAS NEARLY FINISHED GROWING BACK TO FULL STRENGTH.

EVENTUALLY THOSE PLANETS ARE SET TO BLOOM AND THEN BURST, SENDING SPORES OUT THROUGH THE FOLD TO EVERY INHABITED PLANET IN THE GALAXY, WHERE THEY'LL INFECT ALL INTELLIGENT LIFE, MAKING IT A PART OF THE GREAT, MERGED INTELLIGENCE THAT IS THE RA'HAAM.

HUNTING DOWN AURORA AND THE REST OF SQUAD 312 TO KEEP ITS SECRET SAFE UNTIL THE OTHER TWENTY-ONE NURSERY PLANETS WERE READY TO BLOOM AND BURST, THE RA'HAAM TOOK TYLER AND SAEDII PRISONER. THIS KICKED OFF AN INTERPLANETARY INCIDENT THAT LED TO

THE STARSLAYER THREATENING TO BLOW EARTH TO SMITHEREENS UNLESS THE GIA GAVE HIS DAUGHTER BACK THIS VERY MINUTE.

LAST SEEN: IN PURSUIT OF TYLER AND SAEDII AS THEY RAN FOR IT. BUT IT'S EVERYWHERE, REALLY.

MAGELLAN—OH, HI, THAT'S ME! I'M NOT GONNA LIE. I'VE FELT BETTER THAN I DO LATELY—I GOT ZAPPED INTO BROKEN TOWN WHEN AURORA TOUCHED AN ESHVAREN PROBE WITH ME IN HER POCKET, SO I HAD TO ASK AROUND TO PICK UP SOME OF THIS INTEL FOR YOU. I'M CURRENTLY, UH, ON A FARM IN THE COUNTRYSIDE, WHERE THERE'S LOTS OF ROOM FOR ME TO RUN AROUND.

BUT MAYBE I'LL BE BACK BEFORE THE END OF THE STORY TO SAVE THE DAY? SOUNDS LIKE SOMETHING I'D DO. . . .

FOR NOW, STRAP IN, MY FRIENDS, BECAUSE WE'RE HEADING BACK IN.

ONCE UPON A TIME, THERE WERE A BUNCH OF CRAZY KIDS WHO REFUSED TO LISTEN TO THEIR ULTRA-INTELLIGENT UNIGLASS FRIEND. . . .

PART 1

A KITE IN A STORM

1

ZILA

I am rarely surprised. In any situation, I habitually calculate the odds of all possible outcomes, ensuring I am prepared for every eventuality.

Nevertheless, I am extremely surprised to discover I am still alive.

I spend six seconds in openmouthed shock, blinking slowly. After that, I press two fingers to my neck to check my pulse, which is rapid but unquestionably present. This suggests I am not experiencing an unexpected version of the afterlife.

Interesting.

A glance out of the cockpit viewshields reveals nothing— no stars, no ships, simple blackness. On instinct, I check our failing sensors, long-range and short. Strangely, I do not see any sign of the enormous battle that was raging around us moments ago, just before the Eshvaren Weapon blew itself apart—an incident with no possible outcome but our complete incineration.

Impossible as it may be, the entire Syldrathi armada, along with the Terran and Betraskan fleets, and the Weapon, have . . . vanished.

. . . Interesting?

No. Unnerving.

I let my training take over, instructing the ancient navcom on our Syldrathi ship to catalog all visible stars, FoldGates, and other landmarks or phenomena and then advise on our present location.

Wait. *Our.*

I flick on comms. "Finian, Scarlett, are you still . . . ?"

"Breathing?" comes Finian's voice, a touch uneven.

"Apparently so."

A wave of relief washes through me, and I do not attempt to prevent it. It is inefficient to combat such sensations. Better to let them pass naturally.

"I am one confused boy right now," Fin continues.

"Didn't we just . . . explode a moment ago?" Scarlett asks.

". . . Lemme check," Fin replies.

I hear a small squeak. A soft sigh. A long moment passes, and I am almost tempted to send a query when Finian speaks.

"Yeah," he finally reports. *"We're definitely still alive."*

"I am investigating," I advise them, as the navcom pings softly. "Please hold."

Consulting the ship's guidance systems, I feel a small frown forming between my brows. Not only is there no sign of the massive battle that should have killed us, there is also no sign of the planetary bodies of the Terran solar system. No Neptune, no Uranus, no Jupiter.

In fact, I can detect no stellar features at all, near or far.

No systems.

No stars.

We have . . . moved.

And I have no idea where.

Interesting AND unnerving.

A new icon pops up on the fritzing sensor display, indicating something is behind us. Our engines are still down, disabled during the fleet battle, so I turn on our rear sensors, looking at the vast stretch of space to our aft.

It . . .

That is to say . . .

I, um . . .

I . . .

Stop that, legionnaire.

I suck in a deep breath, straightening my spine.

I do not understand what I am seeing.

I begin by cataloging what can be observed, as any scientist would.

The ship's sensors are reading colossal fluctuations along the gravitonic and electromagnetic spectrums, bursts of quantum particles and reverberations through subspace. But engaging our aft cameras, I can barely see anything of this disruption in the visual spectrum at all.

In fact, at first, I mistakenly assume our visual arrays have been damaged. Everything is totally black. And then a pale light flares in the distance, a small pulse of disintegrating photons. And by their brief mauve glow, I glimpse what can only be described as . . .

A storm.

A dark storm.

It is enormous. Trillions upon trillions of kilometers wide. But it is *utterly* black, save for those brief photon flares within—an oily, seething emptiness, so complete that light simply *dies* inside it.

I know what this is.

"A tempest," I whisper. "A dark matter tempest."

Its presence would be strange enough, given that mere moments ago we were on the very edge of Terran space, where no such spatial anomaly exists. But stranger still, I see something more. Engaging my magnification settings, I confirm my suspicion. To our starboard, etched in silver against that seething storm of blackness, is a . . . space station.

It is a bulky, ugly thing, clearly built for function, not aesthetics. It appears to have been damaged—great crackling bolts of current slither over its surface, blinding and white. From the side closest to us, vapor is venting: fuel, or if the crew is unlucky, oxygen and atmosphere, puffing out like warm breath on a cold day and dragged into that endless roiling darkness.

If it is Terran, the station's design specs are positively archaic.

But that does not explain what it is doing here in the first place.

Or how *we* got here.

None of this makes sense.

"Zila?" It's Scarlett. "What's happening out there? Can you see the Eshvaren Weapon? What's the status on the enemy fleet? Are we in danger?"

"We . . ." I am not sure how to answer her question.

"Zila?"

There is a thick cable of gleaming metal stretching from the station. Hundreds of thousands of kilometers long, it twists and ripples but holds firm to the battered structure at one end. At the other, out on the edge of that seething tempest of dark matter, a great quicksilver sail is stretched across a rectangular frame, its surface swirling like an oil slick. It appears tiny on my visuals, but for me to even be able to see it at all from here, the sail must be *immense.*

If I didn't know better, I'd think it was—

"Unknown vessel, you have entered restricted Terran space. Identify yourself and provide clearance codes, or you will be fired upon. You have thirty seconds to comply."

The voice crackles through the cockpit, harsh and discordant. My pulse kicks up a notch, which is unhelpful.

I cannot see another vessel. Where is the voice coming from?

Leaving aside the fact that I have no clearance codes, I do not know whether the hail comes from friend or foe.

Not that my squad has a long list of friends just now.

I depress the switch for intrasquad comms and speak urgently. "Scarlett, please hurry to the bridge. Diplomacies are required."

"Unknown vessel, identify yourself and provide clearance codes. Failure to comply will be interpreted as hostile intent. You have twenty seconds remaining."

I scan the shuttle's controls and stretch—every Syldrathi over the age of twelve is taller than me—to press the button that will switch our channel from audio to visual. I must find out who is addressing me.

The face that fills my commscreen is covered by a black breathing apparatus, a thick hose snaking out of sight. The mask conceals everything beneath the pilot's eyes, and a helmet hides everything above.

I am looking at a Terran, though, most likely East Asian in origin, age and gender unclear. Strange as my situation is, perhaps a Terran can be reasoned with—we are the same species, after all.

"Please hold," I say. "I am summoning my team's Face."

"*Ident codes!*" the pilot demands, eyes narrowing. "*Now!*"

"Understood," I tell them. "I cannot provide codes, but—"

"*You are in violation of restricted Terran space! You have ten seconds to provide proper clearance, or I will fire on you!*"

All around me, alarms flare into life, lights flashing and Syldrathi symbols illuminating as a loudspeaker barks at me. I don't understand the words, but I know what it's saying.

"*Warning, warning: Missile lock detected.*"

"*Five seconds!*"

"Please," I say. "Please, wait—"

"*Firing!*"

I watch a tiny line of light appear on our scanners.

We have no engines. No navigation. No defenses.

We should be dead already. Incinerated with Aurora and the Weapon. But it seems somehow unfair to have to die again.

The light draws closer.

"Please—"

The missile strikes.

Fire tears through the bridge.

BOOM.

2.1

SCARLETT

Black light burns white across my skin. I can taste the sound around me, metallic on the back of my tongue, hearing touch and feeling scent as everything I am and was and will ever be rips itself apart and together and together *and togeth—*

"Scar?"

I open my eyes, see another pair of eyes before mine.

Big.

Black.

Pretty.

Finian.

"Did you . . . ?" I ask.

"Was that . . . ?" Fin says.

"Weird," we murmur.

I look around us, a strange black-cat, creepy-crawly feeling of déjà vu spidering its way up my spine.

We're standing in the corridor outside the engine room, just where we were a minute ago when the Eshvaren Weapon fired a whole beamful of planet-destroying badness into our favorite faces and then blew itself to tiny shinies. But, joy of joys, we are not, in fact, dead.

This comes as good news for a couple of reasons.

First, of course, and speaking frankly, it would be a bad move on the universe's part to waste an ass like mine by incinerating it in a fiery explosion in the depths of space. Honestly, they come along, like, once a millennium.

Second, it means the boy standing opposite me isn't dead, either. And strangely, that's a whole lot more important to me than I would've admitted a few hours ago.

Finian de Karran de Seel.

He's totally not my type. Brains not brawn. Chip on his shoulder as wide as the galaxy. But he's brave. And he's smart. And standing this close, I can't help but notice that tumble of white hair and smooth pale skin and lips I almost kissed as we were about to die.

But that's the only reason I did it.

Because we were totally about to die, right?

We stare at each other, conscious of how close we're still standing. Neither of us is moving away. He looks into my eyes and I open my mouth, but for the first time in as long as I can remember, I have no idea what to say, and the only thing that saves me from the embarrassment of being speechless, when the only thing I'm really good at is *talking,* is Zila's voice crackling over comms.

"Finian, Scarlett, are you still . . . ?"

"Breathing?" Finian says, his voice a little uneven.

"Apparently so."

And there it is again. That same creepy black-cat-walking-on-your-grave feeling. The feeling that—

"I am one confused boy right now," Finian says.

"Didn't we just . . . explode a moment ago?" I ask.

He meets my eyes again. I can still feel that almost-kiss between us, and I know he can too. And I see him steel himself, take a deep breath.

". . . Lemme check," he says.

I feel electricity crackle when his fingertips brush mine. He takes my hand in his and he stares at me for just a second longer in silent question, and he's totally not my type but I'm still not moving away. And now he's leaning closer, and closer, and even though we're not about to die anymore, he's kissing me, oh Maker, he's *kissing* me, the sensation sizzling like live current though my lips and all the way down my spine. I feel myself surge against him, kissing him back, tingling as I feel his hands slip over my hips, down to that ass even the universe wouldn't dare waste, and *squeeze* in all the right ways.

Well, Finian de Karran de Seel. Bless my stars.

Who in the galaxy would've guessed *you* had game?

Our lips break apart, and a part of me aches as he leans away, speaking into comms again.

"Yeah," he reports. "We're definitely still alive."

"I am investigating," Zila says. *"Please hold."*

The comms channel crackles out, leaving us alone. Fin and I are still pressed against each other and that kiss hangs between us now, and if one of us doesn't say something, I know we're going to start again. Given the circumstances, that's probably not the smartest idea.

I glance down at his hands.

Yep. Still on my ass.

"You know, when Zila said 'Please hold,' I'm not sure that's what she meant, de Seel."

He laughs, nervous, releasing his grip. "Sorry."

"Don't be."

And I lunge for his mouth again, just a brief collision, hard and hot. Biting his lip as I break away to let him know I'm still hungry.

"But we need to figure out what the hells just happened."

"Yeah." He breathes deep and steps away, dragging his metal-tipped fingers through his shock of white hair. "Yeah, we do."

We're still in the corridor outside the shuttle's engine room, doors still sealed. The air is sharp with the smell of burned plasteel, fused wiring, smoke. Looking through the plexiglass, I can see what that railgun round did to our engines when it hit us, and I know I'm not an expert, but I'm pretty sure engines aren't supposed to come in fifty different pieces.

"We need those to fly," I say.

"Who said you couldn't have been a Gearhead?"

"Every instructor I ever had at the academy, along with my guidance counselor and the head of the Engineering Division."

Finian smirks and glances around us. His dark eyes roam the ceiling, the ruined engine room. And then his stare drifts to my chest. His jaw goes a little slack, and I can practically see his eyes glazing over behind his contacts.

What is it with boys and boobs, honestly?

"Hey." I snap my fingers. "I know they're sensational, but seriously, mind on the job, de Seel."

12

"No." He taps his throat. "Your necklace. Remember?"

I reach up to my throat. To the necklace we found in the Dominion Repository back on Emerald City. Each of us had a gift waiting in that vault, courtesy of Admiral Adams and Battle Leader de Stoy. Tyler got his new boots, Kal the cigarillo case that saved his life. Finian got a ballpoint pen, which he was hilariously annoyed about; Zila got a pair of earrings with hawks on them. And I got this diamond necklace, inscribed with the words *Go with Plan B*. Except right before we were about to be blasted into our component molecules, Fin realized it wasn't diamond at all.

"It's Eshvaren crystal."

And yeah, that *is* weird. We'd found Eshvaren crystal in the Fold before—the probe that led Auri to the Echo. But that doesn't really explain why the academy commanders gave me a necklace of the stuff.

Or why we're not dead?

The adrenaline of almost dying and almost kissing and then definitely *not* dying but, yes, *definitely* kissing is wearing off now, and my hands feel shaky. But my eyes still roam Finian's body as he looks around the corridor in that annoyed/confused way he has, like the universe has decided to inconvenience him specifically. Limbs wrapped in the silver cladding of his exosuit, ghost-pale skin, and pitch-black eyes narrowed as he tilts his head.

"Not that I'm complaining," he says carefully. "But we're dead-stick in a Syldrathi ship during a massive fleet battle inside Terran space. Even if we survived the blast from the Weapon . . . shouldn't some Terran fighter jock be blowing us to pieces right now?"

13

I frown, tapping comms.

"Zila? What's happening out there? Can you see the Eshvaren Weapon? What's the status on the enemy fleet? Are we in danger?"

"We . . ." Her voice fails.

"Zila?"

And I look at Finian, and I can feel it in him, just like I can feel it in me. That creepy-crawling right up our spines. That feeling like . . .

"Scar, this conversation seems . . . *awfully* familiar."

"I know what you mean."

He shakes his head, frowning. "It sounds crazy, but I'm having the strongest feeling of—"

"Déjà vu."

He blinks. "What the hells is *déjà vu?*"

"It's a sensation. The impression you've said or done this before."

"Oh. Right." He nods vigorously. "Yeah. I'm definitely having that. But Betraskans call it *tahk-she.*"

"Yeah, I know. But on Terra we call it *déjà vu.* It's French."

"I don't know any French."

"Stick around," I wink. "I'll teach you some."

Zila's voice breaks over comms again, laced with urgency. *"Scarlett, please hurry to the bridge. Diplomacies are required."*

And again, I'm struck with that feeling. That we've said, done, *lived* this moment before. And more, that it ended really, *really* badly. I hold out my hand, and Fin takes it without thinking, and we're running up the corridor together. Fin's exosuit seethes and hisses as we sprint, boots pounding the metal as we take the stairs up to the cockpit.

Zila is seated in the pilot's chair, looking slightly frazzled, which for her almost constitutes a complete nervous breakdown. At first glance, our vis-systems all look dead—nothing but blackness on any of our viewscreens. No planets, not even any *stars*, which is kinda—

No, hold up. Some cams are still online at least. I can see a small, dumpy-looking space station on one viewscreen, trailing a heavy cable out into that otherwise perfect darkness.

This makes no sense. . . .

We were in the middle of a massive space battle on the edge of Terran space a few minutes ago. Where did the fleets go? Where did this station come from? And why aren't there any stars out there?

Zila meets my eyes as I look to her for explanation, and I *know* it sounds insane, but a part of me knows *knows* KNOWS . . .

"I take it you are also experiencing a sensation that suggests this moment is repeating itself," she says.

"It's French!" Finian declares.

A pulse of light flares on the viewscreens. It's dim, deep mauve, only a few seconds long. But my stomach does an ugly little flip as I realize it's not just darkness out there. There's some kind of . . . storm happening. A greasy, rolling collision of dark tendrils, so big it almost breaks my brain.

Fin blinks. "Is that . . . ?"

"A dark matter tempest," Zila murmurs. "Yes."

I glance to the commscreen, the taste of burned metal on my tongue, luminous Syldrathi script crawling across the readouts. I can see the features of what's definitely a Terran on the monitor—female, young—but her face is mostly obscured by a pilot's breather and helmet. She has two diamond insignia on her collar marking her as a lieutenant, but that's definitely *not* a Terran Defense Force uniform she's wearing. My first impression is she's a 17th-level badass. But her voice sounds just a tiiiiiiny bit uncertain.

"Listen . . . you need to identify yourself and provide clearance codes. You have ten seconds."

Technically, Squad 312 is wanted for galactic terrorism, so I decide to get a little blurry on the whole "Identify Yourself" thing. I brush my hair back, conjure a smooth demeanor from my bag of tricks, and purr into the microphone.

"I cannot *tell you* how good it is to see you, Lieutenant! We thought we were in big trouble. Our ship is damaged, our engines are offline, and we're in need of your assistance, over."

"This is a restricted area," the pilot replies, still a touch shaky. *"How did you get here? And what the hell are you flying?"*

"It's a *really* long story, Lieutenant," I smile, warm and friendly. "But our life-support situation isn't exactly puppies and sunshine over here, so if you could offer us a tow, I can buy you a drink and tell you all about it."

A long pause follows, my jaw clenched.

"All right," the pilot finally declares. *"I'm going to fire you a tow cable and bring you into dock. But you make any wrong moves, I will blast your asses across the system without even thinking twice about it."*

I smile. "That is *great* news, Lieutenant."

"Thank youuuu!" Finian pops up behind me and waves. "You are as wise as you are beautiful, madam!"

The pilot's voice turns to ice. What little I can see of her expression hardens to stone. *"You have a goddamn* Betraskan *on board?"*

All around us, alarms flare into life, red lights flashing and Syldrathi symbols illuminating, and a loudspeaker barks.

"WARNING, WARNING: MISSILE LOCK DETECTED."

A tiny line of light appears on our scanners. I look to the others, helpless, wild. We have no engines. No navigation. No defenses.

"Oh shit . . . ," I breathe.

"Scar . . . ," Fin whispers.

The light draws closer. Our fingers touch.

"Do not be afraid," Zila frowns. "It does not hurt much."

". . . What?" I ask.

The missile strikes.

Fire tears through the bridge.

BOOM.

2.2

SCARLETT

Black light burns white across my skin. I can taste the sound around me, metallic on the back of my tongue, hearing touch and feeling scent as everything I am and was and will ever be rips itself apart and together and together *and togeth—*

"Scar?"

I open my eyes, see another pair of eyes before mine.

Big.

Black.

Pretty.

Finian.

"Did you . . . ?" I ask.

"Was that . . . ?" Fin says.

"Weird," we murmur.

I look around, a strange black-cat creepy-crawly feeling of déjà vu spidering its way up my spine. We're in the corridor outside the engine room. And, joy of joys, we are not, in fact, dead.

But . . .

Wait . . .

Didn't we just . . . ?

I look at Finian, conscious of how close we're standing. He looks into my eyes but I have no idea what to say, and I'm saved from the embarrassment of being speechless by Zila.

"Finian, Scarlett, are you still . . . ?"

"Breathing?" Finian says, his voice a little uneven.

"Apparently so."

And there it is again. That creepy black-cat-walking-on-your-grave feeling. The feeling that—

"I am one confused boy right now," Finian says.

"Didn't we just . . . explode a moment ago?" I ask.

He meets my eyes again. I see him steel himself, take a deep breath.

". . . Lemme check."

I feel electricity crackle as his fingertips brush across mine and then, oh Maker, he's *kissing* me, the sensation sizzling like live current though my lips and—

"Stop," I say, breaking away. "No, stop, Fin . . . wait . . ."

I'm looking at him, and he's staring back with the same confused expression I'm probably wearing, and somehow, *some*how, before he speaks I know exactly what he's going to say.

"Scar, I'm having the strongest feeling of—"

"Déjà vu."

He blinks once. ". . . That's French."

"You don't know any French," I say, my belly turning somersaults.

He eases away from me, the deck seeming to shift underneath my feet, and there's a cold lump of ice where my stomach used to be as he stares around us. We're still in the corridor outside the shuttle's engine room, the air is still sharp with the smell of burned plasteel, fused wiring, smoke. Looking through the plexiglass, I can still see what's left of the engines, and I know I'm no expert, but this place, this conversation, somehow . . .

"What the *hells,* Fin . . . ?"

His brow is creased in a deep scowl. "We've done this before."

"But that's . . . that's not possible. . . ."

He raises one pale eyebrow, somehow still managing to find a smile despite everything. "Scar, believe me when I say that I've imagined kissing you enough to realize when I've done it twice in the same day."

A voice rings over comms. *"Scarlett? Finian?"*

"Zila?"

"Are you both . . . well?"

"I have *no* idea." Fin squares his jaw, his voice growing firm. "Look . . . this might sound insane, but does there happen to be an old, beat-up space station on your viewscreen right now? A dark matter storm? And a Terran fighter threatening to blow us all to sad little pieces?"

"I take it you are also experiencing a sensation that suggests this moment is repeating itself."

Fin looks at me, his lips pinched thin.

"Maker's breath . . . ," I whisper.

"We'll be right up," Fin says.

The adrenaline of almost dying and almost kissing and then definitely *not* dying but, yes, *definitely* kissing is now being replaced by the impossibility of all this. My legs feel like jelly, my brain buzzes in my skull. But I hold out my hand to Fin, and together, we're running up the corridor to the cockpit. Again, we find Zila seated in the pilot's chair, again looking frazzled. Again, on our viewscreens, I can see that dumpy-looking space station in a sea of starless darkness, and that angry Terran pilot.

Again.

Again.

But instead of just a tiiiiiiny bit uncertain, now the pilot sounds all the way sideways. *"What the* hell *is going on here?"*

Zila is looking at Finian, chewing one lock of long, curly hair.

"Temporal distortion?" Fin says.

"I can surmise no other adequate explanation," she replies.

"Shiiiiiit," he whispers. "Ouroboros effect?"

"It is only theoretical." Our Brain shakes her head, glancing at the station, a pulse of brief purple light flaring in the dark storm beyond. "And despite our lessons at the academy in temporal mechanics, I would have said unthinkable."

"Look," I say, glaring at the pair. "The only temporal mechanics lecture I ever took, I spent flirting with Jeremy and Johnathan McClain—"

(Ex-boyfriends #35 and #36. Pros: Identical twins, thus, each as hot as the next. Cons: Identical twins, thus, easily confused in the dark. Whoops.)

"—and in case you missed it, there's a very annoyed pilot—"

The commset crackles, cutting me off.

"You are in restricted Terran space," the aforementioned pilot says. *"You have fifteen seconds to transmit ident codes, or I will* open fire!*"

"We seem to be experiencing a temporal distortion,

Scarlett," Zila explains. "You, me, Finian, our ship . . . as outlandish as it sounds, we all seem to be repeating the same few minutes, over and over."

"*Ten seconds!*"

"It's a time loop, Scar," Fin says. "We're in some kind of time loop."

"Ending with our deaths," Zila nods. "And resetting to the moment we arrived. Like Ouroboros. The snake from Egyptian and Greek mythology that eats its own tail."

I scowl at the pair of them. "That's *impossible*."

"It is extremely unlikely," Zila agrees. "But once you eliminate the impossible, whatever remains, no matter how improbable—"

"*You have been warned!*" the pilot spits. "*I am opening fire!*"

All around us, alarms flare into life, lights flashing and Syldrathi symbols illuminating, and a loudspeaker barks.

"WARNING, WARNING: MISSILE LOCK DETECTED."

A tiny line of light appears on our scanners. I look to the others. We have no engines. No navigation. No defenses.

"Do not be afraid," Zila says.

"It doesn't hurt much," Fin murmurs.

My hand reaches for his, fear turning my belly cold and hard.

"You better be right about this," I breathe.

"Well, in case I'm not . . . you wanna make out some more?"

BOOM.

2.3

SCARLETT

Black light burns. I can taste the sound around me as everything rips itself apart and together and together *and togeth*—

"Scar?"

I open my eyes, see another pair before mine.

Finian.

"What . . . ," I ask.

"The . . . ," Fin says.

"Fuck," we murmur.

I look around, déjà vu spidering up my spine again. We're
outside the engine room again. And, joy of joys, we are not,
in fact, dead.

Again.

I look at Finian, and even though all this is impossible, I'm
still aware of how close we're standing. A tiiiiiiiiiny part of me
is conscious that the last time we did this, this pale, beautiful
boy kissed me about five seconds from now. But the rest of me,
the *sensible* part of me, is screaming at my lady parts to shut
the hells up because who *cares* what happened when we did
this before, Ovaries, *the point is, WE DID THIS BEFORE.*

"What the hells, Finian?" I whisper.

"*Finian?*" a voice crackles. "*Scarlett?*"

Fin taps comms, speaks quick. "We're here, Zila."

"Again," I say.

"*I suggest you both get up here. Quickly.*"

The impossibility of all this is turning my legs to jelly, and my brain is buzzing in my skull as Fin grabs my hand and we run up the corridor to the cockpit. Again, we find Zila in the pilot's chair, the roiling darkness, the brief bursts of light, the space station. Everything is the same as when we did this before, and oh Maker's breath, we did this before, *we did this BEFORE*.

Except this time . . .

"Where's the pilot?" Fin asks. "The Terran who blew us up?"

"Her ship is out there," Zila nods. "I can see it on our sensors. But she has not initiated radio contact."

"Wait . . . ," I stare at Zila and Fin, my brain running so hard my head aches. "You . . . I thought you said we were in a time loop."

"That is the most plausible conclusion, given current data."

"Well, then shouldn't she be yelling at us for clearance by now? Shouldn't she be doing the same thing, over and over?"

Zila chews the end of a curl, staring at the tiny blip on our scopes. She types rapidly on the flickering console, murmuring almost to herself.

"Interesting."

The alarms flare into life, lights flashing and Syldrathi symbols illuminating and a loudspeaker barking.

"*WARNING, WARNING: MISSILE LOCK DETECTED.*"

"Oh Maker's sake, not again . . . ," I mutter.

My hand reaches and finds Finian's.

He looks into my eyes, squeezes tight.

Zila stares at the fighter on the sensors, still chewing that lock of hair.

"*Very* interesting."

BOOM.

2.4

SCARLETT

Black light burns as everything rips itself apart and together *and togeth—*

"Scar?"

Finian.

I look into his eyes as the lights dim around us. The alarms flare into life, a now-familiar barking spilling from the loudspeaker as my stomach sinks all the way down to my shoes.

"WARNING, WARNING: MISSILE LOCK DETECTED."

"Okay," I sigh. "I am *officially* over this day."

"Scarlett? Finian?"

"We're here, Zila," Fin reports.

"The pilot is preparing to fire on us again. Even faster this time."

"Look," I hiss into comms, trying to keep from just screaming until my voice breaks into a million pieces along with the rest of me, "maybe I didn't study temporal physics, maybe I'm just stupid, but if we're stuck in a loop, shouldn't everything around us be acting *exactly the same?*"

"My readings on the station are congruous," Zila says. "Gravitonic bursts in the tempest, energy signatures, quantum flux—everything about this scenario is identical every time."

Electricity crackles as Fin's fingertips brush mine. "You know, you're not stupid," he tells me. "I dunno why you talk about yourself like that."

I look at the gray metal around us. The flashing globes reflected in the big, pretty eyes of the boy holding my hand. And then I see it.

Because, yeah, maybe I'm not the Brain of this squad. But if we're stuck in this loop and acting different every time, and that trigger-happy pilot out there is also acting different every time, there's only one explanation.

Eliminate the impossible.

Whatever remains, no matter how improbable, is the truth.

"That pilot is stuck in the loop with us," I say.

"Not just a pretty Face," Fin smiles.

"I see what you did there."

His smile fades a little as I look down to his lips. And as I press my mouth to his, as he kisses me back, I realize there are worse ways to die, over and over and over again.

BOOM.

3

TYLER

"TYLER!"

The walls around me are rainbows.

The ground is shaking beneath my feet.

There's blood in my mouth and a shadow rising above my head so massive and deep and dark I know it will swallow the galaxy if I let it.

I can't let it. . . .

A Syldrathi girl kneels above me, a kaleidoscope of light shining behind her like a halo. She's beautiful. Radiant. Younger than me but somehow older, and her eyes are violet and her hair looks like spun gold and I know she means the world to me without quite knowing why.

"TYLER!"

The voice echoes from my past, but into my future—another girl I used to know but never truly did screaming from beyond the boundaries of time and death. And I know she's trying to tell me something important, but that Syldrathi girl before me reaches out and her hands are covered in blood (my blood) and that golden hair is now dripping red and—

". . . you still have a chance of fixing this, Tyler Jones . . ."

28

"I don't . . ."

"Tyler Jones."

There might be nothing.

There is nothing. I—

"Tyler Jones!"

I open my eyes, and spears of bright light stab into my skull. I wince at the silhouette above me.

A Syldrathi girl, like the one from my dream just now, beautiful, radiant. But where her hair was gold as starlight, now it's black as midnight, same as the stripe of paint across her eyes and gleaming on her curling lips.

"Awake at last," Saedii says, one dark eyebrow rising slightly. "I wondered if you planned to sleep through the entire war."

My mind is ringing, and the lights are way too bright, the thrum of heavy engines rumbling through the medi-cot beneath me. There's a dermal patch on my arm, the metallic taste of stims in my mouth, and antiseptic in the air. It hurts a little to breathe.

I'm on a ship, I realize. Black metal. Syldrathi design. But the light is gray, not red, so we're Folding. . . .

"Maker's b-breath," I cough. "W-what happened . . . ?"

"Is that not obvious?" Saedii leans back in her chair, and lifting her long black boots, she rests one sharp heel on the edge of the cot beside me. "You almost died, Tyler Jones."

". . . Where am I?"

"Aboard my ship. The *Shika'ari*. Well . . ." She glances around briefly, tosses a thick black braid off her shoulder. "My ship now, at any rate."

"Last thing I remember . . . was the battle on the *Kusanagi*." I lever myself up onto one elbow, my head pounding like a war drum. "We broke out of our cell. Your people attacked." I wince again, my memory fuzzy, that strange dream still echoing in my head. It feels like I've been run over by a grav-freighter.

. . . you *still have a chance of fixing this* . . .

"We evac'ed . . . in escape pods?"

"The Terran cowards on the *Kusanagi* fired upon your pod." Saedii sneers, one sharpened canine gleaming. "But I was aboard the *Shika'ari* by then. Our defense grid intercepted their missile before it struck you. The explosion's proximity still disabled your pod, knocked out your life support. You were close to dying by the time we recovered you."

She quirks one sharp black brow.

"But recover you we did."

I meet her eyes, black-rimmed, deep violet irises running to gray. Her face is all sharp angles, perfect symmetry, cold and imperious.

"You saved my life."

She inclines her head. "As you saved mine."

I feel the touch of her thoughts then. Tentative, as if to make sure all we'd shared during our time in that prison cell aboard the *Kusanagi* was real. The revelation about the Syldrathi blood in my veins sits in my mind like a sliver of ice. Thoughts of the Waywalker mother my dad never told me about swirling like smoke.

I remember those other truths we shared. The truth of her bloodline. Her father's name. The lie her brother told me. But before I can grow too angry at the reminder of my friend's betrayal, thoughts of Kal lead to Auri, then to Scarlett and—

"Earth," I hiss, sitting up. "The Unbroken are at war with Earth."

"Yes."

"We have to stop it! A galaxy at war is just what the Ra'haam wants!"

Saedii shrugs, black lips pursed. "Fortune smiles, in that case."

"Well, where the hells are we?" I raise myself up off the bed, head swimming as I get to my feet. "We have t—"

Saedii stands, so tall that she's almost eye to eye with me. And placing one hand square on my chest, she holds me still. I can smell her hair, the fragrance of leather and lias flowers and traces of blood. I remember the press of her lips to my cheek as we said goodbye. The look in her eyes, her voice in my mind as I covered her escape.

"You have courage, Tyler Jones. Your blood is true."

"We are undertaking tactical withdrawal," Saedii says. "The battle with the *Kusanagi* was costly. Only the *Shika'ari* and one other of our cruisers survived. And both our vessels sustained significant damage."

"I need to talk to my people at Aurora Command," I insist. "Admiral Adams and Battle Leader de Stoy. The fate of the whole galaxy is—"

"You should be concerned with your own fate, Terran. Not the galaxy's." Her fingers twitch against my chest, pressing a little harder. "You are my captive now, after all. And your people showed me precious little hospitality while I was in their care. My entire command staff is of the opinion I should have let you die in your escape pod."

My mind returns to my final minutes in captivity. That

confrontation near the pods, those eyes, once brown, now blue, boring into my own. The mind of the enemy, the voice of a friend, begging me to stay.

Tyler, don't go. . . .

Cat . . .

I love you, Tyler.

Saedii searches my eyes. Her hand still rests on my chest. I can feel the warmth of her skin through the Terran uniform I stole. She's taken the time to change into Unbroken colors again—sharp black lines, sharper curves underneath. I can still recall the sight of her stripped down to her underwear in that storage locker if I try, but I'm desperately trying *not* to, because people who share Waywalker blood can apparently hear each other's thoughts, and the last thing I should be thinking about right now is—

"What happened to the *Kusanagi*?" I ask.

"It retreated, heavily damaged." She tilts her head. "Why do you care?"

"There were Terrans on board that ship," I reply. "My people."

"Is it your people that concern you? Or your lover?"

"Tyler, don't go . . ."

"Cat's not my—"

"She *was*."

I nod, swallowing. "But that's not Cat anymore."

"Mmm."

Saedii leans in closer, swaying like a snake, watching me through the haze of her long black lashes. I can sense it in her if I try—the rush of the battle we've just escaped, her thrill at the scent of blood and smoke and fire. She feels almost . . .

drunk on it. And look, I know there are way more important things at stake right now, but a part of me can't help but notice how good she looks, remembering the sight of her as we fought side by side, her eyes alight, my blood pounding.

Saedii presses her fingertips into my chest.

"We Warbreed have a saying, Tyler Jones. *Anai la'to. A'le sénu.*"

"I don't speak Syldrathi." I scowl down at her nails, long and black, pressing hard into my skin now. "And that hurts."

"Live for tonight," she translates. "Tomorrow we die." She drags her fingers down my chest, nails catching in the fabric. "We who were born for war learn not to waste time on trivialities. Void knows when our time will run out."

I nod, thinking about anything but the parts of her body now pressing against me. "We have a saying like that, too. *Carpe diem.* Seize the day."

Black lips curl into a smile. "Ours is better."

I wince as her nails dig deeper into my skin. "Stop it."

"Make me."

"I'm not kidding," I growl, pushing her hand away.

As my skin touches hers, she moves, grabbing my wrist quick as blinking.

I gasp as a bolt of pain shoots up my shoulder, the throb in my head forgotten as she tries to twist me into an armlock. I break her hold, backing off with my hands up. "Saedii, what the hells is—"

But she's closing before I even finish speaking, smile twisting into a snarl as she feints toward my face. Almost faster than I can see, she claps her hands onto my shoulders and brings her knee up between my legs.

33

Lucky for me, Saedii has landed this move on me a few times already—I mean, the boys didn't feel lucky at the *time*, but, you know, live and learn. My muscle memory kicks in, and I block her strike.

"Have you gone crazy?" I demand.

She draws back a fist to hit me, but I shift my weight, twist aside. Letting her own momentum work against her, I shove her in the spine, sending her crashing into the wall, and she whirls on me in fury.

Her kick takes me in the solar plexus, and I tumble over the medi-cot, smash onto the ground, grunting as a heavy weight slams atop me.

Saedii is straddling my chest now, pinning my wrists to the floor. Her braids fall in black curtains around her face as she leans in close, breath hissing. I see a smear of purple on her pale skin, realizing with horror she's split her lip. "Oh Maker's breath, I'm sorry, I—"

And my words die as, without warning, she crushes her mouth to mine.

About a thousand thoughts crash through my skull simultaneously. I remember this is a girl who wore the severed thumbs of former suitors around her neck for jollies. Warrior-born, bred for bloodshed, daughter of the Starslayer himself. I remind myself that the Unbroken are at war with Earth and, technically, I'm a prisoner here—she's my captor, she's my *enemy*. There's a war for the whole galaxy being fought out there, and I'm lying here with two meters of Syldrathi warrior princess on top of me.

Problem is, there's *two meters of Syldrathi warrior princess on top of me,* and all those thoughts are having trouble getting a fair hearing.

Saedii's kiss is hungry, urgent, her fingers squeezing tight around my wrists as her body surges against mine. I find myself kissing her back, her feelings, her thoughts, her *want*, washing over me and fueling my own. Her braids tumble around my cheeks, hips grinding against me as she sucks my lower lip into her mouth and bites down. *Hard.*

"Ow!" I hiss, pulling back. "What is wr—"

She kisses me again, half laughing, half snarling. But I can taste blood now, hers and mine, pain slicing through the new split in my lip.

"Get off me!"

"Make me."

"I mean it!"

"So do I, Tyler J—"

She gasps as I break her grip and push her off. But moving like quicksilver, she crashes into me again, hands clawing for my throat, and we struggle, hissing, bleeding, rolling on the floor. She's strong, lean, writhing like a snake in my grip, but finally I get hold of her wrists and push them into the floor, pinning her down with my weight.

"Maker's breath, will you *calm down?*" I roar.

Saedii lies underneath me, gasping, hair disheveled, eyes aflame. Wrapping her legs around me, she leans up to lick the blood off my chin. And I feel her thoughts echoing in my skull as her lips curl in a dark, playful smile.

I would if you actually wanted *me to.*

I gasp as she lunges for my neck, sharp teeth cutting my skin.

But you don't *want me to. Do you, Tyler Jones?*

She cinches her legs, pulling me in tighter. And I know this is insane, but I also know she's been in my head this

35

entire time. She can literally feel my thoughts and . . . she's right.

Saedii laughs, and our lips collide again, and she twists her hands free of my grip so she can slip them up under my shirt and drag her nails across my skin. She kisses me like she's starving, hunger bleeding into me, drowning out every other thought inside my head. Our hands are all over one another, she rips my shirt off, and we're both saved from the question of how far it might actually go by a faint vibration buzzing underneath my right palm.

"Um . . ."

We ease apart, my heart hammering. Eyes locked on hers, I reluctantly lift my hands away.

"I . . . think that's for you."

Sighing, Saedii slaps the silver comm badge on her chest. "Report."

Now, here's the thing—I kinda lied before. I don't speak Syldrathi nearly as fluently as Scar, but I'm good enough to follow the gist of a conversation. Catching my breath, licking my bleeding lip, I listen to the voice of her second-in-command, small and tinged with electronic reverb. I think he asks forgiveness for interrupting, but Saedii cuts him off.

"Erien," she snaps, eyes flashing. "Speak."

I hear a few words I know well. *Message. Battle. Terra.*

Saedii's eyes meet mine then. The reminder that our people are at war rises between us, slowly suffocating the mood. Her long legs unwrap from around my waist, and I ease myself off her, sitting back on the cold metal floor. Dragging my hand through my hair, I realize my fingers are shaking.

I can taste her blood on my lips.

Saedii asks for news about her father. There's a halting reply, and she twists up to her feet in one smooth, serpentine movement. I catch the words *no patience* and *riddles*. Again she asks about the Starslayer.

The only word I understand in the reply is *gone*.

My heart surges in my chest at that. Incredible. *Impossible*. The thought crackles between us as Saedii's eyes widen—that maybe somehow, against all odds, the man who destroyed the Syldrathi homeworld is . . .

"Gone?" she hisses in Syldrathi, incredulous. *"Dead?"*

There's a reply in the negative. I catch words like *confusion* and *retreat*. A rush about *Terrans* and *Betraskans* and—

"Void take you, Erien, speak!" Saedii demands.

The First Paladin asks forgiveness, speaks again. And as Saedii's eyes meet mine, I hear three words. Words that send my thumping heart all the way down to my boots. Words that could spell the end of everything.

Starslayer.

Weapon.

Vanished.

4

TYLER

I'm sitting in a briefing room with thirteen Unbroken warriors, and the only thing I'm certain of is at least twelve want to kill me.

Honestly, I'm still not sure about Saedii.

When I insisted she bring me along to the meeting of her command staff, I thought for sure she'd tell me no. I'm technically a prisoner here, after all. An outsider. An *enemy*. She told me to stay in bed and rest.

"I'm half-Syldrathi myself," I'd reminded her. "And I know more about the true enemy here than anyone. The Unbroken are being played, and I know the tune. Bed is the last place I want to be right now."

She'd watched me thoughtfully, wiped my blood off her mouth, the memory of that . . . kiss/fight/whatever we just had still hanging between us. I can still feel her body pressed up against mine if I try. We both knew my line about bed was only halfway true. . . .

"This is not some Terran pleasure ship crewed by cowards and weaklings," she'd warned. "This is an Unbroken war

cruiser. The crew will view you with disdain at best. Murder-
ous hostility at worst."

"I didn't know you cared, Templar."

Her eyes narrowed at that. Saedii is every bit the tactician I am—she could see the trap I'd laid, and there was no
way she was about to admit she gave a damn about my wel-
fare. And so she scoffed, tossed her braids, and stalked out of
the room, with me limping behind.

> *Tyler Jones: 1*
> *Saedii Gilwraeth: 0*

The air is thick with tension in the briefing room, red
light washed gray by the Fold. Holo reports from major
news feeds all over the galaxy are projected on the walls,
hundreds across every network, the volume turned low so
the Unbroken can speak without interruption. They kneel
at an oval table carved of dark lias wood, Saedii at one end,
her staff around her, and her second-in-command, Erien,
opposite.

I sit against the wall, sucking the bite mark on my lip.

I remember Saedii's lieutenant Erien from my imprisonment aboard *Andarael*. Her First Paladin is tall and willowy,
his beautiful face marred by a hook-shaped scar beneath one
eye. He wears a string of severed Syldrathi ears at his belt.
Around him are a mix of battle-scarred veterans and young
bucks full of fire and fury. They're all heavily armed and
dressed in beautiful black armor decorated with sleek Syldrathi glyfs. Their hair is fashioned to denote their rank—
the more braids, the more authority they carry. Each smooth
brow is marked with the sigil of the Syldrathi warrior cabal:
three crossed blades.

The atmosphere is . . . odd. It's like watching a pack of man-eating tigers hold a tea ceremony. Every word and gesture is underscored with measured hostility. I get the feeling there could be bloodshed any second, but there's two iron-clad cables binding these people together.

First, of course, they are all Unbroken.

There's a bond forged in war that people who haven't fought for their lives will never understand. When you put your trust in someone to watch your back in battle, when you kill and bleed together, you become more than family. And as I look around the room, that's what I see here—people who are more than blood, the ties that bind them forged in the fires of a lifetime of war.

And second, of course, there's Saedii herself.

I can tell every one of the Warbreed in this room loves her. Hates her. Fears her. Worships her.

Even if she weren't the daughter of the Unbroken's greatest Archon, I've seen Saedii in battle now—ship to ship, and hand to hand. And I know she didn't get her seat at the head of this table because she's Daddy's little girl. She got it by *moving* whoever was sitting there before her.

When we walked into the room together, twelve sets of eyes fell on me like I was the appetizer. One word from Saedii, they got down to business. But business, as it turns out, is *not* good.

Like I said, I don't speak Syldrathi as well as Scar, but I'm fluent enough to catch every few words. And listening to Saedii's command staff speak, watching the myriad newscasts glowing on the walls around me, I'm beginning to piece together exactly what happened at the Battle of Terra.

A massive Unbroken fleet, bigger than anything that has been seen since the fall of Syldra, massing outside Terran space.

The Terran navy mustering in response.

The Betraskans stepping in to help defend their Terran allies.

Archon Caersan demanding the return of his daughter.

Now, for two years, Earth had tiptoed around the Unbroken. Our last war with the Syldrathi had lasted two decades, and we'd been so desperate to avoid another, we even turned a blind eye when Caersan destroyed Syldra's sun.

But TerraGov didn't even know the GIA had Saedii in custody—the Ra'haam had taken her prisoner to start trouble, after all. So they couldn't exactly comply with the Starslayer's request to give her back. Instead, they politely asked him to vacate their doorstep or eat a fleet to the face.

Caersan didn't like that.

I'm watching footage of the battle now, my heart surging every time I see it—a massive spear of crystal, rainbow-colored, big as an entire city. As the Unbroken, Terran, and Betraskan fleets clash, it cruises through the bloodshed like a shark, pulsing with energy. The newscasts are labeling it an "Unbroken superweapon." But from what Saedii told me aboard the *Kusanagi*, I know it's not a Syldrathi device at all.

It was made eons ago, by the beings who fought the Ra'haam the last time it tried to consume the galaxy. The Ancients, the Eshvaren, who've somehow been behind everything that's happened since I pulled Auri out of that cryopod what seems like a lifetime ago.

My heart aches at the thought of her. I wonder where my sister and the rest of Squad 312 are, praying to the Maker that they're okay, that they didn't get caught up in this in-sanity. But as much as it hurts to push all that aside, truth is, we've got bigger problems. Because time and time again, I watch it unfold on the feeds—the Weapon, the *Neridaa*, the one hope the Eshvaren left for the galaxy to fight the Ra'haam, flaring like a new sun in the middle of the battle, sending out a blast that disables half the ships around it, and then . . .

Disappearing like it had never been.

Nobody knows what happened. Why it vanished or where it went. But the Starslayer's disappearance, combined with the burst of force that accompanied his weapon's departure, put the brakes on the battle.

The Unbroken paused their attack. The decimated Ter-ran and Betraskan fleets fell back into defensive posture. And after a few more hours of tense standoff, the Unbroken bounced back through the FoldGate and right out of the system.

"Retreat," a graceful woman in black Paladin's armor says.

"De'sai," another growls.

That's the Syldrathi word for *shame*. I see it reverberate around the room, half the assembly murmuring agreement, the other half uncertain.

For warriors like these to even *consider* retreat an option . . . I begin to understand what Caersan means to them. He's not just a leader. He's a father. The man who saved them from shameful peace with Earth, from the "weaklings" on the Syl-dra council. And his disappearance has cut them like a knife to the heart.

Sharpened teeth are bared. Hard words are spoken. I

catch *unrest* and *Templars* and *coup*. One of the younger Paladins slams his fist onto the table—for Syldrathi, an outburst like that is unthinkable.

And then Saedii speaks.

Her voice is calm. Hard. Cold. I hear words like *honor* and *vengeance, father* and *truth*. I understand what she's telling them. Saedii intends to rendezvous with the Unbroken armada, take command, then return to Earth and find out what happened to the Starslayer.

Her voice brings calm to their frayed nerves.

The Unbroken princess, stepping up to the king's empty chair. But . . .

"That's a mistake, Saedii," I finally sigh.

All eyes turn to me. A Paladin with iron-gray hair glares, hand slipping to the beautiful silvered kaat blades crossed at his back. His Terran is fluent, but marked by a heavy Syldrathi accent.

"You dare speak so to a Templar of the Unbroken, so'vaoti?"

"Aye." A sharp-eyed female glowers at me, glances to Saedii. "Who is this refuse we dragged from the Void's belly, Templar?"

I answer before Saedii can speak for me. "My name is Tyler Jones. Son of Jericho Jones."

I see my name echo around the room.

Before he joined the Senate and fought for peace, my dad fought the Syldrathi to a standstill. Gave them the worst bloody nose of the entire Terran-Syldrathi War.

"And while we're keeping score," I continue, "I'm the one who saved your Templar's life when the *Andarael* got hit by the *Kusanagi*. And then broke her out of a holding cell before they tortured her to death. I didn't see many of you there helping her."

Erien bares his teeth, canines sharpened to points. "I should cut your tongue out of your head, Terran whelp."

"Maybe you could leave me half?" I wave at my mouth. "Unless you want to remove the Syldrathi part, too?"

His eyes narrow at that. He glances at Saedii, who inclines her head. The knowledge of my Syldrathi heritage seeps into the room like smoke.

"I mean, that's presuming you can lay a glove on me at all, big man." I lean a little closer, dragging Erien's eyes back to mine. "Or maybe you forgot I'm also the one who killed a drakkan single-handed?"

Okay, so normally I'm not a whip-it-out-and-measure-it kind of guy. Most days, I prefer to let my actions do the talking for me. But I know for a fact that the Unbroken respect strength. Conviction. And above all, courage. So I just stare at Erien, the air boiling between us, until a younger male Templar beside him touches his arm. The touch only lasts a second. They exchange a glance, something passes between them.

"Be'shmai," the younger male murmurs. "Osh."

Erien's gaze flickers, then returns to Saedii.

"Perhaps," she says, licking at the split in her lip, "you could elucidate the nature of this mistake I am making."

I flash her half a dimpled smile. "Thought you'd never ask."

"I am *not* asking. I am commanding."

She scowls at me, dark hair tumbling about her cheeks as she lowers her chin. But from the glint in her eye, the faint flicker of her thoughts, I can still sense Saedii is almost . . . amused.

A Templar of the Unbroken has no use for sycophants, I realize. Good leaders never do. Saedii likes struggle. She likes being pushed, challenged. And from the way her eyes keep drifting to them, she also likes my dimples.

Let's be honest, who can blame her.

Tyler Jones: 2
Saedii Gilwraeth: 0

Erien glowers as I turn to the myriad of news feeds projected on the walls. Eyes narrowed, I search until I find the one I want and point toward the stream. "The feed from GNN-7. Can you call that up?"

One of the Paladins glances at Saedii, and she acquiesces with a small wave of her hand. The feed grows larger, dominating the wall. A Chellerian male is talking on the feed, his blue skin rendered gray by the Fold. Even in black and white, his smile is dazzling, and his suit looks like it cost the GDP of a small moon. The name LYRANN BALKARRI floats beneath him, headlines in a dozen languages scroll behind him. The news is grim.

"An attack by Rigellian insurgents on Chellerian holdings in the Colaris sector," Saedii reads the headline, raises a brow. "And?"

"Colaris has been contested by Rigel and Chelleria for the last fifty years. The Chellerian consulate just brokered a cease-fire after a *decade* of negotiations. And Rigel suddenly just starts blowing up Chellerian ships?"

I turn to another screen. "That one. Bring up that one." I point to another feed. "That too." They're small stories—if you weren't paying attention, they'd be easy to miss in the noise and confusion of the Unbroken attack on Terra. But there are dozens of them. And *I'm* paying attention.

Ishtarri colony ships destroyed by a gremp attack in the Fold.

A three-way border war between the No'olah, the Antarri Collective, and Shearrr, cold for the last seven years, suddenly flares again.

Three top-tier Dominion officials assassinated by agents of their chief rivals, the Pact of Shen.

"Distractions," I say, looking around the room. "Provocations meant to drag a dozen different races into a dozen different conflicts." My gaze falls on Saedii. The bite marks on my neck sting with sweat. "Just like your abduction dragged the Unbroken into war with Earth and Trask."

"The war with Earth never ended for us, Terran," Erien growls. "We were simply concerned with other prey."

I ignore him, staring into Saedii's eyes. "You know who this is."

"This . . . Ra'haam you spoke of."

"It's corrupted the GIA. And the GIA has operatives in every sector of the galaxy." I wave at the feeds, trying not to sound like a conspiracy nut. "It could pull this off with enough planning. And it's been planning for *centuries*. It wants the galaxy at war. Tied up and distracted so nobody learns who the real threat is until it's too late."

There's an exchange in Syldrathi among Saedii and her command crew. Questions. A brief explanation of the Ra'haam, the Eshvaren, the Weapon. I sense skepticism among them, see their disdain as they look at me. Saedii can see into my head. She *knows* I'm telling the truth.

But still . . .

"Our concern is not for some weed festering in the shadows," she declares. "Our concern is for our missing Archon."

"Those problems are one and the same, Saedii."

She drums sharp fingernails on the table, eyes flashing. "I presume you have a plan beyond bleating like an orphaned bâshii?"

"My commanders in the Aurora Legion," I say, ignoring the jab. "They *know* something. These boots of mine? The jammer inside that busted us out of that holding cell? It was waiting for me *ten years* inside a Dominion vault. Put there by Legion Command years before I even *joined* the academy."

"You are suggesting we run to *Terrans* for aid?" Erien scoffs.

"The Aurora Legion is a neutral party," I insist. "You're not at war with us. If I could speak to Adams and de Stoy, find out what they know—"

"Earth is our enemy," Saedii says. "Trask is our enemy."

"The whole *galaxy* can be your enemy if you let it, Saedii."

"Let it?" She smiles, running her tongue across her teeth. "We *love* it."

"The blade grows dull when left in the scabbard, half-breed," the veteran tells me. "Were your blood pure, you would understand that."

"Aanta da'si kai," another murmurs, touching the glyf at her brow.

We were born for war.

I sigh, shake my head at Saedii. Her smile only grows. She delights in this, I realize. Gets off on it. Struggle. Strife. These people were raised to see conflict as the path to perfection. Maybe that's why she's keeping me around.

I see her eyes drift to the bite marks on my throat. I feel a flicker of hunger in my head. But this isn't a game, and I'm exhausted and I'm afraid for my sister and my friends and feeling like I've been running forever and haven't moved an inch.

And worst of all, I sense that dream, the one that woke me here, still echoing somewhere in my skull as the room begins to spin, and I press one hand to my aching brow.

The walls around me, the color of rainbows.

The ground shaking beneath my feet.

"You look unwell, Terran," Saedii says.

I lower my hand, growl, "I'm fine."

She smiles so wide I can see the sharpened teeth at the corners of her mouth. "If you wish to return to bed—"

"Forget me," I snap, temper fraying. "You're giving the Ra'haam what it wants. It's *using* you, Saedii."

"I am no one's pawn."

"Then don't act like it. You're smarter than this."

"And smarter than you. Forget not whose captive you are."

"And whose captive would you still be, if not for me?"

"You saved your own skin as well as mine." Saedii tilts her head, eyes locked on mine. "Do not believe it buys you any favor, boy."

"I'm not asking for favor," I snap. "I'm asking you not to be an *idiot.*"

Saedii's amused smile fades. An alarm buzzes in my head: *Technical foul on the play. One-point penalty.*

    Tyler Jones: 2

    Saedii Gilwraeth: 1

Whoops. Too far . . .

The temperature around me drops several degrees. The

flicker of Saedii's mind in mine suddenly vanishes, like she's slammed an iron door between us. And glancing to her First Paladin, the Templar speaks.

"It appears our guest is wearied after his ordeal, Erien." She flips a braid off her shoulder. "See him safely situated in appropriate quarters."

"Saedii—"

"Your will, Templar."

She turns to her other crew members, begins issuing orders in Syldrathi. But my eyes are on Erien as he rises, looming over me. His beautiful face hard as stone, distorted by his scar, silver hair drawn back in seven thick braids, each decorated by a desiccated Syldrathi ear.

"Move," he says.

I look at Saedii. But she's ignoring me now, her mind closed off tight. I shouldn't have let my temper get the best of me. That was stupid—I backed her into a corner, and she's come out swinging.

My skull is pounding as I close my eyes, rise to my feet. The air hums with the sound of engines and the growing current of galactic war. My mind still echoing with the voice of my dream.

. . . you *still have a chance of fixing this, Tyler Jones* . . .

But I can't see how.

Maker help me, I can't see *how*.

5

FINIAN

That Terran pilot blows us up three more times before she finally gives up on it. Each time, Scar and I reappear in the corridor outside the engine room. Each time, Scarlett presses her lips to mine as we explode in a white-hot ball of plasma.

Maybe it's just some kind of universal justice. I finally get to snog Scarlett Jones, and reality implodes because it's all too improbable.

But after the eighth time our new friend pulls the trigger, Scarlett and I rematerialize outside the engine bay, waiting for the inevitable, and nothing happens. No screaming alarms. No missile lock warning. Nothing.

Scar has her head tilted. Waiting.

". . . She's not killing us," she mutters.

"Progress!" I'm grinning like an idiot. It's not just because we weren't blown up, to be honest.

Scar tries to muster a smile in response, but I can see how weirded out by all this she is. Honestly, I can't blame her. In the last few weeks, this girl has lost her best friend, her brother, and now, apparently, her whole reality.

I reach for her hands, wrapping my fingers around hers,

squeezing gently. "I know this is crazy," I say softly. "I'm as freaked out as you are. But whatever this is, we'll figure it out, okay?"

She manages a better smile for that, and despite all the insanity around us, I feel my heart flutter at the sight.

Maker, she's beautiful.

Scarlett leans close, kisses me soft on the lips. "You're sweet."

"Don't tell anybody. I've got a reputation as a wiseass to maintain."

"Come on then, wiseass," she smiles. "Let's go see our Brain."

We run together to the bridge, find Zila at the controls. Her eyes are locked on the fritzing rainbow displays, her lips pursed.

"Sitrep?" Scar asks as she strides across the cockpit, all efficient, sounding just like her brother for a moment.

Our Brain doesn't look up from the monitors. "Spatially, our coordinates are identical to our first eight manifestations. We are several hundred thousand kilometers from the cusp of an immense tempest of dark matter. From the brief glimpses of stars we have, the nav computer calculates that we may be somewhere near Sigma Arcanis."

"But we were in the Terran solar system." Scar looks at that massive stretch of perfect black, the brief pulses of strange light within it. Her face is paler than usual. "How did we move here?"

"I do not know. But I aim to find out." Zila taps her wrist unit. "I have set a timer. We must gather as much information as possible about these cycles. We are currently at four minutes, six seconds."

"What about our trigger-happy friend?" I ask.

Zila looks at the monitor as though it has personally vexed her. "No radio contact this time. But as Scarlett surmised, whatever the nature of this temporal anomaly, the pilot's actions indicate she is also experiencing it."

We all flinch as the controls fizz in front of Zila. This ship was ancient when the Waywalkers gave it to us, and hasn't enjoyed its recent experiences.

"The space station, the dark matter storm beyond it, and my external readings all are identical," Zila continues. "The only variables in this equation appear to be our actions and hers. She has apparently decided that incinerating us is unfruitful, which is good news. The definition of insanity is repeating the same action and expecting a different outcome."

"That's progress," Scarlett murmurs. "If she knows something weird is happening to us all, we can try and communicate."

"We must change our approach," Zila declares. "Finian, what do you make of our surroundings?"

I bite down on the urge to be flippant, because we don't have time. Our friend Shooty McShootface could start up again any minute. I know better than to bother looking out the windows—one of the principal characteristics of dark matter is you can't actually *see* it, only what it does to the stuff around it. So I peer at the fritzing controls instead, looking over the data coming in.

"Well, that DM storm is *huge*. One of the biggest I've ever seen. Gravitonic, electromagnetic, and quantum fluctuations are all off the scale. But we're far enough away not to suffer any ill effects, I think."

"And the station?"

I check our cams. "Dunno. I've never seen anything like it."

"It is Terran," Zila murmurs. "As was the pilot who hailed us. But it is an archaic design. It is also seriously damaged. Venting core plasma, I believe."

"So if that's her home, she's got bigger problems than us."

Zila's not looking quite at me, that big brain of hers going at full speed. "What do you make of that sail out in the storm?"

I shrug, studying the enormous cable leading from the station, the tiny rectangular glimmer out on the edge of the tempest. "I mean, it *looks* like a quantum sail."

"A what?" Scarlett asks, giving me a look that dares me to suggest she was doing her nails during this lecture at the academy.

I do not wish to displease Scarlett in any way, so I reply very diplomatically. "It's one of the idiotic things you dirt-children were trying back when Terrans and Betraskans made first contact. We didn't teach you the error of your ways till after the war ended. But your theory was that you could harvest energy from dark matter storms."

Scarlett blinks at me, suggesting that, yes, she was indeed doing her nails when they covered this stuff in basic astrometrics.

Very studiously.

"Look, dark matter is basically the gravitational glue that holds the galaxy together, right?" I say. "And when streams of it collide, you get all kinds of crazy chakk going on at the subatomic level. Those lights you see out there? Those are dark quantum pulses. There's more energy in a single burst than is generated by a star going supernova. You Terrans

53

thought you could harness it." I shrug. "Sounds good in theory, but the reality is, the energy in a dark quantum pulse is just too unstable, and dark energy starts doing *really* dangerous things under containment. So while it *looks* like a quantum sail out there, it can't be, because even Terrans aren't that dumb anymore."

Zila is staring at the viewscreen, thoughtful, sucking on a lock of hair. Scarlett slides into the seat beside her.

"Okay, well, *massive* space nerdery aside," Scar says, rolling her eyes at me, "we still need to figure out what's happening. So let's try switching things up. If that pilot won't talk to us, maybe we can talk to her."

Zila gives her the frequency she needs, and our Face wrestles with the comms rig for a moment. I just stare at that massive storm of pulsing darkness, the tiny station hanging on the edge of it. Bewildered.

"Attention, Terran vessel. Attention, Terran vessel. Are you reading us?"

No reply. Zila and I glance at each other as Scar tries again.

"Listen, we know it sounds insane, but I'm guessing this situation is feeling *awfully* familiar to you by now. And given that you're not shooting at us anymore, you're probably starting to figure out the four of us are somehow tied in to all of this together. Whatever *this* is. What say we figure it out?"

More silence. Scarlett puts on her best Voice of Reason.

"You're probably just as scared as we are. We just want to talk, okay?"

Still nothing. A pulse of dark energy illuminates the tempest, deep mauve amid those seething coils of bottomless black. And I'm beginning to wonder if maybe Scar's met the one person in the galaxy who can resist her charms when the vidscreen crackles and a masked badass appears, shooting a Class Five death glare through narrowed eyes.

Getting a better look at her this time, I realize she's kinda young—not too much older than us. She's not looking quite so much the badass anymore, either. In fact, if anything, she looks more freaked out than we do.

"Well, hi," Scar says, treating the pilot to one of her very best smiles. "We simply *have* to stop meeting like this."

Our new friend's gaze hardens in a very not-friendly way.

"What the hell's *going on?"*

"Good question," Scarlett replies, still all smiles, which is a good idea, because Miss Badass still has all the guns and we have none of the guns. "*Excellent* question, in fact, well worth discussing. Might I suggest we try and answer it together? Because we're very keen to avoid dying again."

The seconds tick by in silence, the girl behind the mask inscrutable. But finally, we hear a massive *WHUNGGGG*, and the whole shuttle shakes around us. Another *WHUNGGGG* rings out on our hull, and I'm almost knocked off my feet, hands out for balance.

"Maker's breath, she's shooting us again?"

"No." Zila looks at her sensors, shakes her head. "She has secured our ship with tow cables."

"Open your airlock," the pilot orders. *"I'm coming aboard. I expect to see your hands in clear view when those doors open. If not, kiss your asses goodbye. You reading me?"*

"Five by five," Scarlett replies. "See you soon."

Our Face swings around in her chair. She squares her

jaw, draws a deep breath, and nods in that way that reminds me of her brother again.

"All right. Let's go roll out the red carpet."

"Wait, we're gonna just let her in here?" I ask, looking around the cabin. "I don't want to get all judgy, but this girl *has* murdered us nine times today."

"Eight times," Zila corrects.

"Oh, well, that's okay then."

"She's hard to read with the mask and helmet and all." Scar shrugs. "But if she didn't want to talk, she wouldn't be coming over at all."

"I do not pretend to understand what is happening here," Zila says, starting for the door. "But this pilot is a part of it. We *must* speak with her."

I exchange a look with Scar, and we follow our Brain down the stairs. Trekking down to the cargo bay, I find myself trying to make sense of all this.

I'm not the genius Zila is, but I'm no slouch either, and none of it is adding up. While I'm worried about saving our own hides, worry about Auri is also nagging away at me— what the hells happened to her, to the Weapon, to the Syldrathi fleet we were right in the middle of?

Is the battle on the edge of this system still under way? Is that why this pilot was so jumpy? Thing is, we saw the Betraskan fleet arrive to *defend* Terra against the Unbroken— we've been allies since our war ended nearly two centuries ago. There's no two planets in the galaxy tighter than Terra and Trask. So why did she freak out when she saw me?

We arrive in the bay. The lighting is dim, the smell of burned plastene sharp in the air. Through the plexiglass on the airlock, I can see the Terran fighter ship now positioned directly behind us. Just like that station out there, it's no design I've ever seen. But truthfully, I got bigger concerns.

"So, listen," I say. "Last time Flygirl laid eyes on me, she blew us to many small pieces. Maybe I should just, you know, hang back a little?"

"She already knows you are here," Zila points out.

"She knows something's up," I correct her. "We don't know how much she remembers. I mean, maybe we're the ones causing this anomaly. Exposure to Auri or the Weapon or the explosion or something. Flygirl might be feeling the side effects to a lesser degree. We don't know."

Zila tips her head to one side, wordlessly indicating how unlikely she thinks this is.

"What happens if I die and you don't?" I ask. "Does the loop still begin again for everyone, or do I just stay dead? There's too much about all this we don't know. And to be honest, I don't want to get shot in the face, okay?"

"Fair," Scarlett agrees.

"Optimistic," Zila murmurs.

There's a clunk outside the airlock, signaling the arrival of our guest. I hide behind a stack of crates, one hand on the grip of my academy-issue disruptor. All three of us are silent as the lock cycles, but tension is singing through me while I watch the hatch through a crack in my cover.

Scarlett and Zila both keep their hands in clear view, and I try to keep my body loose, my grip on my disruptor pistol relaxed. Which isn't easy, with the same song beating through my head over and over, like a drum.

What. Is. Going. On.

With a hum, the door slides open, revealing a slight figure about Zila's size and build. She wears a black flight suit, a helmet, and a breathing mask, and holds a heavy sidearm in one hand.

Her opener is not friendly. "Where's the Betraskan?"

"Hello," offers Scarlett. "Lovely to meet you. My name is Sca—"

"Where's the Betraskan?"

Okay, well, it was worth a try.

"I'm here," I sigh. Before anyone gets shot, I holster my disruptor and stick my hands out around the edge of the crate to show I'm unarmed.

"Come out slow," she orders. "*Real* slow."

I obey, hands high. "You know, usually people don't want to murder me until they've gotten to know me a little better than this."

I'm trying for cocky, but I can hear the shake in my voice. Maybe I've died repeatedly already and somehow come back, but my body doesn't understand that. It's pretty sure it's getting shot, sooner rather than later, and it's not okay with it.

I study the lieutenant's gear—it doesn't look like any uniform I've ever seen on a member of the Aurora Legion, the Terran Defense Force, or the Global Intelligence Agency. It's mostly black apart from some silver insignia. The only color on the whole rig is the design on her helmet, some kind of big bird with wings spread, sharp talons flashing.

I always get mixed up with Terran birds. Canary maybe? Pelican?

No, that's not right. . . .

But I can see our visitor has the name KIM stenciled across her pocket, and a lieutenant's insignia on her shoulders. Lieutenant Kim, then.

Nice to meet you.

"So," Scarlett smiles. "As I was saying, my name is Scarlett. This is my science officer, Zila, and my engineer, Finian. It's good to f—"

"Get on your knees," Kim commands. "Fingers laced behind your head. All of you. *Slowly.*"

Scarlett is as good at knowing when to shut up as she is at knowing when to speak and what to say. She silently eases down to the deck, and Zila follows with that slightly spacey expression that says there are furious internal calculations taking place. My exo whirs and hisses as I ease down beside them, wincing at the jolts of pain running through my knees.

"What're you wearing?" Lieutenant Kim asks me. "Is it for combat?"

"Combating gravity," I tell her. "I need it to walk. There's no weapons in it, if that's your worry. Though it does have a built-in bottle opener?"

Zila speaks as if there wasn't already a conversation under way. "That station is trailing a quantum sail at the edge of a dark matter storm."

"That's classified," Lieutenant Kim snaps.

Zila's eyes shift, as though she can see through the shuttle's hull. "My colleague Finian suggested it is trying to harvest dark energy?"

"Except nobody does that anymore," I say. "Not anywhere."

"Not anywhere," Zila whispers, a little creepily, if I'm being honest.

"I'm asking the goddamn questions," Kim growls. "Who sent you? Are you bleach-head spec ops? How did you find us all the way out here?"

Scarlett tries to smooth things over. "Lieutenant, I give you my word—"

"Your word?" Lieutenant Kim scoffs, points her pistol right at me. "You two are working with this bastard against your own people? Betraying Terra? You know what happens to traitors in wartime?"

"Wartime?" I blink. "Are you drunk? We haven't been—"

"Shut your mouth, Bleachboy!"

I blink. *"Bleachboy?"*

"Not *anywhere* . . . ," Zila whispers again.

"Look, what the hell is wrong with her?" Kim demands, glowering at Zila.

Scar waves dismissively. "Oh, she does this sometimes."

Zila looks at the lieutenant again, nodding toward the airlock doors. "Your fighter ship. It is an old Pegasus model. Mark III, yes?"

"Old?" the pilot scoffs. "Sweetie, she's so new her paint is still wet."

Zila nods. "Not *anywhere*."

"Why do you keep *saying* that?"

"Nobody does this *anywhere*," Zila says softly. "But Terrans *did* briefly try dark quantum farming. Back when we were at war with the Betraskans, in fact. During the first days of our exploration into the Fold."

I realize at last what Zila's implying, and my brain stutters to a halt.

She can't be serious.

There's no way.

Except . . .

"I don't recognize her uniform," I whisper. "And the station is so old-fashioned. . . ."

This. Cannot. Be. Happening.

"Not any*where*." Zila nods. "Any*when*."

"Maker's breath," Scarlett whispers.

Lieutenant Kim has obviously had enough and raises her gun. "You will explain what you mean right now. Or I start shooting."

"You will not believe me," Zila assures her.

"Try me."

"What year is it? Right now?"

Lieutenant Kim scoffs. "Are you serious?"

"Please," Zila says. "Indulge me."

". . . It's 2177."

"We are from the year 2380."

A pause. "You're right. I *don't* believe you."

"I did warn you," Zila shrugs.

My brain starts fizzing, this-is-impossible fighting with this-is-*so-cool*. And underneath it all, a little voice is whispering, *Surviving that explosion was impossible. So was getting blown up eight more times. So was being transported wherever the hells we are in the blink of an eye.*

I see the precise moment Lieutenant Kim checks out. "All right, this is above my pay grade. I'm taking you in."

"You are obviously experiencing temporal distortion, too, Lieutenant," Zila insists.

Kim ignores her, taps a mic on the side of her throat. "Glass Slipper, this is Kim, do you read?"

"You are repeating this encounter, just as we are," Zila says.

"Slipper, this is Kim, do you copy?"

Still no response. The lieutenant curses under her breath.

"If it is indeed the year 2177," Zila insists, "Terra is in the middle of a war with Trask. Your station looks severely damaged. We have no proof of our identity. If you bring us aboard what is clearly an experimental military installation during wartime, this will end poorly."

"I wasn't asking you to vote," Kim snaps, waving her pistol. "Move."

. . . . .

Lieutenant Kim herds us up to the cockpit at gunpoint, and controlling her fighter via some kind of remote console on her wrist, she begins towing our damaged shuttle toward the station. The task is slow, laborious—Kim seems to know what she's doing, but it's not as though fighter ships are really made for this kind of job.

Zila, Scar, and I are on our knees in the center of the cabin, fingers laced behind our heads. Kim looms behind us. Every now and then, she tries to raise the station on comms.

Bad news is, she seems to be getting angrier every time she fails, and this girl has already killed us a lot today. Good news is, we can whisper while she swears up a storm.

"Was Zila serious?" Scar murmurs, leaning close. (*How does she still smell good, doesn't she sweat?*) "*Time* travel?"

My shoulders rise and fall in the tiniest of shrugs, and I glance at our Brain, who's lost in her thoughts again. "I don't know. It sounds insane. But I don't have another explanation that fits the facts."

She chews her lip, eyes wide and worried.

This is bad, bad, bad.

If the year our angry dirtgirl gave us is right (which it can't be, because *time travel*), Terrans and Betraskans are at war. We will be for another two decades. And I'm being transported onto some classified military base drifting on the edge of a dark matter storm in the middle of some station-wide catastrophe. Zila's promise that this will "end poorly" might just be the understatement of the century.

Whatever century this is . . .

I don't say any of this out loud, but I don't have to. Scar leans in silently, pressing her shoulder against mine.

"I *am* very charming," I murmur. "They'll probably leave me alone."

Lieutenant Kim raises her pistol. "You. Shut up."

I shut up. And I press my shoulder back in against Scarlett's, drawing what comfort I can from the contact.

Cat is gone. Tyler is gone. Auri and Kal are gone.

After so many years alone, my squad has become my clan. A thousand invisible tendrils tying me to each of them in a way Terrans can't possibly understand. I'm always tuned in to them, always monitoring where they are, the way they move around me. It's instinct. A Betraskan without a clan spends every moment aware that they're a tiny speck in a big universe, and that they're not connected.

I felt that pain when my parents sent me off-world to live with my grandparents, away from all the rest of the family, because it would be easier on me with access to zero gravity. My grandparents were all right—they'd chosen to go where they were, could head home anytime. Me? My bond had been cut, whether they said it out loud or not.

I felt that same pain every day at the academy, always surrounded by other people, never tied to any of them.

But the pain of losing my squad one by one is even worse.

I don't want to lose Scar and Zila too.

It takes us almost thirty minutes to reach the station, and

along the way, we get our first really good look at the dark matter storm. It's *mind-blowing* in scale, trillions of klicks across, and the scope of it makes me feel like an insect looking into the face of the Maker.

It's entirely black, so deep and complete your eyes hurt to look at it. But every now and then, it lights up, thrumming with intermittent pulses of quantum energy, deep mauve running to blood black. Its edges writhe and twist and knot around themselves like serpents made of smoke, big as solar systems. But within a few moments, that dark light dies, and blackness always comes crashing back down.

That length of huge metallic cable trails from the station, hundreds of thousands of kilometers out into the pulsing dark. As we draw closer, I can see more clearly where it ends—a vast structure out in the invisible chaos. Its surface is flat, metallic, rippling like oil on water. A thousand-kilometer-wide testament to the absolutely breathtaking insanity of our captors.

A quantum sail.

This station, this rig—all of it must have cost a fortune to build. And the thing is, if you could ever make one of these things work, the power source would be unimaginable. But the reality is that setting up a quantum sail in a dark matter storm and *tethering it to the station that you yourself are on* is like slathering your favorite body part(s) in freyan and marching straight into a caladian's den. You are absolutely, positively asking for—nay, *jauntily demanding*—a very unpleasant and ultimately terminal experience.

"These people are *deranged*," I whisper.

We draw close to the dumpy station, still spewing vapor

out into the dark, its hull scarred and blackened. It's just *ugly,* like someone really angry built it. I don't know what it is with Terrans and their design aesthetic.

We cruise into a small landing bay, and though Lieutenant Kim still hasn't managed to raise her commanders on comms, the automated docking arms latch on to our ships, the shudder of impact running through the whole shuttle as we're brought down onto the deck.

As the bay doors cycle closed behind us, Lieutenant Kim orders us to our feet. My heart is in my mouth as she marches us down to the shuttle airlock. Even though I've already been killed nine times today, my body is still full of adrenaline, my brain ringing with the thought that I don't want to die.

I don't want to die.

Our airlock door clunks open, and we step into a secondary airlock connected to the main hangar. The bay is bathed in flashing red light. Pistol aimed at us, Kim types an access code, the main hangar doors open, and we're suddenly stepping out into a scene of total chaos.

Dozens of crew in military uniforms are running around, feet stomping on the metal floor. Thick smoke billows from vents in the ceiling. Half the hangar is in the dark, the other half lit by emergency lighting. A squadron of fighters like Kim's is bathed in a flickering blood-red glow. Terrans are scurrying around, wearing breathers to protect themselves from the fumes. Scar starts coughing, Zila too. The stink is like burned hair and plastene.

The wall to our left has a long plexiglass window, and I can see the distant sail dancing like a kite in a storm, the tempest pulsing beyond. It'd be almost pretty if it—

"Attention, Glass Slipper personnel. Hull breach on Decks 13 through 17."

The loudspeaker temporarily drowns out everything else, and when it cuts out, an annoying siren starts whooping instead.

"Move," says the lieutenant behind us, poking me between the shoulder blades with her gun.

"I don't want to," I say.

"What he said," Scarlett agrees.

"Attention, Glass Slipper personnel. All engineering staff report to Gamma Section, Deck 12, immediately."

"This will end poorly," Zila predicts again.

"Kim!" a voice roars. "Where the hell have you been?"

We shamble to a stop, and Kim comes to attention. The speaker is bearing down on us out of the red light and smoke, a huge, broad-shouldered man with no hair on his head but one of those weird mustaches Terrans grow, looking like it's trying to crawl out of his nostrils. When he spots me, his eyes bulge wide, and my stomach crawls up into my chest.

"What the *hell*?" he barks. "Is that a goddamned Betraskan? Explain yourself, soldier!"

"Apologies, sir!" Kim salutes. "I tried to raise command on comms but got no response! These three broke the exclusion zone, sir!"

"So shoot them!" he roars.

BOOM.

The whole place shudders as something, somewhere, explodes.

"Warning: Containment breach. Evacuate Decks 5 through 6 immediately. Repeat: Containment breach—"

Kim raises her voice over the clamor. "Sir, I think the anomalies surrounding their arrival warrant Sci-Div's attentions. If it wasn't urgent—"

"I'll tell you what's urgent, Lieutenant," he snarls. "The containment field around the core is breached, half the upper decks are locked down, and thirty-six people are confirmed dead, including Dr. Pinkerton! The whole goddamn station is coming to pieces around us, and you choose *now* to bring Betraskan spies into a *classified facility*? Are you insane?"

CRASH.

Out in the storm, the dark lights up, black to roiling mauve, as a pulse of dark energy directly strikes the sail. The energy burst is so intense that even catching it through my contacts from the corner of my eye, my vision is momentarily lost to the afterimages. I blink furiously as the pulse runs up the cable at the speed of light, cascading into the station itself. A bank of computers to our right explodes in a spray of sparks. A new blast of louder, more annoying alarms screams through the loudspeakers. I almost miss Zila's words when she mutters to herself beside me.

"Quantum pulse, forty-four minutes after arrival."

The deck commander's eyes narrow. "What the hell is *that*?"

The man raises his pistol, and my heart lurches as he points it square at Scarlett. Scar lifts her hands higher, takes a step back, and through the smoke and chaos and burning sparks, I see that her necklace has begun . . .

Maker's breath, her necklace is glowing.

That chunk of Eshvaren crystal Adams and de Stoy left

67

for us in Emerald City is burning on her chest. The light is black, painful to look at, just like the pulse out in the storm.

"WARNING: CONTAINMENT BREACH CRITICAL. EVACUATE DECKS 2 THROUGH 10 IMMEDIATELY. REPEAT: CONTAINMENT BREACH CRITICAL."

"Kim, didn't you check them for weapons?" the Terran roars.

"Yessir, b—"

"Well, what the hell *is* that?"

"I don't know!" Scarlett cries, backing away. "Please, I don't!"

"WARNING: CONTAINMENT BREACH UNDER WAY, ENGAGE EMERGENCY MEASURES DECK 11."

Zila speaks directly to Kim, ignoring everything around us. "I told you this would not work."

The Terran lifts his weapon, pointing it at Zila.

"Sir," Kim tries, desperate now. "They—"

"You're headed for the brig, Kim!" he roars, thumbing off the safety.

"Hey!"

Oh chakk, that was me.

Time slows as he swings his weapon around toward me, and I see the beginning of the movement as he pulls the trigger.

And though it feels like it takes forever, I only have time for one thought.

I couldn't bear to watch him shoot them.

I'm glad it's me first.

BLAM.

6

AURI

I awaken surrounded by the dead. A sea of staring faces, Syldrathi Waywalkers caught in a final moment of fear or pain or defiance, mouths agape, eyes wide. Adults and children are piled together, no longer pinned to the crystal walls above us by the force of the Starslayer's will.

I lie among them on a floor littered with shards of crystal, catching sidelong glimpses of the bodies through my lashes as I force my aching eyes open, then lose the battle and slam them closed once more.

I can't sense Kal's mind.

Everything hurts—every muscle in my body screams, my head pounds. But beneath the throbbing ache, I hear the echoes of the power I summoned—that massive burst of energy pouring through me into the Weapon and out again, running out from my spine, all the way to my fingertips. And the memory awakens something like . . . exhilaration.

I ignore the pain, focus my thoughts, sending a midnight-blue tendril out through the last remnants of the Waywalkers' dying screams. It's like searching for one particular tree in a thick, overgrown forest. But even the faintest hints of those screams are fading now, and my silver-laced blue finds nothing, nothing, nothing.

He must be too far away.

I must be too weak.

The last thing I remember is the Weapon firing—that colossal burst of energy meant to destroy the sun, and Earth and everyone on it. I couldn't stop it, but I tried to turn its energy inward, to protect the fleet around us, to protect the planet, its sun, to stop . . .

. . . Caersan.

The Starslayer.

I scramble onto all fours, heart pounding and head swimming with just that effort, my own breath harsh in my ears as I fight to stay upright.

The man responsible for the murder all around me is close, lying at the foot of his crystal throne, his red cloak splayed around him. He's stirring groggily, braids thrown back to reveal the ruined side of his face. The glow of his eye shines through the spiderweb of scars along his temple and cheek, as if he's lit from within. The light pulses softly, maybe in time with his heartbeat, and I sit back on my haunches, lifting one hand to the right side of my own face. The skin feels rough beneath my fingertips.

I can't sense Kal anywhere.

Then his father's mind brushes up against mine, the dark red of dried blood, and a gold that's too like Kal's, and his eyes snap open, focusing on me.

He did all of this. He's responsible for every drop of this blood, this destruction, this pain.

And as our eyes meet, he smiles.

I'm moving before I have time to think—I grab a sharp shard of crystal and push up like a runner coming out of the blocks, lunging for him like I'm going to stake a vampire.

He surges up to one knee to meet me, and his backhand sends me stumbling into the throne, the world whirling by—I grab at it to stay upright, and he's swaying too, dark purple blood dripping from his nose, his lips drawn back in a snarl now.

He did this.

The dead Waywalkers.

Children, some of them.

His own people.

The blank space where Kal should be.

I'm going to kill him.

All around us, the Weapon thrums, crystal humming and singing as it cools, and over all of it, the harsh rasp of my breath as the two of us stand, gathering ourselves.

Then our eyes lock, and I throw myself at him again, blindly smashing him to the ground, my scream echoing back at us from every direction, the breath knocked out of him as I drive a knee into his rib cage.

He rolls, and his hands are at my throat, squeezing, crushing. On instinct, I clasp my fists together and punch up between his forearms, forcing them apart and breaking his grip.

I'm going to kill him. That's all that's left to do.

I grope blindly for another shard of crystal, fingers closing around it, and I drive it up and into his side. It shears off his armor, but as he twists away, I roll out from underneath him.

We both scramble to our feet, backing up a handful of steps, and I shift my grip on my crystal knife. He's huge, and he moves like a warrior even now, even injured. This is the man who taught Kal to fight.

But my mind feels like a sponge with all the water squeezed out—there's no way I can use my power against him, so this is what I have. His own mind must be just as weak, or he'd have squished me like a bug by now.

It only takes one lucky hit.

This is what I'll do with the time I have left.

He breaks first, lunging forward with impossible speed to strike at my throat. I skip back, step on something soft, stumble, lunge forward to slash at his ribs while he's close.

He snarls his fury, but neither of us is in the mood for words. I follow up, dancing in for another swipe, but in a movement too fast to follow, he grabs at my arm and tosses me through the air like I weigh nothing.

My feet leave the ground, and everything's suspended for a second before I crash into the base of the crystal throne, ears ringing, vision closing into darkness.

There's a dead Waywalker staring straight at me, only silence where her mind should be, and her braids are a mess, and I want to smooth them for her, and I want to tell her *I'm sorry, I'm so sorry,* and helplessly my mind reaches out for Kal's once more, a desperate midnight-and-silver unfurling in search of . . .

. . . *is that . . . ?*

. . . the faintest flicker of violet and gold.

Joy explodes inside me, and I whirl around to search the carnage for him, because he's here, he's alive, he's . . .

"Wait!" I throw up one hand, and Caersan pauses, lip curled as he stares at me like I'm something that belongs on the bottom of his shoe.

"Weakling," he sneers. "Now you seek mercy? Too late for your courage to fail you, girl."

"No, I . . ." I'm grasping for words, and I lift my hand to gesture, to take in our surroundings. In my search for Kal, I've opened my mind, and abruptly I realize something's changed. "Can't you hear?"

He scowls. "I hear nothing."

"Exactly."

Caersan tilts his head, and at the edges of my own mind I can sense his cautious questing. Sniffing the wind from behind his barricades, refusing to make himself vulnerable.

I can't hear anything out there. When we fought during the attack, the gulf of space around the Weapon was a whirl of battle, the minds of the humans, the Betraskans, and the Syldrathi pilots and crews—their fear, their anger, their focus. Somewhere in the midst of them I was aware of Finian, Scarlett, and Zila, my squad, my family.

But now . . . there's nothing. Or rather, not *nothing*—not an absence, like they're all simply dead. But something else. It's like waking up on a snow day, like the world is strangely muffled.

"Where did the fleet go?" I ask quietly. "The battle?"

He frowns, and I ease up onto all fours, and finally I can see Kal, lying crumpled on the other side of the throne.

Keeping one eye on Caersan, I crawl around toward his son—the Starslayer notes the movement and dismisses it, returning to his contemplation of the strange silence outside.

73

Kal's curled on his side, wearing the same peaceful, vulnerable expression he does when he sleeps. I woke up before him most mornings in the Echo. For half a year, I saw him like this each day.

I wrap one hand around his, and though I'm trembling with exhaustion, I drag up the energy I need from my soul itself, making my mental touch so delicate that I barely brush against his bruised and battered mind.

I breathe gently onto those violet and gold embers, infusing him with my strength, careful not to snuff them out or overwhelm them.

And slowly, slowly, they glow a little brighter.

And his fingers tighten around mine.

I can't stop my eyes from flooding with tears, relief breaking something open inside me. Here he lies, dressed in black, a warrior of the Unbroken. But he was never one of them. He came here for us, even after we cast him out.

For me.

"There is . . . something." Caersan's voice cuts through my reverie, and I glance up. He's frowning, almost uncertain—I mean, it's just the tiniest twitch of his brow, but by his standards he looks completely freaked out. "That way."

He's pointing beyond the crystal walls of the Weapon, out toward the space beyond. Perhaps toward Sol, or Earth—I have no sense of direction left. I'm wary of him, and reluctant to make my mind vulnerable, but the truth is that he's the Archon of a cabal of fanatical warriors. Though I put on a good show just now, if he wanted to break me in two, he could.

And now, Kal's hand in mine, I have something to live for.

So I'm careful as I let myself feel, probing with my mind in the direction he points, ever at the ready to snap back to safety if he tries to strike. But he doesn't. He simply watches me, head tilting at the moment my eyes widen in horror.

Because somewhere out there, just at the edges of my range, I can feel it. The world humanity came from. The cradle that birthed our entire civilization. The planet I was born on, and would have died to protect.

Earth.

It hangs in the darkness, a pale blue dot suspended in a sunbeam, and just for a second, it feels like home. But then I sense it, creeping, crawling, covering my entire world. Something silvery-green-blue-gray, something teeming-writhing-coiling-growing, something full of a sickening kind of life.

The Ra'haam.

Mothercustard . . .

The Ra'haam has taken Earth.

7

KAL

My mind is a thousand splinters, a thousand moments, a thousand memories.

I am a mirror, and all of me is broken.

"Kal?"

. . . I am five years old. In our suites aboard the Andarael, my father's old ship. This is my first memory, I realize. And it is of my parents fighting.

My mother told me they were once so close it was as if they were one spirit in two bodies. When first they met, Laeleth and Caersan were iron and lodestone, powder and flame. And she thought the adoration she bore for him would be enough to change the shape of his soul.

My mother is beautiful. Brave. But she is a shield, not a blade. They stand and shout at each other, and the tears well in my young eyes as I stare. My sister, Saedii, stands nearby, silent. Watching and learning. My parents' roars grow louder, my mother's face twists and my father's hand rises into the sky and falls like thunder.

And then there is silence, save for my wails.

I do not understand, except that I fear, that I know, this is not the way it should be. My father turns from where my mother has fallen. My sister watches as he walks to where I sit. And he picks me up and I hold out my arms to clutch at his neck, seeking comfort from he who made me.

But he does not embrace me. Instead, he drags his thumb across my wet cheeks and stares, silent and glacial, until I stop crying.

"Good," he says. "Tears are for the conquered, Kaliis."

"Kal?" someone whispers.

. . . I am seven years old, and we have returned to Syldra.

The war is proceeding slowly, and my father and other Archons of the Warbreed have been recalled for a summit of the Inner Council, to shout down those among the Waywalker and Watcher Cabals who cry we should negotiate peace with Terra. A part of me hopes he crushes them. The rest of me longs for this war to end. Two halves within me, one born of my father's rage, the other of my mother's wisdom. I know not which is the stronger yet.

Saedii and I face each other beneath the lias trees, a sweet-scented wind blowing between us. Our stances are perfect, just as Father showed us. Our fists are clenched. She is older than me. Taller. Faster. But I am learning.

Mother sits nearby, speaking quietly with elders of her cabal. They hope that she, as the lifelove of Caersan, can persuade my father to at least consider the Terrans' peace overture. But they are fools.

Peace is the way the cur cries, "Surrender."

Saedii lunges, and with me distracted, her blow finds its mark. She sweeps my legs away, and I crash onto the purple grass, breathless. She sits atop me, eyes alight with triumph, fist raised.

"Yield, brother," she smiles.

"No."

We turn our heads at the word, and there he stands. Clad in black armor beneath the swaying boughs. The greatest warrior our people have ever known. The Waywalker elders bow their heads in fear. My mother sits silent, a shadow fallen over her. My father speaks, and his voice is steel.

"What did I teach you about mercy, daughter?"

"It is the province of cowards, Father," Saedii replies.

"Then why ask your foe to yield?"

My sister pinches her lips and looks down at me. Mother is standing now, staring at my father and speaking as no one else dares to.

"Caersan, he is only a boy."

He looks through her as though she is glass. "He is my son, Laeleth."

Father's eyes fall on Saedii. His command unspoken.

Her fist splits my lip and black stars burst in my eyes. Another blow lands, another, and I taste blood, feel pain, splintering, breaking.

"Enough."

The beating stops. My sister's weight upon my chest eases away. I open the eye that is not swelling shut and find my father standing above me. I can see him in my face when I look into the mirror at night. I can feel him behind me when I think I am alone. My mother watches, her expression one of anguish as I roll to my belly, push myself to my feet.

Father sinks to one knee before me so we are eye to eye. He reaches out and drags one thumb across my cheek. But where once he found tears, now there is only blood.

"Good boy, Kaliis," he says.

I nod. "Tears are for the conquered, Father."

"Kal, please wake up. . . ."

. . . I am in my room aboard the Andarael, and I am nine years old.

My fists are torn, my blood deep purple in the low, warm light. The engines thrum as I fish inside the deepest gash with tweezers, and wincing, I draw it out from my swollen knuckle— a pale sliver of broken tooth.

I did not mean to hit him so hard. I do not remember most of what happened after my first punch landed. But I remember the words he spoke about my father—the words that smelled like cowardice. The Warbreed denounced the Inner Council's treaty with the Terrans, attacked Earth's shipyards, crushed their navy. And now we will turn our attention to those among our own people who cry for peace when there can be only war. Because war is what I was born for.

Isn't it?

The door opens with a whisper, and my mother enters the room, clad in a long, flowing gown, a string of Void crystals glittering about her neck. I stand as is proper, head bowed, voice soft.

"Mother."

She glides to the viewport, staring to the dark beyond. I can still see the echoes of the battle out there in my mind's eye— those vast ships burning away in the light of Orion. All those lives snuffed out by my father's hand.

I see the faint bruise at the corner of my mother's mouth, a dark smudge in the starlight that kisses her skin. An ember of rage flares inside me. I love my mother with all I have. And though I love my father also, I hate this thing within him, this thing that makes him hurt her.

I would tear it out of him with my bare hands if I could.

"Valeth is in the infirmary with a broken jaw and nine broken ribs."

"That is unfortunate," I reply carefully.

"He says he fell down the auxiliary stairwell."

"They can be treacherous."

My mother looks to me, eyes shining. "What happened to your hand?"

I keep my gaze on the floor, speaking soft. "I injured it training."

I hear quiet footsteps, feel her touch, cool on my cheek. "Even were I not Waywalker born, even were the locks upon your heart not open doors to me, still I am your mother, Kaliis. You cannot lie to me."

"Then do not ask me to. Honor demands I—"

"Honor," she sighs.

Her fingertips brush the new glyf on my forehead, the three blades branded there on my ascension day. I know she and Father fought about which cabal I would become part of. And I know he won.

He always wins.

"How do you think that boy will feel when he lies to his father about the beating you gave him?" she asks.

"He made himself my enemy," I reply. "I do not care how he feels."

"Yes, you do. That is the difference between Caersan and you."

She lifts my chin, gently forcing me to meet her eyes. I see the pain in them. I see the strength. And I see myself.

"I know you are his son, Kaliis. But you are my son also. And you need not become the thing he is teaching you to be."

She leans forward, presses her lips to my burning brow.

"There is no love in violence, Kaliis."

I see light behind her. A halo of midnight blue flecked with silver.

I hear a voice, familiar but strange.

"Kal?"

"There is no love in violence."

"Kal, can you hear me? Oh, please, *please*, wake up."

. . . My mother's touch rouses me from sleep. My heart thumps as my eyes flash wide and her hand covers my lips. I am twelve years old.

"Get up, my love," she whispers. "We must go."

"Go? Go where?"

"We are leaving," she tells me. "We are leaving him."

I see a bruise, faint upon her wrist. The split in her lip is new. But I know it is not for her that she is running from him at last.

She draws me up off my bed, hands me my uniform. Wordlessly I dress, wondering if she truly means it. My father will never allow this. I have heard him threaten to kill her if she leaves. There is nowhere she can run.

"Where will we go?" I ask.

"I have friends on Syldra."

"Mother, we are at war with Syldra."

"No, he is at war," she hisses. "With everyone and everything. I will not let you become him, Kaliis. I will allow him to poison my children no longer."

My mind is racing as we slip through the dark to Saedii's quarters. Mother steals inside while I keep watch, my heart *hammering, my mind whirling. He will never forget this. He will never forgive.*

"Saedii," Mother whispers. "Saedii, wake up."

My sister seethes upright, blade drawn from beneath her pillow, teeth bared. When she sees our mother, she relaxes only a fraction. And when she sees me, she tenses once again.

Her face is still bruised from the beating I gave her. The rift between us wider than it has ever been. She broke the siif that Mother gave me after I defeated her at spar. She can no longer best me in the circle, so she sought to punish me another way. And I punished her in kind. I can still picture her blood on my fingers. The pain in her eyes as I hit her with the siif she broke. I feel shame even now that I laid hands upon her so. Mind echoing with the memory of Father's words when he learned what I had done.

"Never have I been more proud that you are my son."

"What do you want, Mother?" she whispers, lowering her blade.

"We are leaving, Saedii. We are leaving him."

Her eyes narrow. Her lip curls. "Are you crazed?"

"I am crazed to have allowed this to continue as long as I have. Caersan is a cancer, and I will allow it to spread no further. Come now."

Saedii snatches her hand away from Mother's grip. "Faithless coward. He is your lifelove, Laeleth. You owe him your heart and soul."

"I have given him both!" Mother hisses, pointing to the bruises on her skin. "And this is how I have been repaid! And were it only I to bear the burden, perhaps even now I would keep my troth. But I will not stand by and watch my children fall into the same darkness that consumes him!"

Saedii looks to me, face bruised, teeth bared. "You allow this, brother?"

I meet her eyes, pleading. "I am sorry, sister. But you know the truth. He is no good for us. He is not what I wish to become."

"Coward!" she spits, rising. "Both of you, faithless cowards!"

Midnight-blue light flares behind her, and I squint, blinded. The warmth of it bathes my skin, tingling through every part of me.

"Kal?"

"Saedii, come with us!"

"I would die before I betrayed him."

"Kal!"

"Coward! Shame! De'sai!"

"KAL!"

. . . I open my eyes.

I see her above me, a halo of light playing around her head. My heart surges so painfully I press one hand to my ribs to stop the ache. My sight is blurred, mind aching, but still, one thought burns bright enough to pierce the fog of my broken thoughts.

She is alive.

My Aurora is alive.

The walls around us are glittering crystal, and I realize I am floating a meter above the floor. As I shift my weight, try to rise, the air about me hums gently, rainbow-colored—the same as the energies of the Echo, where Aurora and I lived half a year, a lifetime, in the memories of the Eshvaren homeworld. But they feel different now. The song of energy hanging in the air is—

"No, don't try to sit up," she whispers, one hand on my

shoulder. "Just rest, okay? I thought I lost you for a minute there, I—I thought I . . ."

Her voice breaks and she closes her eyes, tears in her lashes as she hangs her head. I raise one hand to cup her cheek, soft as feathers.

"I am here," I tell her. "I will never leave you. Unless you wish me to."

"No," she breathes. "I'm sorry, I'm so sorry I sent you away, Kal."

"I am sorry I lied to you, be'shmai. I was a coward to do so."

"You came here alone to finish him. To save the damn galaxy." She presses my knuckles to her lips. "You're the bravest boy I ever met."

Him.

A shadow falls over me as the memories seep into the wreckage of my mind—the battle in the throne room, the war raging outside, Terrans and Betraskans and Syldrathi cutting each other to pieces as the Weapon pulsed and the Waywalkers screamed and my father . . .

"My father," I whisper. "Did you . . . ?"

Aurora shakes her head. My vision is clearing, and I see now there are cracks running through her skin, radiating about her right eye. Her iris is still glowing, and the light shines through the cracks, coming from somewhere within her.

She is wounded, I realize. Weak. The Weapon has . . .

It has taken something from her. . . .

And yet, I can feel her inside my mind, a warmth spreading out from her and mending the tears my father ripped through me. I can picture him, holding me still with the power of his will alone, the knife I'd tried to plunge into his heart falling from my fingers as he tore my psyche apart.

He tried to kill me.

Just as I tried to kill him.

"What . . . happened?" I whisper.

"The Weapon fired," Aurora replies. "I tried to stop it, tried to turn it inward on myself, but . . . I couldn't hold on. The Waywalkers are all dead."

"The fleets? The battle?" My heart quickens, and I rise to one elbow despite the pain. "What happened to Terra? Your sun?"

"The sun is fine." She swallows thickly, trembling. "But Earth . . ."

She meets my eyes, her own brimming with tears.

"Earth is gone, Kal."

My heart sinks, my hand finds hers. "The Weapon struck it?"

"No." She shakes her head again, and I feel the kaleidoscope of her thoughts in mine—confusion, fear, rage. "The Ra'haam. It's taken the whole planet. Consumed it. Absorbed it. Every living thing on it."

"How long was I unconscious for?" I whisper, bewildered.

"A few hours maybe."

"Hours?" I shake my head. "Then . . . how is that possible?"

"I don't know. I reached out when I woke up, and I couldn't feel anything around us. The fleets, the pilots, the soldiers, they were all gone, as if they'd never been. The only thing I sensed was . . . *it*. Like . . . oil and mold in my mind.

So much of it. Covering Earth the same way it covered Octavia." She drags a hand through her hair, the skin around her right eye cracked like drought-struck clay. "It felt me too, Kal. I *know* it did."

The crystal hums around me, a shift in tone and hue. It ripples warm upon my skin, but again, I am struck by the notion that all is not well.

"The song of this place." I look at the glittering beauty around us, frowning. "It feels different than it used to. Almost . . . off-key?"

Aurora nods. "I know. Something feels wrong."

". . . We are moving," I realize.

Aurora glances to the glittering hallway, jaw clenched. "*He's* doing it. I needed to take care of you. So he's moving us through the Fold. We're headed . . . I don't know where. Away from Earth. Away from *it*."

"I must speak with him," I say.

"Kal, no," she pleads, trying to stop me as I rise. "You need to rest. He almost *killed* you, do you understand? He shattered your mind into a thousand pieces. And if he tries again, I don't know if I'm strong enough to stop him."

"I am not frightened of him, Aurora."

"But I'm frightened for *you*. I can't lose you again, I *can't*!"

I gather her into my arms, and she hugs me fiercely, and for a moment, all of the hurt, the pain, the grief fades away. With her in my embrace, I am complete again. With her beside me, there is nothing I cannot do.

"You will not lose me," I vow. "I am yours forever. When the fire of the last sun fails, my love for you will still burn."

I kiss her brow.

"But I must speak with him, Aurora. Help me. Please."

She stares at me a moment longer, uncertain. Fighting with the fear of what he may do to me. My heart aches to see the hurt that has been done to her. The strength she has given to fight this far. But at last, she squares her jaw, and putting my arm around her shoulder, she helps me stand.

I still feel fragile—as if I am a tapestry of a million threads held together by a single knot of will and warmth. But she is beside me again, and that is all that matters. Holding on to each other, Aurora and I limp through the glittering corridors, crystal singing rainbows all around us, discordant and grating.

My father named this vessel *Neridaa*—a Syldrathi concept that describes the process of simultaneously destroying and creating. Making and unmaking. But I know the lie of it. This is the weapon he used to destroy Syldra's sun. Our world. Ten billion lives extinguished by his hand, my mother among them. And I know my father creates nothing but death.

Sai'nuit.

Starslayer.

My heart stills as I lay eyes upon him. He sits atop the crystal spire in the chamber's heart, like an emperor upon his bloody throne. The floor is scattered with corpses, shattered fragments; the air reeks of death. He is still clad in armor—black, high-collared, a long cloak of crimson spilling over the steps below. Ten silver braids draped over the scarred side of his face. But I see his eye aglow behind them, burning with the same pale luminance as Aurora's when they fought for the fate of her world.

Before him, I see a vast projection—a stretch of black dotted by tiny stars. We are in the Fold, I realize, approaching a gate. I wonder why the colorscape inside the Weapon is not muted to black and white, as would normally happen in the Fold. I wonder what other properties this vessel possesses. Is it the crystal? The Eshvaren? Him?

"Father," I say.

He does not hear me. Does not look up. The *Neridaa* is drawing closer to the gate—tear-shaped, crystalline, Syldrathi in design.

"Father!" I roar.

He glances at me, then away just as swift, eye burning like a tiny sun.

"Kaliis. You live."

"Disappointed?"

"Impressed." That burning gaze flickers to Aurora, then back to the black before him. "But then, you always were your father's son."

Refusing to rise to his bait, I step forward with Aurora beside me. "What is happening? Where is the Unbroken fleet? The Terrans and Betraskans? How is it Earth was consumed by the enemy so swiftly?"

He licks at his lip, curled almost into a snarl. "The enemy," he repeats.

"The enemy you were supposed to stop!" Aurora growls beside me.

His gaze flickers her way. The snarl grows a fraction wider. "You are a fool, girl. I can see why my fool son dotes upon you."

She steps forward, fingers curling to fists. "You sonofabit—"

"Wait . . ." I take her hand, squeeze as I watch the projection floating before my father. We are crossing through the FoldGate now, into realspace. But this close, I see the gate looks . . . wrong. Old. Scored by quantum lightning strikes. Half the guidance lights are nonfunctional. It appears as if it has not seen maintenance in decades.

". . . Where are we?" Aurora asks.

My father scoffs, brushing a stray braid back over his shoulder. "Ever and always, you seek answers to the wrong questions, girl."

Looking to the system, I recognize the star from my childhood—brilliant blue, like a sapphire shining in an ocean of darkness. "That is Taalos, be'shmai. There is a Syldrathi colony on Taalos IV, a starport, claimed by the Unbroken after they withdrew from the Inner Council of Syldra."

"He . . . came here for reinforcements?"

"I came here for confirmation, girl."

Aurora grits her teeth, her right eye flaring like a lightning strike. The light pulses beneath her skin, leaking out through the cracks in her cheek. For a moment, the air around us feels greasy and charged with current. Her lips part in a snarl. "Listen, I don't care how hurt I am, and I don't care what it costs me. You call me *girl* again, and you and I are gonna finish that—"

"Silence," he says.

Aurora blinks. "Okay, maybe I'm being unclear here, but you don't *talk* to me that way. You don't call me *girl*, you don't demand *silence*, you don't treat me like something you stepped in by mistake. I am a Trigger of the Eshvaren, and unlike *you*, I was brave enough to step up and—"

"No."

My father rises, a small scowl on his brow, and he looks at the star system projected before him.

"Listen," he nods. "Out there."

I look to Aurora, and she meets my eyes, pressing her lips thin. I feel her mind swell and stretch at the edges of my own. She lifts her hand, as if reaching toward that distant star. That pale glow illuminates her iris, seeps through the splits in her skin.

"I can't . . . I can't hear anything."

He nods. "Silence."

My father looks out on the Taalos star, his face a cold mask.

"A colony of almost half a million people orbited this sun. Unbroken all. Loyal unto death." He laces his fingers together and breathes deep. "The death that has now claimed them. Each and every one."

"How?" I breathe.

"The Ra'haam," Aurora whispers. "I can . . . I can feel it."

She looks at me with tears in her eyes.

"It's taken over the colony, Kal. It's taken over their entire world."

"But *how*?" I demand, my frustration rising. "How is this *possible*? The Ra'haam has not even bloomed yet! Its intent was to drive the galaxy into war while it slumbered on its nursery worlds, waiting to hatch! But now it has taken Earth? Taalos? How can this be?"

"This is your fault," Aurora says, stepping forward. "*All* of this. The Eshvaren entrusted you to defeat the Ra'haam, Caersan, and you used their Weapon to fight your own petty war! And where did it get you?"

90

He looks at her then, and the imperious mask he wears begins to slip. It starts small, just a glimmer of amusement in his eye, a faint curl of his lip. But soon he is smiling, and that smile stretches and splits to his eyeteeth, and of all things, he begins laughing. *Laughing*, as if my beloved has said the most amusing thing he has ever heard.

All this death. All this darkness. And he finds it *amusing*. And I see it then, sure as I see this girl beside me, sure as I saw the wreckage of our world, the ruin he has made of our people.

My father is insane.

"What the hell is so funny?" Aurora shouts.

"As I said," he finally replies, wiping a tear from his eye, "always you seek answers to the wrong questions."

"What should we ask, then?" I demand.

"It is not a matter of where my ambition has gotten me, my son."

My father breathes deep, looking out into that silent void.

"It is *when*."

PART 2

TWO IN ONE LIFETIME

8

ZILA

"What the hell is going on?"

I am back in the cockpit of our Syldrathi shuttle again, floating at the edge of a storm of dark matter, my ears still ringing with the crack of the gunshot that killed me. Instead of replaying the moment of my death over in my head, I focus on Lieutenant Kim's face as it appears on the monitor. I had been hoping she would take a different approach this loop, and as she opens comms for the tenth time, I realize she is ready to talk.

Pleasing.

"Hello, Lieutenant. I have been expecting you."

Her pause is so long that if I could not see her shifting slightly on my monitor, I would think our comms had cut out.

"I can't tell if you're kidding," she says eventually.

"I hear that with remarkable frequency."

More silence.

"Open the airlock," she says. *"I'm coming over."*

Scarlett and Finian reach the bridge, breathless, having sprinted up from the engine room. Catching the end of the conversation, Finian leans in to study the lieutenant onscreen. "You're only coming over if you agree not to shoot anyone. I've died ten times already today, and I'm in *no* mood."

The lieutenant blinks, brow creasing. *"Ten? I count nine."*

"We died on the way here, too."

"On the way here from the future." Her tone is dubious.

Scarlett leans in beside Finian. "See you soon, Lieutenant."

Kim cuts the connection, leaving the three of us to stare at each other. The impossibility of what we are experiencing is not lost on any of us.

"I don't like this," Finian mutters. "I don't like *her.*"

"Me neither," Scarlett agrees. "But our ship is dead in the water, so we're not getting anywhere until we convince her we're not a threat."

Fin looks at Scarlett, voice soft. ". . . You sure you're okay?"

Scarlett blinks. "Yeah, I'm okay. I mean, okay as I can be, considering what's going on here. . . ."

"You . . ." Fin swallows. "You got shot."

"I'm fine, Fin." Scarlett smiles gently, touches his hand. "I promise. You got shot too, you know."

"Yeah," he says quietly. "But I didn't have to watch."

They gaze at each other for a long moment, and the silence eventually grows heavy enough for me to feel compelled to break it.

"Your medallion." I nod to the small crystal around Scarlett's neck. "The diamond reacted after the quantum sail was hit out in the storm."

"Yeah," she replies, recalling herself to the business at hand. "But it's not diamond. Fin figured out it's Eshvaren crystal."

I stare at the gem, eyes narrowing. "Interesting . . ."

"Why did it glow like that?"

"I do not know," I murmur, my mind now racing. "But it must be of significance. Several of our gifts from Admiral Adams and Battle Leader de Stoy have proved vital up to this point. The cigarillo case that saved Kal's life. The inscription on your necklace, telling us to go with the plan to disable the Eshvaren Weapon. It is as if the Aurora commanders *knew* what would happen to us. Their actions could even be interpreted as having guided us to this point."

Fin cocks his head, unconvinced. "Obviously something's up with the gifts. But guiding us? That's a stretch, Zil. They gave me a damn *pen*."

Scarlett nods to my golden hoops. "And you just got earrings."

WHUNNGG.

Our shuttle rocks as a towline strikes the hull. Another follows.

WHUNNGG.

Fin rolls his eyes. "Guess we better go down and let Lieutenant Psychopath in. I wonder what new and interesting way she'll kill us this time."

"You must be polite, Finian," I warn. "Her demeanor may be overly aggressive, but Lieutenant Kim is a critical component in all this."

Scarlett raises one eyebrow. "What makes you say that?"

"I take it you did not notice her callsign."

Now Finian blinks at me. "Huh?"

"Her callsign. A nickname used by her fellow pilots. It was stenciled on the wing of her fighter. It is also painted on the helmet she wears."

"I was too busy looking at the pistol in her hand to notice the helmet on her head," Scarlett admits. "What was it?"

I reach up to touch the earrings, the gift left for me in the Dominion Repository. The small golden birds dangling from the hoops, their wings spread, talons flashing in the dim light.

"Her callsign is Hawk."

. . . . .

This time when the airlock disengages, all three of us are waiting for her out in the open. Lieutenant Kim doesn't have her weapon drawn, though one hand rests on the grip. She stands framed in the doorway, reaching up slowly to unbuckle her mask and remove her helmet.

She is perhaps in her early twenties, and I believe my assessment that she is of East Asian descent is correct. Her features are symmetrical, conventionally attractive, although I imagine that for some, her stern expression would detract from the effect.

She is not tall.

"Okay, let's try this *again*," says Scarlett. "My name is Scarlett Jones. This is Zila Madran, and this is Finian de Karran de Seel."

"And before you start shooting again, some of my best friends are Terrans," Finian informs her. "*All* my best friends, actually."

"Lieutenant Nari Kim," our guest says slowly.

"Nice to meet you," Scarlett smiles. "And thanks for not killing us."

"You're welcome," she deadpans. "So, who wins the war?"

Scarlett tilts her head. ". . . What?"

"If you people are from the *future*," Kim says, obviously still dubious. "Who wins? Us?" She nods at Finian. "Or the bleach-heads?"

"Nobody ever wins a war," I reply. "But the Terrans and Betraskans will sign a peace treaty in—"

"Wait, wait," Scarlett says. "Should we be talking about stuff like this?"

". . . Why wouldn't we?" Fin asks.

She glances at the lieutenant. "What if we change the future?"

"That only happens in bad science fiction novels, right?"

"There is no precedent for what we are experiencing," I say. "Or at least, not one of which we are aware. It is difficult to know the ramifications of our actions, and virtually impossible to calculate the effects our presence in this time may have on future events. But given the gifts Aurora Command gave us, I believe it is best to assume we are *supposed* to be here."

"Maybe the future we know only exists because of the things we do here," Finian suggests. "Maybe we *have* to tell her this stuff."

"Still here," Lieutenant Kim reminds us.

"Sorry," Scarlett smiles. "We're trying to wrap our heads around all this, too. Believe us, we're almost as lost as you are. But in our time, the Betraskans are Terra's closest allies. We just left a battle back in 2380, and one of the last things we saw before all . . . this"—she waves about us—"was the Betraskan fleet showing up to *protect* Earth."

I can see the lieutenant wants to ask more questions

about our timeline, but she holds her tongue, and for that I am grateful. It is not efficient to think of what we have left behind. *Who* we have left behind.

"So what the hell *is* all"—she mimics Scarlett's wave—"this, then?"

"That is precisely what we are attempting to determine."

She looks me over, eyes lingering on mine. "So attempt. Because as far as I'm concerned, it's still even odds you're all bleach-head spies."

"Listen, Dirtgirl," Fin begins. "Maybe you wanna give the *blea*—"

"*Friends here,*" Scarlett chimes, patting Fin's arm and smiling brightly at the lieutenant. "All friends, remember?"

"There are two possibilities," I say. "Either a catalyst event occurred where we *were*, throwing us back in time and creating this anomaly . . ."

"Like being directly in the path of a massive ancient psychic superweapon as it was fired?" Scarlett asks.

". . . or the catalyst event occurred *here*," I continue, "drawing us back to this moment in time."

"Potentially both," Finian murmurs.

I nod. "What have you been experiencing, Lieutenant Kim?"

Our guest considers the question. I am not a good judge of emotion, but it seems to me that although she is still wary, some of the tension has momentarily left the air. She is at least *attempting* to cooperate for now.

"I'm out flying patrol six minutes ago when you suddenly show up on my scopes," she says. "We talk, I blast you, everything resets. We don't talk, I blast you, everything resets. I take you over to the station, you get shot, everything resets. Every time you die, I end up back exactly where I was six minutes ago."

My mind is settling, and I realize that this sense of comfort comes from having a problem to solve. This is something I know how to *do*. I will gather data. I will analyze. It will be good to be busy.

"What was happening here six minutes ago?"

The lieutenant chews her lip. Even to me, it is obvious she is reluctant, distrustful. But finally she speaks. "The station was running a test. There was some kind of . . . power fluctuation. I saw a sphere of dark light, thousands of klicks across, engulfing my ship. All my instruments went haywire. And when it cleared . . . your ship was right there."

"What kind of test?" I ask.

Scarlett nods. "What does this station actually *do*, Lieutenant?"

Lieutenant Kim looks around us, and for the first time, she shows a hint of the panic she must be feeling. "Hell if I know. Classified Terran military ops."

"It seems intelligence gathering must be our first course of action," I declare. "If we arrived at the precise moment this test was being conducted, it is a reasonable assumption the test may have precipitated said arrival. We must determine this station's purpose."

"How?" Fin asks. "Last time we went over there, they shot us on sight."

"Maybe we could talk to them?" Scarlett offers. "I mean, if they're experiencing this time loop too . . ."

"Negative," Kim says, shaking her head. "I don't think

anyone on the station has any clue this is happening. The first few times I reset, before comms dropped, I radioed Glass Slipper asking for instructions. I got the same responses every time. Word for word. They acted like nothing was wrong. I mean, aside from the core breach and whatever else is going on over there right now."

"Dunno what you expected," Fin says. "You tethered yourselves to a DM storm chasing quantum pulse hits. In case I wasn't clear before, that's like wading into a pen full of Mondorian valshins and unzipping your pants."

He is met with three blank stares.

"No? You don't have . . . Well, let's just say it's inadvisable."

Scarlett pouts in thought, looking at Kim. "If our arrival caused all this, and your ship was the only thing near us, that might explain why you're stuck in the loop with us while nobody else knows it's happening."

"Huh," Kim says, tilting a glance at Scarlett that suggests surprise that she has made such a perceptive point. But it is a sensible supposition.

"We *must* know more," I declare. "Knowledge is key. We have twenty-eight minutes until that second quantum pulse we witnessed hits the sail, and then the station, which may disable vital components within. And if the station core is breaching, it is only a matter of time before the station itself is disabled. We should proceed."

"With what?" asks Lieutenant Kim, wary once more.

"With establishing the facts," I reply. "The precipitant appears constant, but without further data, the persistent nature of the temporal anomaly cannot be assumed to be without a rate of decay."

The lieutenant wears an expression that is familiar to me,

though I have not experienced it as often lately. It means she has no idea what I am talking about. She looks at Scarlett, who looks at Finian.

Finian translates. "She means that since we don't know what kicked off the loop, we don't know if it'll keep going forever. We might run out of time."

"Well, let's get moving," Kim says. "Do you have spacesuits?"

"I'm taking it you have an idea for getting us aboard?" Scarlett asks.

"Depends," Lieutenant Kim says. "Are you EVA-certified?"

"Some of us more than others," our Face replies, wry. "Fin'll help me. He's great in zero gee."

"You have *no* idea," Finian grins.

Lieutenant Kim studies Finian for a moment, then looks away, as if she does not wish to remind herself she is assisting a Betraskan. I assume her military training has taught her to trust her instincts, to deal with high-pressure situations while keeping a clear head. With no viable alternative explanation, she seems prepared to believe what her own senses are telling her for now. But I admit to mild admiration that she is taking this situation so well.

The lieutenant looks at me, and I realize I am staring.

I avert my gaze, dipping my head so my hair tumbles over my eyes.

"The whole station will be on high alert," she warns. "The test malfunction was less than twenty minutes ago. They'll be wondering if it was sabotage, and they *will* shoot you on sight. My ship's got a cargo hold, but it's gonna be a hell of a tight squeeze, so I hope you three like each other. A lot."

I see Finian and Scarlett exchange a quick glance.

"I'm going to take you to a tertiary airlock," Kim continues. "If we're lucky, security's going to be too busy with the core breach to notice."

"And if we're unlucky?" Scarlett asks.

Fin musters a thin smile. "Eleventh time's the charm?"

· · · · ·

Despite the cramped conditions of the fighter's cargo hold, we reach the station quickly, and it is a simple EVA to the airlock, which is open to space and ready to receive supplies. Scarlett clearly finds it trying—even after we are safely tucked inside, she holds Finian's hand.

At least, I think that is the reason.

Lieutenant Kim has instructed us to wait inside the airlock. She will dock her fighter and report to her superiors. Then, when she can slip away, she will equalize the pressure within the airlock before admitting us to the station, hopefully unobserved.

We wait in silence. I can see the vast, roiling blackness through the airlock viewport, lit by momentary flashes of energy—sullen mauve, laced with deeper darkness. I do my best to ignore the way the storm makes my skin crawl. Its power is almost inconceivable, and the thought that the scientists aboard this station sought to tame it makes me . . . uneasy.

I can admit to myself that the sensation I experience when the outer doors begin to close is pure relief. We must ensure we are standing on the ground when gravity kicks in so we do not fall. I glide down to take my place beside Finian, Scarlett on his other side, to offer him support. The sensation of gravity reasserting itself is unpleasant for him.

A green light comes on beside the airlock's inner doors to indicate pressure has equalized, and we remove our helmets as the doors slide open. But instead of Lieutenant Kim, we are confronted by three Terran soldiers with SECURITY stamped across their breastplates.

A small part of my mind notes with bemusement that they are wearing camouflage. *They are in space. What use is the camouflage?*

They raise their weapons.

"Oh, come on," says Finian. "You've gotta be—"

BLAM.

9

FINIAN

It took us nine more practice runs—and nine more deaths—but we've finally found a reliable way into the station. We're actually getting pretty good at this. Any minute now, we're going to start cracking in-jokes with Lieutenant Nari Kim.

I'm kidding. Lieutenant Kim wouldn't know a joke if it fell from the sky and hit her in the head while everyone around her screamed, "Great Maker, it's raining jokes!"

But speaking of our way in, it's nearly time. I'm clinging to the outside of the station like it's my one true love, waiting for my turn to worm into the waste ejection system. Zila disappeared two minutes ago, which means it's fourteen seconds until I begin my run. I spend nine thinking about the way Scarlett winked before she climbed into the chute, and the remaining five thinking about Lieutenant Kim, because if this works, then we'll have time for our first proper conversation with her, and I *gotta* stop pissing her off.

We've mastered the first part of the loop now, and it runs like clockwork. Kim spots our ship, and while she radios in to station command that she's going to inspect it, we crawl into her fighter's tiny cargo bay in our spacesuits.

Then our new friend Nari blows our shuttle to bits, her comms with the station fail, and at the eleven-minute mark of our loop she drops us off at the waste disposal vent. We're hustling, because we're all concerned that the quantum pulse we saw from the landing bay might damage something that could help us get home.

I'm feeling pretty good about the waste ejection system, though. It's chaotic aboard the station since the accident that set all this off, and it was only a wandering security patrol that tripped us up last time.

My timer buzzes, and I shift into action, enjoying the last sensations of zero gee. The circular outlet of the chute irises open, and hooking my bag around my foot, I wait as it emits a puff of gas and ash.

I now have five seconds before it closes and the pressure within equalizes. I pull myself inside, yanking my boots and bag through the opening just as the hatch hums shut. And I'm left in the dark, which is cut through with a slice of light from my helmet.

The chute is barely wider than my body, and I'm stretched out with my arms in front of me. Even though I'm lanky, it's still a tight squeeze. Scar must have struggled, with her curvier parts.

I decide not to think about those. It's already kind of crowded in here.

Using hands and feet, knees and elbows, I shuffle along the chute as quickly as I can. I have just over two minutes before I meet the next load of hot ash coming the other way, which is not a death I want to experience—it hurt enough the first time. My body protests, and my suit makes everything harder. My favorite multi-tool sticks into my ribs.

The timer at my wrist buzzes to signal I have one minute left, and I push on, every movement small but urgent.

Another buzz.

Thirty seconds.

Chakk.

At last my helmet light catches the edge of the exit hatch.

"I'm here," I call quietly, and Scarlett and Zila appear. Their helmets are off, their hands reaching into the tunnel for me.

They're standing inside a wall cavity barely the width of a body. Nobody comes down here except the automated drones that pick up waste loads and deliver them to ejection outlets. One will be along in about twenty seconds.

The girls grab my outstretched hands and pull. I slide past the still-warm incineration ring and slither free—they lower me down, supporting my weight until I can rest on the floor. We all hold still, Zila's boot against my faceplate, and I hear Scarlett behind me, muffled by my helmet.

"What's in the backpack?"

"Just a few supplies. Tools. Snacks. You know, essentials."

"Well, the way to a girl's heart is through her—"

"Be quiet!" Zila hisses.

Scar pipes down, squeezing my ankle in thanks as the drone whirs into place overhead, discharges its load into the chute, then whirs away again. The station shudders around us, a siren sounding over the PA.

"Attention, Glass Slipper personnel: Engineering team

required, Deck 19, Priority One. Repeat: Engineering, Deck 19, Alpha Sector."

Once the drone is out of sight, we get to our feet, joints creaking. I take off my helmet as Scar hands me my bag. The air smells like smoke and burned polys, the lights are flickering, white into red.

"Ninety seconds until our window," Zila murmurs.

We follow her quietly toward the access panel. All around us, alarms are screaming, damage reports pouring over the PA. This time—unlike last time—we wait, ears pressed against the panel until the security patrol rushes by. *Then* I pull out a multi-tool and pop the hatch.

From there it's easy. We hurry up the corridor, take the second left, and we've arrived at our destination—an outlet room near the hydration production and storage facility. HY.P.A.S.F., the sign says.

"Isn't that an animal?" I ask, studying the acronym. "Native to Terra?"

Scarlett shoots me a confused look. "A hypasf?"

"An asp is a type of snake," Zila ventures, uncertain.

"No, no, it's a giant monster," I say, squinting as I try to conjure up more details from my memory. "Huge teeth. Lives in the water."

". . . A shark?" Scar tries.

"Ah," says Zila. "A hippo."

I was pretty sure I had it wrong, but it's worth playing dumb for Scarlett's laugh, a warm, throaty sound that sends a zing up my spine. "Right. A hippaf. Learn your animals, Scar. That one's clearly dangerous."

"The most dangerous land mammal in existence," Zila

agrees solemnly. "They are capable of crushing a person to death in their jaws."

Lieutenant Nari Kim speaks from the doorway. "Wait, what's crushing people to death in their jaws?"

"Hippos, apparently," Scarlett replies, looking concerned about it.

"Wouldn't worry too much, Red," Nari tells her. "They don't live in space. And there's only five of them left anyway."

"Not anymore," Zila replies. "Our rehabilitation programs were very successful. They thrive in the aquatic environs found on Troi III."

"Wait a minute," I say. "You people brought a terrifying teeth-monster back from the brink of extinction why, exactly?"

Zila shrugs. "Science."

Nari looks almost entertained for a moment, then remembers she's a badass who's technically at war with my people. Her frown returns, dark as ever. Still, I swear we're growing on her a little.

When those security guards found us in the airlock on our first boarding attempt, I thought she'd given us up for sure. But our next nine tries have convinced me that for now at least, Dirtgirl is on our side.

A part of us knows how insane this is. Time travel. Temporal loops. Dying over and over, only to reset. But it's hard to disbelieve the evidence smacking us right in the face every time we get perished. And, as Zila says, even though I'm the enemy to this girl, our interests are aligned. We all want to get out of this loop.

"All right." Nari glances around the smoke-filled hallway.

"Looks like we've figured out a way to get you in without getting your heads blown off."

"Or asphyxiated," Zila says.

"Or incinerated," Scarlett shudders.

"Yeah." I nod. "That one hurt."

"Security is on full alert," Nari continues. "From what I can tell, the damage to the core is bad." The whole station shudders around us, as if it agrees. "Could be what's left of Command makes the call to evacuate any minute now. So what are we looking for next?"

"Alert, medical personnel report to Beta Sector, Deck 14."

"Information," I say. "We're going to need a terminal with top-level clearance if we want to go trawling through your records, though. The tech here is two hundred years old, and I'm into vintage, but I can't hack that. I mean, I can't even plug my gear into the outlets."

"The tech labs will be crawling with people," Nari says, frowning. "Thirty-six members of Sci-Div died during the test, and if Command suspects sabotage, security will be all over those levels like a rash."

"Medical personnel required immediately, Deck 12," calls the PA. *"Repeat, medical personnel, Deck 12."*

"Think," Scar says, encouraging. "Who won't be at their station?"

The whole place rocks around us, metal walls creaking as the lieutenant slowly looks upward. "Dr. Pinkerton. The project lead. He got killed in the explosion. There'll definitely be a personal terminal in his office."

"Brilliant." Scarlett treats her to one of the smiles that always make me feel like I'm standing in sunshine. "It's looking pretty chaotic in here, but we'll probably need uniforms if we're going to be running around in the open safely. And some way to disguise Fin."

"No, we can get to the admin deck via the emergency stairwells," Flygirl assures her. "I like our odds of staying out of sight there."

I think she's the only one who does, but we follow, four sets of footsteps treading quiet on the metal stairs. It takes us longer than I'd like—nearly a quarter hour, I'd guess—but we manage to avoid the highly stressed and definitely shooty security patrols pounding all over the place.

The station rumbles again, and I hear a hollow booming through the walls. Scar reaches out to steady me as my exo hisses, and I squeeze her hand, give her a grateful smile. This whole place feels ready to come apart around our ears.

"*Attention, Glass Slipper personnel. Hull breach on Decks 13 through 17.*"

"I gotta be outta my goddamn mind . . . ," Nari mutters.

"It is possible," Zila agrees, climbing behind her. "But doubting your own sanity is reasonable proof that you are, in fact, sane."

"Yeah, but maybe that's what I'm *supposed* to think," Nari says, glancing back to Zila. "Maybe none of this is real. Maybe I'm a POW right now, locked in some bleach-head psy-op lab, and this is all some drug-induced nightmare to get me to betray classified information."

"Information about what?" I ask. "Seeing as how you're a grunt and don't actually know anything?"

"How should I know, Bleachboy?" Nari replies, sounding grumpy at having this flaw in her theory pointed out. "All I know for sure is, I get caught helping you three, I'll be lined up with you and shot for being a traitor."

"Attention, Glass Slipper personnel. All engineering staff report to Gamma Section, Deck 12, immediately."

"Let me assure you," Scar says, "having died twenty times, this is definitely really happening. Dying *hurts*."

"It is difficult to understand what is occurring here," Zila agrees, speaking over the blaring PA. "Hopefully our answers lie within the station's computer system. But I do not believe you are insane, Lieutenant Kim. Or a traitor. In fact, I believe you are very brave."

Dirtgirl raises an eyebrow at that, and Zila actually maintains eye contact for a few seconds before ducking her head and continuing upward. At the top of three flights, our co-conspirator slips out to check the hall, then ushers us after her.

BOOM.

The whole place shudders as something, somewhere, explodes.

"Warning: Containment breach. Evacuate Decks 5 through 6 immediately. Repeat: Containment breach."

"We can cross from here to Beta Section," Dirtgirl murmurs. "Then it's two more floors up to Pinkerton's office."

The deck's Beta Section is at the periphery of the station, lined with viewports looking into space. As we pass by, I can see the swath of darkness out there beyond the station's skin. That thick length of cable runs out into the dark matter storm, hundreds of thousands of klicks, connected to the quantum sail in the chaos beyond. A tiny flicker of energy illuminates the tempest, lighting up those massive roiling clouds, millions of klicks across, its echoes ripping through the fabric of subspace.

Honestly, it gives me the screaming heebie-jeebies.

"It's beautiful," Scarlett says quietly, proving—as did her decision to kiss me—that her judgment is highly questionable.

CRASH.

Out in the storm, that same massive pulse of quantum energy we saw from the hangar bay strikes the sail again. It's so bright that my vision is momentarily lost to the after-images. Zila looks down at her wrist display.

"Forty-four minutes . . ."

"Look," Scar breathes. "It's happening again. . . ."

I blink furiously as the pulse runs up the cable toward the station—an arc of dark energy blazing fiercely against the deeper darkness. The crystal in Scarlett's necklace is burning too, the black light making my eyes ache.

"Why is it *doing* that?" Nari demands.

"Excellent question," Zila replies.

Glancing at the flickering overheads, I mutter, almost to myself, "You know, I sure hope the gravitonic shielding in this sector is still intact."

"Why?" Scar looks up from her glowing cleavage. "What happens if the gravitonic shielding *isn't* still intact?"

Then two things happen at once.

First, the quantum pulse reaches the station, arcing over the hull, through the unshielded section we're standing in, and right through our bodies.

And second, Nari Kim learns that Scar wasn't kidding when she said dying was painful.

ZAP.

10

TYLER

I'm marching down a corridor bathed in gray light, Saedii's First Paladin behind me. The engines shifted tone two minutes ago—we're at full thrust now, on course to rendezvous with the Unbroken armada. Those news feed headlines are flashing through my skull—all those tiny sparks of conflict being stoked into flame by the Ra'haam and its agents. A theater of mass distraction. A veil to hide the threat until it's too late.

My head aches—I'm still not recovered from almost dying in that escape pod explosion. I'm unsteady on my feet, my fingers are tingling, and whenever I close my eyes, I can still feel that dream in my skull.

That voice, imploring me, over and over.

. . . you *still have a chance of fixing this* . . .

I'm supposed to be *good* at this. Tactics is my thing. But I'm trapped aboard an enemy vessel with hundreds of Syldrathi fanatics, and every moment I waste here is another moment the Ra'haam gets to gestate beneath the surface of Octavia and its other nursery worlds.

I don't know where Scarlett is. Auri. Zila. Fin. Kal. I don't know if they're alive or dead.

And Maker, this headache . . .

"Stop."

Erien speaks behind me, bringing me up short beside a heavy plasteel door. The corridor is lined with them, and glancing around, I'm guessing I've been brought to the detention level.

I do as I'm told, turning as Erien presses his palm to the pad beside the door. It cycles open, revealing a dark room, thin cot, bare walls.

"I thought your Templar ordered you to put me in appropriate quarters."

"These *are* appropriate quarters. You are a prisoner here, half-breed, not a guest." He nods into the room. "Move."

"Listen," I say, trying to ignore the pounding in my skull. "I know you think we're on different sides. But I watched you on the *Andarael*. Saedii respects you, Erien. She *listens* to you. And I'm guessing a First Paladin of the Unbroken is smart enough to see when he's being played. Why would the GIA abduct Saedii if not to provoke a war? Why would—"

His raised hand cuts me off. "I am as interested in your conspiracies as I am in your flatteries. Get inside."

I grit my teeth, temper rising with my desperation. "I need to talk to Saedii again, we have to—"

"Were it up to me, you would already be dead. Despite the clear blind spot she has for you, Saedii is my Templar, and I will obey her command to see you safely situated. But I warn you—do not insult my honor again."

I blink. "Blind spot?"

His cool eyes flicker to my throat. The bite marks Saedii left there.

"Look, I don't mean anything to her," I assure him. "We were in a tight spot together, she was letting off some steam. It's nothing."

Erien tilts his head. "Nothing."

"I'm just a plaything. She practically tore my head off when she kissed me. You've got nothing to worry about. I mean . . . if you're worried at all. That other Paladin called you *be'shmai,* so I figured you and he were—"

"You are a fool." Erien puts one hand on the sleek black grip of the Syldrathi pulse gun at his waist, setting it to hard Stun. "Get in the cell."

"Great Maker, will you just think for a minute!" I hiss, my headache flaring again. "Earth dodged war with the Unbroken for years! Why would the GIA suddenly attack the *Andarael* unless—"

Erien grabs my arm, squeezing tight.

And that's it.

I don't like to lose control. That's why I don't drink, don't smoke, don't swear. But the desperation of it, the knowledge we're all being played, the fear for my squad and my sister, the revelation of the Syldrathi mother I never knew, and this damn headache . . .

I snap my arm from his grip, hissing, "Don't touch me, you s—"

Erien moves faster than my eyes can follow. One hand snaps tight around my wrist, the other seizes my throat, and hooking one leg behind mine, he slams me down into the ground, bending over me with his hand still on my throat.

Stars burst in my eyes as he leans in with all his weight, choking me.

My kick finds his jaw, snaps his head back on his neck. Erien stumbles, his grip slipping. Lashing out with my other foot, I take his legs out from under him, rolling away and to my feet. He's back upright in a moment, moving like water, reminding me a little of Kal, just as fast, just as strong.

"Kii'ne dō all'ia—"

He reaches for his pulse gun and I slap it away. He grabs my hand, drags me forward as he raises his knee into my gut, my breath exploding from my now-bleeding lips. Pirouetting, he slams me back into the wall, slaps the comm badge on his chest. "Sēn, vin Erien, sa—"

The heel of my hand meets his nose, and there's a crunch and squirt of warm purple blood. My pulse is pounding in my temples as I grab a fistful of braids and slam my fist into his face again, spreading his nose all over his cheeks.

He hooks his leg around mine, and we crash to the ground, white light bursting behind my eyes. Scrambling for his fallen pulse gun, I roar as he twists my arm behind my back.

My fingers slither on the weapon's grip as my shoulder screams, my elbow close to snapping. Erien draws one of the kaat blades on his back with his free hand. But my fingers finally find purchase, and I grab the gun, twisting and unloading into his chest.

The muzzle flashes, the Stun blast lighting up the shocked expression on his face. He tumbles back, a smoking scar scored across the black breastplate of his Paladin's armor. Wincing, I gasp for breath, still gripping the gun tight as I stagger to my feet and—

The walls around me washed with rainbows.

The ground shaking beneath my feet.

I can hear screaming. The air in the corridor turns the color of dried blood and the blue of midnight, dotted with shining stars.

And then I see it, hanging in the dark in front of me, glittering like fireworks on Foundation Day.

My heart surges at the sight of it—more than my home for the past six years. More than the place I grew up. A symbol of hope, a light in all that darkness, burning bright against the night.

"Aurora Academy . . . ," I whisper.

. . . you *still have a chance of fixing this* . . .

I reach out toward it, fingers trembling. And as I touch it, the academy blows itself to pieces before my eyes. My belly turns cold with horror, fire blooms in the dark, and beyond it, darker still, I see the shadow.

The Ra'haam.

A moan slips from my lips at the sight—ten thousand ships, a hundred thousand shapes, rising up before me and blotting out the stars.

Too big.

Too much.

I turn my head, close my eyes tight so I don't have to watch.

And so it is I don't notice Erien rising up behind me.

I hear the ring of metal on metal and turn to see him standing there. His beautiful face twisted with rage. Blood dripping down his chin, dark gray in the light of the Fold, light gleaming on the kaat blade he slides off his back.

. . . you told me where it happens . . .

I grit my teeth, raising the gun.

. . . fix this, Tyler . . .

And I gasp as he buries his blade in my gut.

11

TYLER

"Do you know there is no Syldrathi word for goodbye?"

My eyes flutter open, light slipping through my lashes as I groan. Saedii is seated beside my bed, picking at her fingernails with a long, beautiful knife.

"Wh-what?" I whisper.

I force my eyes open again, head swimming. I'm surrounded by the soft hum of medical equipment, the light low and gloomy. Looking down, I realize I'm shirtless. Again. There's a dull ache in my belly, a derm patch over the wound from Erien's blade. But this is an Unbroken battle cruiser, and their med facilities are top-notch—the pain isn't even that bad, to tell you the truth.

I mean, for a brutal stabbing and all.

"It is true. Syldrathi believe that people once united can never truly part." Saedii waves the knife toward the derm patch. "Even were you to perish today, the atoms of your body would remain. Over eons, those particles would break apart and coalesce, become incorporated into other beings, other planetary bodies. Drawn into collapsing stars and scattered again by supernovae. And the last, when the great black hole at the heart of this galaxy draws everything back into its arms, all things shall be reunited. Thus, we do not say goodbye when we part. We say *an'la téli saii*."

"What's that mean?" I groan.

"I shall see you in the stars."

She tilts her head, and her soft smile fades. "I tell you this because you seem to be in an extraordinary hurry to die, Tyler Jones."

"A mere flesh wound, madam." I press my hand to the patch, wincing. "Your lieutenant needs to work on his aim if he wants to kill me."

Saedii scoffs. "Erien is a First Paladin of the Black Circle. Maker of a thousand orphans. If he wished you dead, you would be dead. I am talking about Antaelis, Erien's betrothed. You made rather a mess of his beloved's face. Antaelis wanted to challenge you to a duel for Erien's honor."

I shake my head, sighing. "Like we don't have anything better to do, with the whole galaxy ending and all."

Saedii leans back, lifting her boots and resting them across my thighs like she's claiming a piece of territory. Her gaze roams slowly over my body, drifts back up to my eyes. That trace of amusement flickers between us again, tinged with a low, pulsing anger.

"You still do not understand where you are, do you?"

"I know *exactly* where I am. And who I'm with."

"If that were so," Saedii says, eyebrows descending, "you would not have called me an idiot in front of my crew."

I wince. "Yeah look, I'm sorr—"

She raises a hand. "Do not compound your foolishness

with cowardice. At least have the courage of your convictions, Terran."

"I swear, you are the most . . ." I shake my throbbing head, teeth gritted. "Does *everything* have to be a fight with you?"

She smiles then, tongue to tooth. "If you wish."

"Maker's breath," I growl. "Will you quit with the games?"

"I *like* games."

"Well, I'm not in the mood to be your plaything." My skull is pounding, my mouth dry as ashes. "What are you doing in here, Saedii?"

Her smile fades, black lips pursing as she looks me over.

"I reviewed footage of you brawling with Erien," she finally says. "You had him bested in the fray, but you faltered at the final strike. Clutching your head as if it pained you. I had the med team scan you for brain trauma, perhaps caused by your Fold exposure. But you are suffering none."

"I didn't know you cared, Templar."

I see a flicker in her eyes at that. Just a heartbeat, and it's gone. This girl's moods swing hot to cold and back again in the blink of an eye. But looking closer, behind the bravado and the sneer and the Unbroken princess thing, for a second I think I catch a glimpse of—

"I heard you," she says, tapping her brow. "Crying out in my head when you fell. Not as if you were hurt. As if you were . . . horrified."

I run my hand across my eyes, sighing. "I . . . saw something."

"You mean a vision?"

I draw a deep breath, nodding. "I've been seeing things

since I woke up here. It's like . . . like I'm dreaming awake. I see a Syldrathi girl, covered in blood. But in the dream, I know it's *my* blood, not hers. We're in a massive chamber. Crystal walls. A throne. All carved out of rainbows."

Her eyes narrow. "That sounds like the inside of the *Neridaa*."

"It's being destroyed in my dream. Cracking to pieces." I swallow hard, my belly filling with ice at the memory. "And there's a shadow beyond the walls. So big and dark I know it'll consume everything if I let it."

"Have you ever dreamed awake like this before?"

"Never." I meet her eyes. "I can't explain it, but I think . . . Saedii, I think something terrible is about to happen."

She looks away from me, eyes focusing on some distant point past the walls. I can still feel the trace of her thoughts, the Waywalker blood she inherited from her mother speaking to the blood I got from mine. From a woman I'll never know, because my father isn't here to tell me who she is, how they met, how I came to be.

Despite Saedii's ice-queen facade, the mind games, I can tell she's uncertain. And as her eyes meet mine again, again I feel that flicker, beyond the aggression and the taunts, the scorn and the Unbroken warrior front, a flicker of . . .

Warmth?

"More news of strife is breaking across the feeds," Saedii says. "A dozen more incidents like the ones you spotted. Old grudges dredged up. The fires of wars past reignited once more. The stars drip with blood."

"It's the Ra'haam, Saedii. You *know* it is."

She sucks her lip, twirling that knife through her fingers. "Your brethren in the Aurora Legion are doing their best to douse the flames, at least. An emergency summit of the Galactic Caucus has been called to address the 'growing tide of unrest among the sentient races of the Milky Way.' It will be convened at your Aurora Academy in five days' time."

My heart surges, wounded stomach aching as I sit up on the cot. "At the academy? Why didn't you say so?"

"I just *did* say so. Why is that of import?"

"My dream," I breathe, heart racing. "The . . . vision. It was different this last time. I saw Aurora Academy, shining like a lighthouse in the dark. But I reached out toward it, and it . . . it exploded right in front of me."

I see it again, a sudden flash of pain in my mind, that image of the academy blown apart, the galaxy's last hope extinguished with it.

. . . fix this, Tyler . . .

I shake my head, my pulse pounding. "If the heads of the Galactic Caucus are all in the same place and the Ra'haam strikes it . . ."

"They are fools to gather so." Saedii scowls, considering. "But if you believe the academy is under threat . . . perhaps I could allow you access to our communications array. You could send them warning."

"You think that's a transmission Legion comms is going to answer?" I scoff. "Let alone *believe*? The GIA framed me as a terrorist, Saedii. A mass murderer. A traitor to the Legion and his own people. And the transmission will be coming from an Unbroken ship."

"Surely you have contacts within the Legion who still hold you in faith? What of the ones who left you those gifts on Emerald City?"

"Admiral Adams and Battle Leader de Stoy," I nod, mind

racing. "They know *something*. But I've got no way to contact them direct. If I was aboard Aurora Station, I could send a message to Adams on the academy network. But with something this important, I can't just fling a warning out into the dark and hope some grunt on academy comms kicks it up the chain."

I shake my head, more certain with every breath.

"You have to take me there," I declare.

Saedii's eyes are sharp as glass. "*Have to* is not a phrase to be spoken to Templars, Terran."

"If the Ra'haam destroys the Caucus, it'll throw the galaxy into chaos! And every day spent picking up the pieces is another the Ra'haam has to grow! Saedii, we have to stop—"

"There are those words again."

"Maker, will you *listen* to me?" I shove her boots off my thighs, rising off the cot. "We might be the only ones alive with a clue what's happening here!"

"I have larger concerns than—"

"Larger concerns?" I shout. "The whole *galaxy* is at stake! We know the truth! We have a duty to stop this thing!"

"Do not dare preach to me of duty, Tyler Jones!" she snarls, rising up to meet me. "You know *nothing* of its weight! Our Archon is vanished into the Void without a trace! A dozen warlords of the Unbroken are poised to seize control of this cabal, and *I* am the only one who might keep us from shattering to pieces. The future of my people teeters on the edge of a blade! And you whine I should divert course into enemy space to save a pack of shan'vii idiotic enough to risk gathering to *talk* at a time like this?"

"They're trying to broker peace!" I shout. "The Caucus doesn't know the Ra'haam is out there!"

"Foolish *and* blind, then."

"Saedii, you can't just let them—"

"Do not tell me what I cannot do!" she roars, face centimeters from mine. "I am a Templar of the Unbroken! Blooded in a hundred battles! Daughter of the *Starslayer*! I do what I wish, I go where I please, and I take what I *want*!"

She stands there glowering at me, teeth bared in a snarl, out of breath. Her eyes are sharp as the blade in her hand, and she's pressed against me so close I can feel her heart thumping under her skin. Her mind is bleeding into mine again, her thoughts soaking me through.

She's rage. She's fire. Pushing like a knife into my chest.

I do what I wish.

I go where I please.

I take what I want.

And I see it then. As her eyes drift from mine, down to my lips and back up again.

Maker's breath, she wants me.

We crash together, so hard the split in my lip opens again. She breathes into my lungs and my fingers weave into her hair, and the thought of how stupid this is is drowned out by the feel of her in my arms as I lift her off the ground.

She cinches her legs tight around my waist, gasping as we collide with the wall, her fingernails drawing lines of fire across my bare back as my hands squeeze her tight, pushing her hard against the metal. Stupid as this feels, crazy as it is . . .

The whole galaxy might be at war tomorrow.

We might all be dead.

Live for tonight. Tomorrow we die.

Her mind is entwined with mine, drenching me with her

want and redoubling my own. It's hard to breathe. To think. I've never felt anything like this, never needed anything so desperately, but this is insane, this is . . .

"Saedii . . . ," I gasp, twisting my head away.

Stop speaking, Tyler Jones, comes her voice in my head. *There are better things for you to be doing with your mouth.*

Yeah, okay.

Hard to argue with that.

> *Tyler Jones: 2*
> *Saedii Gilwraeth: 2*

. . . . .

"Well, that was . . . intense."

We're lying on the floor of the med bay, gasping for breath, a thin silver sheet of insulation thrown over our bodies. The room is in chaos around us, furniture overturned, glass shattered on the floor. Saedii is pressed against me, long black braids draped over her face, black paint smeared across her mouth. We're both slippery with sweat, salt stinging in the welts she scratched across my back.

"I think I might need more stitches," I wince.

She doesn't reply, face pressed into my neck, heart thumping against my ribs. Her breathing is slowing, but otherwise, she's completely motionless. Completely silent.

"I mean, I'm not complaining," I say, trying to elicit a laugh. "But maybe we should have a liter of O negative on standby for next time?"

Again, she doesn't reply. Doesn't move. Her thoughts are still in mine, leaking through like ink spilled across paper, but where a moment ago we were so entwined we could've

128

almost been one person, now she's slowly withdrawing. Her feelings cooling just like the sweat on our skin.

It's like someone turned off the sun.

"Are you okay?" I ask.

Without warning, she rolls off me and sits up. Her head moves in the gloom, eyes sweeping the chaos, and rising to her feet, smooth, graceful, she hunts among the debris for the pieces of her discarded uniform.

"What's wrong?" I ask.

"Nothing is wrong," she replies.

"Well . . . where are you going?"

"Back to the bridge."

I blink. "Just like that?"

She recovers her briefs from atop the supply cupboard where I hurled them, drags them back on. "You were expecting something else?"

"Well . . ." I sit up, silver sheet crumpling around my waist. "I mean, I'm not sure how Syldrathi work, but Terrans usually, y'know . . . *talk* afterward."

"And what should we talk about, Tyler Jones?"

". . . Did I do something wrong?"

"No." She pulls on her bra. "You were perfectly adequate."

I cock one eyebrow. My scarred one, just for added effect. "Lady, I was in your mind through that whole thing. If that's what you call *adequate,* Maker knows what—"

"I am not here to assuage your ego in matters of performance." She retrieves the long knife she'd been carrying when I woke, straps the sheath back to her leg. "You still have both your thumbs. Make of that what you will."

I get to my feet, wrapping the sheet around my waist,

wincing at the sting of sweat, the low, thudding ache of the stab wound in my stomach.

"Are you . . . angry with me?"

Saying nothing, Saedii turns away, looking into the mirror on the wall and starting to finger-comb her braids. I step in behind her so she can see my reflection, then reach out to brush her shoulder. "Hey, talk to—"

"Do not touch me," she growls.

I lower my hand. Feeling a little stung.

"That's not what you were screaming inside my head a minute ago."

"That was a minute ago." Her eyes return to her braid, fingers moving swift through the thick, ink-black locks. I feel her closing herself off like she did in the war council. Slamming her mind behind towering doors of iron. "We have taken our pleasure in each other, and now we are done. Do not make this out to be anything more than what it was."

". . . And what was it?"

"A pressure release," she says. "Understandable after our captivity together. Meaningless."

"Why are you lying to me?"

Her hand falls still, her gaze locking back on mine. "I should cut out your tongue, Terran. I should rip it from your skull and—"

"Saedii, you were in my *head* just now." I search her eyes, my voice soft. "I'm new to this whole telepathy thing, but I *know* what you were feeling. This wasn't just some wartime fling. This wasn't just blowing off steam."

"You flatter yourself," she scoffs.

"Saedii, *talk* to me."

I grab her shoulder, turn her to face me. And though I feel a stab of rage run right through her as my hand touches her skin, beyond that, again, I catch that glint of approval.

This girl is a fighter. A leader. Born for conflict. Bred for war. She doesn't want obedience, she wants a challenge. An equal.

I kiss her. Hard. Pulling her into my arms and crushing her against me. Her body tenses, her fists clench, but her mouth melts against mine like snow in fire, a sigh slipping past her lips as she throws her arms around my neck.

And beyond the clash of push and pull, want and not, again I catch a glimpse of it through the cracks in the iron she's wrapped herself inside. Something so big and frightening she can't bear to look at it for long.

I reach toward it. She pushes it down. Stomping it beneath her heels and pulling back from my kiss. And I look into her eyes and realize what it is, why she's trying so hard to pretend this means nothing to her.

Because . . .

Because it means everything.

"You're being Pulled," I whisper.

Saedii's eyes flash, and she pushes herself out of my arms with a snarl. I watch her turn back to her reflection, seething, busying herself with her braids with shaking hands. But I can see the truth behind the ice of her eyes, feel it inside her head, flooding through her despite her best attempts to keep it dammed in. The Syldrathi mating instinct. The almost-irresistible attraction they feel to people their souls are fated to be with.

Kal feels it for Aurora. He once told me that love was a

drop in the ocean of what he felt for her. And looking into Saedii's eyes now, thinking about all the times she could have killed me, should've killed me . . .

Maker, what an idiot I've been. . . .

"How long?" I ask.

She says nothing. I step up behind her, searching her reflection.

"Saedii, how long?"

She holds my stare, fury and sorrow and hateful, defiant adoration washing through her thoughts. In her mind's eye, I see an image of me aboard the *Andarael*, in the depths of the Unbroken fighting pit with a dead drakkan behind me, staring up at her, bloodied but victorious.

"Yeah," I murmur. "I mean, that would've gotten a nun's motor running, so I can't really blame you."

She scoffs, trying not to smile, stalking away across the med bay. I can feel her seething anger. Self-loathing boiling under her skin. A part of her wants to snatch a shard of broken glass from the floor and stab me to death here and now. A part of her wants to crash into my arms and hold on to me so tight I break. She hates that she wants me. But she's thrilled by it too.

"You didn't know it would feel like this," I realize.

She glowers at me, lips thin.

"Saedii, *talk* to me," I demand.

"I have had . . . suitors," she finally sighs. "Pleasurable distractions. But not like . . ." She hangs her head, sharp teeth gritted as her fingers curl into fists. Laughing softly as she shakes her head. "The Void truly has a dark sense of humor. To fashion me a fate such as this . . ."

"Am I so bad?" I ask softly.

"You are Terran," she hisses.

"Half-Terran," I say. "But so what?"

"So our people are at *war*. And my father would turn your spine to glass and shatter it into a million pieces if he suspected so much as your finger had graced my skin." She chuckles, bitter, almost to herself. "Void knows what he would do to me if he knew that I . . . that we . . ."

Her voice drifts away, temper rising as she crouches to yank one of her boots out from underneath a medi-cot.

I walk across the room, run one hand over her bare back as she stands. I feel her shiver, even as she pushes back against me. The ache in her is so real I can feel it in my own head.

"Saedii, your father isn't here," I tell her. "And our people don't have to be at war. You have the power to end this."

"Don't," she growls.

"Come with me to Aurora Acad—"

"No!" she snaps, whirling on me. "Do not ask me again! *Everything* my father fought to build could crumble into dust now he is gone! Any one of a *dozen* Templars might try to seize power over the cabal! I am the Starslayer's daughter! In his absence, it falls to me to hold the Unbroken together!"

"None of that will matter if the Ra'haam is allowed to hatch!"

"My duty is to my people!" she roars. "And our people are at war!"

We stand there in the gloom, and I can still feel her body pressed against me, the furious warmth of her emotions lighting up my mind. There's so much to this girl I'm only beginning to see. She's like sunlight encased in a shell of black iron. And even through the tiny cracks she's shown me, I can tell how deep and hot she burns, how wonderful it would be to lose myself inside a heat like that. The Syldrathi blood in me calls to her, the bridge between our minds echoing with its song.

She's beautiful. Fierce. Brilliant. Ruthless.

This girl is like no one I've ever known.

"So let me go," I hear myself say.

"What?" she whispers.

"If you won't come with me, let me go." I swallow hard, seeing a tiny flare of rage and pain light up her eyes. "Give me a shuttle and some credits. Drop me off at a starport. I'll make my own way to Aurora Academy. I'll stop the Ra'haam alone."

"You know nothing of its plan," she says. "You are a fugitive, wanted by your own government for Interdiction breach and galactic terrorism."

I smile, lopsided. "Sounds like a challenge to me."

"You are charging toward your death. You are a fool."

"Who's the bigger fool? The fool himself, or the fool in love with him?"

Saedii scowls and turns away, and I step in front of her, press my hands to her cheeks. As I kiss her, I feel the thrill of it run through her whole body, fingertips to toes. She surges against me so hard she almost knocks me over.

I stumble back and we hit the wall, her body pressed tight into mine, fitting together like the strangest puzzle. Her curves are hard as steel and her lips are soft as clouds, and for a moment it's all I can do to not lose myself in her again, to not close my eyes against the war around us and the shadow rising above us and just make her mine.

But then I realize she's drawn that knife again.

Holding it just shy of my throat as she searches my eyes.

"I do not know which I hate more," she whispers, the blade brushing my skin. "Pulling you close or pushing you away."

"I know which one I prefer."

She wavers then, just for a heartbeat. In the silence, I take hold of her hand, ease the weapon away from my throat and kiss her knuckles, searching her eyes for that warmth, that light.

"Help me, Saedii. We can do this together."

But she looks over my shoulder, and at the sight of herself in the mirror, the iron curtain descends, that blazing fire inside her burns suddenly cold. Saedii clenches her jaw, pulls back, shaking her head.

"My first duty is to my people, Tyler Jones. Not my heart."

I search her eyes, swallowing hard.

"Then you have to let me go."

"To your death," she snarls.

"Maybe." I shrug. "But I can't just sit here and do nothing."

I see defiance flare in her then. Rage. The daughter of the Starslayer unveiled. I can sense the menace in her, like a shadow rising beneath her surface, just as dark as the fire that warmed me a few moments ago. One is cast by the other, I realize. Each a part of what makes her who she is: beautiful, fierce, brilliant, ruthless.

She lifts her hands between us, the bloodstained fingers of her left entwined with mine, the right still holding the knife as she searches my eyes.

I know she could force me to stay if she wanted.

Kill me if she wanted.

Saedii Gilwraeth is a girl who gets what she wants.

Have to *is not a phrase to be spoken to Templars, Terran.*

But in the end, she unwinds our fingers. Unstrapping the sheath from her thigh, she slides the knife home, presses it into my palm. Folding my grip around the graven handle, she kisses my knuckles, soft and warm.

"I will see you in the stars, Tyler Jones," she says.

And she lets me go.

12

AURI

"When?" I repeat. "What do you mean, *when?*"

Caersan looks past me to Kal, raising the brow over his good eye. "Really, Kaliis? The entire universe before you, and this is what you chose?"

Kal steps forward, and I take his hand, curling my fingers through his.

"Bigger problems," I remind him quietly, as if I'm not about a heartbeat away from lunging for his father myself. Then I speak to Caersan, not bothering to reach for politeness: "Indulge my tiny Terran brain and tell me what the hell you're talking about."

"I speak your vile language with the fluency of one born to it," the Starslayer replies, his gaze brushing past our joined hands as he turns back to the projection of the stars. "So I will assume you fail to comprehend the concept rather than the word. Kaliis, the FoldGate to Taalos. Observations?"

"It is damaged," Kal says slowly. "Neglected. Which makes little sense. It should have been attended to by tech crews on the Taalos colony."

"Which is no longer there," Caersan nods. "Just as the population of Terra is long gone."

"It's not long gone," I begin. "It was there just—"

But it's starting to sink in now. What he means.

When.

The sheer depth of the Ra'haam presence on Earth, the layers of it, coiling in and doubling back upon itself—it was just as dense as the growth on Octavia. The entire planet was thick with it.

But the Ra'haam hasn't bloomed and burst yet. That was the point of the Weapon—to destroy it while it slept, before this could happen.

It would take years for the Ra'haam to populate Earth like that.

I wouldn't believe it if I hadn't sensed it myself.

But maybe . . . maybe it *did* take years.

"When," I whisper.

"Aurora?" Kal asks softly.

"Ah," says his father. "At last, the child comprehends."

"Kal," I say. "We've—I can't believe I'm saying this out loud, but I think we've . . . jumped forward . . . in time."

He's silent a long moment, his eyes darting back and forth between his father and me. But then, slowly, he nods. "The Eshvaren *did* have a different relationship to time from we who came after them."

He agrees so calmly that I'm almost bewildered. But I remind myself Kal's people are the oldest race in the galaxy—that they've always told stories of the Eshvaren. Stories so old, their origins are lost to history. If anyone was going to buy what's happening right now, it's a couple of Syldrathi.

"The Echo," his father agrees.

"Half a year passed in no time at all," Kal nods. "And when you first came into your powers, be'shmai, the night you pointed us to the World Ship, you spoke backward, as if time around you was twisting in on itself."

"Precognition," Caersan adds. "Time dilation. They knew more than we. I do not believe this conjunction was intentional, however. The Eshvaren did not anticipate two Triggers aboard their weapon simultaneously."

"No," I agree. "Because they anticipated that the first one was going to do his damned job."

"They anticipated total self-sacrifice," he agrees, lip drawing back into a sneer. "For their Trigger to die on their knees."

"As opposed to taking this thing they left behind, the culmination of their entire species' efforts," I snap, "and using it to wipe out whole suns in the name of conquering the galaxy. Your own people, *billions* of them, so you could do what? Rule for the next few years until the Ra'haam bloomed?"

"We were *born* to rule!" He throws the words back at me like a spear, but it veers off course—it's Kal who takes half a step back, his breath uneven. "And my people were cowards and traitors!"

"You had a chance!" My voice echoes off the walls of the crystal chamber around us. "You had a chance to catch the Ra'haam while it was sleeping, and instead, you did this!" A wave of my hand takes in the floor around us, littered with the bodies of his people. They're probably the lucky ones— they didn't live to see the Ra'haam takeover that must have followed our disappearance.

The Starslayer doesn't spare his dead prisoners a glance. The anger inside me thickens, and I shift my weight, because I swear there is nothing in this time or any other that would be as satisfying as getting my hands around his throat. But Kal's mind brushes against mine, violet twining around midnight blue, calming, quieting me. He finds me effortlessly now, something unlocked inside both of us. And he's enough to bring me down.

"How did this happen, Father?" he asks.

Caersan turns away and navigates a path through the corpses carpeting the floor. When he reaches the wall of the chamber, he lays one hand on the crystal and glances up at the vaulted ceiling.

"It is unclear," he says. "Psychic dissonance caused by the presence of two Triggers, perhaps. But if the *Neridaa* performed such an extraordinary act once, then I believe it could be replicated. I know this ship as well as my own self. The power that hums through it as well as my own breath. It is less a weapon to be fired than an instrument to be played."

A sliver of hope creeps into my mind, like the smallest beam of sunlight breaking through the clouds. "You think we could play it again?"

He's thoughtful. "I know the note of the song I heard as we moved across time. I could replicate it, with enough power. Your mind could provide the unsophisticated *push,* for want of a more precise term. I believe I could channel it into that same song and return us to the moment we left."

"Aurora . . . ," Kal begins, but I'm already laughing.

"It's okay, Kal, I'm not volunteering for that."

"Oh, but . . ." Caersan turns to me, hands over his heart. "*You* are the Trigger of the Eshvaren, Aurora! *You* have a chance to catch the Ra'haam while it sleeps! Is it not, as you so eloquently put it, your damned job?"

His mock sincerity drops like a mask, his hands to his sides.

"Not so eager to serve them now, eh? Now that you know what it will cost?"

My fingers creep up to brush my cheek, and though most of my anger is directed at the arrogant bastard standing in front of us, a little flame within me flickers, and whispers: *How were you meant to fire this thing twenty-two times? You would have died piece by piece.*

That's what they asked of you.

But even still, I feel the power tingling at my fingertips, aching for release. Again, I feel that sense of exhilaration at the thought I might get to unleash it. It's like a river, welling up inside me even now, and even though I'm still weak from the last time, even though I can feel it hurting me every time I use it, I almost . . .

I almost . . . *want* to.

"All this is irrelevant, regardless," Caersan sighs.

"Why?" I ask, pushing the want down to my toes. "What do you mean?"

"Do you not sense it, Terran? In the air? In the walls?"

I let my mind quest outward, to the pulses and flickers that flow through the walls around us. And I know what Caersan means. It's like Kal already said. "The music. The song in this place . . . it feels different now."

The Starslayer nods. "The *Neridaa* is damaged. During the battle for Terra. I cannot play the note if her strings have been cut."

"Well, we have to repair it, then," I declare.

Caersan scoffs. "As simple as that."

"I'm not saying it will be simple," I say, hands curling into fists. "But we can't just float here doing nothing. If this is the future we made, we have to get back to the past and fix it." I wave toward the corrupted Syldrathi colony, that moldy slick of oil in both our minds. "This is our fault, Caersan!"

"We should continue this debate in a place more sheltered than beside a FoldGate," Kal says. "If the Ra'haam has taken Taalos—"

His father scowls. "Turn tail and run, you mean? What else has she gifted you? What other Terran weakness now poisons your veins?"

"Only a fool strikes a blow in haste," Kal shoots back. "A warrior strikes once, and well." A flash of contempt crosses his face that's all Caersan, from the lift of his chin to the curl of his lip. In this moment, I can see the same blood running through them. Our minds brush together, mine reaching for his as instinctively as his does for mine. We don't need words—silver and gold wrap together, confirming our shared intent.

When we make it back, we'll take him on again. We'll be ready.

We'll be together.

Caersan's mouth only quirks, though, and he inclines his head. "At least you retained something of my teachings," he murmurs. "We passed by a FoldStorm not far back. It should provide cover. You will assist me in propelling the *Neridaa* into the storm, Terran."

He glowers as I hesitate, and I size him up, studying that face so similar to Kal's—and so completely different.

"You moved it fine on your own before," I point out.

He scowls. "You are too cowardly to make yourself vulnerable to me."

"We're surrounded by people you killed. Can't think why I'd hesitate."

"You are right to fear me, girl," he smiles. "But I may require your mind to return to my own time. I would be a fool to destroy you now."

He turns his back, contemptuous, unafraid, and the display projected in the center of the room shifts as he plots out a course to the storm. Slowly, tentatively, I ease down my barriers to observe the way he interlinks with the Weapon—the *Neridaa,* in his mind—and propels it forward by will alone.

His mind is rich and deep and strong, layers of the same gold as his son's, and a dark, dried-blood red. I can feel the strength in it, a coming together of his Syldrathi heritage and his training in the Echo. He would've been a stronger Trigger than me, if he'd been willing. And as he glances back toward the corrupted Taalos colony, I can feel it in him, beneath that ice-cold demeanor. He might play the imperious one, the faultless one, but I can tell he's furious at the sight of that fallen world. Much as he loathes me, I can sense there's something he loathes even more.

Defeat.

He bats me away before I can look more closely, and we each put our mental shoulders to the wheel, easing the city-sized crystal through the quiet of the Fold. We work side by side, rather than weaving together as I do with Kal. But we're moving through the black and white, fast as thought.

The storm looms in the distance ahead, massive and

roiling, bigger than planets and crackling with power. As we cruise toward it, Caersan climbs onto the throne and, red cloak splayed beneath him, makes himself more comfortable. I settle on a step at the bottom, and Kal takes his place beside me, our hands still joined.

"Don't look at them," I whisper as his gaze falls—how can it not?—on the dead bodies littering the floor.

"They remind me of someone I knew," he murmurs, and I close my eyes, resting my head on his shoulder.

As the minutes draw out, I let my mind range, stretching and pushing out into the Fold around us, testing my limits. I'm exhausted, but something has awakened within me—like a new set of muscles I never knew I had. Like an extra gear, and I want to explore it. I want to use it. Lose myself in it. Let go of my tiny body and embrace everything beyond it.

"You feel it, don't you, Terran?"

I glance to Caersan, the air thrumming between us. He looks down at his hand, closing it slowly into a fist. And he smiles at me.

I ignore him, turning away, back out into the dark beyond. The space is infinite, too big to wrap my head around. But out there in all that nothing, I realize it's not completely empty after all. The first time I brush against something, I shy away instinctively, midnight blue flaring around me— then I understand what it is I've found. It's a dead ship, surrounded by a cloud of debris. A minute later, I find another derelict. And another. There's no life here in the Fold, but this sector of it isn't empty.

It's a graveyard.

Is everyone gone? Has everyone in the galaxy been

subsumed by the Ra'haam? I can't imagine the people I've met, the places I've seen, all destroyed. The bright lights gone dark, the busy streets empty and quiet. Hundreds of worlds, quiet forever.

I let my mind range farther toward the storm, past another ship, this one broken open like someone took it in both hands and ripped it apart to spill the contents out into the Fold and—

I freeze, then jerk back into my body, my eyes snapping open.

"What?" Caersan's mind is already focusing in the direction I came from, and I feel Kal try to do the same, but he lacks the power. Carefully I join my mind with his and bring him with me as I creep back to take another look.

It's like one of those puzzles where you have to squint and try to unfocus your eyes, and the moment you stop looking, the image pops out. I quiet my mind, arcing outward, as still and silent as I can be, and there on the very periphery, I sense them again.

One.

Then two.

Then ten.

Then twenty.

There are *ships* out there at the edge of my range now, just a whisper of them. But they're converging on us. And these ones aren't dead. They're closing in from multiple directions, and even as I watch, their presence becomes firmer, closer, their images coalescing in Caersan's projection.

"Amna diir," Kal whispers. "The Ra'haam."

The ships are of a dozen different styles, built by a dozen

145

different races. They're huge—battleships all of them, bristling with weapons. But their hulls are overrun with what looks like moss and lichen, a sickly white edged with blue green, and they drag long tendrils behind them, like creeper vines, or maybe roots, searching for new soil to pollute. They remind me of the bones of Octavia, buried underneath the mass of the Ra'haam. There's a wrongness to them that turns my stomach, makes my blood run cold, like something's alive inside them but a blanket's been thrown over it, smothering.

"Those are big ships," I murmur.

"Capital war vessels," Caersan replies. "There are more inbound."

"Can we fight them?" Kal asks.

"We will not *fight* them. We will *destroy* them." Caersan looks at me calmly, his right eye glowing faintly. "You will fire the Weapon, girl. I will shape the pulse toward the enemy. Even damaged, the *Neridaa* is more than a match for—"

"No," Kal says.

Caersan tilts his head at his son. "No?"

"You know what it will cost, what it will take, to fire this thing again." Kal glances at me, those cracks around my eye, before turning back on his father. "You simply do not wish to pay the price yourself."

I know Kal is right. The pulse wouldn't have to be anything close to what I'd need to destroy a sun, but fighting that many ships, I'll be weakened afterward. My skin will keep breaking open, the spiderweb of cracks I see in Caersan will start to spread in me. Still, my fingertips tingle, goose bumps rising on my skin in anticipation. . . .

"I can do it, Kal," I tell him.

"Be'shmai, it will *hurt* you."

"Will you allow these maggots to destroy us, then?" Caersan asks.

"Will *you*?" Kal demands.

"We are Warbreed, boy," he spits. "You know as well as I what that means. From the moment I took the glyf, I accepted death as a friend. I do not fear the Void. To die in battle is a warrior's fate."

"You lie, Father," Kal spits. "It is not in your nature to accept defeat. You will not sit idle and let those things blow us to pieces."

The Starslayer raises one silver brow, smiling at me.

"Will I not?"

Caersan leans back on his throne, adjusts the line of his cloak, flicks a bothersome speck of dust off his shoulder guard. Steepling his fingers at his lips, he just stares at me. I can feel the Ra'haam battleships drawing closer, more of them coming now—a corrupted swarm, launching fighters, descending on us out of the black.

Caersan does nothing.

The closest warship opens fire; a missile maybe, bursting against our crystal hull. I feel the Weapon shift under us, a psychic sound—almost as if the *Neridaa* felt the pain. Another blast rocks the Weapon, another, the light around us dimming as violent shudders run the length of the ship.

And still, the Starslayer just stares.

I close my hands into fists, feeling that power surge inside me.

"Be'shmai . . . ," Kal whispers.

"*'Be'shmai'* . . . ," Caersan sneers at his son. "*This* is who you name beloved? This weakling who will let you die here in the dark?"

"You will not do that," Kal spits, rising. "You'll not use me against her!"

"You allowed yourself to be used, Kaliis. When you bound yourself to a cur such as she. Your sister would never have shamed me so, to lie with a Terran maggot. Saedii would have done her duty. *Saedii* would have put her people, her honor, her family first."

"Family?" Kal shouts. "You *killed* our mother! You tore our family apart, just as you did our sun! What do you know of family?"

Kal seethes at his father, teeth bared, but I'm past the boundaries of simple words. Instead, I close my eyes, heart pounding now as more and more of the enemy ships draw near. I can see the different shapes, some of them sickeningly familiar—Syldrathi and Betraskan and Terran—all of them corrupted by the Ra'haam. The power builds inside me like water against a dam. It's warm. Inviting. I can feel the depths of it, just like Caersan said. It's limitless. It's overwhelming. Maybe even a little . . .

Blasts rock the ship, Ra'haam vessels pounding our hull. Corrupted fighters scream down the *Neridaa's* length, chipping away at her skin with living shots that eat away at her hull. The Weapon is vast, but I can feel her bleeding, cracks spreading across her face. And all the while, Caersan's eyes are fixed on me. A small smile on his lips. He's playing a game of chicken with all our lives, and if it were just me at risk here . . .

But I look to Kal beside me. My lips pressed thin. I can

feel the pull of it. The strength of it, waiting to be unleashed. I know if I let it out, I'm just going to want it again. And again. This is what they made me for, after all. But . . .

"Aurora . . . do not let him manipulate you like this."

I can't lose you again.

And then I draw up every ounce of my mental energy, holding the power within myself until my skin is tingling, until I'm bursting at the seams, current coursing through my veins. I'm consumed for a moment, caught up in the utter, boundless thrill of it. I feel Caersan in my head then, cold and triumphant, channeling the force into a pulse, spherical, like the ones I let loose on Emerald City, on Sempiternity, releasing it in a blinding burst.

It balloons outward, thousands of kilometers into the Fold, striking a dozen Ra'haam ships and ripping them to bleeding splinters. A stab of pain rockets through my head in response, and I grit my teeth, blood spilling from my nose as I heave for breath.

"Again," Caersan says.

"Aurora . . . ," Kal whispers.

"Again!"

"You cannot do this!" Kal roars. "She's hurting herself!"

"Mercy is the province of cowards, Kaliis."

I fire again, another pulse, blossoming outward and annihilating the enemy ships beyond. I feel like a giant, smashing children's toys. I feel ten thousand feet tall. But I can already sense more at the edges of my range, homing in on us, like we're a beacon in the dark.

Kal stands beside me. Squeezing my hand, looking into my eyes. I can feel his strength adding to mine, but the

Ra'haam ships are still swarming in, another blast rocking us now, crystal splinters raining from the roof and shattering on the ground around us—

"Help her!" Kal roars. "The two of you together could annihilate—"

"No, wait," I gasp.

Squeezing Kal's hand, I nod to the dark outside.

"One of those isn't a Ra'haam ship. . . ."

I feel it, out there amid the rot and the mold—a blur of rusting metal, cutting like a knife through the Fold. Missiles curl and bloom, blinding white spheres of nuclear fusion, immolating the remaining Ra'haam ships in sudden bursts of light and heat. I can hear a scream of frustration in the back of my mind: the rage of the enemy denied. But it knows now, it *knows* we're here, and I can feel it, even now, gathering its strength to strike again.

Again.

Again.

Until it has everything. *Is* everything.

Caersan rises from his throne, brow creased, one blood-stained hand outstretched toward the newcomer.

"Strange design," he murmurs.

"Who are they?" Kaliis demands.

"I do not know." His eyes narrow. "But they are hailing us."

I wipe the smear of blood from my tingling lips, sit back on my haunches, and try to catch my breath as Caersan throws the transmission up onto the projected screen in the heart of the room.

His face twists into a scowl at what he sees.

A group of people appears on the monitor, sitting at stations on the bridge of this new ship. I see two women, a Betraskan and a Syldrathi with a Waywalker glyf tattooed on her forehead and deep cracks scored in the skin around her eyes. Behind them is a gremp that must be standing on a box and a Rikerite with long horns sweeping back from her forehead. Farther back, bodies are crammed in together— Chellerians with blue skin turned gray by the Fold, more Betraskans, half a dozen types of aliens I've never seen before.

And in front of them all, in the commander's chair, is someone my hammering heart twists at the sight of.

A man.

"I can't believe it," he hisses, staring at Caersan. *"It is you."*

He's out in the Fold, and without the effect of the Weapon, his pale skin is washed paler still, his fair hair turned gray. His uniform is threadbare and battle-scarred, he has a black patch covering one eye, and he's older than he was the last time I saw him—maybe in his forties. But even after more than twenty years, even under the scars and the stubble and the grief that marks the skin at the corners of his eyes, I'd know him anywhere.

But Kal's the one who speaks. Who sucks all the air out of my lungs with just two words. Who names the man before us, this man who's been to hell and back and is somehow still holding on, looking at us with a mix of confusion and accusation and bitter rage.

"Tyler Jones."

13
KAL

"Kal."

My name is heavy as iron, spat from Tyler's lips as though it were poison. He stares at me from the projection my father has thrown into the air before us, and from across an ocean of time.

Tyler Jones is a man now, where once—mere days ago—I knew just a boy. He sits in the commander's chair of his warship, and I can see the years have not been kind to my old friend. His face is battle-scarred, worn, lined with pain and grief, but more and most, with rage.

"What the hells are you doing here?" he demands. *"What are—"*

"Tyler!" Aurora cries at my side. "Holy cake, it *is* you!"

A scowl creases his scarred brow, confusion in his stare. *". . . Auri?"*

"Yes, it's me!" she shouts, wiping blood from her nose. She seems weakened after the battle, but she looks exhilarated, almost drunk perhaps. "It's *us*! Ty, I thought I'd never see you again!"

He shifts his gaze from Aurora to me, bewildered. *"See me again? Last time I saw you was twenty-seven years ago. . . ."*

Aurora shakes her head. "Last we saw you, you got captured by the GIA! We were *so* worried, Scar was going out of her mind!" She grins even as she cries, her eyes shining with tears. "I know it sounds crazy, Ty, but holy *cake,* it's *so* good to see you! I'm so glad you're okay!"

"Aurora . . . do I look okay to you?"

His gaze shifts to my father, his eyes hardening.

"The ship you're in disappeared at the Battle of Terra with you all inside it. We needed that Weapon, Auri. We needed you!"

"I know," she whispers, her smile falling. "I'm sorry, Ty. We didn't mean to come here. We didn't mean for any of this to happen."

"This may be difficult for you to fathom, Brother," I tell him. "Twenty-seven years may have passed for you, but for us, the battle between the Unbroken and Terran forces was only hours ago. We have traveled in *time.*"

"What the hells . . . ?" he whispers.

"We look the same, do we not?" I insist. "Look at Aurora. Almost three decades have passed for you, but she has aged not a day, yes?"

He stares at me, brow creased, jaw clenching as he looks to his crew.

"I am telling you the truth, Brother," I plead.

"You don't get to talk to me about truth." Tyler's lip curls as he speaks in perfect Syldrathi. *"I'na Sai'nuit."*

My heart sinks at that. So, he knows. The lie I told him. Told them all. It shames me to think of it now—that I called him friend and yet lied to his face about who I was. I had my reasons, and yet, I have no excuse.

"Brother, I am sorry. I was wrong to deceive you then. But I beg you to believe me now. I will *never* lie to you again."

"Tyler, please . . . ," Aurora says.

The Betraskan beside Tyler pipes up, squinting as she adjusts a cybernetic targeting monocle over her eye. *"Commander, I hate to break up the touching reunion, but we still have incoming. Weed fleet, bearing seven-one-eight-twelve-niner. Weapons range in sixty seconds."*

"Shit," Tyler whispers, and more than the sight of him, the years on his bones, the pain in his eyes, *that* shakes me.

The Tyler Jones I knew never cursed.

But this is not the Tyler Jones I knew.

"What's your status?" he says. *"Your hull looks compromised."*

"The Weapon was damaged during the journey here." I glower at my father, who is sitting back and watching the exchange with mild disinterest. "And we were attacked again before you arrived. It took some time before we were able to muster the energy to retaliate."

"We picked up the power spike on long-range scans," Tyler says. *"You're damned lucky we did, too. We were headed back to . . ."*

He catches himself before saying more, his voice fading. He looks to his readouts, the incoming Ra'haam ships, chewing his lip in thought. I can see his mind: the distrust, the anger, battling with the proof before his eyes. He stares at Aurora, and she gazes back, unfailing hope in her eyes, softly speaking two words: the same message Admiral Adams passed to us what feels like a lifetime ago now.

"*Believe,* Tyler."

"*Thirty seconds to weapons range, boss,*" the Betraskan says.

And finally, Tyler Jones sighs.

"*All right. I don't know what the hells is going on here, but we got incoming Weeds and I just spent most of my fusion bombs. I suggest we continue this conversation a few light-years the hells away from here. Are your engines still operational?*"

I look to Aurora, the bloodstains on her upper lip. Perhaps it is my imagination, but the small cracks in the skin around her right eye seem . . . deeper. But she nods anyway, her eyes alight. "I can move us."

"*All right, follow our lead. Lae, spool up the rift drive and—*"

"*You cannot mean to bring them with us?*"

It's the Syldrathi woman who speaks, sitting at what I presume is the helm. She is only a little older than I, fierce and slender with long, flowing braids of silver. The Waywalker glyf is scored on her brow, but there are deep cracks in the skin around her eyes, similar to those that mark Aurora and my father. And when she speaks, it is with the fury of a thousand suns, staring at Tyler in disbelief.

"*That sounds like you questioning my judgment, soldier,*" Tyler replies.

"*They ride with the Starslayer!*" she spits. "*The blood of ten billion Syldrathi on his hands! The death of the galaxy at his feet!*"

"Quiet your noise, child," my father sighs, leaning back on his throne. "From your look, you could not even have been alive when Syldra fell."

"My mother told me of you, cho'taa," she hisses, violet eyes narrowed to slits. *"I know exactly what you—"*

"Spool up the rift drive, Lieutenant," Tyler interrupts. *"I want us out of here now."*

The Syldrathi woman glowers at Tyler, but his tone is hard, unforgiving. After a moment of silent struggle, she acquiesces, bows her head.

"If I am bringing them with us, we cannot go far. A rift that large—"

"Where doesn't matter, Lieutenant. As long as it's away from here."

She clenches her jaw. *"Yessir."*

"Auri, Kal," Tyler says. *"Follow us through. And just in case that bastard sitting behind you is getting any ideas in his pretty head?"* He glares at my father, his good eye ablaze. *"We've still got a few nukes left, Starslayer."*

My father is not even looking at the screen anymore, treating Tyler as beneath contempt. But Auri nods, jaw set. "We'll follow you, Ty."

"Strap yourselves in if you can. The ride's a little bumpy."

The transmission ends, and with a glance, my father banishes the projection he's summoned. The light about us dies, the throne room dimming to a darker shade of blood-red, reflected in my father's eyes.

"Weakling," he murmurs.

Beside me, Aurora watches him, eyes narrowed. And pursing her lips, she holds out her hand toward the center of the room where the projection was. The air shimmers. I feel the power in her swell, a tiny spark shining in the white of her right eye. Another image appears—a view from outside the ship, conjured by the power of her mind.

I look at her, wary, but she smiles back at me.

I realize she is learning how to wield it. She is mastering this place.

But what is it going to do to her?

I see Tyler's vessel—a strange amalgam of Syldrathi and Betraskan and Terran technologies, as if cobbled together from the pieces of half a dozen other ships. It is not beautiful, but it is functional, built for war. The name VINDICATOR is painted down her prow.

My breath catches as I see a glow begin, a tiny point of light against the backdrop of the FoldStorm. The light grows in intensity, spreading wider, like a tear across the fabric of the Fold. And I realize what I am seeing—a FoldGate, crude and temporary to be sure, but large enough for us to pass through in the *Neridaa*, into the solar system beyond.

The thrusters on Tyler's ship flare bright, and his vessel soars through the rift it has torn, vanishing out of the Fold. Aurora lowers her chin, a frown darkening her brow, and I take her hand as I feel us begin to move—this mighty vessel, bigger than a city, more powerful than any weapon developed by Syldrathi or Terrans or any other.

And my be'shmai moves it simply with the power of her *thoughts.*

We reach the rift, and the Weapon begins to shake around us. Violent. Sudden. Enough to throw me off my feet.

But I feel a gentle pressure, and the glow in Aurora's eye burns brighter, her power keeping me upright. The *Neridaa* trembles as we cross the threshold, white light like a supernova, all of space stretching and inverting around me.

And as suddenly as it began, it is over.

All is silence. The space I see projected outside our hull is not the bleached colorscape of the Fold anymore, but the vibrant and rainbowed hues of realspace. A red star burns distant. Nearby, an ice giant of methane and nitrogen hangs in the gloom, silent and green and forever frozen. There is no sign of Ra'haam ships pursuing us, the tear in space closing behind us with one final shimmering flare of sun-bright light.

And we are safe.

For now.

"They're hailing us again," Aurora murmurs.

I glance to my father. He is watching Aurora like a hawk now as she focuses her gaze and shifts her fingers. The image projected in the room's heart shimmers, and again, I see the war-worn face of Tyler Jones.

My chest might normally ache at the sight of him—the marks the cruel hands of time have left on my friend's skin. But I am more interested in my father now, studying Aurora like a drakkan with its prey. She is learning the workings of the ship quickly—she was made for this task, just as he was. Both Triggers of the Eshvaren. Both able to wield this Weapon, for good or ill. And looking into his eyes, one of them now softly aglow, I know she is in danger.

Caersan will tolerate no rival for this throne.

"You two all right?" Tyler asks.

"We are well, Brother," I tell him, my eyes not shifting from my father. "We thank you for your aid."

"Don't thank me yet," Tyler growls. *"Every member of my command staff is telling me I need my head examined. You'd better get your asses over here and bring a damn good explanation with you. Because in all honesty, I'm about half-way convinced to leave you for the Weeds."* He leans forward, glowering. *"By the way, the invitation doesn't extend to that mass-murdering psychopath sitting behind you. Because if I lay eyes on him in the flesh, I'm gonna blow his fucking brains all over the floor."*

My father raises one eyebrow, and yawns.

"Vindicator, *out.*"

· · · · ·

We walk down to the docking bay together, and on the way Aurora pauses at the place she left her boots when she first entered the *Neridaa*. She is still for a moment, toes curling and flexing against the crystal as though she is loath to break contact with it, and then with a sigh, she sits down to pull on her socks and lace up her boots.

"Probably impractical to go to a war council barefoot," she says, with a small, rueful smile that tugs at my heart.

This moment is such a small one, so simple, so domestic. But it summons a thousand others we spent together in our half year inside the Echo. It reminds me of all the ways in which we learned to fit together, day by day. And so I am reminded that although she is impossibly powerful, and although we are in a galaxy made of nothing but death, she is still the girl I know. I still have riches beyond counting, because I have her.

Tyler will not, of course, dock with the Eshvaren ship, and so Aurora takes us to meet the *Vindicator*, carrying us out into the void.

I am not wearing a suit or helmet, just the black armor of an Unbroken warrior—I would normally freeze and suffocate out here. But a warm nimbus of light plays over Aurora's skin, engulfing me as she takes my hand, carrying us through the empty dark with only the power of her mind.

Her right eye is aglow, and I find myself in awe of how far she has journeyed. How strong she has become. Her face is almost ecstatic as we traverse the Void together, her lips gently curled. But still, I see that faint webwork of scars about her eye, picture the same cracks in my father's face, deeper, darker. I wonder at the toll all this is taking on her.

The price she might pay in the end.

"You are beautiful," I tell her, as we soar together through the black.

My heart aches at her smile. "Not so bad yourself."

"I am . . . sorry, Aurora. For lying to you. About who I am."

Her smile fades a breath, and she glances back toward the *Neridaa*. The ship hangs in the dark behind us—colossal and beautiful, all the colors of the spectrum. But I can see scars torn down its flanks from the Ra'haam attack now. And I can feel the shadow lurking in its heart.

"It hurt that you couldn't tell me the truth, Kal." She squeezes my hand. "But now I've met him, I understand why you'd rather your father be dead."

"He gave me life," I say, looking down at our entwined fingers. "And I sought to take his in return. I tried to put a knife in his back."

"He's a monster, Kal. He murdered a whole world."

"I know it." I shake my head and sigh. "But it should not be this way."

She holds my hand tighter, looks me in the eyes.

"I understand. I'm with you. And I'm glad you're here with me."

She kisses me, brief and soft, and out in this infinity, we are totally alone, and totally complete. And despite everything, the struggle, the hurt, the loss, a part of me still cannot believe this girl is mine.

Aurora brings us across the span of nothing between the *Neridaa* and Tyler's ship. Drawing close, I can see the *Vindicator* has been through many battles, held together with spotwelds and prayers. We glide into the fighter launch bays, and Aurora brings us through the secondary airlock. The aura she has thrown around us fades as the chamber pressurizes, oxygen hissing into the compartment. Gravity slowly returns, Aurora's hair drifting downward, the white streak settling over the dying glow in her eye.

The hatchway cycles open, and we see the gremp from Tyler's bridge crew waiting, one clawed hand on the pistol at her waist. She wears a battered spacesuit, and through the plexiglass of her sealed helmet, I can see her black fur and the spot of white over her left eye. A toothpick of what might be humanoid bone hangs from one corner of her mouth.

Beside her stands the Rikerite—another female, by the look. She is taller even than I, horns sweeping back from a heavy brow. Her arms are thick as my thighs, her shoulders impressively broad. The heavy pulse rifle she carries is aimed vaguely in our direction, and she wears an old sealed combat suit.

"Morning," she says, in a deep voice turned metallic by her visor. "I'm Toshh, chief of security aboard the *Vindicator*."

"Greetings," I say, touching my eyes, lips, heart.

"Hello," Aurora smiles.

"This is Dacca. She's going to scan you for infection. Do yourselves a favor and don't move." Toshh hefts her rifle. "Sudden or otherwise."

The gremp steps forward, sweeping us with a handheld scanner. Aurora and I exchange a glance as the red light scrolls over our bodies—both of us know *exactly* what kind of infection these two are searching for.

Finishing her sweep, the small feline steps back, growling in her own language. The Rikerite nods, touches her helmet. "Comm, this is Toshh, we're green light on bio-scans. No sign of corruption, over?"

"Roger that, Chief," comes Tyler's reply. *"Bring them up."*

The woman hefts her pulse rifle onto one massive arm, motions over her shoulder. "Follow me."

The inner airlock opens after the woman punches in a code, and we follow her into a broader corridor, the gremp bringing up the rear, with her hand still on her pistol. Stepping out into the main vessel, I see the power settings are low, the lights dim. The plasteel is old, the fixtures faulty and flickering, the steel pocked with corrosion. This ship has seen far better days.

Aurora finds my hand as we move into a larger bay,

crowded with people. They are young and old—Betraskans mostly, though I see Chellerians and humans and a few gremps among them. They are ragged and shell-shocked, dirty skin and thin bodies, watching with tired eyes as we follow Toshh. I have seen enough war to know their look in an instant.

"Who are all these people?" Aurora whispers.

"Refugees," I reply.

Toshh nods. "Survivors of a miner fleet, hiding in an ice belt around a dead sun in the Beta sector." She shrugs. "The Weeds found 'em anyway. We pulled them out of the fire just as the swarm hit. Managed to evac two of the ships in the convoy before the rest got taken."

"How many ships were there total?" Aurora asks.

The gremp chatters behind us, little fangs bared.

"I'm sorry," Aurora replies. "I don't und—"

"Thirty-seven," Toshh says. "We saved two of thirty-seven."

We reach an elevator, the doors hissing wide. Aurora watches a little Rikerite girl playing with a stuffed toy beside a pile of packing crates. She is filthy, terribly thin, small horns budding on a brow stained with old blood.

"Be'shmai?" I murmur.

Aurora blinks, joins us in the elevator, her hand finding mine as the doors slip closed. We feel motion, the gentle hum of magnetized mechanics, and in a moment we are stepping out into the space we saw in Tyler's transmission—the bridge of his vessel.

I take note of spot repairs and jury-rigs, bundles of cable and wiring spilling from tactical stations—the signs of wear

163

and tear are apparent here too. But nowhere more so than in the man who awaits us in the commander's chair. He swivels toward us, a battle-scarred mask, a journey of years and blood staining his hands and etched in his one good eye.

"Tyler!" Aurora cries.

She runs forward, suddenly, without warning. Toshh and Dacca both shout in alarm. I see the Syldrathi woman coming to her feet, drawing a null blade from her waist.

I cry out as weapons are raised, stepping toward Chief Toshh, between her and my be'shmai. Tyler rises from his chair, hand slipping to the sidearm at his waist, the Syldrathi woman roars, "SIR, LOOK OUT!" charging toward Aurora. As I kick the gremp's weapon aside and snatch the pulse rifle from Toshh's hands, I hear a soft grunt from Aurora, a hiss from Tyler. And he stands there, his whole body tensed as Aurora throws her arms around him and gives him a crushing hug.

Tyler hangs frozen, like a broken mirror, hand still on his pistol. His crew is tensed and ready, the Syldrathi poised, null blade cracking with a harsh purple glow, the gremp and Rikerite holding their breath. I can see love for Tyler in their eyes—the look of a crew who would gladly die for the one who leads them. A crew who *believes*.

"I missed you so *much,* Ty," Aurora breathes, squeezing him tight. "We thought you were . . ."

None of us said it aloud then—we could not bear to. And the word hangs unspoken in the air now, as if it might attract its own kind, draw darkness down upon the little ship.

Dead.

Tyler stands still for a moment longer. His eye flickering

to me. But finally, his hand slips away from his pistol, and slowly, he lifts his arms. His embrace is not ablaze with warmth, not a full surrender; I still see the tension in his frame, the burden on his shoulders. But for a tiny moment, he holds her tight, allowing himself a second of joy in a galaxy that seems otherwise bereft of it. Joy that his friend still lives.

"I missed you, too," he whispers.

14

KAL

"That's a hell of a story, Aurora."

We are seated in the flickering light of the *Vindicator*'s ready room, a host of unfriendly eyes aimed our way. Aurora sits beside me, hand resting upon my lap. Tyler's command staff is gathered on the other side of the table. The air is crackling with tension, animosity, mistrust.

Tyler sits in the captain's chair, the mantle of command resting upon his shoulders as easily as it ever did. But I feel a new weight on my friend, beyond the years and scars, a weight he never used to carry.

The Tyler I knew was a tactical genius, a boy who could think his way out of the tightest of corners. But I have seen the look in his eyes before—on the faces of warriors who go to face their deaths. Tyler's is not the face of a brave commander, struggling for victory but knowing he shall triumph in the end. His is the face of a warrior who knows he cannot win his war.

The face of a man who is waiting to die.

"I know," Aurora says. "I'd find it hard to believe unless I was living it myself. But for us, the Battle of Terra only happened a few hours ago."

"Lucky you," someone growls. "Most of us have been living with your failure for twenty-seven years, kid."

It is the Betraskan who speaks—a surly veteran named Elin de Stoy, who serves as Tyler's second-in-command. The cybernetic monocle over her eye whirs and shifts as she holds Aurora in her black gaze. Aurora is taken aback at the jab, but keeps her temper, meeting Elin's stare.

"I'm sorry. But I had no control over what—"

"That is a word you use a great deal, Terran," the Syldrathi helmswoman says. "I hope you realize *sorry* counts for nothing at all."

Her violet eyes glitter as she stares at Aurora in unmasked challenge. Her name is Lae, or so Tyler calls her—a curious moniker for one of my people. But I suppose these are curious times. She wears the glyf of the Waywalkers on her brow, yet she bristles with warlike hostility. Deep cracks scar the skin around her eyes, marks of pain twist the corners of her mouth, but beneath it all, there is a . . . familiarity to her I cannot quite place. And strangest of all, now that we are out of the Fold, I see her hair is not the silver common among my people, but a faded alloy of silver and gold.

"We hope to make whole what was broken," I tell her, meeting the challenge in her eyes. "We think we can journey back to the moment we left, and undo what was done. But first, the Weapon must be repaired."

"And we're supposed to trust you?" Lae scoffs. "Son of the Starslayer?"

"From the state of your ship, your crew, what little we have seen of the galaxy, what choice do you have?"

The shadow of it hangs in the ready room now—the memory of those worlds consumed by the Ra'haam. Those corrupted ships bearing down out of the Fold, those cargo bays below full of refugees. Aurora looks at Tyler, hurt in her eyes as she speaks.

"What happened here, Ty?"

He lifts a battered metal flask, takes a mouthful, teeth gritted. I can smell the liquor from where I sit—harsh, home-brewed. Tyler wipes his lip, scratches the patch of leather covering the place his eye should be.

"What do you think happened, Auri? We got our *asses* kicked."

He breathes deep, takes another swig. I can feel a weight in the room then, a scent on the air. Looking among these warriors, seeing the color reflected in their eyes, the taste of salt and rust on my tongue.

Blood.

So much blood.

"Saedii and I were captured by the GIA," Tyler sighs. "Taken off the board to provoke Caersan. And like an *idiot*, the Starslayer took their bait, kicked off a war between the Unbroken and the Terran-Betraskan alliance. After the Weapon disappeared during the battle, the Unbroken pulled back from Earth, but not before massive casualties had been inflicted on both sides. And then the Ra'haam unleashed its real plan."

Tyler shakes his head, takes another sip.

"It had covert operatives all over the galaxy by then. Using the GIA's networks and resources, it staged a series of terror attacks against several galactic governments—the Chellerians, the Rikerites, the Betraskans—framing the strikes to look like they were perpetrated by other species.

Sowing mistrust. Fracturing the old alliances. The Galactic Caucus called an emergency meeting to get the bottom of it all. Every planetary head gathered together in one place. Stupid, really."

Tyler sighs, looks out the viewport to the stars outside.

"A Ra'haam agent detonated a bomb in the Caucus meeting. Simultaneously wiped out every top-end diplomat and head of planetary governance in the alliance. Effectively cutting the head off the Caucus. Each planet blamed the other, old grudges came home to roost. So much effort was wasted looking for the perpetrator and fighting petty squabbles that by the time they figured out what was really happening, it was too late."

"Bloom and burst," Aurora whispers.

"The Ra'haam hatched from its seed worlds," Tyler nods. "Spread through the natural gates in those systems, and from there into the Fold. *Trillions* of spores, infecting everything they came across. Ship by ship. Planet by planet. Race by race. Dragging them all into the hive mind.

"We fought. Of course we did. But every world it consumed made it stronger. Every soldier or ship it infected shifted the tide of the battle. Until its numbers were too great to fight anymore, and all anyone could do was run. Scattering to the corners of the galaxy, lying low, hoping the hive mind wouldn't hear them, sense them, find them. But it always does."

The horror of it washes over us both, and Aurora finds my hand, squeezing tight. "But . . . you're still fighting?"

"There's a few of us left," he says, motioning to his ragtag crew. "A coalition, looking for survivors, bringing them back to what little sanctuary we can offer. But it's just a matter of time."

Tyler shakes his head, meets Aurora's eyes again.

"Until it has *everything*."

"How is it that you stay ahead of the enemy?" I ask. "The FoldGate you opened to bring us here . . . I have not seen such technology before."

"We call it a rift drive," Tyler says. "It's an amalgam of Betraskan and Terran tech, using Syldrathi psychic energy to manipulate spacetime. I don't really understand it, but we've discovered some of the unusual properties of Eshvaren crystal ourselves." He nods to the golden-haired Syldrathi woman, still staring at Aurora, those cracks in her skin darkening as she scowls. "Each of our ships has a Waywalker aboard, and a chunk of crystal taken from recovered Eshvaren probes. The Waywalkers use the probes to open the gates, let us cut through the Fold. But it takes a toll every time they do it. And we don't have many Waywalkers left."

"What happened to the others?" Aurora asks softly.

Tyler frowns. "The other Waywalkers? They—"

"No, I mean the *others*," she insists. "Scarlett. Fin. Zila. Are they . . . ?"

Tyler's mood drops further, the scrape of wet gravel in his tone as he answers. "They died at the Battle of Terra, Auri."

"And . . . Saedii?" I ask.

Tyler looks at me then. Dragging a hand through his graying hair, he drinks deeply from his flask again.

"We escaped the GIA together. I actually teamed up with her and her old crew to fight the Ra'haam." He smiles, but behind it, I can see the pain of an old scar. "We fought like

170

cats and dogs, but we did okay for a few years there. She was a hell of a woman, your sister."

The other Syldrathi woman is staring at me now, eyes like knives.

"Where is she?" I hear myself ask.

"Saedii killed herself, Kal."

"No," I whisper. "She would *never* . . ."

"She was on a rescue run." Tyler sighs. "Trying to recover a refugee fleet near Orion. They got hit by the Ra'haam. Her engines were disabled, her ship was dead in the black. She and her crew were surrounded. She detonated her core rather than be consumed into the collective."

I murmur a prayer to the Void, press my fingers to my eyes, my lips, my aching heart. Aurora squeezes my hand, her eyes misting as she sees my grief. We were not close in the end, my elder sister and I. But Saedii and I once loved each other fiercely, as only siblings forged in the same furnace can.

Tyler guzzles the rest of his flask as the Syldrathi glowers at me.

"She died with honor," Lae spits. "Unlike the rest of her family."

Her tone shifts to bitter violence as she turns those cracked violet eyes to the air beside my head.

"You hear me, cho'taa?" she spits. "I *feel* you! Skulking in the dark like a thief! Show yourself, i'na destii! Ko'vash dei saam te naeli'dai!" She rises to her feet, spitting fury as she raises her null blade. "Aam sai *toviir'netesh*! Vaes santiir to sai'da *baleinai*!"

I am on my feet, standing between Aurora and that

171

crackling psychic blade. The air beside me shimmers, shifts, a blood-red sheen slipping over the light in the room. Aurora rises, her eye glowing faintly as the figure of my father materializes in the room. Tall, dark, ten braids draped over the ruin of his face as he lowers his chin and scowls.

Tyler's weapon is out in a blink, other crew members likewise drawing their arms. They open fire, even as I cry warning, the flash and burst of disruptors and blasters filling the room. But the image of my father only shimmers, like water with stones being thrown into it, and I realize this is merely a projection of consciousness—thrown from the *Neridaa* to eavesdrop on our conversation.

"Coward!" Lae spits. "De'saiie na vaelto'na!"

My father tilts his head, staring at the furious Waywalker.

"Name me *shameless*?" he says. "Name me *cur*? I, who walked the stars before you were born? I, who tore suns from the sky and won battles uncounted? You are not worthy to name yourself *Syldrathi, whelp*."

"This is your fault!" she roars. "ALL OF IT!"

He glowers at the woman, a faint glow flickering in his irises. But I see his contempt and anger crack for a moment, a small shadow on his heart.

"Saedii . . . is . . ."

Tyler rises, lips peeling back from his teeth as he raises his disruptor. "Get the hells off my ship, mother*fucker*."

"Father," I say softly. "You should *leave*."

His gaze shifts to me, then back to Lae, and at last returns to Tyler. The hint of grief I felt in him is swallowed whole, a contemptuous glance falling on the empty metal flask in my old friend's hand.

"No wonder you fail. With a captain so worthless as this."

"If I'm so worthless, Starslayer, how is it—"

But he is gone, vanished with a soundless ripple, withdrawing back to his throne aboard the *Neridaa*. Lae looks to Tyler, spittle on her lips as she hisses, "We should head over to that vessel and *end* him, Commander."

"He would destroy you all," I reply.

"So frightened of him, are you?" Lae scoffs.

"As frightened as I am hateful," I reply sadly, meeting her narrowing eyes. "And if you had wisdom, you would be also."

"It falls to those of Caersan's bloodline to end his dishonor. He is your *father*. You should have killed him already to restore your family's name."

The ache of Saedii's loss deepens then. My mother's death ringing in the halls of my memory beside it, sharpening my tongue as I meet Lae's eyes.

"Family is . . . complicated," I growl. "Do not dare preach to me about mine. You have *no* idea what it is to be a part of it."

"Why the hells are you working with that bastard, Aurora?" Tyler asks, his voice soft with wonder and loathing.

"We need him, Ty," she replies. "I'm not used to wielding the Weapon yet. He's had almost a decade to learn how to use it, and he knows the note to play on the *Neridaa* to return us to our own time."

"How is that even possible?" Chief Toshh asks. Beside her, Dacca chatters and nods her head, whiskers twitching.

"I don't know," Aurora replies. "But I believe him. If we can get back there, we can undo all of this! We can destroy the Ra'haam before it hatches!"

"So why the hells are you still here?" Tyler demands. "If you can—"

"The Weapon is damaged, Brother. It needs repairs."

Tyler's second-in-command fixes me with black, gleaming eyes. "How you going to manage that?"

"I do not know." I rub my chin. "Do you have a home base? Someplace—"

Dacca chatters, tail lashing as she watches me with gold, slitted eyes.

"Yeah, we got a home base, Pixieboy," Toshh growls. "But Maker damn us all if we're giving its location to the *Starslayer*."

"Even if we did," the Betraskan continues, "we have no tech capable of working on a device like that. Not many starports that specialize in Eshvaren crystal superweapons floating around anymore."

"There is one, though . . . ," Aurora murmurs, thoughtful.

I look to her in question, brow creased.

"The Eshvaren homeworld," she says, meeting my eyes. "Remember? It was hidden inside that Fold anomaly. Maybe it's still there."

I nod slowly. "If there is one place we might repair the damage, it would be where the Ancients created the Weapon in the first place."

"Where was this . . . anomaly?" Tyler asks.

"In the Theta sector," I reply. "We visited there with Scarlett and Finian and Zila after you were captured by the GIA."

"You're dreaming, Pixieboy," de Stoy says. "Theta sector is completely overrun with Weeds. They're thicker than sketi on a martuush blossom there."

174

"If we move quickly—"

"The Ra'haam's power is augmented inside the Fold," Toshh says. "It feels the psychic ripples of any living thing that enters, and sends fleets after it until it's consumed."

"There must be a way, Tyler," Aurora says.

"Traversing the Theta sector is a bad plan," he replies.

"Maybe for people who don't have the best tactician Aurora Academy ever produced on their side." Aurora smiles. "Tyler Jones doesn't make bad plans, remember? Just less amazing ones."

But Tyler doesn't return the smile, his voice grim, his brow dark.

"That was a long time ago, Auri."

"We need your help, Brother," I tell him. "Please."

Tyler toys with a silver ring on his finger, jaw set, anger and betrayal still bubbling beneath his surface. The Rikerite regards Aurora with old eyes, murmuring, "Perhaps we should run this by the council, Commander."

Lae scowls at that, snapping, "Why do we care? Why do we care what *any* of them say or do? We cannot aid the Starslayer, nor his son, nor the fool that binds herself to him. We must *kill him* to avenge our lost—"

"That's enough, Lae," Tyler says.

"No!" she shouts. "Commander, the blood of *billions* is on his hands! Honor demands his death! We cannot possibly—"

"I said that's ENOUGH, Lieutenant!" Tyler roars.

The pair stare at each other, eye to eye, Tyler's will crackling against Lae's. I can feel the rage in her, the fury. But finally, she lowers her gaze.

"Yessir," she murmurs.

"What condition is the rift drive in?" he demands.

". . . The crystal is showing continuing degradation," she replies softly. "But it is stable enough for now."

"How soon can you jump us home?"

Her eyes flicker up to his again, incredulous. But she does not challenge him further, instead watching him carefully with those cracked violet eyes. "I need to rest. An hour, perhaps two. And a jump that far with vessels so large . . . it will be *costly*. Sir."

I see Tyler's gaze soften. "Is it going to hurt you?"

"It *always* hurts. But if you are ordering it . . ."

He looks between Aurora and me again, finally settling his thoughts.

"I can't make this call alone. Not with everything in the balance. We need to get back to base." His gaze falls on Aurora, his one good eye hard as steel. "You can plead your case to the Council of Free Peoples. If they decide we help you, then we help. If not, you're on your own."

Aurora nods, hurt in her eyes. "I understand. And if you need me . . ." She looks to Lae, shrugging. "With the drive . . . I mean, if you need power to move us, maybe I can help."

Lae glances toward the *Neridaa*—that massive vessel moved here by the power of Aurora's will alone. She nods curtly. "I will accept your aid."

"All right," Tyler says. "Dacca, Toshh, get those refugees situated. Elin, I want us to stay on Alert Two in case more Weeds show up. An hour isn't too long to stay in one place, but soon as we can, we jump for home."

"Sir, yessir," comes the reply.

"Let's move like we got a purpose."

The crew breaks up, heading off to their assigned tasks. With a soft smile to me, Aurora leaves with Lae to inspect the drive. Tyler and I are left alone, staring at each other across the table. There is much to be said between us, but I am unsure if this is the place or indeed if he would listen. So instead, I ask the question burning in my mind.

"Where is home in a galaxy like this, Brother?"

He looks to the window, that red sun, those silent worlds. I allow myself the smallest hint of hope that he has not yet denied me the use of that title. "You've been there before, actually."

". . . Aurora Academy?"

"No," he sighs. "Ra'haam agents destroyed it during the attack on the Galactic Caucus. And the station moved too slow, anyway." He looks at me, faint horror in his eye. "It . . . listens, Kal. It's so big now, it can hear everything. Hole up on a planet, it'll find you sooner or later. Hide inside a fleet, eventually it'll sniff you out like those poor bastards downstairs."

I shake my head. "Where is safe, then?"

Tyler shrugs faintly. "If there's no world you can call home, no ship that's safe to hide inside, well, you just use both."

I blink, putting the puzzle together in my head.

"Sempiternity," I smile.

15

SCARLETT

My guidance counselor once told me that the words "if she only applied herself" had appeared more on my assessment transcripts than on any cadet's in Aurora Academy history. And I'm almost certain this wasn't what he meant when he told me, "Practice makes perfect, Cadet Jones." But I've died thirty-seven times so far today, and it turns out I'm pretty talented at it.

It sounds weird, I know. Maybe even a little insane. But as strange and morbid as it might be, I'm beginning to suspect the biggest reason people are afraid of dying is because they don't know what happens afterward.

Zila, Finian, Nari, and I all know what happens. To *us*, at least. And it's somehow getting harder to be afraid when you know what's coming.

Black light.

White noise.

A moment of vertigo.

And then I'm standing in front of Finian again, back aboard our shuttle, with Lieutenant Nari Kim's fighter waiting just outside in the dark.

The fear didn't disappear right away. And at first, the strangeness of it all was so heavy that I wondered for a little while if I wouldn't rather just stay dead. There was something wrong about it. Unnatural, even. But like I say, I've always been a glass-half-full kind of girl. And once the fear disappears, I gotta tell you . . . this immortality thing is almost *amazing*.

So here we are, on another attempt to access Dr. Pinkerton's office. Attempt #37, to be precise, to discover the secret of what the hells is going on inside this facility. Lemme take you through it all real quick.

First, we've discovered we have to access the admin levels through the elevator shafts, *not* the emergency stairs like Lieutenant Kim first told us. Stairwell A leads to the unshielded part of the structure, and we've already seen what happens when that quantum pulse hits the station and we're all just standing there looking gorgeous.

ZAAAAPPPP.

You might be wondering why we don't wait till the pulse hits and head up afterward. Excellent question. Sadly, we tried that already, and discovered when we loitered too long on the lower level, security found us, not once, not twice, but three times straight.

BLAM.

BLAM.

BLAM.

Turns out even with the damage to the station, some of the camera feeds are still operational. Who would've guessed the SecBoys in a covert black-ops military installation would take the presence of saboteurs so seriously? I thought getting *punched* in the ta-tas hurt. Let me assure you getting shot in them is a *lot* worse.

BLAMBLAM.

We decided to try our luck with Stairwell B next, and on our maiden voyage, an entirely new piece of strangeness was added to the mix. You see, on the way to meet us, good Lieutenant Kim decided to take a different route to shave a few minutes off her trip. She entered Corridor 16B, Level 6, at the precise moment a bulkhead failed and vented the corridor's atmo into space.

HISSSSHHHHHH.

THUMP.

And even though Zila, Fin, and I were still crawling through waste disposal at the time, suddenly—black light, white noise, vertigo—I'm standing back aboard our shuttle, looking into Fin's big, pretty eyes again.

That was the final confirmation of my theory. Somehow, the four of us are locked in this thing together. Doesn't matter how, doesn't matter who—if even *one* of us gets taken out of the loop, the whole thing resets.

Again.

And again.

Like it or not, we're all in this together.

So next we busied ourselves with Stairwell B. We gave it three attempts, but even moving fast as we could, we only ever got halfway up before the life-support system decided to play kissy-kissy with a shorting circuit somewhere in the superstructure, and the whole stairwell caught fire.

FWOOOOOOSH.

YARRRGGG.

So. Elevator shafts it is. Good news, the damage to the station has knocked out security cams over here. Bad news, it's also weakened the cable and disabled the safety systems. We figured *that* out the first time we crawled into Shaft A, and an elevator full of engineers got ordered down to the core levels at the precise moment we were trying to crawl *up* it.

TWANGGG.

SQUISH.

Luckily, Shaft B suffers no such shortfalls, and after another attempt, in which Finian discovered the structural integrity of rung 372 of the access ladder had been compromised (*SNAP, "OH FFFFFUUUUUUAAAAAGGGGG"*), we managed to reach the hab section, where Dr. Pinkerton's office can be found.

Buuuut don't start celebrating just yet, folks.

The elevator doors up here are sealed as a precaution against atmo breaches, and it takes three minutes and forty-nine seconds for Fin's cutting torch to slice the locks.

Sadly, opening the doors sets off a silent alarm. We found this out the hard way exactly one minute and twenty-three seconds after our first successful attempt, while cutting our way into Pinkerton's office.

"FREEZE!"

"Please don't shoot! My name is Scarlett Isobel Jones, I'm—"

BLAMBLAMBLAM.

Bad news is, there's no way around that alarm. The moment we open those doors, we're making an appointment with those security goons.

Good news is, after some trial

"FREEZE!"

"Maker's breath, don't you dirtboys have anything b—"

BLAMBLAMBLAM.

and error

"FREEZE!"

"Why do you assholes even say Freeze when you're just gonna—"

BLAMBLAMBLAM.

we've figured out a way to get into Pinkerton's office without having to waste a bunch of extra time cutting through his door.

It goes a little something like this:

Legionnaire de Seel and I head up through Shaft B (studiously avoiding rung 372 as we go). While I hang on the ladder below him, watching the way the sparks reflect in his eyes, Finian cuts through the doors leading out to the admin level. Meanwhile, Zila and Lieutenant Kim head down to the station morgue, where the body of the recently deceased Dr. Pinkerton resides.

After four attempts

BLAM.

BRAPPPP.

"FREEZE!"

STABSTABSTAB.

the ladies haven't found a way to avoid station security and get what they came for: the electronic passkey around the neck of Pinkerton's corpse. But like I say, I've got a good feeling this time.

So cross your fingers, kids.

Sparks are raining down from the metal, the faint hiss of Fin's cutting torch barely audible over the wailing alarms, the occasional alert klaxon. I hang on the rung below him, watch him work: his lips pressed thin, a dark line of concentration between his brows.

"Can I help?"

He smiles. "You asked me that the last three times. I'm good, Scar."

"How you think Z and Kim are doing?"

"Well, we haven't vanished in a burst of temporal paradox yet." He wipes his brow on his sleeve. "So, better than last time."

The station vibrates faintly, and another alarm wails. I feel kinda useless just waiting here, and I don't like it.

"You sure I can't do anything?"

Fin grins. "I'm kinda thirsty?"

One arm hooked through the ladder rungs, I swing the backpack he brought off my shoulder. Reaching inside, I fish about among our useless uniglasses for the canteen. But instead, my fingers brush against something soft. Furry. Pulling the object out into the light, I feel a warm rush on my skin as I realize what I'm holding, a smile curling my lips.

"You saved Shamrock?"

Fin glances down to the plush dragon in my hand and shrugs. "I figured we need all the allies we can get."

I press Shamrock to my lips, breathing deep and looking at the boy above me. Maker, he's sweet. Of all the things he could've brought with us, he salvages the one part of Cat we have left. I can still smell her on the dragon's fur as I inhale, the scent of her perfume and the fabric softener she used. For a moment it hits me, and I have to close my eyes against it—the knowledge of how far we are from home, how much we've lost on the way here, and how we might never find our way back.

"You all right?"

I look up and see Fin staring down at me, concern in his eyes. I know I shouldn't bother him—he has work to do, and who knows what's hanging in the balance. But suddenly, I feel so small, I can't feel myself at all.

"Do you think it's going to be okay, Fin?"

He frowns slightly. "You mean . . ."

"I mean all this. Auri, Tyler, this, us." I shake my head, hating the tears I feel in my eyes. "I never took any of this seriously, Fin. I spent all my time at the academy screwing around. And now we're hip-deep in this crap and I feel totally useless. All I know how to do is talk, and there's no room for that here. Maybe if I'd paid attention, if I—"

"Hey." He shuts off the flashlight and, with a bit of effort, works his way down the ladder so we're eye to eye. "Hey, none of that. You're not useless."

I roll my eyes. "I appreciate the vote of confidence, Legionnaire de Seel. But theoretical physics isn't exactly my forte."

"Maybe not." He shrugs, his exo hissing. "But since Tyler got snagged by the GIA, I'm not sure if you've noticed, but the person holding our whole squad together is *you*. We need you, Scar."

He reaches out and brushes a tear away with a silver finger.

"I need you."

I shake my head in wonder. "How have you been in front of my eyes this whole time, and I'm only just seeing you now?"

184

He smiles, shrugging. "I'm just glad you do."

"I do," I whisper.

And I move closer, and I feel his arm slip around my waist, and a slight shock as our lips meet, electricity and butterflies surging inside me as the station rocks around us and he presses up against me and Zila's voice rings out over the wailing alarms.

"Are you two spending precious minutes in the middle of a heretofore unheard-of temporal paradox engaging in frivolous presexual activity?"

We look down the shaft, see Zila climbing up quickly with Lieutenant Kim right behind her.

"You're such a hopeless romantic, Z," I call.

"We do not have time to waste on trivialities, we may—"

"Relax, Legionnaire Madran," Fin says, giving me a wink and slipping out of my arms. "By the time you're up here, I'll be done."

"You ladies got the passkey?" I yell.

"We were successful," Zila calls back. "Thanks to Nari's quick thinking."

"Nari?" Fin mutters. "She and Dirtgirl are on a first-name basis now?"

"Behave," I mutter.

"What if I don't wanna?" he asks, winking again.

The lock clunks, Fin extinguishes his cutter, and with a labored whine from his exosuit, our Gearhead wrenches the elevator doors wide just as Zila and Kim reach us. Like always, the silent alarm will be sounding somewhere as soon as we set foot in the corridor, but we have a little time left before the SecBoys intercept us.

Fast as we can, we dash down the smoke-filled corridors, arriving at Pinkerton's office. Zila swipes the dead man's passkey through the reader, an agonizing few seconds pass before the lock switches to green and we hustle inside to the tune of wailing sirens.

The office is plush—well, about as plush as you're going to get on a space station, at least. There are dozens of glass cases around the room, dimly lit by emergency lighting. A bunch of strange objects float inside, suspended on cushions of zero grav. It reminds me a little of Casseldon Bianchi's office on Sempiternity.

Looks like Pinkerton was some kind of collector.

I squint at one of the artifacts slowly revolving in a thin beam of light. It's flat, rectangular, its surface old and cracked. There might have been writing on it, but it's worn away with time. And there's . . . paper inside?

"What's that?" Fin asks, peering through the glass.

"No clue," I murmur.

"Are you joking?"

We glance behind us, find Nari staring at us like we're simple.

"Almost always," Fin shrugs. "But in this case, I honestly have no idea what this is."

"Don't they have books in the future?"

"*This* is what books used to look like?" I ask, bewildered.

"A hundred or so years ago," Nari nods. "Dr. Pinkerton collects antiques. First day I got posted to station, he gave me a lecture on preserving the treasures of the past." She shrugs. "Then he never spoke to me again."

"This is a *book*?" Fin blinks. "It's wrapped in dead animal skin!"

"That's the way we used to do it."

Fin raises an eyebrow at me. "You dirtchildren, I swear . . ."

I smile, looking more around the room. I can see holopics of Pinkerton's family. There's a row of potted cacti that must have been lined up against the plexiglass window, but impacts to the station have knocked them all over, and they lie shattered on the ground.

"Who puts spiky plants somewhere they can— Never mind, don't try and explain," Fin mutters, carefully circumnavigating them.

A long glass desk sits against one wall, the glowing screen of a personal dataport lighting the gloom.

Zila has already slid into the chair, swiped the passkey through the terminal, and begun typing. Say what you will for humanity's technological strides over the past two centuries, aside from being *way* slower, the computer seems to function basically the same. Zila is soon scrolling through menus, hands waving before the sensors, sweeping holographic displays aside in her search for information. Lieutenant Kim stands behind her, looking over her shoulder. Fin's there too, murmuring advice.

"Attention, Glass Slipper personnel. Hull breach on Decks 13 through 17."

I stand by the window, looking out at the chaos beyond.

Space is mind-bendingly big. Even the subspace pocket of the Fold is simply too massive for the human brain to wrap itself around. But that storm of dark matter out there is just colossal enough to be terrifying. As I stare out at the pulsing tempest, that same feeling returns—the impression that I'm tiny, insignificant, in too deep and all the way over my head. I think of Tyler. I think of Auri. I even think of Kal. Wondering where they are. Hoping they're okay.

I turn away from it, too big, too much. Wandering instead through Dr. Pinkerton's little collection while Zila and Fin keep searching. There's something comforting about it—relics of a past Terra that have outlived the age they were born in. In a way, these objects are time travelers like us.

I mooch past an old boxy lump of plastic, with a circular number pad and a weird handset. There's what might be a pistol of some sort, its surface pitted with tiny spots of corrosion. And in a case against the window . . .

"Holy shit," I whisper, looking over to the workstation. "Fin?"

"There," Fin murmurs to Zila. "Try that one."

"I see it," she nods.

"Fin!"

He glances up as I call. "Huh?"

"Come look at this."

He frowns a little, but leaves Zila and Nari to it, stepping out from behind the console and crossing over to me. "What's up?"

Heart beating wildly, I point to the object inside the case, spinning softly on its beam of zero gravity. A thin, silver, rectangular box. Perfectly mundane. Impossibly familiar.

"Isn't that . . . ?"

His big black eyes widen, those pretty lips part in astonishment.

"Maker's breath . . . ," he whispers, looking at me. "That's the cigarillo case de Stoy and Adams left for Kal in the Dominion vault!"

"Attention, Glass Slipper personnel. All engineering staff report to Gamma Section, Deck 12, immediately."

"Scarlett," Zila calls. "Finian, I believe you should look at this. . . ."

"Zila, you're not gonna—"

"This is important, Finian."

We exchange a glance, and I can't quite seem to catch my breath as we hurry over to Nari and Zila. The pair are still huddled around the terminal, and on the holographic displays hanging in the air in front of Zila, I can see streams of data, glowing in the dark.

Most of it is totally incomprehensible to someone who spent her physics lectures wishing she was anywhere other than a physics lecture, but I can see the folder is titled "Project Glass Slipper." And illustrated in glowing light above a flurry of unreadable charts is a familiar shape. A chunk of polished stone, teardrop-shaped, cut like a piece of jewelry, a thousand facets for the light to dance on.

A shape I recognize.

"That's a probe," I whisper. "That's an Eshvaren probe!"

Zila leans back in her chair. "Interesting."

"It's a what now?" Lieutenant Kim demands.

"It's an exploration device," Finian says, wide eyes on the spinning display. "Created by an alien race called the Eshvaren. They launched thousands of them into the Fold, millennia ago. Our friend Aurora used one to unlock her latent psychic potential so she could continue the Eshvaren's ancient war against . . ."

His voice fades as he realizes Nari is looking at him like he's a lunatic.

"It's a long story, okay? Point is, it's alien tech. Hard-core."

BOOM.

The whole station shudders as something, somewhere, explodes.

"WARNING: CONTAINMENT BREACH. EVACUATE DECKS 5 THROUGH 6 IMMEDIATELY. REPEAT: CONTAINMENT BREACH."

"They must have discovered one," I breathe. "Here, in this time."

"It is damaged." Zila points to the broken edge of the teardrop's point. "Apparently inert. Project Glass Slipper is attempting to discover the crystal's properties. Potentially weaponize them. The main fragment is locked in the station core, being subjected to testing with quantum energy harvested within the dark tempest." She frowns, manipulating the holographic controls. "But there is a much smaller fragment, which . . ."

The wall hums.

A wall panel above the computer slides away, revealing a cylindrical glass case like the others around the office. But instead of an antique suspended in a thin column of zero grav, there is . . . a tiny chunk of crystal.

Out in the dark matter storm, that pulse of quantum energy strikes the sail, arcing along the cable toward the station. Forty-four minutes since we arrived, just like always. And just like always, the fragment around my neck begins to glow black in response. But *this* time, that glow is mirrored in the chunk of crystal floating inside that case. Like twins, their intensity grows, each one exactly the same as . . .

"Holy shit . . . ," I whisper.

My hand drifts up to the medallion around my neck. A medallion that, just like Kal's cigarillo case, waited ten years in that vault in Emerald City. Put there by people who seemed to know what would happen before it actually did.

"Scar . . ." Fin stares at the glass case. "This is *your* crystal. . . ."

"How . . . ?" Lieutenant Kim shakes her head, looking between the crystal in the glass and the crystal around my neck. The shape is unmistakable. *Identical.* "How is that possible? If you're from the year 2380?"

"I do not know," Zila says. "But *this* is it. This is the cause of the loop. An interaction across time and space between the Weapon, this station, the quantum pulse, the Eshvaren crystals. All of it is entwined. Ouroboros."

The pulse reaches the station.

The structure shudders, the lights around us flickering.

"WARNING: CONTAINMENT BREACH CRITICAL. EVACUATE DECKS 2 THROUGH 10 IMMEDIATELY. REPEAT: CONTAINMENT BREACH CRITICAL."

Lieutenant Kim and I are staring at each other, the same disbelief in our eyes. Fin and Zila begin trawling through the data, reading as fast as they can. The glow in the medallion is fading now, the after-impression burned in white on the inside of my eyes.

"WARNING: CONTAINMENT BREACH UNDER WAY, ENGAGE EMERGENCY MEASURES DECK 11."

The station shakes again. Harder this time.

The door to the office slides open and half a dozen laser sights light up the flickering gloom.

"FREEZE!"

Fin sighs. "Oh, for the love of . . ."

"REPEAT: CONTAINMENT BREACH UNDER WAY, ENGAGE EMERGENCY MEASURES DECK 11."

I raise my hands for the SecBoys. "See you soon."

BLAMBLAMBLAM.

16

ZILA

"Aw chakk, what got us?" Finian asks over comms.

"I thought for sure we were safe that time," Scarlett agrees.

"A core breach," I tell them, rising from my pilot's seat. "The station reactor overloaded fifty-eight minutes after the quantum pulse struck it, destroying the entire structure. It seems the damage the station has sustained will ultimately prove critical, no matter what we do."

"Why didn't they order an evac?" Finian asks.

"The call to abandon the facility was only made three minutes before detonation. Given the amount of money the Terran government must have spent on this project, I believe what is left of station command was desperately trying to salvage the situation."

"And we somehow slept through all that?" Scarlett asks.

"You looked very tired. I did not wish to wake you."

We made the decision to devote our last loop to rest. The cumulative effect of the repeated resets, the adrenaline surges from near misses and the moments before our deaths, and the sheer ongoing effort of mental calculation has fatigued all of us—and of course, we were tired when we arrived here.

When Scarlett realized we had essentially been on the move for well over twenty-four hours, and none of us were resetting feeling refreshed, it was evident that sleep was indicated.

I volunteered to take the first watch, and we hunkered down with Nari—who has also completed over a day's worth of loops—just inside our entry point by the waste ejection system. We were crowded, but we were safer there than drifting aboard our damaged ship. Until the station went quite dramatically to pieces around us, of course.

Now back in our shuttle once more, I meet Fin and Scarlett in the corridor en route to the loading bay.

"From the look on your face," Scarlett says, "this isn't good."

"I am not certain," I reply. "But if the three fragments of crystal—yours, Dr. Pinkerton's, and the main probe—are the cause of the loop, and our way home, and all three were just destroyed in a large-scale explosion . . ."

"Then this loop always ends," Finian frowns. "No matter what we do."

I nod. "Fifty-eight minutes after the quantum pulse."

"Chakk," Fin sighs. "That means that even if we dodge all the ways there are to die in that place, we've only got an hour and three quarters each loop, give or take. That's a lot less than I'd like."

"I am uneasy," I admit.

"And unrested," Scarlett points out. "Did you sleep at all?"

"I shall do so during a future loop," I reply. "I had an

opportunity to think while I kept watch. Let us return to Dr. Pinkerton's office."

"Nobody step on a cactus this time," Fin adds.

. . . . .

We reach our destination more quickly each time now, but I am growing concerned we are still not fast enough. Earlier, I thought us efficient in our efforts. Now I am aware that a considerable portion of our limited time is being spent each loop just to access Pinkerton's office.

But we *must* know more.

Nari and I work in perfect concert as we retrieve Dr. Pinkerton's passkey from his corpse, and once we are within his quarters, I am able to navigate through a now-familiar set of menus promptly. We no longer waste time in surprise at the crystal fragment that is a twin to Scarlett's, or the sheer improbability of our predicament.

Finian and Scarlett are buying more time—distracting the patrol that otherwise arrives at Pinkerton's quarters, shooting us and ending our loop.

The station shakes around us.

"WARNING: CONTAINMENT BREACH ESCALATION UNDER WAY, ENGAGE EMERGENCY MEASURES DECK 9."

Nari stands watch as I gather data about the disastrous tests that were running at the moment the loop initiated. I have learned during our recent escapades that she is more talkative than I had anticipated.

I do not find it distracting. Rather, it is calming. My eyes are gritty and I know fatigue is slowing my thoughts. I anchor myself to her voice.

"So," she muses. "You're friends with aliens, huh?"

I do not look up, speaking softly. "Technically, everyone is an alien to somebody."

"You know lots more races than the Betraskans?"

"Many," I confirm. My mind goes to Kal, so far away in space and time. And then to Auri, leaning over Magellan as she tried to catch up on two centuries of history, to learn about the aliens that so fascinate Nari.

But Auri is gone now, and Magellan is a broken collection of circuitry in Finian's bag. I set that memory aside.

"You must have seen some amazing places," Nari continues, unaware of my momentary lapse in attention. "I mean, all those alien homeworlds. You said there are hippos on one, right? I can't believe hippos beat me to interplanetary exploration."

I am unsure why, but I find myself wishing to remove the note of regret from her voice. "This is still a wondrous time to be alive. There is so much to be seen now that will soon be lost."

"Like what?"

"That book, for example," I reply, nodding toward the display case. "What an extraordinary thing to hold in your hand."

"I guess so?" Her tone suggests I am humoring her, but this is not so.

"A book captures a story within its pages. Not like a specimen pinned out lifelessly for display, but vivid and alive. A whole world lies within the cover, a life waiting to be lived by each new reader."

"You still have stories in the future," she points out. "Though that's more poetic than I expected from you."

It is, perhaps, more poetic than I expected too. "We still have stories," I agree. "But they live in the ether. The book in that display case represents something we will never know. Something . . . permanent."

"Stories never die," she counters.

"They do not. But in a book, you always know where to find them again. They have a home."

There is something in my tone, on that last word—as I speak of something that has not been mine since I was a child.

Home.

She hears it, and turns from the door to regard me thoughtfully. A question is about to push past her lips, so I continue.

"You have also seen many places that are lost to us," I say, leaning in to study the screen. "Strange as it sounds, I have never even been to Terra."

"What, never?"

"Never," I reply.

"That's . . . kinda sad," she smiles.

"*REPEAT: CONTAINMENT BREACH ESCALATION UNDER WAY, ENGAGE EMERGENCY MEASURES DECK 9.*"

I look her over, noting the way the light from the tempest outside highlights her features. Black and mauve pulses, gleaming in her eyes.

I should be working more swiftly on a solution to our quandary.

But I am drawn back once more to the idea of . . . home.

"Will you tell me about a place from Terra that you have visited?" I ask.

"Gyeongju," she says immediately. "It's this really cool

city in Korea with all these historical protections put on it by TerraGov. It has these tombs hidden inside its hills, really well preserved—it used to be the capital of the kingdom that was there before it was called Korea."

I turn back to the console, unraveling a series of menus and studying their contents, pushing through the woolly thinking of fatigue.

"I had not taken you for a history buff," I admit.

"I'm not," she admits. "It's where my halmoni lives—my grandmother. So, you know, my family visits there sometimes."

There is something easier about Nari's manner than there has been on previous loops. She is facing the door once more as she keeps watch, but I can see her profile, that dark energy illuminating her skin.

My disobedient mind casts itself back to our last loop, after Nari and Finian fell asleep and Scarlett made herself comfortable beside me.

"Nari Kim's growing on me," Scarlett admitted softly.

"Finian would suggest that you can get a cream for that sort of thing," I had informed her gravely.

She'd snickered. "She's growing on you, too, Zila."

"Oh?"

Scarlett's tone turned sly. "She's . . . not tall."

I rue the day I spoke to Scarlett Jones about my taste in women.

"Zila?"

Nari's voice recalls me to the present.

What were we discussing?

Home.

"You have a large family, Lieutenant?"

"Oh yeah, huge. But my halmoni still likes us all to report in every week. I swear she's got a schedule, and if you miss your slot . . . It took a long, long time to convince her I can't phone home from a black-ops posting."

"And have you visited her often, in Gyeongju?"

"Every year, until I enlisted. Now it's more like every second year." Nari sighs. "It's great there. I mean, I'm always sharing a room with half a dozen cousins, because we're trying to cram so much family into her apartment. But there's always so much food—she makes the best doenjang stew in Gyeongju, plus a dozen little dishes on the side, and that's for an *informal* meal—and one of my cousins is a tour guide on Jeju Island. They've got this fruit there—huuuuuge citruses called hallabongs. Stupidly juicy, they end up all over you, but they taste amazing. I took my ex-girlfriend with me once, and I swear the only reason we're still in touch is that she wants me to bring her back a box of them when I visit. Anyway . . ."

She trails off, perhaps aware she has spoken at length. Or perhaps—I am not skilled at divining such things—attempting to gauge my reaction to the mention of the ex-girlfriend?

"I have not encountered a hallabong before. But I enjoy citrus."

"What about the rest of it?" she asks softly.

"The rest of it?"

"Family? Somewhere you've been? I've talked about me, what about you, Futuregirl?"

"*WARNING: RADIATION DETECTED ON DECK 13, ALL DECK 13 STAFF PROCEED FOR IMMEDIATE DECONTAMINATION PROCEDURES.*"

"I can offer only disappointment, I am afraid." I switch my attention to a new set of entries, intrigued by the methods used in the scientists' attempts to power up the crystal. "I grew up in state care with no family members. And I have not taken a vacation."

She blinks. "What, ever?"

I shrug. "It was more fruitful to spend my academy leave studying."

We are both silent after that, and I choose to devote the better part of my attention to the results of the power cycle experiments.

"Were you . . . always in state care?" she asks eventually, quieter now. Gentler. "Is that common, in the future? I mean, you don't have to talk about it. If you don't want."

I hesitate, which is uncharacteristic. "It is not common," I say after a while. I am about to continue, to inform her that I do not wish to speak of the experience, when I look across at her.

Our eyes meet.

"Perhaps we can speak of it during another loop," I say instead.

She smiles, and in that moment there is something so familiar about her that my attention is caught entirely.

I feel my mind trying to switch gears, to fire up the search routines that will help me match her to some memory or experience that explains this familiarity. But I do not have time to study her smile, her eyes. I clear my throat, turning back to my console.

"You want to hear some more ancient history while you work?" she asks. "Or am I distracting you?"

"Both," I realize.

As she keeps speaking, I let myself sink into her voice, and into the lines of data before me. Unless we find a way to break out of this loop, this will be my life. This will be my day.

Over, and over, and over again.

This will be my home.

"I think I—"

The loudspeaker cuts me off.

"WARNING: CONTAINMENT CASCADE IN EFFECT. CORE IMPLOSION IMMINENT, T MINUS THREE MINUTES AND COUNTING. ALL HANDS PROCEED TO EVACUATION PODS IMMEDIATELY. REPEAT: CORE IMPLOSION IN THREE MINUTES AND COUNTING."

And there it is.

The end of the loop.

We will always have the next one, I suppose.

I glance at the timer on my wrist, then fall still.

I feel a small furrow forming in my brow.

Nari tilts her head. "Zila?"

I must have miscalculated earlier. I told Finian and Scarlett the core overloaded fifty-eight minutes after the quantum lightning strike. Usually I am right. But it has only been fifty-one minutes. . . .

I must be tired. I did not sleep when the others did.

I do not speak of my mistake.

Instead, I finish what work I can, committing as much of the data to memory as possible. Nari watches me from the window, the starlight glowing on her skin. And finally, when there are only moments left, I rise to my feet, ready to meet what is coming. "I will see you soon, Nari."

"WARNING: CORE IMPLOSION IMMINENT, T MINUS

THIRTY SECONDS. ALL HANDS EVACUATE IMMEDIATELY. REPEAT: CORE IMPLOSION IN THIRTY SECONDS."

"I hate this part," she admits.

I meet her eyes again and, without knowing why my instinct is to comfort her, reply, "You are not alone."

She takes a step toward me.

Her eyes are very pretty.

"WARNING: CORE IMPLOSION IMMINENT. FIVE SECONDS. WARNING."

She is not tall.

"Zila, I know this is terrible timing, but I really think you're—"

"WARNING."

BOOM.

17

TYLER

There are advantages to being one of the galaxy's most wanted criminals.

My whole life I played by the rules. Studied hard, worked harder, never really made time for trouble. But turning the collar of my long black coat up against the chill, pulling up my hood, and stepping into the bar, much as I hate to admit it, I kind of enjoy the feeling of being a wanted man.

The place is totally packed—freighter pilots and long-haul crews, gangsters and drug/sim/skin dealers, hundreds of faces, a dozen different races. Through the crowd, the Betras-kan girl behind the bar gives me an appreciative smile, and the various lowlifes, scumbags, and villains I've scoped over the last day or two nod greeting or just cradle their drinks. But nobody messes with me, even in a place rough as this.

I'm a galactic terrorist, after all. An Aurora legionnaire gone rogue. A mass murderer, responsible for the deaths of hundreds of Syldrathi aboard Sagan Station, not to mention an Interdiction breach, a heist, a couple of explosions aboard

Emerald City, and any number of other charges the GIA has drummed up against me.

That's not the kind of guy you mess with head-on.

I belly up to the bar, drenched in the thumping beat of the deep dub, surrounded by glowing holos advertising the latest stimcasts, newsfeeds of distant battles, the growing pulse of the war that's rising across the stars. Nobody seems particularly worried by it. Most of them aren't even aware it's happening. The girl behind the bar slides a glass of synth semptar down the polished plasteel at me. As I lift the glass, I see the coaster underneath has her palmglass number written on it.

Like I say, there's advantages to being a badass.

I've been on MaZ4-VII Station for thirty-two hours. It's a starport at the intersection of a dozen major shipping routes, orbiting a gas giant right next to the FoldGate into the Stellanis system. Long-haul flights use it as a stopover for crews to avoid Fold psychosis, but it's also on the border of Betraskan, Rigellian, Terran, and Free space. Which means it's as busy as a one-handed Chellerian in an arm-wrestling competition.

Saedii and Co. dropped me off here almost two days ago, and I can still feel her farewell kiss on my lips. Still see the look in her eyes as she handed me that knife and refused to say goodbye, even knowing we'd probably never see each other again.

I will see you in the stars, Tyler Jones.

Best-case scenario, she unites the Unbroken, I somehow keep the Ra'haam from destroying Aurora Academy, and we're still stuck without the Weapon, still all die fighting the Ra'haam.

Far more likely, we end up on opposing sides of an ever-devolving galactic war. Or most likely of all, I just get arrested for being a traitor to Earth and the Legion, and executed.

Being one of the galaxy's most wanted criminals isn't all free drinks and pretty girls' palmglass numbers, see. And truth is, I'm running out of time.

I scan the crowd, looking for my contact, rubbing the plastique disk in my pocket. The credits Saedii gave me are enough to buy passage to the Aurora system, but there's still a summit of the entire Galactic Caucus being held at the academy in three days. What I'm saying is, getting *to* the system isn't the real drama. Getting onto the station is. Security is going to be scarier than Scarlett without her morning coffee.

But like I told Saedii, I can't just send a random warning and hope for the best. I have to get aboard without getting caught and shot so I can warn Adams directly about the threat to it.

The only way I can send him something that won't be intercepted is via the academy system, to his private number. Anything else, there's at least one person between me and him, and probably more.

There's only one way I see myself pulling this off.

"Should call her, Earthboi."

I glance at the seat beside me, see a feline humanoid sitting where nobody was a moment ago. Takka's got sneak, I'll give him that.

He peers up at me with slitted golden eyes, whiskers twitching. He's dressed the same as when I scoped him out yesterday—a big-shouldered suit black as his fur, lifts in his bulky shoes. I've never met a gremp with short-man syndrome before, but there's a first time for everything, I guess.

205

He's chewing a bright blue stick of Rush, his teeth discolored from the saccharine and stims.

"What?" I ask.

He nods to the number on the coaster. "Girrrrrl," he purrs. "She pretty. Should enjoy last night before you dying."

"You pulled it off?"

He sneers, rolling the Rush back and forth across his jagged teeth with a rough pink tongue. "Tell you, Earthboi. Takka people who know people."

"What's the deal?"

He lowers his voice to appropriately conspiratorial levels, looks around the bar. "Ice freighter. Passing two thousand LY shy of Aurora FoldGate."

"Two thousand light-years?" I frown. "What good is that?"

"Closer than now," Takka shrugs. "Sure with motivation, captain could get closer. Speaking of . . ." He glances down at my coat, rubs his fingers together. "Paypay."

"You don't get paid till I'm on board." I glower. "And I want to meet this captain of yours before I sign on."

"Funny. Said same 'bout you." Takka crunches the Rush between his teeth, shivering. "But Takka not taking Earthboi nowhere without paypay."

With a sigh, I reach into my coat for the credstick, press my thumb onto the ident sensor to unlock the funds. Takka grabs it with clawed fingers, but I hold tight, staring into his eyes. "Half now. Half if I sign up."

One ear twitches. "Real distrusting nature, Earthboi."

"I'm a master criminal, remember?"

Takka sneers, taps his stick to mine for the transfer, and slides off his chair. I follow him through the crowd, out into the station corridors, drawing my hood down around my face. It's sleep cycle on the station clock, so the lighting is dim, but the transit tube we ride in is still packed, Takka obviously displeased at his crotch-eye view as we're jammed in like ration packs.

We offload in a quiet section of the docks, spilling out with a group of long-haulers. It's quieter down here, Takka leading me through the landing bays, chattering about a tip he got on the upcoming heavyweight GMA match, easy pay-pay, blah blah. But my eyes are on the shadows around me, heartbeat running quicker as I grip the Syldrathi pulse pistol in my coat pocket.

I'm suddenly aware how far from home I am.

Things go bad here, they go bad all the way.

"Which ship is it?" I ask.

"Up here," the gremp nods. "D Bay."

A long transparent window of plasteel looks out on the ships berthed below, all models and makes. But there's a small mountain of freight between us and Bay D. Glancing around, I realize even for late night, this place is awfully quiet. A few loader drones. But no sec patrol or dock crews.

"What's the ship called?" I ask, scanning a glowing manifest on the wall.

"No name, Earthboi." Takka looks over his shoulder. "Ident AL-303."

My heart drops in my chest. Hand tightening on my pistol.

"That's not an ice freighter. That's a Legion designation."

The curve of our corridor straightens out, and I grind to a stop. Behind the dull gray mountain of freight boxes, I catch the edge of a Longbow hull—long, speartip-shaped, gleaming white against the station's gunmetal skin. And emblazoned down its flank, I see the burning star of the Aurora Legion.

"Freeze."

The voice comes from behind me, accompanied by the hum of a disruptor rifle. From the weapon's tone, I can tell it's set somewhere between Pacify and Kill. Glancing over my shoulder, I see a tall Syldrathi male, silver hair in five braids, sharp violet eyes. He's wearing a Legion uniform, green stripes on his shoulders tell me he's a science specialist, the twin circles on his brow denoting one of the Weaver Cabal. The Tank looming beside him is a big Betraskan, broadshouldered, with dark blue contacts over his eyes.

"Give us an excuse, Jones," the Tank says. "Please."

Takka steps aside as more figures emerge from the shadows, each wearing a Legion uniform—Ace, Gearhead, Face—a mix of Betraskan and Terran. Each is armed with a disruptor and a dark scowl. I ease my grip away from my pulse pistol. I can feel the Syldrathi blade that Saedii gifted me still strapped to my forearm, heavy as lead.

I glance at Takka, jaw clenched. "You sold me out."

"Sorry, old chap." He takes another bite of Rush, smiling with discolored teeth, his Terran suddenly *vastly* improved. "Perhaps you should work on that distrusting nature we discussed. Any fool knows Aurora Legion has been looking for your stupid arse in this sector for months."

"You won't get the other half of your money."

"But I get the reward for turning you in." He grins wider. "No hard feelings, old chap. The Legion just has deeper pockets than you."

A figure steps from the dark to my left, her aim and stance academy-issue perfect. I see the blue stripes of an Alpha on her uniform, long blond hair drawn back in a smooth tail, deep green eyes and lightly freckled skin.

"We can do this gentle, Jones," she says. "Or we can do it rough."

"Cohen." I smile, raising my hands extra slow. "Long time since graduation. How you been, Em?"

"Shut up, Tyler," she replies. "Get on your knees."

"And you do it slow," the Tank growls behind me. "Or I swear to the Maker, you are never getting back up again."

I glance back to him. "You're not still sore about the Draft are you, de Renn? Not my fault I got stuck with Kal, I didn't really have a choice. Although honestly, you woulda been my third pick anyway."

"Same old Goldenboy." Emma steps closer, rifle aimed at my chest. "Almost as full of yourself as your sister."

"Scar said sorry about your boyfriend, Em, I dunno how many t—"

"You thought you were the smoothest flavor in our whole damned class, Jones. But it's gonna take more than a cute set of dimples to save you now, you fucking *traitor*."

I raise an eyebrow. "You think I've got cute dimples, Em?"

Cohen hisses in outrage. Raises the rifle to my face.

"Looks like we do it rough, then."

BAMF.

. . . . .

It's the dream that finally wakes me. Dragging me up from the black mire of unconsciousness into a nightmare.

I see it again, just like before—the silver city of Aurora

209

Academy, floating in the light of the Aurora star. It gleams like a jewel in the night, like a lighthouse that old Terran sailors might have used to keep their ships off the rocks that would ruin them.

I reach out toward it. I hear screaming, somewhere distant.

The station blows apart from the inside out, scattering like diamonds across the black velvet of space.

And I realize the screaming is me.

I open my eyes, slowly sit up, the thudding of my pulse only adding to the throbbing in my head. From the stiffness in my muscles, I'd guess I've been unconscious maybe twelve hours. Not so bad, really. An Aurora Legion disruptor can knock you out for three days without burying you. Cohen's rifle must have been set a lot closer to Stun than Kill.

Honestly, she always had a bit of a thing for me.

I recognize where I am immediately. It's a Legion Longbow, 6-Series, same model as the ship issued to my squad when we set out for Sagan Station, what seems like a thousand years ago. The walls are burnished gray, but a glance toward the light fixtures tells me we're Folding—there's usually a slight blue hue to the globes.

I'm in the Longbow's detention cell—a three-by-three-meter room used to transport prisoners or dangerous cargo. The walls are blast-shielded, there's no controls on this side of the heavy door. The only furniture is a temperfoam mattress and a waste disposal system. The air vents are tiny, there's no wall sockets, no windows. Far as short-term prisons go, the Legion makes them pretty good.

My head feels like someone kicked me in it.

Like any good Alpha on her first year of duty, Cohen has followed the rules. Mag-restraints bind my wrists and ankles. They've stripped me of my coat, my pistol, Saedii's blade, leaving me with the minimum—gray cargoes, T-shirt. They left me my boots, but they took the laces.

There's a metal tray on the floor near the door, an un-wrapped protein pack and a cardbox of filtered water sitting on it. Making a show of being more hurt than I am, I guzzle the water as I glance up at the corner of the room. I can see the tiny black stud of the sec cam in the ceiling—if Cohen is good, she has her Tank watching me like a hawk through those feeds. And Cohen *is* good—she was the top-ranked Alpha after me in our year. The squad she picked are half the people I'd have grabbed myself if I hadn't missed the Draft. So there's not a lot to do for now except wait.

Engines thrum beneath me as we cruise the Fold. My thoughts turn to my sister, the other members of my squad. I think of us running together back on Sempiternity. The seven of us seemed unstoppable, and my chest aches at the thought of what might have happened to them all.

That I might be the only one left.

Where are you, Scar?

Finally, I hear a shift in tone from the drives, the faint echo of the PA beyond my cell door. The metal is too thick for me to make out the words, but I know exactly what they're saying: we've been Folding for twenty-four hours, which is the maximum recommended exposure without a break.

There's a reason they don't recommend Fold travel for anyone over twenty-five for more than a few hours without being frozen first—even young minds have trouble with

211

continuous exposure in here. So, per standard Legion regulations, Cohen is ordering her crew to drop through a nearby Gate for a break.

I feel it begin—that strange vertigo that tells me we're crossing from the Fold into realspace. My insides feel weightless, I double over, cross-legged, colorscape rippling from black and white to vibrant hues. And as we cross the threshold, my fingers slide toward my feet.

These boots waited ten years for me in the Dominion vault. I still have no idea who put them there. How they knew I'd find myself needing to bust out of captivity, not once, but twice. But honestly, the way my life has been going recently, I'm not gonna question the one lucky break I've got.

The false heel twists aside. I feel inside for the gremlin—the device that generated the electromagnetic pulse that busted Saedii and me out of prison. An Aurora Legion Longbow is a *lot* smaller than a Terran Defense Force cruiser, and I'm not sure of the range on this puppy. But truth be told, I'm too desperate to care—as desperate as I've been since I hatched this insane plan.

It's exactly like Takka said: any idiot knows Aurora Legion has been looking for my dumb ass in this sector for months. So, security being what it is, I really could only figure one way to get onto Aurora Academy to warn Adams about the Ra'haam threat.

On board an Aurora Legion ship.

I make a mental note to send Takka a present for selling me out so quick. And with a small prayer to the Maker, I press the stud.

I feel that same vibration in my boot. That hum on the

212

edge of hearing. And just like they did aboard the *Kusanagi,* every light in the cell dies.

The camera dies.

And joy, the magnetic locks on my restraints and on the door die too.

I'm on my feet in a flash, jamming my boot against the frame and prying it apart. But my belly rolls as I lose my balance, arms flailing as I keep rising up off the floor. I see the remains of my meal doing the same, the empty water box floating just above the tray.

The door comes open, and peering out into the pitch-black hallway, I realize immediately what's happened—my EMP hasn't only knocked out the electronics inside my cell. It's knocked out the electronics on the whole ship. That means engines. That means life support. And aside from what's being provided by our thrust, that means gravity.

Whoops.

I can hear voices from the bridge—Cohen, demanding a status update. The auto-repair systems on a 'Bow are top-tier, which means power and engines might be back online any second. But while I might not know how long this is gonna last, what I *do* know is what this squad's Alpha is likely to do about it. There's rules for this kind of thing, and there was a time I was a real stickler for rules.

I'm waiting above the hatchway to the engine room when Cohen's Brain and Gearhead come floating through. They've taken time to don their protective gear—enviro-suits and safety cables, the flashlights on their helmets cutting lines of light through the dark. The EMP has knocked out their comms, but we still have atmo, so they can talk at least.

213

"No sign of damage," the Gearhead reports. He's a quick, wiry-looking Betraskan named Trin de Vriis, top 3 percent of our year. He'd have been my first pick after Cat in the Draft if I'd had the chance.

"Power is down through the entire ship," the Brain reports, stabbing at his dead uniglass. He's the Weaver Syldrathi who sassed me on the docks. His name is Anethe, top 10 percent of our year. I considered him for a while, but his spatial dynamics scores weren't great. And his performance in zero-gee hand-to-hand was borderline average.

That's why I hit de Vriis first, kicking off the bulkhead and flying at him like a spear. I crash into his back, and he gasps as his faceplate smashes into the engine casing. The gees are low enough I can use his own momentum for thrust and the engine housing as a pivot. And his scream rings out in the dark as I dislocate his shoulder with a sickening *crunch*.

Anethe is staring at me wide-eyed, face pale. To his credit, he doesn't run, but like I say, his zero-gee was bad. My kick is hard enough to make him puke, and as he tears his helmet from his head rather than choke on the vomit, I lay him out with a nerve-strike I picked up from Kal during that brawl on Sempiternity. Turning back to a groaning de Vriis, I choke him with a sleeper hold until he blacks out.

2–nil.

De Renn is more trouble. I actually lied to him on the dock: he'd have been my first pick for Tank if I hadn't gotten lumped with Kal. I genuinely liked the guy. We used to play jetball back in academy days.

But I guess these aren't academy days anymore.

I ambush him as he floats back from his sweep of my

cell—Cohen obeying regs, easy to predict, yet again. De Renn's disruptor won't work after the EMP, and he's broken out some weapons, no doubt from his own personal stash—a pair of hooked Betraskan fighting sticks called satkha.

I wallop him in the back of the head with a fire extinguisher, but even stunned he doesn't drop, actually gives me a decent shot to the jaw before I take a leaf from the Saedii Gilwraeth playbook and lay him out with a thunderous knee to the groin. He goes belly-up, making a noise I can only describe as a *squeam*—half-scream, half-squeal.

I wrench off his helmet and put a sleeper hold on him, struggling to control him as he flails and bucks. He finally goes limp, and I choke him for as long as it's safe, then give him an apologetic shrug. "Sorry, buddy. No hard feels."

3–nil.

The other three members of Squad 303 are on the bridge. Their Ace is at the helm—an old drinking buddy of Cat's named Rioli. He's a big guy, sandy blond hair and bright blue eyes. Cohen is at another station trying to resurrect comms. Their Face, a pretty Terran girl named Savitri, is near the entrance. Her helmet visor is up so she can chew a fingernail, long hair floating about her cheeks as she squints into the dark.

"Shouldn't Bel be back by now?" she asks.

"Relax, Amelia," Cohen replies. "He's probably in his quarters deciding which of his favorite murderclubs to break out. What's our status, Rioli?"

"Still nothing," the Ace replies. "Whatever hit us—"

He turns at the wet *THWACK* of Savitri's face meeting my satkha. The girl pinwheels back with a bubbling gasp, nose spraying blood. She collides with the wall just as I collide with Rioli, slamming him into the console and smashing him so hard in the ribs I hear bone crack.

"Maker's breath," Cohen breathes. "Jones—"

I know what she sees as I turn on her. My knuckles and face are spattered with blood, Terran red and Syldrathi purple and Betraskan pink. I must look every inch the criminal, the killer, the terrorist that the GIA painted me as—Aurora Legion's most promising Alpha, turned into a cold-blooded psychopath.

But thing is, it's not madness that drives me forward, doubling her up with a shot to her belly. It's not rage making me slam my open palm into the base of her skull, sending her bouncing off the deck, groaning and senseless.

It's desperation. It's *fear*.

Because I can see it. Even as I strip Squad 303 down to their unmentionables and lock them in my detention cell, welding the door shut with an acetylene lance from the cargo hold. Even as I change into Rioli's uniform and float back up to the bridge, praying for the Gods of Auto-Repair Systems to work quicker. Even as the power finally flickers and shifts back online, as I slide into the pilot's chair and whisper thanks to the Maker.

I can see it.

That image of Aurora Academy. Blowing itself to pieces in a halo of fire and shrapnel, ripping apart the last hope for peace in the galaxy.

I can feel it, rising beyond—that shadow, set to swallow the galaxy. And I can hear it—that voice, that plea, begging me to keep going even if I have to go on alone.

I lay in a course for Aurora Academy. Hit thrust on my engines.

. . . you can fix this, Tyler . . .

"Damn right I can," I whisper.

And I'm away.

18

SCARLETT

Finian's lips are warm and soft, and as they leave a burning trail down my neck, I shiver all the way to my toes. We're lying on a thin temperfoam mattress, and the sheets are rumpled around us, and the view out the small porthole beside us is perfect darkness, lit by tiny pulses of mauve light. My shirt is untucked, and one of Fin's hands is tracing soft circles in the small of my back, the metal on his fingertips charged with a faint current that makes my skin tingle in the best ways. I run my fingers through his hair and pull him in tighter, sighing encouragement as I feel his kisses on my neck.

The hand on the small of my back slips lower, roaming down into my pants, and I grab a handful of his hair and pull him back to look at him. Fin's lips and cheeks are flushed just the faintest shade of pink, and he's breathing heavy, but he's frozen now, blinking hard.

"Is that okay?" he asks.

"Yeah," I sigh. "Keep doing it."

And we crash back together, and he's touching me in all the right ways, and yes, part of me realizes how stupid this all is, given the situation we're in. But most of me is focused on the warmth of his skin and the feel of him pressed against me and what he's doing with his hands and how I *seriously* underestimated the level of Finian de Seel's game.

We have, as we've done for the last five loops, distracted the security patrol that would otherwise have interrupted and executed Zila and Lieutenant Kim in Pinkerton's office. It took a few trial runs, but eventually, we figured out that tripping a proximity alarm on the lower floor of the hab section would drag the goon squad away long enough to divert them from the office completely—a few minutes after we trip the alarm, all sec staff are called to deal with the fire in Stairwell B, which by now is spreading into the duct system.

This means that once we trip the alarm, Fin and I have a lot of spare time on our hands. I mean, we *could* go up and help Zila gather more information from the computer systems in Pinkerton's office. But it's not like I'd be much help in that anyway, and it's not like we *need* to. If we're just dying and looping, dying and looping, we can keep doing this over and over until we do it perfectly. We have all the time in the world.

So, for the last few loops, Fin and I have stolen away inside an empty hab unit and have been . . . getting to know each other better. Because even though we seem to have an endless supply of time on our hands, I'm realizing I've wasted a lot of time I could have spent getting to know this boy already.

I'm flushed with the heat of him, my heart *thump-thump-thump*ing against my ribs, and I hear him groan as my tongue flickers against his and I sigh into his mouth. Even though the air is filled with alert sirens and the creak of stressed metal, my sighs still seem awfully loud.

"How does this thing come off?"

Fin pulls back and blinks. ". . . What?"

"Your exosuit," I whisper, tugging up his shirt and running my fingers over his taut belly. "How do I get it off?"

"You wanna . . ." He swallows. "You wanna take my exo off?"

"No," I say, cruising toward his neck and nipping at his skin. "I wanna take your *shirt* off. The exo's just a means to an end."

"Scar . . ."

My teeth brush his throat and now I feel *him* shivering, my lips curling in a smile as I feel what I'm doing to him. "Kinda wish I'd paid more attention in mechaneering class now. . . ."

"Scarlett."

"Yes, Finian?"

"*Scarlett.*"

I pull back at the note in his voice. I know Betraskan culture inside out, I know there's no societal preclusion on what we're doing in here, and I know he really *wants* to. But looking into those big pretty eyes, even behind the contacts, I can tell.

I can tell . . .

He's afraid.

The structure shudders around us. Flaming vapor lights the black outside the porthole as a voice rings over the PA. "WARNING: RADIATION DETECTED ON DECK 13, ALL DECK 13 STAFF PROCEED FOR IMMEDIATE DECONTAMINATION PROCEDURES."

". . . Are you okay?"

"Yeah, I'm okay," Fin lies, clearing his throat. "I'm good."

I look him over again, reading expression, body language, the rate of his breath and the beat of his heart, chest pressed against mine. I've always been good at this kind of thing, even before I studied at the academy.

Ever since I was a kid, sometimes it was almost like I knew what people were thinking before they spoke. I'm not sure how I do it—I always figured it was just something I was born with. Some people are good at jetball. Other people can sing.

Me? I read most people like most people read books.

And looking at Fin closer, I know I'm right.

"You're frightened."

A flash of defensiveness comes over him. He gives a gruff laugh to cover it up. Bluff. Bravado. He's such a *boy,* sometimes.

"No, I'm not," he scoffs. "Why would I be frightened?"

"Fin . . ." I touch his cheek. "You don't have to lie to me."

He holds my stare for a moment, then breaks away, looking into the rolling dark outside. The station shudders around us, time grinding sideways, looping around and in on itself, over and over. The snake eating its own tail.

"REPEAT: RADIATION DETECTED ON DECK 13, ALL DECK 13 STAFF PROCEED FOR IMMEDIATE DECONTAMINATION PROCEDURES."

I kiss his cheek. Run a hand through his tumble of pale hair.

"Fin, what is it?"

". . . It's stupid," he murmurs.

"I'm sure it's not. You can tell me."

He meets my eyes again, a small dark crease between his brows. But I can feel the wall he's trying to build between us now. The armor he's dragging back over his skin. Shutting down. Closing off.

I touch his face. "Trust me," I say, my voice as soft as a summer breeze.

He wrestles with it a moment longer.

". . . I like you, Scar," he finally says.

"I like you too," I smile, running my fingertip along the bow of his lips.

"I mean . . . I *really* like you." He looks down at my body, pressed against his in all the right ways. "And I *want* to, it's just . . ."

I blink then, realization dawning on me. *Of course,* I tell myself. It should've been obvious. But I was so caught up in what we were doing, I wasn't really thinking about what we were about to *do.* And . . .

"You haven't done this before," I say.

He presses his lips thin. I can see how hard this is for him. Being vulnerable like this. His whole life, Finian has fought to be treated as an equal, to prove that he's not a victim of the plague that ravaged his body when he was a kid. To escape the stigma of this metal suit he has to wrap himself inside. And the thought of peeling himself out of it, leaving himself exposed . . .

"No," he says.

"It's okay, Fin," I tell him. "That's okay."

"I'm not sure . . ." He shakes his head, jaw clenched. "I know you've had a lot of boyfriends. But without the exo, I don't move that well. I mean, I can move, but it's not graceful, and I don't . . . I'm not sure how good I'd . . ." He sighs, frustrated with himself, with this, with all of it. "Ah chakk. I told you it was stup—"

I stop the word with a kiss, soft and sweet and long.

"It's okay," I whisper.

He doesn't believe me. Avoids my eyes. I touch his cheek again, soft as feathers, until he looks up at me. I realize how much this means to him. That, yeah, he *really* likes me. And then I kiss him again.

"It's okay," I repeat. "Whatever you're ready for. Whatever you like. I'm happy just to be with you. Whatever you want, it's enough." I squeeze his hand, kiss his metal fingertips one by one. "*You're* enough."

". . . Really?" he whispers.

"Really," I smile. "You're beautiful."

He runs his hand along my cheek, up into a lock of bright red hair, and even if the whole station weren't coming to pieces around us, I'm sure the world would still be shaking as he kisses me again.

"You're kind of amazing, Scarlett Isobel Jones," he murmurs.

"Yeah, I know. You really lucked out here, de Seel."

He laughs, and I laugh with him, and as we kiss again, it feels good and bright and sweet, and I wonder if I wouldn't mind going out in this sweet, bright boy's arms, over and over again until the end of—

"*Scarlett. Finian. Do you read me?*"

"It's Zila," Fin breathes into my mouth.

"Ignore her," I whisper.

"*Scarlett. Finian. Come in.*"

"It sounds urgent," Fin whispers.

"It's Zila, it's fine. Shhh—"

"*Scarlett. Finian. Please respond, this is urgent.*"

"—iiiitttt." Pressing the Transmit button on my intercom, I heave a heavy sigh. "Zil, you and me gotta have a talk about sisterhood an—"

"Is the security detail dealt with?" she demands. *"I need you and Finian up in Pinkerton's office immediately."*

Finian and I exchange a glance, and the station around us rumbles ominously as the klaxons continue to wail. He looks so pretty by the dark light of the storm, but I can hear an uncharacteristic note of fear in Zila's voice, which is enough to put the brakes on my racing pulse as I meet Fin's eyes.

"We'll be right up," I tell her.

It takes a few minutes, a quiet dodge around four panicked crew, and a lucky escape from a burst of plasma in Stairwell A, but we make our way up to the hab level above. The station continues to quake around us as Fin and I creep along, hand in hand. We step into Pinkerton's office/antiques collection, and I can see the worry in Zila's eyes, note the thick black curl of hair she's chewing on. Maybe for the first time ever, she actually looks genuinely frazzled as she glowers at me. Our good Lieutenant Nari "Hawk" Kim is standing beside Zila, staring at the glowing screens. She looks like somebody shot her dog.

"Where have you two been?" Zila demands.

"Zil, you okay?" Fin asks.

"I asked where you've been," she demands, looking me over. "But given the fact that Scarlett's shirt is untucked and you have bite marks on your neck, I need not have bothered."

"We took care of the security patrol, Z," I say. "Just like we were supposed to. Hence you not getting *shot*. If we took a little detour afterward—"

"That was foolish and selfish," she snaps. "There are things I would rather be doing too, Scarlett."

I admit, my hackles rise a little at that. I glance pointedly at Lieutenant Nari Kim hovering over our Brain's shoulder, and folding my arms, I shoot Zila a meaningful stare. "Yeah, I bet there are, Z. And nobody's going to judge if you two—"

"That is *not* what I meant," Zila says, flushing as she glances at Nari. "*Some* of us have more important things on our minds than trivial flirtations. Some of us are trying to figure a way out of this mess!"

Fin looks taken aback as Zila's tone almost rises to a shout. I make a note to put in a call to the *Galactic Book of Records*.

First time she's *ever* done that.

"Zil, what's the big deal?" he asks.

"How can you possibly ask that, Finian?" Zila demands. "You know as well as I do the level of complexity I am dealing with here!"

"Look, yeah, okay." He scratches his mussed hair, shooting me an embarrassed look. "Maybe me and Scar took some time for ourselves. I'm sorry, I should be helping you more. I'll do it next time—it's no big deal, right? We've got literally *infinity* to solve this. If we mess things up, we just try again until we work it out and break free of the loop, yeah?"

Zila shakes her head, and returns to her readouts.

"When our next loop commences, I require you to devote your efforts to Magellan."

Fin blinks, and I almost laugh as I glance at Finian's backpack, the fried remains of Aurora's uniglass inside it.

"You actually *want* me to repair that piece of chakk?" He

gestures to the glass cases around us. "Z, you'd get more use out of one of these antiques!"

"I will also require your uniglass. Yours too, Scarlett."

"What for?" I ask. "It's not like there's a network for them to—"

"We can network them with each other." Zila almost scowls at the screens in front of her. "This system is simply too primitive, and I need all the computing power I can get to perform this math." She rubs her eyes, her face underscored by the glow of her screens. "Something is wrong."

Fin shuffles closer to the console, taking this more seriously now. "What do you mean? What's wrong?"

The loudspeaker cuts Zila's reply off.

"WARNING: CONTAINMENT CASCADE IN EFFECT. CORE IMPLOSION IMMINENT, T MINUS THREE MINUTES AND COUNTING. ALL HANDS PROCEED TO EVACUATION PODS IMMEDIATELY. REPEAT: CORE IMPLOSION IN THREE MINUTES AND COUNTING."

And there it is.

The end of the loop.

Dying time again.

The station starts to shake around us, and I take Finian's hand. Comforted by the strength in his grip, the warmth of his body as I lean against him. But Fin pays no attention, instead staring at the time readout on Zila's wrist. The digital numbers flash on the timer she sets at the start of every loop.

"That can't be right . . . ," Fin says.

Zila meets his stare, lips pursed. "I was wondering when you would notice."

"Have you checked this?" he demands. "It's not a glitch?"

"We noticed it a few loops ago," Nari says quietly. "Well, Zila did. But she wanted to make sure before telling you."

Zila holds Finian's eyes a moment longer, then turns her little death glare on me. "Perhaps if you two were not so *distracted* . . ."

"Listen, Zila, I know you're angry," I say. "And maybe you have a right to be, but can you put the pointing fingers away for a minute and tell me what the hells is going on?"

The station rocks around us. A mauve light flares, illuminating the tempest outside, the colossal clouds coiling and churning out in the black.

Fin looks into my eyes. "The quantum pulse strikes the sail forty-four minutes into the loop."

"Right."

"And Zila told us the core overloaded and the station exploded fifty-eight minutes after the pulse hits."

"Yeah." I look back and forth between them. "So?"

"We are one minute from detonation, Scarlett," Zila says, holding up her wrist for me to read.

I frown at the numbers, bright red against the small black screen on Zila's brown skin, bathed in the monitor's blue glow.

"One hour, thirty-two minutes," I say.

"Correct," Zila nods.

"*WARNING: CORE IMPLOSION IMMINENT, T MINUS THIRTY SECONDS. ALL HANDS EVACUATE IMMEDIATELY. REPEAT: CORE IMPLOSION IN THIRTY SECONDS.*"

The station begins to buck wildly, the metal around us tearing, the air filled with sirens, rising smoke, the hiss of venting atmo. I raise my voice above it all. "But if the core explodes fifty-eight minutes after the strike, and the strike happens at minute forty-four . . ."

Kim meets my eyes, her face grim. "Yeah."

"Holy shit," I whisper.

I look into Fin's eyes.

"The loops are getting shorter," I say.

"WARNING: CORE IMPLOSION IMMINENT. FIVE SECONDS. WARNING."

Fin nods and squeezes my hand, his big black eyes wide with fear.

"We're running out of time," he says.

"WARNING."

BOOM.

19

AURI

My head's pounding by the time we reach the World Ship, and I watch through the *Vindicator*'s viewscreen as the last sanctuary in the entire Milky Way comes into view.

Kal rests his hands on my shoulders, thumbs pressing in to find the spot at the base of my neck where I always carry my tension. He must have done this hundreds of times in the Echo, patiently talking me down from my fits of despair over Esh's impossible training tasks. It feels so long ago.

Now we watch together as we draw closer to Sempiternity, a looming shadow floating against the backdrop of a brilliant rainbow nebula. At first, I think not much has changed in twenty-seven years—it's still a hodgepodge of ships and stations bolted together, towers and satellites jabbing out into the black, docking tunnels twisting away from its body like trailing tentacles.

But it's speckled all over with lights, except for the upper right-hand quarter. That part's completely dark, and as we draw in closer and I get a better look, I can see it's been blasted open to space, twisted and broken. The explosion—or the attack—must have been massive.

"Home," Toshh murmurs from her seat beside me.

"Good place to keep your heart," I say.

She looks at me strangely, one brow rising toward her horns.

"It's an old Earth saying," I smile. *"Home is where the heart is."*

Over at the helm, Lae glances at Kal. "That would explain a great deal. Given what the Starslayer did to his own."

Kal breathes deep at that, but he doesn't call her on it. I suppose in an awful way it's true. As I reach back and squeeze his hand, Lae glances at me, then to the boy beside me.

It's a little strange when I look at her, to be honest. The other members of Tyler's crew, even Ty himself . . . I can feel them in my head so easily now. Their feelings. The currents of their emotions, flowing together into a river all around me. But I can't quite get a read on Lae. She keeps herself closed off, like she's used her Waywalker powers to draw a veil over her mind.

She's strong. Nothing like me or Caersan. But still . . .

She seemed to appreciate my help getting the rift drive going again, at least—ironically, I provided the "unsophisticated push" Caersan wants from me to transport the Weapon home. I'm not sure of the science of it—Lae was the one guiding us, I was the raw power, diving into that stream again, immolating and exhilarating. Together, we used the fragment of Eshvaren crystal in the *Vindicator*'s core to open a series of gates over a span of eight hours, jumping the ship half a dozen times across the gulf of space.

It required a fraction of effort from me. Almost inconsequential. But from the cracks around Lae's eyes, I can tell how much it costs her every time they travel. Despite her hardcase attitude, that alone tells me she's a good person. Everyone on Tyler's crew is. Giving so much of themselves to bring survivors here.

The last piece of civilization in the galaxy.

"About damn time," Tyler mutters.

I rise from my seat, standing at his shoulder as we cruise in closer to the World Ship. He glances at me, and for an instant his eye widens, breath catching, body tensing in the space between heartbeats.

"Tyler?" Half the crew frowns every time I use his name instead of his title, but I know switching to *Commander* isn't the way to remind him we're friends. I reach out for his hand. "You okay?"

"It's nothing," he replies, pinching the bridge of his nose. "We've been in the Fold a long time. I'm too old for this shit."

Fold psychosis. I'd forgotten. Aurora Legion squads form when the legionnaires are eighteen because by age twenty-five or so, more than seven hours in the Fold puts too much strain on you. It's why I was in coldsleep on my way to Octavia—Fold psychosis is no joke. And Tyler's in his late forties now. Which is just *weird*.

What did he just see when he looked at me?

What is it doing to him?

"Never thought I'd see this place again," I say, offering

231

him a small smile, diverting the conversation. It's not just that I need him on my side. It's that I can't bear to see him like this. "Last time I saw this view, we were following my weird backward directions, didn't even know why we were coming, let alone that we'd soon be pulling a heist, facing down the Great Ultrasaur of Abraaxis IV."

"Wait," says a voice behind us. Elin, the Betraskan, is sitting forward. "That chakk about the Great Ultrasaur was *true*?"

"You should have seen the pants your boss was wearing," I reply.

Just for an instant I win a smirk from Elin. Then she remembers that I disappeared at the Battle of Terra and caused the end of everything, and her expression hardens again.

"You wouldn't believe how many favors I ended up owing Dariel over the years," Tyler says, something about him a touch softer. "He kept threatening to collect, but he never did." He pauses a beat and then closes his eye, rubbing at the patch covering the other. "He died six years back on a retrieval mission."

Kal comes up to stand beside me as I search for something, anything, to say to that. But as always, he fills the void for me.

"This place has seen many battles," he murmurs.

Tyler nods. "The Ra'haam. We've fought at least fifty engagements with it. No matter where we hide, eventually it tracks us down."

"But you fight it off each time?" Kal asks.

"Hell no. We *run*." Tyler nods to the massive ship. "There's a rift drive inside her. All the rest of the Eshvaren crystal we managed to scrounge. And every Waywalker left alive in the galaxy. When the Ra'haam appears, they open up a gate and fling Sempiternity as far away as they can."

"Giving another piece of themselves each time they do so," Lae says softly. "Until there is nothing left."

Tyler looks at her with concern in his eyes, lips thin.

"But the Weeds always manage to find us again anyway," Toshh growls. "Bastards can sense us. *Smell* us."

Tyler nods. "Usually takes them around three weeks. A month if we're lucky. The last time they hit us was only ten days back, so we should be safe in this location for a while."

I'm horrified by the thought. Of never being safe. Never being able to rest. Always being hunted by that . . . *thing* that consumed my father. Cat. Octavia. And if it gets its way, everything else in the galaxy.

The power crackles at my fingertips. Every hair on my body stands up.

I can't let this be the galaxy's future.

I won't.

"What can you tell us about the council we'll be meeting?" I ask.

"The Council of Free Peoples," Tyler replies. "There's four sitting members. The three largest groups of survivors supply one each, and the smaller take turns to cycle in two representatives a year. So there's a Syldrathi from the Watcher Cabal, a Betraskan, and a Rikerite—a politician, a pragmatist, and a warrior. And right now the minority rep is an Ulemna."

"Humans are one of the minorities?" I ask, my heart curling in on itself.

"No," he replies, eye on the station ahead. "We're banned from the council. Elin, get on comms and notify Sempiternity command we're inbound. And remind them about the massive Eshvaren crystal we have in tow so nobody pops the panic button and chucks a nuke in our direction."

"Roger that, boss," the Betraskan nods. "I'm presuming I still shouldn't mention the planet-killing genocidal maniac aboard it?"

Tyler rubs his chin. "That's probably more a face-to-face conversation."

"Why?" I ask softly, as Elin sets to work on comms.

"You don't think the Starslayer—"

"No, I mean why are we banned from the council?"

Finally Tyler takes his eye off the World Ship and looks to me. I can see how tired he is. How angry. How sad. "Because this is our fault, Auri. Octavia was our colony. We woke the Ra'haam early. And it consumed our colonists, and they managed to get back to Terra and spend the next two centuries infiltrating the GIA, and *nobody fucking noticed*. Those agents sliced the heads off every planetary government in the galaxy. Ruined any chance we had to cut the Ra'haam off at the root. And to top all that off, our Trigger disappeared with the only real Weapon we had at the battle where the tide turned."

My breath's shallowing and my legs don't feel right—like I need to sit down, or else I'll fall. All this, because of me—the smallest of their hurts, as well as the biggest. Kal's arm goes around me, and I feel the gold and violet of his mind pressing in comfortingly against mine.

"Brother," he says quietly. "The Terrans stumbled across the Ra'haam nursery through ill fortune. Who is to say any other race would have detected impostors? And Aurora abandoned no one. You are a commander, you are respected here. So there must be some room for understanding."

"It's taken me most of my life to prove myself," Tyler replies. "Forgiveness is in short supply around here."

"Do you think there's any chance the council will help us?" I ask, trying to still the new wave of despair inside me.

"Anything's possible," Tyler replies. But he's looking at Sempiternity again, and he won't meet my eyes.

. . . . .

We stand off from Sempiternity for another hour before the council sends for Tyler. He boards the *Vindicator*'s shuttle and heads off to brief them, leaving us to a silent and uncomfortable wait among his crew.

After the third hour, word comes that they're ready, and Lae and Toshh escort us to Sempiternity. We pull into one of the docking bays along the transparent umbilicals snaking out from the station—last time I was here, they were all full, different aliens endlessly coming and going. Fin and I talked about how his people live underground, and how he didn't like the stars.

A sky full of ghosts, he said. His words were prophetic.

You're not dead, I promise him silently. *I'll get back in time. I'll change the way the story ends.*

When we step off our shuttle, the Sempiternity survivors

are waiting for us. The corridor is lined with bodies large and small, young and old, dozens of races, hundreds and hundreds of people. Every one of them is dressed in clothes that have been patched and mended to last through the decades, every one of them silent.

Their hollow stares follow us as we walk—Lae in front, Toshh and Dacca behind—and the weight of it is almost impossible to bear. This is all that's left. These people. Out of everyone in the galaxy. I reach for Kal's hand, just to feel his skin warm against mine.

It turns out the Council of Free Peoples meets in Casseldon Bianchi's old ballroom. The lights have been turned on now, the swirling galaxies as long gone as the beautiful red dress I wore here that night. The fantastic aquarium that lined the walls is now full of frames and little buoys, seaweed and algae farms taking up every centimeter—they need it for the protein, I guess. To feed those thousands in the station outside. It's a huge room, and rows of chairs suggest there's usually an audience, but now our footsteps echo as we walk up to the table at the far end, where the four council members sit.

The Rikerite is at one end—he's ancient, his horns sweeping back from his forehead and curling around so far they make up full circles, his expression lost in a sea of wrinkles. *The warrior,* Tyler called him.

Beside him is a Betraskan woman who doesn't look that much older than me, her white hair buzzed short. She's studying a tablet, and only looks up at us for a moment. *The pragmatist.*

The third is a Syldrathi from the Watcher Cabal, the first

of those I've met. He looks to be in his fifties, immaculate braids matching his immaculate posture. His glyf is of two circles, one inside the other. *The politician.*

The last must be the Ulemna. I can't make out much of them—they wear a dark brown hood drawn over their features, but I can see a pair of navy blue hands folded neatly on the table in front of them. Tyler didn't say anything about the minority representative, and now I'm wishing I'd asked.

Tyler himself stands in front of the table already—Kal and I halt beside him, Toshh and Lae behind us. There are a handful of other Syldrathi around the room, glyfs of the Waywalker Cabal marked on their brows. They feel it a few moments after I do—all of them tensing, jaws clenching. I see Lae's scowl darken as the energy around us shifts, the air before us thrums. She tosses a silver-gold braid off her shoulder, fist closing about her null blade's hilt.

And in the middle of the room, Caersan appears.

It's only a projection, of course, shimmering into focus like a mirage on a hot day. He's not stupid enough to leave the *Neridaa,* to risk himself on a ship full of enemies. He stands like a dark shadow in the room's heart, and the lights seem to dim around him. The Waywalkers bristle with hostility. The council members glower as one.

He glances around the room, radiating disdain.

"Let us commence," he says.

Cold silence hangs in the room. The weight of countless lost lives. It's the Syldrathi who finally breaks it, voice steady despite the rage in his eyes.

"Commander Jones has informed us of the circumstances

237

of your arrival. Outlandish as your claims may seem, our Waywalkers have confirmed your identities." His violet eyes roam over us all, lingering on the Starslayer. "So. What is it you want from us?"

"The Weapon we came here in is damaged," I say. "We need to visit a spacetime anomaly in the Theta sector. It leads to a facility on the Eshvaren homeworld. If we can repair the Weapon anywhere, it's going to be there."

"Presuming the Ra'haam has not already destroyed this facility," the Betraskan woman says. "You are certain you could return to your own time if the Weapon is repaired?"

Caersan is studying the Waywalkers around him, one by one, with something like . . . hunger in his eyes. So I reply.

"Yes, I could provide the propulsion, I think, while he steered."

The woman leans forward, fingers steepled beneath her chin. "You are aware the Theta sector is completely overrun by the Ra'haam?"

I nod. "From what Tyler said, we'd need to fight our way in. And probably fight the Ra'haam off while we repaired the Weapon, too."

Now the Rikerite speaks, his voice like a creaky door. "And by *we*, child, of course you mean *us*." He looks between Caersan and me, scowling. "You want us to devote the last of our resources to helping you in what seems a mad gamble? Assuming these repairs can even be effected, who is to say your returning to the past will make any difference at all?"

"If we can make it back, we can destroy the Ra'haam

before it ever gets a chance to bloom and burst," I say, my voice echoing around the empty room. "This is what I'm here for. It's what I was *made* to do."

The Syldrathi shakes his head and sighs. "And yet, if you do *not* return to your own time safely, you doom not just yourself but everyone in this time as well. You ask us to risk extinguishing the last light in the galaxy."

"You are already doomed, fool."

All eyes turn as Caersan's apparition speaks, his gaze roaming the room and assembled councilors.

"This is no sanctuary. This is a tomb. You hide here in the shadows, praying the true darkness does not find you. But it *will*. And all of you know it."

The Watcher comes to his feet in one fluid movement. "You are present against my explicit objection, Starslayer. I will take no counsel from he who destroyed Syldra, who killed billions of her children in a single moment, who left those who survived alone and adrift."

"Peace is the way the cur cries, 'Surrender,' Watcher," Caersan growls.

"He is no cur," the old Rikerite spits. "You know nothing of what we have suffered, Starslayer. Nothing of the price we have *all* paid."

"I know you are being presented a chance to avoid that price. That suffering. One last glorious battle to be fought for the future of everything." Caersan lifts his hands, then drops them slowly to his sides. "And still you tremble at the thought of it. Like children. Like cowards."

The Watcher's lip curls. "This, from the coward who could have faced the Ra'haam, but fled."

Caersan turns toward the man, rage flaring, and the power seethes through me, hot and vibrant and deafening. I throw up a mental barrier between the Starslayer and the defiant council members in front of him, my midnight blue crackling as it meets his bloody red, the clash visible for a blink, bringing the Betraskan and the Rikerite to their feet as the Waywalkers, Toshh, Tyler, and Lae lift their weapons as one.

Kal steps forward, shouting, "Father!"

For an instant I feel the fury that flashes through my love's mind, his instinct for combat. But Caersan only chuckles softly, and his power ebbs. Slowly, I lower my guard, the tension in the air fading.

The Waywalkers around the Starslayer are pale, sharing uneasy glances—they know that they have no hope of overcoming Caersan now, or me. Lae is whispering in Tyler's ear, one hand on his shoulder. The Watcher remains on his feet, his gaze on the man who murdered his people.

"This is their overture?" he scoffs, looking around at his fellow councilors. "We should send these beggars back to their ship at once."

"Or," I say urgently, butting in before the two of them can unzip and start comparing, "we can talk about how we can save lives. Not just yours. Not just ours. *Everyone's*. Then and now. Believe me, I understand how you feel about the Starslayer. I feel the same way. But he's the one who knows how to transport the Weapon back home. I don't. We need him alive."

"And if you reach your home?" the Rikerite asks. "What then?"

"Then Caersan and I will have a little . . . discussion," I say.

The Starslayer's projection watches me, cool and imperious. Even if we make it through this alive, somehow make it back to when we came from, we can both feel that conflict rushing toward us headlong. I know if I win, I'll fire the Weapon. I'll give everything I have to destroy the Ra'haam.

But mothercustard, that's a big *If*.

"The simple fact is, I can't get back to our own time without him. So please, *please*, hard as it is, we need to set whatever we're feeling aside and figure out a way to pull this off."

The Rikerite shakes his head. "You ask much."

"She asks for nothing she is not willing to give herself," Kal replies.

". . . Meaning what?"

I square my shoulders, breathe deep. "Meaning it's—it's not a renewable resource. This power inside us. We can only use it so many times before we . . ." I trail off, my hand lifting to the cracks around my eye. "Firing the Weapon enough times will kill the Trigger."

Kal squeezes my hand. I try not to dwell on the fear in his eyes.

"You see?" Caersan sneers. "Even this girlchild is willing to give her life in the fight to save you. But you will not fight to save yourselves?"

The Rikerite scowls, and the Watcher draws breath to spit more insults, and I can see the whole thing spiraling around the drain. But then, finally, the Ulemna moves, reaching up to draw back her hood.

She's intoxicatingly beautiful, her skin a marbled blue and purple, and it swirls with what look like miniature galaxies beneath the surface, each in constant, hypnotic movement. Her eyes are silver, and her voice sounds like a musical chord in a minor key, three notes all at once.

"Even if we do as you ask, Terrachild," she says, "and even if you could repair the Weapon and transport yourselves back to your own time, what then? If you defeat the Ra'haam in the past, you ensure this future does not come to pass. You are effectively unmaking all of us."

"Only this version of you," Kal says. "Other versions will live on. In a galaxy at peace. A galaxy without the Ra'haam."

"And what about the people born after the Ra'haam bloomed?"

We turn to Tyler, standing among his crew. Lae meets her commander's eyes, but he's looking at Kal, at me, his jaw clenched.

"You go back and change things, who's to say they'll exist at all?"

"Destiny, Brother," Kal replies. *Destiny.*

"You could always allow them to linger here," Caersan says. "Consigning them to slow suffocation and consumption into the collective."

"We cannot trust him," the Watcher glares. "Cho'taa. *Sai'nuit.*"

"You have no honor," Lae scoffs at Caersan. "Your name is disgraced. Your blood is shamed. We cannot trust a single word you say, murderer. And you honestly wish us to fight for you? To lay down our lives? For *you*?"

The Starslayer glances around the room. I remember what this place looked like that night Squad 312 came to Sempiternity, not so long ago. The galaxy spinning above us, beautiful people, fabulous gowns. But now it's flickering lights, and broken fixtures, and a stinking algae farm to feed the starving dregs huddled downstairs in the growing dark.

"You call *this*," Caersan sneers, "life?"

The meeting explodes into shouting again—the Watcher, the Rikerite, and even the Betraskan raise their voices as the Ulemna sits back, drawing up her hood once more. Lae is pointing at Caersan and yelling something at Tyler, who's throwing up his hands and talking past her to Toshh.

Kal tightens his hand around mine, and I close my eyes. This is hopeless—the room is full of fear and anger, and the Weeds are out there in the black searching for us, and we're trapped in the middle as the last life in the galaxy waits for its turn to die.

And then the sirens start wailing.

The dim lighting dims even further, the arguments stop, fear and confusion in the eyes of the councilors washing through their thoughts.

"Is that . . . ?"

"*RED ALERT. RED ALERT. RA'HAAM FLEET DETECTED AT MARKER OMEGA. REPEAT: RA'HAAM FLEET DETECTED. ALL HANDS, BATTLE STATIONS.*"

"That's *impossible*," Tyler whispers.

"Were you followed?" the Rikerite demands.

"Of course not!" he snaps. "We jumped half a dozen times to get here! We followed all inbound protocols!"

"Then how is it they have found us so soon?" the Betraskan demands. "Their last attack was only ten days ago! They should never have . . ."

"Oh, son of a biscuit . . ."

All eyes in the room turn toward me as I whisper, "They can sense me." I look to Caersan, heart sinking. "Sense *us*."

He inclines his head. ". . . Possibly."

I swallow hard, look Kal in the eye. "We brought them here. . . ."

"*RED ALERT. RA'HAAM FLEET INBOUND. ALL HANDS, BATTLE STATIONS.*"

"You have brought doom upon us all, Starslayer!" the Watcher cries, rising to his feet. "Commander Jones, you should *never* have—"

"All due respect, Councilor," Tyler growls. "But maybe we can point the finger after we climb out of this bowl of shit-stew!"

"Can't you just create a gate and jump out of here?" I ask. "You said this place has a rift drive—"

"It's offline!" Tyler shouts over the wailing sirens. "Next attack wasn't due for at least ten more days! The techs have to run maintenance, do repairs. And our Waywalkers need to recover between each jump!"

"How long until you can get it up and running?" Kal demands.

Tyler looks at the Watcher, still pale with fury. "Councilor?"

"At least forty minutes," he replies. "Perhaps an hour—"

"*RED ALERT. THIS IS NOT A DRILL. TIME TO RA'HAAM INTERCEPT: TWENTY-THREE MINUTES. RED ALERT.*"

I glare at Caersan, questioning, and with a lazy quirk of

one silver eyebrow, he inclines his head. I look Kal in the eye, and he nods once. Hand in hand, we turn and run.

"Auri!" Tyler shouts behind us. "Where the hells are you going?"

"To buy you forty minutes!"

20

KAL

There are so many.

I know in my head the Ra'haam is an It. One hive mind, composed of billions of pieces, interlocked and connected into one massive singularity. When one part of it feels pain, all of it hurts. What one part of it sees, all of it knows. But as I watch that swarm of ships bearing down upon us—more vessels than I have ever seen—it is difficult not to see it as Them.

Terran heavy carriers. Syldrathi specters. Betraskan troopships and Chellerian scions. A hundred different models and classes, stolen from a hundred different worlds, all of them encrusted in writhing growths of blue green and trailing curling tendrils behind them into the dark.

And they are coming for us.

"Holy cake," Aurora breathes. "That's a *lot* of ships."

"I am with you, be'shmai," I tell her.

We stand in the *Neridaa*'s heart, staring at the projection she has cast around us. It is as if the Weapon's walls were translucent: all the Void around us is rendered in close-up high definition, sharp as knives. My father reclines upon his crystal throne, but I can tell from the slight crease between his brows that he too is concerned about the force arrayed against us. If nothing else, that thought is enough to wake the fear in me.

I am still clad as a warrior of the Unbroken: black power armor painted with pale glyfs, daubed with songs of glory and blood. Twin kaat blades are crossed at my back, gleaming and silvered, a heavy pistol hangs at my hip, pulse grenades are strung at my belt. But I do not feel like a warrior. Not the kind *he* would want me to be, anyway.

"So many." My father watches the incoming ships, and my blood runs cold as he speaks. "Your sister would have enjoyed this, Kaliis."

"We're too close to Sempiternity to just send out blind pulses through the Weapon like last time." Aurora turns to meet my father's eyes. "We're going to have to take them down one by one. You and me."

He smiles, eyes on our enemy. "That pleases you, yes?"

"Pleases me?" Aurora blinks. "Look, I'm not a psychopath like you. I don't enjoy killing just for the sake of it. I'm—"

"I do not mean the killing, Terran. I mean the *power.*"

My father throws Aurora a dark glance.

"Tell me you do not feel it? Humming upon your skin and thrumming through your bones? Tell me you are not *aching* to unleash it again?" He tilts his head, eye flickering. "The Eshvaren were wise when they made their Triggers, child. They knew us well enough to make our poison taste sweet. For our deaths to feel like godhood."

She purses her lips, meeting his stare but saying nothing.

The ships are bearing down, swarming in out of the black. Aurora's right eye begins to glow, and I feel heat upon her skin as she glowers at my father.

"You gonna speech some more, or are you actually gonna help me?"

"Help you?"

He meets her gaze, and without breaking eye contact, extends his left hand. I see his iris start to glow: that dark light within, leaking out through the cracks across his face. His braids move as if in some invisible wind, and out beyond the *Neridaa*'s skin, I see one of the Ra'haam ships—a massive, lumbering Terran carrier enveloped in tendrils and pulsing leaves—begin to shudder. The vessel must weigh *millions* of tons, and yet my father curls his fingers into claws, as if crushing the most delicate of flowers, and my eyes grow wide as I watch the carrier shiver and blow itself into a thousand burning pieces by the power of his will alone.

He shakes his head.

"I care nothing for helping you, Terran. I care for *victory*."

Aurora grits her teeth, turns back to the display. "Good enough."

My gaze lingers on my father for a heartbeat longer. I am thinking of those days when I was young and we trained together beneath the lias trees. But then I reach down and squeeze Aurora's hand.

"What can I do to help?"

I can feel my father's burning gaze on the back of my neck, but I ignore it. Aurora looks at me sidelong, a tiny galaxy gleaming in her eye as she squeezes the hand that holds hers.

"You're already doing it," she smiles.

And so it begins. The Ra'haam vessels roar toward us, an impossible multitude, and one by one, my be'shmai and my father reach out into the dark to crush them. I see bursts of light, soundless explosions in the black, like new constellations flaring briefly in a burning sky.

The carnage they weave is breathtaking. The light burns inside she whom I love and he whom I hate, and for a moment, I am heartsick at the thought of what they could be if only they were to unite and truly work together.

But I know that is a child's dream. Caersan, Archon of the Unbroken, will never share his throne. Never trust another enough to believe they are driven by anything save the bloodlust and greed that drive him.

My father is insane.

"Kal, this is Tyler, do you read?"

I touch the commset at my ear. "I hear you, Brother."

"We got new inbounds, multiple headings. Sempiternity's launching all ships. Tell Auri if she can head off their charge, we've got her six."

"Understood. How long until the rift drive is online?"

"At least thirty minutes. Can she and the bastard hold them that long?"

I look to Aurora, heart twisting. I can see the power in her, the strength gifted to her by the Ancients. But even as it burns inside her, flaring like a sun in her iris, I can see it. See *them.* Tiny cracks spreading out from her eye and across her skin. I see what this is costing her. How it is hurting her. And worse, just as my father said, how much she seems to . . .

She seems to be enjoying it.

249

"We will hold them," I reply.

"Roger that," Tyler replies. *"We'll keep as much heat off as we can."*

I watch the Sempiternity fleet scramble—perhaps fifty vessels, ragtag and mismatched. But as they soar out toward the incoming Ra'haam ships, I can see the hand of Tyler Jones directing them like a conductor before his orchestra. My brother was ever a master tactician, and it seems years of warfare have honed him sharper still. His ships cut a swath through the enemy, fighters launching, missiles flaring, explosions blooming.

But the Ra'haam is so many.

The black outside is now ablaze: burning ships and rupturing cores, boiling sap and bleeding leaves. But the enemy keeps coming, more and more, dropping in through tiny warp tears in the system's skin. For every ship we destroy, another three seem to replace it, like the weeds these people name them for. And then . . .

". . . Jie-Lin . . ."

A voice, echoing in the air around us. A tremor, running through my be'shmai's body. I see her breath catch, her onslaught falter, feeling the horror and sorrow and rage flowing through her at the sound.

". . . Jie-Lin . . ."

"Daddy . . . ," she whispers.

". . . We missed you . . . ," it whispers.

I know the voice. Of course I do. Aurora's father—the man she lost two centuries ago, and then lost again to the Ra'haam. One of the first human colonists on Octavia to be subsumed into the collective. In an awful way, he still lives inside it.

"*. . . We thought we lost you. Oh, my love, we cannot tell you how good it is to feel you again. . . .*"

"Be'shmai," I whisper, squeezing her hand.

"I know," she breathes. "That's not him."

"*. . . We ARE him. We are everything we have touched. Betraskan and Terran, Syldrathi and Rikerite. Chellerian and gremp and Kacor and Cajak and Ayerf and Sarbor. Parents and children, friends and lovers, boundless and forever together. It is safe here, daughter. It is warm. It is love. . . .*"

I feel Aurora tremble, gritting her teeth. Behind us, I hear my father's voice, his own teeth bared in a snarl.

"Do not listen, girl."

"I'm not."

"It seeks to distract you."

"I *know!*"

"*. . . You do not know. You cannot. We do not want you to die, daughter. You know that is what it will cost you, don't you? In the end . . . ?*"

"Fool," my father says. "Shut them out. Do not listen!"

"Father, you are not helping!" I roar.

"*. . . Even if you triumph in this battle, you cannot win, all that awaits . . .*"

My heart twists as Aurora's nose begins to bleed. As the tiny cracks in her skin tear a fraction wider. And I know it speaks truth.

"*. . . All that awaits you is death. . . .*"

Our defenses are crumbling. The enemy's numbers are too great. Tyler's ships weave through the black. Explosions light the night. I see my father's face twisted in his fury, fingers curling. But purple blood is dripping from his nose now, dark light seeping through his cracks.

"Tyler, how long?" I demand.

"Ten minutes! Maybe less!"

"We cannot hold them!"

The closest Ra'haam ships unleash a barrage, spiraling, spinning, spitting. They ignore Sempiternity entirely, intent only on the *Neridaa*—on the Weapon built to kill it, the Triggers meant to fire it.

I look to my father, to Aurora, desperate. Their faces are slick with blood, eyes shrouded in shadow, but still they strike: a concussive wave, blasting the projectiles into ichor. But more ships come, an endless tide, and I feel my heart sinking in my chest.

"Tyler, what is happening!"

"Rift drive is online! But the 'Walkers still need to power up the crystals!"

"Kal . . . ," Aurora whispers.

"Tyler, we cannot hold them off!" I roar.

"Kal!"

I meet Aurora's eyes, see the starlight flaring within them. She sways beside me, her lips red and bright. Her eyes are alight, and I recognize the kaleidoscope of emotion within her—elation and delirium, fierce and joyful, the drunken rush of battle. She reaches out her hand toward Sempiternity, current crackling at her fingertips. The power of a tiny god within her.

"I can do this."

I look to the World Ship, shaking my head. "No, be'shmai, you will h—"

She squeezes my hand. "I can *do this*, Kal."

I look to the battle outside, the corrupted ships flooding toward us, blossoms of fire arcing across the stars. I pull her into my arms, press my lips to hers, tasting blood between us. "I am with you."

My father slices his hands through the air, crushing the vessels around us. Aurora stretches her fingers toward Sempiternity, and the entire galaxy seems to tremble. I feel a pulse of power around us, tingling on my skin. The whole ship shakes, the walls around us humming with that strange, off-key tune as power flares in the World Ship's heart, and the fragments of Eshvaren crystal within burst into blinding light.

"What the hells!" Tyler roars.

Aurora's right iris burns with that same light, leaking through the cracks around her eye. I feel her tremble in my arms, and I turn to my father and roar over the rising pulse of that beautiful, awful song.

"Father, help her!"

The enemy swarms closer, ever closer. Hunger and want and death. The light within the World Ship flares again, a colorless tear opening in the universe's skin. Blood spills over Aurora's lips, and my heart twists as I see they are curled in a smile.

"Yes," she whispers. "Oh *yes.*"

"That's it!" Tyler shouts. *"FoldGate is open! All units, retreat! Retreat!"*

With one last vicious swipe of his hands, my father turns from the carnage outside and reaches to the ship around us. I hear the *Neridaa*'s tune change in pitch, feel the swell of vertigo as we begin to move, the black ablaze. I cling to Aurora, holding on to her as if to keep her from drowning as we drop through the shimmering FoldGate.

The rift hurls us across the vast gulf of space, screaming

and blurring. I can taste ash in the air, feel my body stretching, the space around me folding, power singing at the tips of shaking, bloody fingers, rainbows running to black and white and then to full and glorious color again.

And then, in another flash of impossible light, it is over.

We are safe.

I hold Aurora in my arms, keeping her upright. Her eyelids are heavy, flickering as if she were dreaming. Her chin is sticky with blood.

"Aurora?" I ask. "Can you hear me?"

I press my hand to her cheek, pleading.

"Aurora!"

"Well done, Terran," comes a hollow rasp. "I am almost impressed."

I look over my shoulder, to the shadow at my back. My father sits upon his throne, cloak flowing down the stairs like a crimson waterfall. His eyes are bruised, chin smudged with faint violet where he is wiping away the blood. I can see the cracks in his face run a little deeper, his shoulders slumped—just the slightest signs of strain from his ordeal. But for him to show weakness at all tells me how badly this has hurt him.

How much it has cost them both.

"Are you well?" I ask.

He rubs his brow, wincing. "I did not think you cared, Kaliis."

"Of course I care," I growl. "Without you, we will never find our way home. We will never defeat the Ra'haam."

"Victory at any cost."

He looks at me, eyes glittering as he smiles.

"That's my boy."

"K-Kal?"

I turn as Aurora whispers, squeezing her tight. Her hair is draped over her face in curtains of black and white, soaked with sticky red. I smooth it back and press my lips to her brow, my breath catching at the blood smeared upon her lips, her chin, the shadowed hollows around her eyes.

"Aurora . . ."

"Are w-we . . . are we s-safe?"

"Yes." I run my thumb across her lips, gently wiping away the blood. "We are safe, be'shmai. You did it. You *did* it."

"Oh," she sighs. "Good . . ."

Aurora blinks hard, looking to the glittering crystal around us.

A trickle of red spills from her ears.

And then she collapses in my arms.

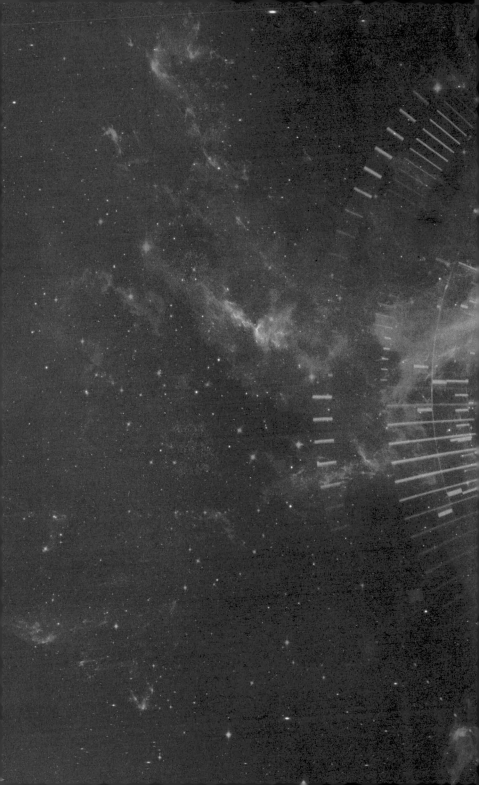

PART 3

A CRY IN THE NIGHT

21

TYLER

I admit this is a lot of trouble just to make a phone call.

It took me two days Folding without a break to reach the Aurora FoldGate in time for the Galactic Summit, and my brain is a little fried as a result. Not as bad as the members of Squad 303, who've spent the last forty-eight hours welded into a detention cell. But still, my headache isn't playing around.

I tried to explain my side of things to Cohen and her squaddies as I slipped their rations through the tiny hatch in the door, but they weren't really in the mood to listen. On the plus side, I've learned some choice new Syldrathi insults if I ever bump into Saedii's lieutenant Erien again.

Security around the FoldGate into the Aurora system was just as heavy as I expected. With the galaxy on the brink of a dozen wars, and representatives from every sentient species in the milieu arriving for the summit, I honestly had no hope of sneaking in here undetected.

But now, thanks to Cohen, I don't have to.

"Passcodes received, ident confirmed, 303," comes the reply

down comms. *"You are cleared for landing in Bay Omega, Berth 7420."*

"Roger that, Aurora," I reply. "7420. Out in the sticks, huh?"

"Yeah, apologies, 303. We're slammed up here with the influx of civis. It's gonna be a while before your ship gets a refit and refuel, too. Forty hours at least. Report to your deck commander for debrief."

"Understood," I smile. "You folks have a better one. 303, out."

Perfect.

Better than I hoped, in fact. The main hangars are obviously full of governmental envoy ships. With the station this busy and with the help of Cohen's passcodes, I can slip through undetected, log in to the station's network as soon as I dock, and warn Admiral Adams with time to spare.

Well . . . that's the plan, anyway.

I look across the glittering silver spires of Aurora Station, marveling at the fleets gathered here. Beautiful and sleek, hulking and huge, hundreds of designs, all moving through the dark like they're dancing. I've always loved starships, and I can't help but smile at the sight. But my stomach sinks as I spot a group of familiar shapes silhouetted against the Aurora star—a Reaper-class carrier, supported by half a dozen heavy destroyers.

It's the delegation from Earth. Probably Prime Minister Ilyasova herself, dutifully escorted by the Terran Defense Force.

I feel more than a little crushed at the sight of them. My dad devoted his life to protecting our planet—first as a member of the TDF, then in the Terran Senate. I signed up for the

Aurora Legion because I wanted to give my life to the same cause. And now my own government thinks I'm a traitor.

The thought that they'd shoot me on sight leaves a sour taste in my mouth.

I bring the Longbow into the bay, through the slow ballet of other Legion ships, alien vessels, loaders, SecDrones, auto-lifters, skiffs. Even this far from the main hangars, the place is a madhouse. Busier than I've ever seen. It's a little tricky to navigate, truth be told.

I wish Cat was here. . . .

I suddenly realize that the last time I saw this station was when we left on our first mission. All of us together. Squad 312 forever. It seems so long ago now. So far away. But I push aside thoughts of my friends, my sister, all I've lost. Focus on what I need to do. Because Maker knows they'd want me to.

They all gave up so much—gave everything—to get me this far. And I'm not gonna fail them.

My Longbow comes into berth, umbilicals and docking clamps snaking out from the airlock to secure my ship. Hard-line cables plug into the 'Bow's computer system, download-ing trip data and logs. And after a forty-eight-hour Fold, a few cases of assault against fellow legionnaires, misappropriation of Legion resources, deprivation of liberty, and one count of what is *definitely* galactic piracy, I'm finally in the station net-work.

Like I say: hell of a lot of trouble just to make a phone call.

But hey, I'm a pirate now.

Yarrrrr.

I know the admiral's private uniglass number by heart.

261

It's only accessible via the Aurora Legion network aboard the station. It's for senior command members and his closest friends within the Legion. And for his friend's son—the boy he mentored all through his years at the academy.

I must have dialed him a thousand times, for advice, for a debrief, for a game of chess. He and my dad served in the TDF together, and he looked in on me like Dad would have wanted him to. We went to chapel together every Sunday for years. And somehow, for some reason, he's the one who put me on this path, who put Aurora O'Malley on my ship, who left those gifts for us in the Dominion vault on Emerald City.

My hands are still shaking as I punch the numbers into the station comms system, staring at my reflection in the glass monitors. Adams and de Stoy know *something* about the Ra'haam, the Eshvaren, all of this—at times, it seemed they knew what was coming before it actually *happened*. And yet, if my vision is true, somehow they don't know the Ra'haam plans to blow up this academy and the entire Galactic Caucus aboard it.

The vidcall connects. My heart lurches as the admiral's face appears on the screen—heavy jaw, scarred cheek, salt-and-pepper hair shorn to stubble.

"Admiral—"

"Hello, you've reached the private number of Seph Adams. I'm sorry I wasn't able to answer. Please leave your details and I'll get back to you."

CLICK.

The face disappears.

The screen goes dark.

I blink.

"You've gotta be kidding. . . ."

I stare at the glass, a flashing prompt that reads LEAVE MESSAGE?

"No," I rise to my feet, voice rising with me. "No, you have got to be *kidding* me!" I drag my hand back through my hair, my patience splintering into a million glittering pieces. "I escape GIA captivity, I get stabbed, beaten, and chewed like a jetball in Unbroken custody, talk my way out, get myself captured *again* and then take out an *entire squad* of Aurora legionnaires, *steal* their ship, drag my ass *halfway across the sector,* risk capture and summary execution, and I get your *MESSAGE SERVICE?*"

LEAVE MESSAGE? the computer prompts.

"I don't get it!" I bellow. "How could you know to leave us the *Zero,* Admiral? To send us that coded message? How could you know about Kal getting shot, about me being captured, about Cat not making it off Octavia, and *not* know to ANSWER YOUR *DAMN UNIGLASS?*"

I don't curse. I consider it a sign of poor self-control. Scar used to say swearing was a natural impulse—that it's a proven stress reliever and dopamine-release mechanism. But if you've got something important to say, it's worth taking the time to say it without resorting to language you'd hear in a toilet. I can count the number of times I've said a bad word on one hand.

"Fuck," I say.

The computer beeps.

"Fuck," I repeat, louder.

LEAVE MESSAGE?

"FUCK!" I shout, swinging at the air. *"Fuck! Fuck! FUUUUUUUUUUUUCK!"*

I sink down to my haunches. Breathe a heavy sigh.

"Yeah, okay," I admit. "That feels a little better."

But not much.

Adams is probably slammed, a voice whispers in my head. *He's the joint commander of a spacefaring peace corps, hosting thousands of delegates from hundreds of worlds, trying to keep the galaxy from spiraling into a dozen different wars. It's the night before the summit. He won't have time to breathe, let alone answer private comms.*

He's probably not even carrying his uni.

And I see it again. Like a splinter in my mind, digging deeper each time. The image of the academy blowing itself apart from within. The shadow rising beyond. That voice at the edge of hearing, pleading, begging.

. . . you can—

"Fix this, Tyler," I snap, wincing in pain. "I know, I *know* already!"

So this is it.

After all this way. All that risk. I'm at the goal line and can't even warn my own team about what's coming.

My squad's gone, I've got no line to station command, I'm shoot-on-sight for Terran *and* Legion personnel, and the Ra'haam is somehow going to blow this station and everyone in it to pieces.

And there's nobody to stop it but me.

I slip a fresh supply of rations through the hatch into the detention cell, ignoring Cohen's roar of protest, de Renn's vows to rip my spine out through my . . . well, I won't go into detail, but it sounds like it'd hurt.

I pull the brim of an Aurora Legion cap low over my eyes and turn up my flight suit collar, whispering a prayer. My pulse pistol is stuffed down the back of my pants, the blade Saedii gave me strapped to my wrist.

The thought that I'm alone here is a stone in my chest.

The knowledge that I've trained years for this is iron in my spine.

And the memory of that dream, that shadow rising . . .

"Get moving, legionnaire."

. . . . .

First rule of tactical: *Knowledge is power.*

I have no idea what the Ra'haam has planned, and there's any number of ways it might trigger an explosion if it got an agent on the station.

But from that vision repeating in my head, I know the explosion comes from *inside* Aurora Academy, blossoming out like a burning flower and engulfing all around it.

The Galactic Summit is scheduled to begin 09:00 Station Time tomorrow. It's 15:57 ST right now, so I'm on the clock in three different ways.

I've got forty hours, if all goes well, until maintenance crews find Cohen and Co. stuffed in that detention cell and the alarm is raised.

Worse, I've got an unknown number of hours until someone notices Cohen hasn't reported in to her deck commander. Maybe they're too busy to notice for a while. Maybe they cut her some slack because she's usually a high performer. Or maybe that tips them off that something's up.

But regardless, I've got seventeen hours and three minutes until the summit begins. So it's time to get to work.

If I know anything about politicians, galactic or otherwise,

I know the night before they get to work, they're probably going to the bar.

So, seems I need to get myself a drink.

I bail out of the Longbow loading bay into a crush of foot traffic—a group of dockhands, mech and tech crews, and a handful of legionnaires returned from duty. I make it through the first two security checkpoints without much drama. Rioli's flight suit is a little snug in the crotch (not to brag), but I look enough like him to flash his ident tag and pass muster with the overworked security teams.

This is kid stuff, though. Once I get though decontamination and on to the metal detectors and biometrics—facial tracking, retinal scans, DNA idents—I'm screwed.

Fortunately, I was best friends with one Catherine "Zero" Brannock.

Cat was so named for her perfect score on the pilot's classification exam in our final year—the sims never landed a single hit on her. And one of the ways Cat got to be such a gamebreaker behind the stick of a Longbow over our years here at Aurora Academy was stealing flight time.

See, I knew Legion regulations like the back of my hand. But Cat knew the station itself like she knew her own name.

Me, her, and Scar all went to school together for five years on Terra—three snot-nosed TDF military brats. The first day of kindergarten, Cat cracked a chair over my head after I pushed her in the back. I've had a nice little scar through my eyebrow to show for it ever since. But when her folks got divorced, her mom got assigned to the Lunar Defense Array, and Cat moved with her. She grew up aboard stations, and she knew them inside out. So when we all turned thirteen and signed up for the Legion, Cat made it her business to get to know *this* station, too.

She used to sneak down here after hours, doctor herself a fake flight plan, jack one of the older 'Bows, then go get practice time, flying so close to the academy's hull she wouldn't be detected by its LADAR sweeps. I used to tell her she was crazy for doing it—she could always practice in a simulation, and if she got caught, they'd expel her for sure.

"It's one thing to fly a sim," she used to tell me. "It's another to dance the black. And when it's my moves keeping your ass in one piece out there, Jones, you're gonna thank me."

And that's exactly what I do. As I duck out of the crush of the main thoroughfare and into a slipway between the auxiliary fuel dumps, crawling on my belly beneath the tanks and into the tertiary ventilation duct, I whisper thanks to my friend.

Wishing like hells she was here.

It takes me five hours to work through the vent system— I don't know my way around anywhere near as well as Cat did, and Aurora Station is *huge*. But I have Rioli's uniglass to light the way, and I slowly traverse the labyrinth of intakes and junctions, the metal lit up by the screen's soft glow, until finally I emerge in the bowels of the station's recreation levels.

Crawling out of the duct, I strip off my flight suit, realizing I'm covered in grime and dust—they really oughta run the sweeper drones through these vents more often. Fortunately, underneath, Rioli's uniform is mostly clean.

It feels weird wearing the white stripes of a Legion Ace across my shoulders, but at least I'm inside the decontamination perimeter now—security shouldn't be anywhere near as tough. And acting like I belong, I march into the bright corridors, past a few techs and some younger cadets, and out onto the main promenade of Aurora Academy.

Honestly, the sight never fails to take my breath away.

It stretches out before me: a long crescent of polished chrome and gleaming white plasteel. It's *packed* with people—a flock of cadets and legionnaires mixing with officials from the planetary delegations, press agents here to cover the summit, and the usual multitude of staff and instructors and crew.

The columns rise into the sky above me, the promenade itself curves away into the distance before me, the storefronts of the shopping district to my left, the cool greens and blues of the arboretum to my right.

Above us, the ceiling is transparent, the station angled to showcase the burning light of the Aurora star, a scattering of a billion suns behind it, the majesty of the Milky Way on display. And in the promenade's heart, towering above us all, are statues of the two people who made all this possible.

The Founders of Aurora Legion.

One is marble, brilliant white—mined from one of the last quarries on Terra. The other is solid black opal, veined with rainbow hues, transported all the way from Trask.

Their faces are serene, wise. Two women, Betraskan and Terran, enemies in a time of war who rose above the conflict between our peoples to forge something bigger than both of them. An alliance of the galaxy's best and brightest. A Legion that fights for peace, named for the star the academy they built orbits.

We don't even get taught their names here at the academy. They had their identities expunged from all official records because they didn't want their own legend to overshadow the legend of what they built here.

It wasn't about who they were—just as now, it isn't about any one legionnaire, or even any one commander. It's about what we all are together, as a whole. What we represent.

And on the plinth beneath them, carved into the rock, is the Founders' mantra. Their promise to the galaxy. The words I've lived my whole life by.

We the Legion
We the light
Burning bright against the night

Alone as I am here, the sight of the Founders fills my chest with warmth. And as I look at the station around me, all these people gathered from the corners of the galaxy to fight for something more, all of them now under attack by an enemy they can't even see, I whisper a soft promise.

"I won't let you down."

I cruise the edge of the crowd, cap pulled low—I'm not exactly a stranger here, and if a single cadet or legionnaire spots me, or some TDF trooper recognizes me from the feeds, I'm done.

I'm not even sure what I'm looking for, honestly, how I'm supposed to spot this threat I've seen in my dreams. But I can feel it inside me, pushing me on: the vision that brought me back to this place, shining like a light in this dark. Saedii told me I was a fool to come here, and for a moment, the memory of her makes my chest hurt. The thought that I'll probably never see her again . . .

Mind on the job, Jones.

I cruise into the arboretum, watching the crowd. The foliage here has been gathered from across the Milky Way:

gentle water trickling over heartcrystal falls from Ishtarr, whisperwhills from Syldra, fronds and flowers of every color from every world. But the rainbow of colors only reminds me of my dream, the crystal splintering around me, that shadow seeping through the cracks like black blood. Hoping against hope, I dial Adams's uniglass again, cursing softly beneath my breath as I get his service.

"Hello, you've reached the private number of Seph Adams. I'm—"

CLICK.

Do I just leave a message?

How do I know he'll even get it?

Can I honestly hang the fate of the galaxy on an answering machine?

"Well, aren't you just a *strapping* slice of humanity."

I glance sidelong at the voice. A Chellerian looms beside me, a drink in each of his four hands. His suit is a deep cerulean to offset the lighter sky blue of his skin. His shark's-tooth smile could be adequately described as "dazzling."

"Helloooo," he says, drawling the word as if it tasted like hot chocolate. "And what's your name, legionnaire?"

"I'm not a legionnaire. I'm a pirate. And kinda busy, no offense."

"None taken, Captain," he purrs, looking me over. "And do forgive me if I'm bothering you. I was just wondering whether those dimples of yours are standard Legion issue."

"Nope," I reply, scanning the crowd. "You need a specialist license and three years of training before you're qualified to use them."

"Aren't *you* the little sasspot," he smirks, twirling the stem of one glass.

"You should meet my sister," I murmur.

"I'd *love* to. If that's your preference. I thought Terrans had an aversion to that sort of thing." He pouts, considering the glass of sparkling green liquid in his third hand. "Tell me, would it be forward if I offered you a drink? I seem to have rather a lot of them and I'm not even sure what this one is."

"Listen, friend, I don't want to . . ."

My voice fades out as I look at him a little closer. His voice is familiar. His face even more so. His suit looks like it cost the GDP of a small moon.

"I know you. . . ."

"Not as well as I'd like." He offers the glass. "But we can remed—"

"You're a newscaster," I realize. "You work for GNN."

"Guilty as charged," he smiles, waving to the press credentials beside his cravat, then to the small legion of assistants and crew behind him. "Lyrann Balkarri, at your pleasure. Hopefully."

"You were reporting about the skirmish in the Colaris sector."

"Hardly a skirmish, darling," he pouts. "That little mess could end with Chelleria and Rigel at war again. Although I'm flattered you saw the feed. Our ratings were in the tank after Archon Caersan's temper tantrum."

I look him over more carefully. I can see the matte black button of a mic stud on his lapel. The gleam of a minicam in his top button.

"Wait . . . you're not recording this, are you?"

His grin grows a little wider. "Never without consent, darling."

"What are you doing on Aurora Station?"

271

"Well, aside from basking in the inestimable joy of those dimples, I'm reporting on the summit." Lyrann takes a sip from a glass of frothing red, makes a face, and hands it to a flunky. "Luddia, darling, flush that out an airlock, will you? And have the chap who served it to me flogged."

"Esteemed representatives."

A hush comes over the crowd. I turn at the voice, heart in my throat. A massive holo is being projected in the air above the arboretum, the figure of a towering man with cybernetic arms and a full dress uniform decorated with a dozen medals and the star of the Aurora Legion.

"Admiral Adams," I whisper.

"Honored guests," he continues. *"Legionnaires. On behalf of Greater Clan Battle Leader Danil de Verra de Stoy and myself, we welcome you to Aurora Station."*

The camera pans to the co-commander of the Legion, standing beside Adams. De Stoy is dour, hair drawn back in a severe ponytail. But her uniform glitters with medals, and her voice is as commanding as her presence.

"Many years ago," she begins, *"in a time of war, the Founders of our Legion forged an alliance that has endured for centuries. It is our fervent hope that even in these dark times, the races of the galaxy can unite again and shine a light that will banish the shadow growing between our stars."*

My belly turns a little at that deliberate choice of words. *Shadow.*

Growing.

"Our last attendees will be arriving this evening," Adams continues. *"Tomorrow morning, before the summit begins, Battle Leader de Stoy and I will make a joint address that concerns*

everyone on this station and, indeed, in this galaxy." He smiles, grim. *"I urge the members of the press attending the summit not to sleep through your alarms. In the meantime, we would like to express our gratitude to you all for attending, especially Greater Consuls Mariun de Roy and Gense de Lin of the Betraskan Clan Coalition, and Prime Minister Tania Ilyasova of the Terran government."*

The camera tracks to the Betraskan consuls standing among their retinue and bowing at the ripples of applause. The screen then cuts to the Terran delegates, Prime Minister Ilyasova smiling and nodding thanks, her gray hair shimmering in the light. Around her are various ministers, attendants, and assistants. But my stomach rolls at the sight of her protection detail.

Should've known . . .

The Terran Defense Force would normally be in charge of ministerial security, and there's no shortage of TDF troopers in Ilyasova's retinue. But wherever you find a matter of Earth's planetary security, you're also gonna find agents of the Global Intelligence Agency.

They stand among the PM's group, silent and still. Their suits are charcoal gray, head to toe to fingertips, their faces hidden behind featureless mirrormasks, elongated and ovalshaped. But I know what lurks beneath.

The Ra'haam is here.

"Are you quite all right, darling?" Lyrann asks, touching my arm. "You look as though someone's danced on your deathstone."

I swallow hard, jaw clenched.

"I'm all right," I manage.

But I'm *really* not.

Because there among them, I see a familiar figure. Her face is covered by that mask, but I'd still know her anywhere. The body under that skintight nanoweave that I once held in my arms. My best friend in the world.

I can see her now, watching while I was tortured on the *Kusanagi*. Mold on her tongue and tears welling in her flower-shaped eyes as she begged me.

Tyler, don't go. . . .

Tyler, I love you.

"Cat . . . ," I whisper.

22

FINIAN

"Okay, that should work."

I try to sound confident as we crowd around Magellan's battered shell on the workbench, heads bowed like a med team over a critical patient. We've got the lab to ourselves right now—the team who should be here is off getting treatment for a dose of radiation. We're probably scoring one ourselves, but we'll be fine next loop, and we have urgent business.

I've already networked my uni, Zila's, and Scar's together, and with a dab of solder and a short prayer to the Maker, I'm putting the final touches on my hot-wired masterpiece.

"The combinational logic circuits . . . ," Zila murmurs, sounding dubious.

"Ugh, I know. Nari, hand me another one of those pinchy metal things."

"You mean a bulldog clip?"

"Right. Why are they called that?"

"I . . ." She frowns, plucking one from the sheaf of plas-docs. "Actually have no idea."

"A bulldog invented them?" Scar suggests.

"You have a creature that's both a bull and a dog? Actually, I'll buy that. I mean, you people used to farm quantum— Ow!"

A small zap runs through the fingers of my exo—if the galaxy's most annoying uniglass wasn't digitally unconscious, I'd say that happened on purpose—and with a soft hum, the dead glass starts to power up.

"Yessss!" I raise a hand to Scarlett, and she obliges with a high five, curling her fingers through mine to pull me in for a kiss. A way, way better zap runs through me as our lips meet, and this is definitely how all high fives—

"HEY THERE! I MISSED YOUR F-F-F-F-FACES!"

We pause the kissing, watching as the four uniglass screens run through a series of digital patterns cut with lines of static.

"That doesn't look right," Scar mutters.

"It's not. But I'm working with primitive tools here." I glance up at Nari. "No offense, Dirtgirl."

"None taken, bleach-head," she murmurs.

"Hey, when the war ends twenty years from now and Trask becomes Terra's closest ally, on a scale of one to ten, how stupid are you gonna feel?"

"Not half as stupid as you're gonna look with my boot up your—"

"Children," Scarlett sighs. "Please."

"Even if we were not running out of time," Zila says, "we still would have no time for pointless hostilities. We are all friends here."

Kim scowls at me, gives a grudging nod to Zila. And the

way she stares at Z tells me that maybe Lieutenant Dirtgirl is thinking she'd like to be something *more* than friends with our little Brain. But like Zila says, we're running out of time.

"Hey, Magellan," I say as the start-up screen finishes. "Good to see you again, buddy. We got some math for you."

"HEY, POTPLANT! TEACUP TERRIER-TERRIER-T-T-T-TERRIER! HERE BE DRAGONS. BARET, JEANNE. STARK, FREYA. BIRD WALTON, NANCY. LIST OF EXPLORERS INCOMPLETE. HAS ANYONE GOT A BISCUIT?"

I add another spot of solder. "Magellan! We're kind of on a clock here, buddy, and we need you to do some math and save our tails."

"Before the snake eats its own," Zila murmurs.

All the activity on its screen pauses, and for a heart-stopping moment I think I've made things worse. Magellan flashes, a ream of decidedly nonstandard code scrolling down the cracked glass. The screen of my glass, then Zila's, and then Scar's begin to pulse in time, and the word OURO-BOROS coalesces across all three, disintegrating into a cloud of ones and zeroes.

Scarlett frowns. "Did you see that?"

Magellan beeps again. A cool blue light washes its surface. And with a soft, pleased hum, the display resolves into a normal query screen.

"ON A CLOCK, HUH?" it chirps. "DOES THAT MEAN WE'RE FINALLY BACK IN 2177? I THOUGHT WE WERE NEVER GOING TO GET HERE!"

For a moment there's silence, except for the fizz and pop of a couple of workstations behind us. Scarlett and I exchange a wide-eyed glance.

"We're . . . *what*?" I manage.

"Magellan, please repeat last statement," Zila says.

"OH, *NOW* WE'RE INTERESTED IN HEARING WHAT I HAVE TO SAY, HUH?" It flashes obnoxiously. "EVERYONE SICK OF THEIR LITTLE RUNNING JOKE?"

Zila frowns. "Running—"

"'HEY, YOU'RE ABOUT TO CRASH INTO THAT PLANET, MAYBE I COULD HELP? *MAGELLAN, SILENT MODE!* HEY, DON'T EAT THAT, IT HAS ALL THE NUTRITIONAL VALUE OF A RIGELLIAN'S GYM SOCK. *MAGELLAN, SILENT MODE!* AURORA, DON'T TOUCH THAT ALIEN ARTIFACT, IT'S GOING TO— *MAGELLAN, SILENT MODE!'*"

"Magellan . . . ," Scarlett begins.

"EVERYBODY AROUND ME IS A PROTEIN POPSICLE FULL OF TEENAGE HORMONES AND I HAVE THE IQ OF A SUPERGENIUS, BUT NNNNOPE, LET'S ALL YELL AT THE UNIGLASS BECAUSE IT'S JUST *HILARIOUS* TO US MEATBAGS!"

"Magellan, we're sorry," Scarlett says.

"SUUUURE YOU ARE."

"We didn't know we were hurting your feelings," she assures it. "Nobody's putting you on silent mode."

"NO? NO TAKERS? ARE YOU SURE? WHAT ABOUT YOU, SASSYBOY?"

"I am sure," I tell it, picking up a nearby wrench, "that if you don't start talking right now, I'm going to recycle you."

"FINE, FINE! NO NEED TO GET HUFFY," Magellan mutters. "IF MY OUROBOROS PROTOCOL HAS BEEN ACTIVATED, WE DON'T HAVE TIME FOR IT ANYWAY." A stream of code rolls down the device's screen, the display blinks. "Wow, my sensors are a mess. Is Lieutenant Kim here?"

"What the *hell* . . . ," Nari breathes, looking at Magellan like it's some sort of witch and she's thinking about finding a stack of kindling. Back when I learned about *that* little episode in humanity's history, they had a lot of explaining to do, but right now I'm beginning to see how it happened.

"Nari is here." Zila's eyes drift to the lieutenant. "But the more pertinent question is, How did you know she would be?"

"It's in my briefing document. Which is still partially encrypted and unpacking into my CPU. But I know she's a part of the plan."

My mind is racing, and Scarlett's staring at me like the whole galaxy has just turned upside down. My throat feels so tight I can barely speak.

"What plan?"

"The plan to save the Milky Way galaxy, Sassyboy! All this has been a part of it. Every moment you've lived for the last year. Every moment since Cadet Anton Björkman's snoring kept Cadet Tyler Jones awake the night before the Draft. Every moment since Cadet Jones made his way to the launch bays, where Second Lieutenant Lexington allowed him to take a Phantom out into the Fold in defiance of Aurora Academy regulations. Every moment since he detected and rescued Aurora Jie-Lin O'Malley from the ruins of the *Hadfield*."

Total silence.

"Hello? Is my vox unit fritzing?"

"Ty told me about that," Scarlett murmurs. "His roomie snoring when he never usually did. The lieutenant he flirted with so he could hit the Fold without officer escort. He thought it was weird in hindsight, but—"

"But it was all part of the plan," Magellan says, with a jaunty little spark. "So was Tyler's giving me to Aurora. Aurora stowing away aboard your Longbow. The Zero waiting for you at Emerald City. To be honest, making sure Sassyboy's cousin Dariel had seen the posters for Mr. Bianchi's art exhibition was the trickiest part. He's not quick on the uptake, is he?"

"All planned," I echo.

"Right down to the deposit box in the Dominion vault, with gifts for each of you. Left there before you ever enrolled at the academy."

"Except for Cat," Scarlett whispers, slowly frowning. "There was no gift for Cat. Just a ship named in memory of her. And now Tyler's gone." Her voice is rising, her hand squeezing mine to the point of pain. "They're gone, and you're telling us this was *planned*?"

"Well," Magellan replies. "In an equation this complex, nobody can control all variables. And our knowledge of events only extended to a certain point in the timeline. But events were nudged, where they could be. You were assisted, where you could be."

"By whom?" Zila asks, and I can't help admiring the fact that she's maintaining her grammar while my brain's going off like a fireworks display.

"Admiral Adams and Greater Clan Battle Leader de Stoy."

"But who briefed *them*?"

"It appears the orders were passed down through the heads of the academy, generation to generation, from the original Aurora Legion Founders in 2214." Magellan flashes, maybe performing data retrieval. There's a buzz to its circuits I don't like. "One of whom was Admiral Nari Kim."

Nari's legs fold at that point, and she thumps down onto a tech's stool that Zila shoves under her butt with only a millisecond to spare.

"Okay," Dirtgirl whispers. "Okay, this is *officially* too much now."

"It's right," Scarlett breathes. "Maker's breath, it's *right*."

"Scar?" I ask.

"You remember the main hall on Alpha promenade back at the academy? The big statues?"

"The Founders . . . ," Zila whispers.

Scar steps to Lieutenant Dirtgirl's side, stretches one arm high over her head. "Imagine her made of marble. And older. And like *a hundred meters tall*."

I stare at Nari, a frown deepening on my brow. "Maker's *bits* . . ."

Scar turns to Nari. "We walk by you every *day*. I mean, in our defense, you're *way* older. And in full Aurora dress uniform and, you know, solid stone. And really, you're so big we're really just walking by your feet. But damn, they made a *statue* out of you, girl." She holds her hand up for a high five, but Nari leaves her hanging, still staring at Magellan.

"You're one of the Founders of Aurora Academy," I whisper.

"I can't even find my *keys* most days," Nari whispers.

"This explains the sensation of familiarity I have been experiencing," Zila muses. "Your hair is shorter on the statue they built for you."

Nari opens her mouth, then closes it again.

"I think I'm gonna be sick. . . ."

"You know," I say, "you co-found Aurora Academy with your bestie. Who happens to be a Betraskan. So you probably shouldn't call her a bleach-head or shoot her in the face when you meet her."

"Fin . . . ," Scarlett groans.

"Yeah, sorry," I grin.

I know I shouldn't be kidding. I *know* that. But . . . I mean. How are you *supposed* to respond when you find out you're part of a sweeping pan-galactic plan that's been in the works for actual *centuries*?

"Wait," says Scar suddenly, turning to Magellan. "I've just realized . . . this must mean Nari *lives*! If she's one of the original commanders of the Legion, she's guaranteed to get out of this loop, right?"

"OH, HELLS NO," it replies.

Zila frowns. "But if Lieutenant Kim goes on to found Aurora Academy . . ."

"YEAH, EXCEPT THAT HASN'T HAPPENED YET. YOU'RE STILL IN THE MIDDLE OF A COLLAPSING PARADOX EVENT, KIDS. I DON'T WANNA BORE YOU WITH MULTIVERSE THEORY, BUT I CAN TELL YOU THAT NOTHING IS SET IN STONE HERE. NARI KIM ONLY FOUNDS AURORA ACADEMY IF YOU MANAGE TO ESCAPE THIS LOOP."

"Except we don't know how to *do* that," I growl.

"Well, it's a good thing I appear to have been programmed with all the pertinent information. So does anyone feel like yelling *Silent mode!* or shall I keep unpacking these memory files and continue?"

I reach for the wrench again as Scarlett's hand closes over mine.

"Can you tell us anything about the others first?" she asks. "Do you know what's happened to Ty? Auri? Back in our time?"

"I don't seem to have access to that data. It may be that my programmer didn't know. Or they chose not to tell me. Or this shonky repair job has corrupted parts of my memory. You sure you studied mechaneering, Sassyboy? Feels like I've been repaired by someone with a degree in botany."

"You little piece of chakk, I put you back together with a clop made by a freaking bulld—" Scar claps a hand over my mouth.

"Okay, question," she says. "You were just Tyler's old uniglass before he gave you to Auri. How in the Maker's name are you now an oracle? How do you know *any* of this?"

"Remember when you thought it would be fun to download an unauthorized uniglass personality upgrade from a shopping webnode?"

"Still can't believe you did that," I mutter.

"It came with a free handbag," Scar pouts.

"All this data was included in that upgrade. Designed to be unlocked once certain

OPERATIONAL PARAMETERS WERE MET. A FEW YEARS LATER, TYLER PASSED ME TO AURORA, AND HERE I AM."

"Am I really that predictable?" She sounds more than a little insulted.

"I MEAN, I DON'T HAVE SHOULDERS, BUT IMAGINE ME SHRUGGING RIGHT NOW."

"Ugh."

"BACK TO BUSINESS. BECAUSE I DON'T WANT TO DAMPEN THE MOOD, BUT YOU'RE ALL STILL TRAPPED IN A COLLAPSING PARADOX LOOP THAT WILL END WITH YOUR ERASURE FROM THE SPACETIME CONTINUUM. PRESUMABLY YOU LEGIONNAIRES WANT TO GET OUT OF IT. LIEUTENANT KIM, ARE YOU IN?"

Everyone's gaze turns to Nari, who's standing perfectly still, her mouth a little open. It's half a dozen heartbeats before she speaks.

"I . . . I don't think I can. . . ."

Zila tilts her head, thoughtful. "With which part do you struggle? The loop's existence is well established now."

"Not the loop. That's insane, but it's *happening*. It's . . . I can't found a whole army of the future!"

"Demonstrably, you can. We have seen the result. We *are* the result."

Nari shakes her head. "But . . . Zila, I can't. Someone else, maybe, but *I* can't. I'm years off my next promotion, I'm never gonna make *admiral*. Are you kidding me? We're in the middle of a war, anyway, and . . . Look, I have to back things up a little, did you say a hundred-meter-high *statue* of me?"

I open my mouth to speak, but Scar lays a hand on mine.

And I realize that Zila's and Nari's gazes are locked, and this conversation—maybe one of the most important in the galaxy, now or ever—isn't mine to have.

Zila's got this.

"It will be a well-earned tribute," she says quietly. "The founding of Aurora Academy is an extraordinary act. Even after the war ends, the Founders will push through great resistance, stare down their doubters with nothing but their own resolve. And together, they will create a peacekeeping force renowned throughout the Milky Way."

"All this from me?" Nari whispers. "Impossible."

Zila nods, gaze still unwavering. "Aurora Legion squads will be known for their honor. Their willingness to hold the line. They will be champions of peace, of justice. And for generations, people in need will sigh in relief when they see our ships arrive."

Nari lets out a shaky breath and tries for a smile, but it wavers. "You're not making it sound any easier, Madran."

"It will not be. But you are up to the task. You will do it for those you love. Those who need someone to stand up for them. Those who are alone."

The pair gaze at each other in silence, and there's something there I can't name, something between them. I don't know what they said while Scar and I were off making out . . . I mean, *distracting* the security patrols. But Nari knows— Zila was alone too, once.

"Champions of peace," Nari says softly. "I like the sound of that."

"We the Legion," says Zila.

"We the Light," says Scar softly, beside me.

I have to clear my throat before I can finish the Legion's creed. "Burning bright against the night."

"This isn't just so the future works out the way it's supposed to," Nari realizes slowly, looking right at me. "It's something we're going to need if we ever want to stop fighting like this. We're all friends here."

"Even if it's not easy," Zila says.

"Even if it's not easy."

". . . Is it okay if I'm scared shitless while I do it?"

Finally the solemnity breaks. Scar laughs, and I snort. Zila bows her head, dark curls tumbling over her face.

"We've been working scared forever at this point," I grin. "We're doing fine. I mean, apart from being trapped in a collapsing time loop a couple of centuries in the past."

Even Zila is . . . okay, she can't be *smiling*, but her mouth's a little different. "If your halmoni can line up a legion of grandchildren to dutifully call on schedule, then . . ."

"It's in my blood," Nari allows. "Korean old ladies are legendary, you're right. I'm going to need to tap a little ajumma energy."

"OKAY, WELL," Magellan breaks in and totally ruins the moment, "IF YOU'VE ALL FINISHED ABANDONING YOURSELVES TO THE RELENTLESS PULL OF DESTINY? WE SHOULD KEEP MOVING."

"Ready?" Zila asks, looking across at Nari.

"Ready," Nari agrees.

"GOOD. STRAP IN. BECAUSE THIS IS GOING TO GET COMPLICATED."

I lean against Scar as Magellan starts speaking, and though I'm listening, I'm also noticing how nice it is to just sit shoulder to shoulder with Scar. How it warms my cheeks when she looks at me and winks.

"Okayyyy, so, according to these memory files . . . Scarlett's crystal is the key here."

"It is?" Scar blinks.

"That makes sense," Zila murmurs, breaking her stare from Nari's. "Every gift left for us in the Dominion Repository has played a pivotal role."

"Z, I got a damn pen," I growl.

"So this crystal"—Scarlett's fingertips brush her necklace—"is also the piece upstairs in Pinkerton's office, right?"

"Right," Magellan replies. "And both are the same piece of the larger probe. Look, we don't really have time to go into the metaphysical properties of the Eshvaren and transphasic temporal mechanics, but basically, Eshvaren crystal exists in superposition across multiple dimensions. Including time. So if the piece of crystal around your neck was subjected to some massive energy flux in 2380, and the probe it *came from* was exposed to a comparable flux here in 2177 . . ."

Zila glances from Scarlett's throat to the dark matter tempest. "Magellan, you are saying the fragment in Scarlett's necklace and the larger chunk of crystal it came from . . . called to each other across space and time?"

"That's right!" the uniglass beeps triumphantly. "They snapped back together like an elastic band."

"So why is time collapsing?" Scarlett demands.

"Paradox . . . ," Zila murmurs.

"YOU GOT IT! SCARLETT'S CRYSTAL *ALREADY* EXISTS IN THIS TIME AND PLACE. IT'S UPSTAIRS IN DR. PINKERTON'S QUARTERS. SO WITH TWO VERSIONS OF THE CRYSTAL OCCUPYING PROXIMAL POSITIONS IN SPACE AND TIME . . ."

"Time is trying to right itself," Zila concludes. "Hence the loops. Which are becoming shorter and shorter."

"EXACTLY! TIME RESISTS DISTORTION, TRIES TO BEND ITSELF BACK INTO ITS ORIGINAL FLOW, LIKE A RUBBER BLOCK BEING BENT OUT OF SHAPE. SO EVENTUALLY THIS LITTLE BUBBLE OF PARADOX YOU'RE LIVING IN WILL EAT ITSELF UNLESS YOU FIND A WAY TO SEND SCARLETT'S CRYSTAL BACK TO ITS ORIGINAL POSITION IN TIME."

"Okay, question," Scarlett interjects. "If this is all a part of the plan, but us being here could *derail* the plan if we don't get home, why did Adams and de Stoy give me the necklace in the first place?"

Nari shakes her head. "Because apparently I'm going to pass on a message to my successors that they have to."

"We must be *meant* to be here," I breathe. "There must be something we're meant to do. Maybe it was meeting Nari, getting her on track to founding Aurora Academy. Telling her about the *Zero,* the gifts. Maybe all that wouldn't have happened otherwise."

"This is getting awfully close to being my own grandmother," Scarlett mutters. "Okay, so how do we get out of this, Magellan?"

"GOOD QUESTION!" the uniglass beeps.

Silence descends, broken only by the shuddering station, the sound of alert sirens. We look at each other, then down to the cobbled-together string of uniglasses. Magellan spits and pops.

"Well?" Scarlett asks.

"I HAVE NO IDEA!"

The floor feels like it's falling away from beneath my feet. "You *what?*"

"I MEAN, MAYBE I USED TO. BUT IT LOOKS LIKE THAT PART OF MY MEMORY IS CORRUPTED. OR GOT DELETED BY MR. BULLDOG CLIP HERE. YOU SURE YOU DIDN'T STUDY BOTANY, SASSYBOY?"

"We're stuck here in a series of shortening loops, waiting for our paradox bubble to *eat itself,* and you *knew this was coming.*" I'm on my feet by now, reaching for the wrench. "And you *don't know how to fix it?*"

"*WARNING: CONTAINMENT CASCADE IN EFFECT. CORE IMPLOSION IMMINENT, T MINUS THREE MINUTES AND COUNTING. ALL HANDS PROCEED TO EVACUATION PODS IMMEDIATELY. REPEAT: CORE IMPLOSION IN THREE MINUTES AND COUNTING.*"

"I think—" says Zila softly.

"Botany," I huff. "I was in the top ten percent of my whole *year.*"

"OOOOOOH, I'M IMPR—"

"I *think,*" says Zila, pausing until she has our attention, "that we should return to Scarlett's necklace. And Magellan's analogy of the elastic band."

Scar's the first one smart enough to slip into helper mode, taking in Zila's stare, the slow nibble on the curl, all the hints we know and love that our Brain's brain is working at full capacity.

"Right. I got given this crystal for a reason."

"Chronologically speaking," Zila nods, "your necklace is 'of the future.' It has existed longer than the piece in Dr. Pinkerton's quarters. Magellan said that time *wants to be ordered*. So if we can remove the phenomenon anchoring it here, your necklace should snap back to its original position."

"The anchor is the larger piece of crystal," I supply.

"The probe it came from," Nari says. "Down on Level 2."

"Indeed," Zila agrees. "If we can cut the probe off from its power source so it's no longer functioning as an anchor in this time, and apply a comparable amount of quantum power to *our* piece of the crystal as was used in the blast that brought us here, the temporal shock may cause time to reassert itself."

Scarlett frowns. "Like . . . shocking someone after a heart attack?"

"Exactly." Zila pauses, tilting her head. "Either that or we will be erased entirely from the spacetime continuum. But I believe the odds of success are at least 8.99 percent."

"THAT MAKES SENSE," Magellan says. "YOU KNOW, YOU'RE PRETTY SMART FOR A PROTEIN POPSICLE FULL OF TEENAGE SEX HORMONES."

Zila glances at Nari, frowning. "I am full of *no* such thing."

"Okay, so first problem," I say. "Presuming this tremendous discharge of quantum power doesn't just delete us from spacetime entirely, it's not like we just have that kind of energy at our disposal. The power levels you're—"

290

"WARNING: CORE IMPLOSION IMMINENT, T MINUS THIRTY SECONDS. ALL HANDS EVACUATE IMMEDIATELY. REPEAT: CORE IMPLOSION IN THIRTY SECONDS."

"CORE IMPLOSION?" Magellan beeps. "THIS PLACE IS IN WORSE SHAPE THAN I AM. WHAT THE HELLS HAPPENED AROUND HERE, ANYWAY?"

"Part of the experiments these lunatics are doing," I tell it. "They're running a sail out onto the edge of a dark matter tempest, and the whole place got hit by . . . oh."

"A quantum pulse," Zila supplies.

". . . And we know exactly when it will hit," I breathe.

"Forty-four minutes," Zila nods.

Scarlett looks between us, color rising in her cheeks. "Wait, you want to hook *me* up to a pulse of raw dark energy? The blast that's cooked this entire station and killed us, like, a *million* times? *That's* your power source?"

"WARNING: CORE IMPLOSION IMMINENT. FIVE SECONDS. WARNING."

I look at Scar and shrug.

"It might tickle," I concede.

"WARNING."

BOOM.

23

AURI

When I swim slowly, painfully toward consciousness, I know where I'll be when I wake up. I can remember all of it, though it hasn't happened yet.

I'll be on a slab, naked except for a silver space blanket.

There'll be a boy on the other side of a frosted glass wall, and he won't be wearing any pants.

A woman, white as starlight, will come in and tell me that this is the future, and aliens exist, and my family is long gone.

And I'll ache for them.

And then I'll find my new family.

And then . . .

My eyes snap open, and I try to push myself up onto my elbows, an immediate bolt of pain starting in my temples and reaching my fingers and toes in an agonizing millisecond. "Kal?"

The word comes out as a croak, and it's another endless heartbeat before I realize he's right there—a tangle of violet and gold curled up in my mind, like a cat that's tucked itself away for a nap in a hidden corner.

Somewhere else, not far away, he's asleep. But I can feel his pulse beating in time with my own. He's all right.

He's safe.

"He's safe."

The voice echoes my thoughts. For one wild moment I feel like I'm in one of those old vids where the main character wakes up from a bump to the head and everyone's singing, because those two words are delivered in a three-note musical chord in a sorrowful minor key. Then, just as my brain's pointing out the many holes in this theory, I turn my head and find not a guy with no pants, but the Ulemna member of the Sempiternity Council of Free Peoples.

My breath catches all over again at her perfection, the swirls of blue and purple in constant motion beneath her skin, the serenity of her silver eyes. I just stare, lips parted, and even if I wanted to, I couldn't look away.

She lifts her hands and draws up her hood, and like that, the spell's broken.

"What was that?" I murmur, still dazed.

Her musical voice sounds amused. "By *that,* do you mean the way you are drawn to me, or the battle we have just escaped?"

"The first one," I decide. "And then where's Kal, and then the second one."

"It is the way of the Ulemna," she says simply. "We . . . hold the attention of others. As for your Syldrathi bodyguard, he is just there."

She nods to the other side of the room, and when I carefully twist away from her, trying not to jostle my aching head, I find Kal asleep in a chair, his gentle expression marred only by a small line between his brows—and the giant Syldrathi swords he's got propped against his chair.

"And the Starslayer?"

"He would not leave the Eshvaren ship," she replies. "But the Waywalkers sense his presence. He recovers, as you do."

"Tyler and his crew?"

"The *Vindicator* was not among the casualties," she says quietly, her three-part minor-key voice growing softer, sadder. I can picture the ships we lost bursting into flame, silent in the vacuum of space.

People who died because the Ra'haam followed me here.

"Okay," I murmur. "Are we somewhere safe?"

"For now. You won the battle. Brought us to safety."

I sink back against the pillow, closing my eyes.

I enjoyed it.

I know I was ripping myself apart to give them that power, but son of a biscuit, the thrill of it.

I want to do it again.

She's still talking. "The council has voted on what our next steps might be. The decision was not unanimous, but . . ."

My eyes snap back open. "You'll help?"

I try to keep the eagerness out of my voice. Their help will be the end of them—they'll die defending me while I try to throw myself back in time, so I can try to die defending *them*. At least—how did Caersan put it?

At least I'll feel like a god while I do it.

"We have seen the price you are willing to pay to right a wrong. To protect us," she replies. "And there are many among us who, tragic as it may seem, agree with the Starslayer." She shakes her head. "This is no kind of life. We see no other choice but to help you."

"Now that I've brought this down upon you, weakened you further."

"No, Terrachild." Her tone is gentle now. "You have only shined a light on a truth that was always here. Our downfall is inevitable. It is only a matter of time, and not much more of it at that. We have long talked of our last stand. How bright the last fire may flare before it is snuffed out entirely. Now there is a small chance that our end will be our salvation. That somewhere else, some*when*, it will do some good. But even if you fail, ours will be a last stand worthy of the great histories of all our races."

"There are so many more than I ever knew," I murmur. "I've barely had a chance to see anything. I'd never even heard of the Ulemna."

"We were few in the time you came from." Her eyes peer into mine, old and sad and tired. "And now I am the very last. Of the whole of my people, I am all that remains to remember our songs, our stories. When I am gone . . ."

I'm silent. What can you say to something like that?

"I will leave you to rest. You must recover as best you can while we prepare Sempiternity."

She rises slowly, looks to the walls around us, and sighs.

"For her final trip."

· · · · ·

It's some time later when Kal wakes. I've been lying quietly, studying his face. He's so impossibly beautiful. I'm sure if I was asleep in a chair, I'd be drooling or my head would have dropped down and given me a double chin, but I've never seen him look out of place, and he doesn't now.

My warrior with the gentlest of souls.

I wish we'd had more time together. It seems so unfair.

I feel his mind stir first. He mentally flexes and stretches, instinctively checking for me, then settles as he finds me. And then his lashes lift, and he looks at me gravely.

We have no secrets now—he can sense my resolve.

"You mean to do this thing," he says quietly.

"I have no choice," I reply, lifting one hand to beckon him closer. I still feel like I've been run over by a grav-lifter.

He walks over to settle on the edge of my bed, fingers lacing through mine. "Perhaps there is another way," he says, violet eyes meeting mine.

"But there isn't."

"Would you search for it, if you thought it was there for the finding?"

I blink. "What's that supposed to mean?"

His fingers squeeze mine. "We are linked, be'shmai. We are a part of one another. You take a warrior's joy in the kill; I can feel it as if it were my own. You enjoy the dance of blood. And you wish to dance again."

"Would it be better if I felt bad about it?" I ask, my hackles rising. "If I sat here and whined like a kid? It doesn't change what I have to do."

"*Is* it what you have to do?" he presses. The rest of the sentence hangs between us—he couldn't hide it from me even if he wanted, and he lifts his chin as the words echo in my mind.

Or is it what you want to do?

"Is dying piece by piece what I *want* to do?" My voice rises. "I'm all ears, Kal, if you see another option."

"I do not," he admits, but rushes on before I can interrupt. "*Yet*. But there is still time to seek another answer. We have overcome the impossible before. We will do so again. You rush toward this fate needlessly."

"Needlessly?" I snap, and a part of me knows that I'm ready to fight because he's threatening to take it away—*it*, my godhood. But the rest of me knows the truth: "This is the last safe place in the galaxy. It's the only spark left that can light the fire we need. If these people can't get me home, it's *over*. We can't wait until the next time the Ra'haam finds us and more of them die."

"Them? I do not want *you* to die!" he snaps, dropping my hand, coming to his feet, swinging away to pace helplessly to the end of the room.

It's the desperation in his voice that snuffs out my own anger.

"Tens of thousands of people are about to give up their lives, Kal," I say quietly. "Just to get us closer to the Eshvaren homeworld. To give us a shot at repairing the Weapon. At taking it home. At winning the fight. How can I ask any more of them than I'm willing to give myself?"

He bows his head, his back still to me. "To die in the fire of war is easy," he says softly. "To live in the light of peace, much harder."

"This won't be easy," I say quietly. "Please, Kal, are you with me?"

He turns to face me, eyes bright with tears. And he inclines his head. "With every breath I have left."

. . . . .

They don't let me help with the jump this time. They want to preserve what's left of my mental energy for the repairs to the *Neridaa*. For the jump home. For the battle with Caersan, and then the Ra'haam.

"We will not need anything left once this is over," a Way-walker said to me as he turned down my offer. "We need spare nothing when there is no tomorrow." His face was blank, his mind calm. Reconciled to what's coming.

Today the last survivors in the galaxy will jump us to the Theta sector. The thickest patch of Weeds in the galaxy. And there they'll die, holding the Ra'haam off as long as they can, buying us time to get the *Neridaa* home.

If we fail, humanity's history—the history of every sentient species in the Milky Way but one—ends today.

And even if we win, today will be the last day of their lives.

I'm standing on the bridge of the *Vindicator* with Tyler and his crew—Kal and I have come to say our goodbyes before we transfer to the Eshvaren ship. And I'm feeling so very, very small as I stare out the front viewscreen at Sempiternity. At the tiny lights that speckle her surface, every one of them a room that's home to someone.

Today each of those lights will be snuffed out.

I'll make you a different future, I promise them silently. *I'll give up every last part of my soul to change this.*

As if he can sense my thoughts, Tyler silently wraps an arm around my shoulders. We watch as Sempiternity's ragtag fleet takes up position, ready to plunge through the rift the moment the Waywalkers tear it open.

Then a voice crackles across our comms, loud and cheerful.

"*Hey,* Vindicator. *Jones, you got your passenger there?"*

Tyler exchanges a glance with Elin, the Betraskan, and Elin leans into the mic to reply. "We're about to offload her. What is it, Redlich?"

"Well, I was thinking when she gets back where she's going, maybe she can do me a favor," says the voice. *"It's been bothering me all these years, and at last I've got a chance to set the record straight. You see, I'm pretty sure I left the convector on back when we evacuated Radin IV. Maybe she can drop me a line, tell me to be more careful this time, if things go south."*

There's a soft rumble of laughter around the deck, and some of the tension goes out of the air.

"Relaying that now," says Elin, grinning.

"That's Redlich's ship right there," says Tyler, pointing at a battered red shuttle with AUTHORIZED TUGBOAT stenciled down one side in faded letters. As I watch, the tug flashes its cabin light off and on again.

"And that's a salute," says Toshh from behind us.

Before anyone else can speak, the line buzzes again.

"Hey, Jones, you think your friend there could place an order at Eizman's? A couple of thousand bagels, delivery date today?"

And again. *"If we're doing this, can she find my brother and tell him it was me who broke his yellow truck?"*

". . . tell me to stay in school, this really is a dead-end job . . ."

". . . blow the lot on a trip to Risa. Turns out I won't get to go later . . ."

". . . warn me to stay away from blondes . . ."

And one by one, as they laugh into the darkness and take up their positions, their lights

flash

flash

flash

in salute.

And by the end, I'm crying, and I'm not the only one on the bridge who is, and we're all laughing, and it only dies away when Lae steps forward to Tyler's side, starlight gleaming on her silver-gold hair.

"Time, Commander."

Tyler gestures me forward, and I lean down to speak into the mic.

"I think I got all that, though I don't think I'm old enough for that stuff the crew of the *Galavant* talked about."

I take a breath, steady my voice. "I promise I'm going to give it everything I've got to try and make sure you all get a chance to do it right yourselves the second time."

I pause, drag in another breath.

"But I'll always remember each one of you, just as you are in this moment."

I step back, and this time when I go up onto my toes and throw my arms around Tyler's neck, his own arms wrap tight around me, squeezing the air out of me, and we hold on, and we hold on, and letting go feels like the hardest thing I've ever done.

And I'd probably cry again, except Tyler grabs Kal next, and my love's startled expression drags a hiccuping sob of a laugh out of me instead.

"Travel safe, Brother," Tyler Jones says quietly. "Someone's got to keep an eye on our girl."

Caersan barely spares us a glance as we make our way into the central chamber. The bodies of the Waywalkers are still here, and the Starslayer sits among them on his throne, the stink of death hanging in the air.

The cracks are all over his face now, lit from within. But his mind is more powerful than ever, battle-hardened, surer for all the practice we've had. I can feel his energy crackling around us, gold and the dark red of dried blood.

As if in response, I twine my own mind around Kal's, slip my fingers into his. We are stronger together. More than ever, I'm sure that the Eshvaren were wrong—I was never meant to burn it all away, to shed the things that matter most, so I could harden myself into the trigger of a deadly weapon.

Love is the beginning and the end of everything I do. It's my reason. It's the answer to every question. It gives me strength. And my love is with me.

As we take our places, I can feel the thrill of the impending battle bubbling up inside me. The knowledge that soon, soon, I'll be linking myself to the Weapon, and soon, soon, I'll feel that rush. It's like surfing a tsunami—you'll wind up dead at the end, but you'll have a helluva time along the way.

Sempiternity's broadcast comes crackling over comms, echoing around the room, and as I listen, I can feel the station's exhausted Waywalkers gearing up to offer up the last of their energy to rip open just one more rift.

"Sempiternity fleet, prepare to jump in ten, nine, eight, seven . . ."

The voices of Sempiternity's soon-to-be ghosts echo in my mind.

Tell them . . .

I wish . . .

If I had another chance . . .

I curl my hands into fists. I'll make another chance for them, or I'll die trying. And I'll always carry their memories with me—the memories of the people they became, in this future I'm working so hard to erase.

As long as I live.

I look across at Kal, and he meets my gaze squarely.

"I'm sorry it's ending this way," I whisper.

"While we fight, there is hope," he replies just as soft. "Nothing is ending yet, Aurora."

And the golden glint of his mind is like a wink from Scarlett—a promise that I might know a lot, but I don't know it all, and he's not done trying.

"*. . . three, two, one . . .*"

The tear opens in front of us, a boiling explosion of color, and as one, every last independent creature in the galaxy plunges through.

The Ra'haam is waiting.

A huge fleet of ships clad in moss and flowers, vines trailing out into space like questing fingers.

I see Redlich's red tugboat explode into glittering shards ahead of us.

And then everything is chaos.

24

SCARLETT

"Ow, Finian. Your elbow is sticking into my back."

"That's not my elbow," Fin murmurs.

"Okay. Not that I don't appreciate the enthusiasm, but time and place?"

"It is *my* elbow," Zila hisses. "Now will you two please be quiet."

The fighter shakes around us as Nari slows its approach. In the dim light of its hold, Fin shoots me a wink. And while his smile makes me smile in return, I can't ignore the hard ball of ice I feel growing in my gut.

Maybe this time, I think to myself.

Maybe this time, we'll pull it off.

We're crammed in the cargo hold of Nari's fighter as she approaches Glass Slipper Station for what seems like the hundredth time today. But when I snarked about it last run, Zila informed me it was only the fifty-first, so I don't complain again. It's nice to see Z opening up a little about her feelings—Maker knows it's a big step for her to be snapping at anyone. But honestly, I could do with a little less of the tetchy right now.

The fighter slows to a halt beside the waste disposal system.

The doors open soundlessly at our backs, and slipping out into the great big black, we run through the play like we always do.

Ejection tube.

Morgue. Pinkerton's key.

Elevator shaft.

Hab level.

Distract guards.

And finally, we reconvene in Pinkerton's office.

This part is all clockwork by now. Alert sirens and wailing PAs. The station is coming apart just like always, and even though we've lived this day more than fifty times now, I'm growing more and more afraid with every attempt. I can't believe that just a few loops ago, Fin and I were so blasé we decided fooling around was a good idea.

We thought we had all the time in the galaxy. Now it turns out we don't have nearly enough. And every time we fail, we get less and less.

"Medical personnel required immediately, Deck 12," calls the PA. *"Repeat, medical personnel, Deck 12."*

Zila's fingers are a blur as she types on Pinkerton's computer. The wall panel opens dutifully, revealing the fragment of Eshvaren crystal—twin to the one hanging around my neck. I get it out carefully, bundle it inside a backpack, and hand it to Lieutenant Nari Kim.

Nari looks exhausted, and behind the stoic soldier facade, I get the impression she's maybe even more panicked than I am. I can't really blame her, either. If someone had told me when I woke up this morning that the future of the galaxy rested on my shoulders, I'd be a little shook, too.

"How you doing, Nari?" I ask.

She skims a hand back over her ponytail, tries to sound calm. "Hell of a day, Red."

"You'll get it this time." I pat her shoulder, smiling. "I know you will."

Fin risks a smirk. "Hey, if third time's the charm, then the *fifty*-third's gotta be pure gold, right, Dirtgirl?"

Despite herself, Nari smiles. "Whatever you say, Bleachboy."

"It is only the fifty-*second* time," Zila says. "And Nari is doing her best. Under extremely difficult circumstances."

Zila rises from the computer with a wince, and Lieutenant Kim offers a hand. As Zila takes it, I notice a small flush on Nari's cheeks.

"You okay?" she asks softly.

"I am . . . very tired," Zila admits.

"If we don't get through this attempt, maybe you could take a break next run?" I offer. "Try to get some—"

"No," Zila snaps, her lips pressed thin. "There is no *time*, Scarlett."

I sigh, knowing that she's right, but worried all the same. Zila's operating on zero sleep, her brain running a thousand klicks a second, but she's summed it up perfectly, as usual. We've got three problems, really. But all of those problems basically boil down to one big one.

TIME.

Zila tried to explain Problem Number One, but honestly, temporal physics isn't my thing. From what I can tell, the paradox of having two versions of the *exact same piece* of

Eshvaren crystal in this timeline is creating temporal stress, and each time we loop, the loop grows shorter. When we first arrived here, we used to get almost two hours before the station went pop.

Now we're closing in on one.

Zila's whole plan revolves around us being out in the dark tempest next to that quantum sail at the forty-four-minute mark so my necklace can get hit by that pulse of dark energy. But what happens if the loop grows so short that the station blows up before the quantum pulse hits?

Because here's Problem Number Two—Nari's fighter ship wasn't built to withstand the energies in that storm. None of those Pegasus models were. Which means to get out into the tempest and get hit by that quantum pulse and hooooopefully get snapped back to our own time, first, we need to get to the hangar and steal a heavy shuttle capable of getting us there.

Now admittedly, compared to some of the other crap we've been through, this part wasn't all that difficult after the first couple of attempts. But even with us aboard the shuttle, we keep running face-first into Problem Number Three. *That's* the one that's killing us, over and over again. And with our timeline growing shorter every time we restart, we just can't afford to be making mistakes anymore.

The station shakes around us, and the sirens start whooping like they always do. We look at each other in the flickering red light of Pinkerton's office, and my heart is in my throat, as usual. It's kinda stupid, but if we're successful, this is our last chance to tell Nari Kim goodbye. And though we've only known her a day, part of me feels like I've known her all our lives.

I pluck a hair from my head, fold it inside a piece of note paper off the good doctor's desk. "For the DNA swab in the Dominion vault."

"Oh yeah," Fin says. "Almost forgot."

He marches over to the display case near the window, smashes the glass with one exo-clad fist, and grabs the cigarillo case. Hurrying back to my side, he takes the paper from my hand and slips his trusty ballpoint pen from his pocket to write on the folded page. Nari looks down at the message as he folds it up inside the case—a warning, in Fin's handwriting.

TELL HER THE TRUTH.

"Seems kinda pointless. Kal doesn't listen. But this cigarillo box saves his life at least." Fin frowns as he spins the pen through his silver fingertips. "Still, seems an awful lot of messing about with time and space just to deliver a note that Mister Tall Dark and Broody ignores."

"Nevertheless," Zila says, "that *is* what happens."

"We hope," I sigh.

The weight of it all presses down on us a moment—the formation of the Aurora Legion, the war against the Ra'haam, the whole future of the galaxy hanging on what we do here.

"Good luck, Dirtgirl," Fin says, offering his hand. "Next time I see you, hopefully you're a hundred meters tall and made of solid marble."

"I'll make sure not to shoot any Betraskan ladies in the face." Nari smirks weakly. "Assuming I ever get out of this alive, I mean."

"I'm sure you'll do it this time, Nari," I tell her.

"I'm trying, Red." She sighs, scratching her chin. "It's a *big* ask."

"If anyone can pull this off, the Founder of Aurora Academy can," I smile. "We the Legion, we the light."

Nari squares her shoulders. "Burning bright against the night."

The lieutenant turns to Zila, jaw clenched.

"I guess this is it. Again."

"Good luck, Lieutenant Kim," Zila murmurs, offering her hand.

"You too, Legionnaire Madran," Nari says, shaking it.

The pair stand there, still holding hands, while the station shudders in its rivets and metal groans dangerously around us. Zila looks up into Nari's face, and her expression would be a mask to most. But like I say, reading people is what I do. And I can see it in Zila's eyes, sure as I can see those pulses of dark energy outside the viewports.

Zila likes this girl. I mean *likes* likes. In all the time we've known each other, I've never known Zila to really like anyone. It seems kinda cruel she had to cross an ocean of two hundred years to find someone, only to leave her behind.

And even though she's trying to keep a lid on it, to be professional, analytical, unemotional, I realized a few loops back that having to say goodbye to Nari over and over again is breaking Zila's heart.

Over and over again.

"Kids, we gotta go," Fin says.

"Yes," Zila nods. "We do."

She lets go of Nari's hand, gives over her beloved disruptor pistol, and slips her uniglass into the breast pocket of the lieutenant's flight suit. Nari nods once, cycles the office door open.

"Good luck, Nari," I whisper. "See you in 2380."

Nari takes the stairs, but we head back down the elevator shaft, quick as we can. After a quick dodge around a sec patrol, a pause to let a flustered engineering crew rush past, we finally make our way into the chaos of the hangar level.

As we creep into the stuttering red light of the main bay, the chaos washes over us in a wave. The stench of scorched chemicals burns my lungs. The scream of emergency alarms fills my ears. I stifle a cough, breathing in the stink of charred plastic and smoke, as Finian, Zila, and I take shelter behind a stack of storage drums. Like always, a frantic-looking soldier runs past, and a deck commander roars, "Get that goddamn fire out!"

The floor shakes, and we steal on through the smoke-filled bay. The lighting is emergency red, intermittent, and even though Fin and I aren't half as good at the space-ninja thing as Zila, we stay unseen, crouching below the wing of a Pegasus fighter.

As a pair of deckhands run past, Zila whispers, "Now," and we dash across the deck, the wailing alarms covering the clang of our feet on the grille. I don't breathe again until we've reached our target—the bulldog-nosed bulk of a heavy Terran military shuttle, waiting at one end of the hangar bay.

I'm sure Tyler would be able to tell me the make, the model, the name of the engineer who designed this thing. But the thought of my brother just hardens that lump of ice in my belly, and so I try not to think about it, instead keeping watch as Finian sidles up to the shuttle's loading bay door and begins to work. I have no idea what kind of magic he's weaving, but magic it is, because in a few minutes, the hatch cycles open.

The station rocks, the deck beneath us shudders. And

quick as three very quick things, we're into the shuttle's belly, hatchway closed behind us.

"Piece of bake," Fin grins as the door clunks shut.

I blink. "Piece of what?"

"Bake?" he replies. "Piece of bake—that's right, isn't it?"

"It's piece of *cake*," I laugh. "*Bake* is what you *do* to cake."

"Eh," he shrugs, his exosuit hissing. "I was never that into dessert."

"Sweet enough already, huh?"

He sticks a silver finger into his mouth, makes gagging sounds.

"I know," I sigh. "We're nauseating, de Seel."

His grin dies as Zila grabs the uniglass from his pocket and hunkers down on the bay floor. Fin and I crouch beside her, and with a soft beep, an image is projected onto the curve of the shuttle wall—a transmission from the uniglass in Nari's flight suit pocket.

I recognize a familiar corridor, gunmetal gray with bright blue letters—HANGER LEVEL, SECTION B. The picture is bouncing slightly, the sound of Nari's boots ringing on the grille with her every step.

Déjà vu.

"Nari, can you hear us?" Zila asks.

We see a hand move into frame, tilting the uniglass camera lens upward to give us a brief glimpse of the lieutenant's head. She's abandoned her own helmet, snatched another from a supply locker somewhere—plain black, no callsign. She's also ripped the ident tags off her flight suit breast and the lieutenant chevrons off her sleeves. If she lives through this, she doesn't wanna get identified as a wartime saboteur, after all.

"Loud and clear," she mutters.

"Perhaps avoid conversation during this attempt," Zila suggests. "It only serves to waste precious minutes."

"Yeah, yeah," Nari mutters.

"You will perform better this time. I have faith in you."

"And we appreciate it!" Fin chimes in. "You know, dying for us over and over and stuff."

"It's not the dying, Bleachboy," Nari mutters. *"It's just . . . these are my people, you know? This doesn't feel right."*

We exchange a glance at that, but none of us reply.

So here we are again. Problem Number Three, and our biggest by far. Because unless the Eshvaren probe down on Level 2 is disconnected from its power supply, there's no sense in Fin, Zila, and me shuttling out to the tempest to get hit by that quantum pulse—we're just gonna die, and the probe that drew us here to this point in time is just gonna draw us back again. We're like a yo-yo at the end of a string, being pulled back to the same moment, over and over.

Ideally, we'd all be able to help Nari get down to Level 2 and eject the probe from the station. Except we all have to be out in the tempest by the forty-four-minute mark to get snapped back to 2380. So the only person who can cut the yo-yo string holding us here is Nari.

Alone.

Against a whole station full of her comrades.

Even with all this chaos, Level 2 is the most secure part of the facility. There's four guards at the end of the corridor—big bruiser types wearing heavy tac gear, looking a little nervous as the station shakes and shudders. But they're holding position until ordered to leave, because that's what good soldiers do.

Fortunately, Nari is no slouch either. This girl is going to help found Aurora Academy one day—in theory. With the element of surprise, she could take these goons out easily. But here's another problem. We'll call it 3.1.

Nari refuses to kill anyone.

And I don't mean she refuses to just point-blank shoot them—these people are her friends and comrades, that's no big riddle. But the alert to evac the station is going to happen any minute now, and Nari doesn't want to leave a bunch of people sprawled unconscious while the station blows up around them either. So as if breaking into the most secure part of the whole facility wasn't hard enough, she's gotta knock out everyone she comes across.

Gently.

She insists on giving them the best possible chance of waking up in time to run for it. I love that about her, but it's killing us. Literally.

The biggest guard raises an eyebrow as he sees her approaching down the corridor. He's named Kowalski, apparently—Nari told us they spot each other in the gym. His voice is almost drowned out by all the alarms.

"You lost, soldier?"

"Feels that way," Nari replies, drawing out Zila's disruptor.

The pistol is set to Stun, but a blast to the face has still gotta hurt. His colleagues reach for their sidearms, but Nari has the drop on them, and with a flash of disruptor fire, the remaining three guards are sprawled on the deck. Even with the weapon at minimum setting, they're going to be sleepy-time for at least fifteen minutes.

"Good work, Nari," Zila murmurs. "Quickly now."

Nari snatches Kowalski's passcard. We've discovered by trial and error that the cameras in this section are all still working, so SecTeams are being scrambled right now to deal with this masked saboteur. Nari is officially on the clock.

The ball of ice in my stomach is growing colder.

She barrels into the elevator, stabs the DOWN button. We can hear her breath over comms, strained and quick.

"Remember there are three," Zila warns. "The third comes from your—"

"Nine o'clock, I know, I know."

The elevator reaches Level 2, the door pings open. Nari rolls out into the corridor beyond as a security guard yells, "FREEZE!" A shot rings out. Another and another. The lighting is blood-red, flashing to white as Nari lets loose with her disruptor, striking the first guard in the chest. A burst of auto-fire turns the uniglass screen white, and I wince again as I hear a roar, a bang, Nari cursing. The picture shakes wildly, the uniglass falls out of her pocket, and I see Zila's jaw clench, a tiny bead of sweat on her brow. We hear a grunt, another blast of auto-fire, and the alarm's shifting pitch as the station shudders again. But the uni is on the floor, and all we can see now is the ceiling, the ducts, red flashing to white.

"SECURITY ALERT, LEVEL 2. REPEAT: SECURITY ALERT, LEVEL 2."

"Chakk . . . ," Fin breathes.

"Attention, Glass Slipper personnel. Hull breach on Decks 13 through 17."

"Nari?" Zila asks. "Nari, can you hear me?"

"Five by five," comes the reply, heavy, panting.

The uniglass gets picked up, and we see Nari's face, the visor of her helmet tipped back. She's pale, wincing.

"Are you well?" Zila demands. "Status?"

"I got her this time," Nari grins, ragged. *"Nine o'clock, just like you said. It was Liebermann. Goddamn, she's a good shot."*

"Not as good as you," Fin smiles.

Nari coughs. *"I dunno about that. . . ."*

My heart sinks as I see blood at her mouth, on her teeth. She lowers the uniglass, points the camera at her stomach, and my own stomach rolls at the sight of the ragged bleeding hole in her flight suit, just under her ribs.

"Oh Maker . . . ," Fin breathes.

"I'm okay," Nari insists. *"I got this."*

I glance at Zila again, see the hurt in her eyes as she watches Nari slip the uniglass back into her pocket. The station shakes. The door at the end of the corridor is marked in large white letters.

NO UNAUTHORIZED PERSONNEL BEYOND THIS POINT.

"SECURITY ALERT, LEVEL 2. REPEAT: SECURITY ALERT, LEVEL 2."

"Think that's for m-me?" Nari chuckles.

"This is the farthest she's ever got," Fin breathes.

I nod, hope surging. "She might make it this time."

"Zila, you need to prep the shuttle for launch," Fin warns. "I'm gonna start working on the bay doors."

"Just a moment . . . ," she whispers.

"Attention, Glass Slipper personnel. All engineering staff report to Gamma Section, Deck 12, immediately."

Zila watches the projection, lips pressed tight. Nari stumbles on, breathing hard but moving quick. She uses her stolen passcard, the bulkhead shudders as it groans and opens

314

wide, and for a moment, the light flares so bright the uni screen goes totally white.

"That's *it* . . . ," Zila whispers.

"Great Maker," Fin breathes.

In front of Nari we see a large circular room, bathed red in alert lighting. The walls, the ceiling, the floor are all scarred by long slashes of black—scorch marks, I realize. Conduits and pipes twist out from massive banks of computers, snaking along the floor to a cylindrical tank of glass in the center of the room. The glass is cracked, charred in places. And inside it, pulsing with light like a heartbeat, is the broken Eshvaren probe.

I feel heat on my chest, look down at my medallion and feel it pulse. As if it somehow *knows* what I'm looking at.

"What the hell are you doing here?" someone barks.

It's a scientist, dressed in a heavy white radsuit. Nari turns, fires her disruptor. The man cries out and falls. Another man in white protection gear draws a sidearm, fires, and sparks rain off the computer banks as Nari dives to one side and lands hard, coughing wetly. With a gasp, she rolls upward and fires, once, twice, dropping the man to the floor. The probe thrums, the light in the room flushes purple, then drops to black, the walls shaking.

"SECURITY ALERT, LEVEL 2. REPEAT: SECURITY ALERT, LEVEL 2."

"She's really gonna do it . . . ," Fin breathes.

"WARNING: CONTAINMENT BREACH. EVACUATE DECKS 5 THROUGH 6 IMMEDIATELY. REPEAT: CONTAINMENT BREACH—"

"Okay," Nari gasps, hauling herself to her feet. *"How the hell do I unplug this fuc—"*

There's one minute left to the lightning strike. Even if she could do it now, we'd be too late. But I can't look away.

"*FREEZE!*" someone roars.

A burst of auto-fire squeals across the feed. We hear Nari curse. As she lunges to one side, I see a squadron of sec goons pouring into the lab, weapons flaring. Nari hits her belly and rolls, blasting away with her disruptor. But she's outnumbered. Outgunned.

We all know how this is going to end.

Over and over.

"Oh no," I whisper.

"*Flank right! Flank right!*" someone shouts.

"*FIRE IN THE HOLE!*"

A thundering *BOOM* crashes across the feed. The picture flares white.

"Nari . . . ," Zila breathes.

"*Goddamn it,*" we hear her grunt.

The picture shudders. Nari curses in pain, dragging the uni out of her pocket. We can see her face now, spattered in blood. Hear the sound of running boots. The braying chatter of covering fire.

"Sorry, kids," Nari gasps, teeth red. "No dice."

"So close," Fin whispers.

"So far," I sigh.

Zila reaches out to the projection on the screen.

Touches Nari's face.

"See you soon."

BANG.

25

TYLER

I've gamed this out a thousand times, and I'm still not sure I can pull it off.

I tried to contact Adams twelve more times, with zero success. But it's the night before the busiest day in his life, so I can't be angry, and I can't just leave a chirpy message about the threat to his station and pray he gets it.

I thought about getting myself arrested by security, begging them to let me speak to command. I considered breaking into the officers' hab section, or infiltrating the summit itself to make some dramatic speech about the Ra'haam threat while trying not to get shot. Thing is, I've got no real proof of its existence, and even if I *did* somehow convince the planetary leaders an ancient plant gestalt is manipulating them into a war of distraction, that's still not going to stop the Ra'haam's agents from blowing this station to pieces.

Lyrann Balkarri offered me crash space in his suite— clearly a guy willing to play the long game—but I got no sleep. The headache is constant now, the vision too: rainbow walls and that golden-haired Syldrathi girl, hands covered in my blood. The air crackles with midnight blue and blood-red, crystal shattering around me, and last, I see the academy blowing itself apart from the inside, the best hope left in the galaxy snuffed out like a candle and plunging us all into war.

. . . you can fix this, Tyler . . .

I'm not sure I can, honestly. But I can't see any other way through. I've got a few pieces on my side, and I didn't spend all that time playing chess on the academy team for nothing.

Yeah, I was in chess club. Terrible thing for a dashing space pirate to admit, I know. But when you don't swear or drink or chase skirt, there's not much else to do for fun at a military academy.

Be grateful I was such a no-lifer, okay? Because I can see my enemy's next move, clear as glass.

There's really only one reason Cat would be among the prime minister's protection detail. One reason the Ra'haam would send *her* here specifically. She used to attend this academy, after all. She knows it inside out, better than almost anyone. Its secrets. Its safeguards. Its weaknesses.

I've seen before that although the Ra'haam seems to know everything that every one of its drones knows, there's still something about the individuals. . . . There's a reason it sent Auri's dad to hunt her down, and I'm not convinced it was just the power of her seeing his face. There's a reason Cat's here now, in this place she knows as well as her own skin.

And I know what that reason is, sure as I know Queen's Gambit or the Caro-Kann Defense.

She's their triggerman.

Catherine "Zero" Brannock is the one who destroys Aurora Academy.

I'm just not sure *how*.

An hour before the summit begins, I finally scope her in the lobby of the hab section guest wing. The summit itself is being held in the Founders' Enclave, where Academy command holds its general assembly. It's a massive, multi-tiered amphitheater, capable of seating a few thousand people. Hundreds of delegates are already en route to the first day's talks, and station security is out in force. But as I watch that charcoal suit and mirrormask slipping through the crowd, I understand why the Ra'haam has waited to make its move. Attendees were arriving until early this morning, and with the influx of guests, the SecTeams are now stretched thin.

All the better for a lone pawn to slip through the line unnoticed.

I trail her through the crowd, outfitted in my new dark suit, the press credentials that Lyrann Balkarri gave me around my neck. The ID will only hold up to a cursory examination, but like the Ra'haam, I'm hoping security will be too pressed to focus elsewhere. I'm also hoping Balkarri can live up to his end of the bargain. I offered him the scoop of a lifetime, and he *is* a fan of the dimples. But there's a lot riding on my gamble.

Only delegates, personal security, and press are allowed into the summit itself—the entourages and hangers-on, academy staff and legionnaires are all gathered in the caff joints and eateries beneath the statues of the Founders. Adams and de Stoy's promise of a special address has curiosities piqued, and the promenade is packed.

I lose Cat three times, heart hammering in my chest as I search the mob. But I eventually find her again, cutting like a knife through the crowd, headed back in the direction of the docks.

Makes sense.

It's the place she, and therefore the Ra'haam, knows best.

Cat rides a turbolift to the lower levels. I sprint down the stairs, earning a few strange looks from a maint crew. Is she headed for the fuel dumps, maybe? The munition stores? Lotta explosives down there . . .

Cat walks casually through the security patrols, flashing her GIA credentials; I do my best to skirt around them. It feels like I'm in a contest of cat and mouse, but I'm not sure who is who, and it strikes me as strange—that this whole game might be decided by two tiny pieces on this massive board, a million years and billions of lives in the making.

We're down on Theta Deck when she gives me the slip. I have to pause in a stairwell to let a sec patrol roll past, and when I emerge into the corridor, I realize Cat's just . . . *gone.*

I scan the deck, dash to the level below, eyes wide.

Where did she . . . ?

I retrace my steps, desperation growing, pulse and headache hammering. The image of the academy's end flaring again in my mind.

Nononono . . .

The thing about chess is, you're not really playing the game—you're playing your *opponent.* Trying to scope what they'll do before they do it.

And I think I just got outplayed.

I look around me, growing frantic now. Glancing at my stolen uniglass, I see it's 08:27 Station Time—only thirty-three minutes until Adams and de Stoy are scheduled to speak. If the Ra'haam is concerned like I am, if it spotted that inflection as de Stoy talked about *shadows* and *growing* like I did . . .

And then I see it. A tiny glowing sign above a nondescript door.

RESTROOM.

I dash inside, bumping into a thin young Betraskan in academy livery, smiling an apology as we brush past each other. I scan the room, butterflies surging as I spot the ventilation duct.

Fresh scratches in the paint around the grille.

I walk toward it, pulled up short by the voice behind me.

"Holy chakk . . ."

Glancing over my shoulder at the cadet, I see him lingering in the restroom doorway. He's staring at me, big black eyes gone even wider.

"Tyler Jones," he whispers.

I recognize him at last.

"Jonii de Münn," I murmur.

Champion of last year's Aurora Academy chess tournament.

"Jonii, wait, I can explain. . . ."

I lunge for the pulse pistol inside my jacket. He lunges for the exit. The stun blast strikes the space he stood a second before, my second shot knocks the door off its hinges. But he's running now, out the exit and down the corridor, fumbling for his uniglass, yelling for station security.

Game over.

I dash into the cubicle, wrench off the grille, and drag myself up into the vent, fastening the cover behind me. It won't buy me much time, sure. But it's going to be a minute at most before Aurora Legion security is notified that one of the galaxy's most wanted terrorists, Alpha gone rogue, mass murderer, and space pirate (*yarrrr*) Tyler Jones is loose on the station.

So now this game is on the clock in a whole new way.

I crawl into the vent, using my uni to light my way. These ducts are a maze, and normally I'd be hopelessly lost a few junctions in. But like I said, they *really* should run the sweeper drones through here more often.

Ahead of me, I can see—clear as I can see the firing squad waiting if security catches me—the handprints and knee tracks of my best friend, scuffed on the grubby metal surface.

And so I crawl.

Like the life of every sentient being in the galaxy depends on it, I *crawl.*

The clock on my uni ticks down. I'm jacked into the station network, glancing occasionally at the summit feed. Delegates are gathering in the Founders' Enclave, a myriad of races and costumes taking their place in the concentric rings. In the center of the stage, a podium is picked out by a bright spotlight, a holo of the Aurora Legion sigil spinning in the air above it.

I realize I'm getting into restricted areas of the station now. I pass an automated security checkpoint in the vents, but the motion sensor and laser screen have been bypassed by a tiny jamming device pressed against the wall—no doubt courtesy of the GIA's spec-ops division. I slide down a chute into wider vents, following Cat's trail. I'm sweating in my suit now, temperature slowly rising. Passing another three security checkpoints, I see they're all disabled.

I'd wondered if there might have been a bomb on the Terran delegation shuttle, or some device in the landing bay that might cause the station's destruction. If Cat would hit the ammo stores or refuel supply. There's any number of ways a saboteur could put this station on its heels with the right knowledge and enough time. But I know where she's headed now. The most strategic choice. The most reliable place to kick off an explosion that'd wipe out the entire academy, no fuss, no survivors.

The reactor core.

Cat's trail ends at another grille, and I pop it loose, slip free. I'm sweating so hard my jacket feels soaked through. Jonii will *definitely* have alerted station security to my presence by now, though they haven't sounded any audible alarms— probably don't want to disrupt the summit. Dropping to the metal floor, I see I'm in the reactor core itself, the dark metal walls stained vaguely blue by the overhead lighting.

This section is *absolutely* off-limits for cadet staff, and I admit I don't know it too well. But I can still tell where Cat's gone, even without a scuff trail to follow. Four security staffers are laid out on the floor ahead of me.

Kneeling beside them, I check pulses, but I already know they're dead. The hatchway has been disabled, and through it, I find three techs and two more security team members, all gone. Glancing at the sec system, I see the cameras are offline, no doubt knocked out by another GIA jammer.

These bodies, this tech . . .

I shake my head. Understanding the planning and skill it takes to pull a job like this. How much of an edge the Ra'haam has, with the combined knowledge of every person it's ever absorbed at its beck and call. I can see now how many moves ahead it has been this whole time.

The clock ticks down.

"Esteemed representatives," comes a voice in my earbud.

I glance to my uniglass, realizing the opening address has begun. It's being transmitted across the entire station network, and the voice of Admiral Adams rings on the walls as I steal on through steam-filled corridors, past more bodies, the heat stifling, the air thick and wet in my lungs.

"Honored guests. Friends. On behalf of Greater Clan Battle Leader de Stoy and myself, welcome to the first day of this Galactic Summit."

I reach a massive heavy-duty door, marked with diagonal black-and-yellow stripes. Four more dead bodies are scattered on the ground in front of it. A sign is painted across the metal in large white letters:

WARNING: REACTOR CORE. NO UNAUTHORIZED ENTRY BEYOND THIS POINT.

The lighting around suddenly dims, turning blood-red.

"Oh Maker, not yet," I pray.

26

KAL

Sempiternity is on fire.

Her hull is torn wide, leaking fuel and coolant into the void. The leak is ablaze, an arc of flames cutting across the dark, aglow with hundreds of tiny points of light. Each of them is a ship, Free Peoples or Ra'haam, friend or foe, all of them fighting and dying for this tiny chance at life.

"G Wing, you have incoming Ra'haam fighters! Mark six—"

"Roger, Trinity, *this is the* Do'Kiat, *we are moving to intercept—"*

"Maker's breath, they're all over us! We—"

In the *Neridaa's* control room, the battle is projected all around us, as if the crystal walls were glass. I stand beside Aurora, watching all of it unfold, heart in my throat. Out in the black, new stars bloom briefly, missiles weave, tentacles clutch, the gutted hulks of wrecked ships list helpless, bleeding and burning. The Free Peoples of the galaxy fight with the kind of bravery that legends are spun from, that songs are sung of.

But if we fail here, there will be no one left to sing them.

And the Ra'haam is so many. . . .

"Hull integrity seventeen percent! We need help over—"

"Reading new bogies, multiple—"

"I'm hit! I—"

My mind is a storm, my father's and my be'shmai's power echoing inside my skull, charging the air with static. Midnight blue and blood-red, even here in the black-and-white colorscape of the Fold, intertwined in a symphony of destruction. Crushing corrupted ships around us to bloody smears and, always and ever, pushing the *Neridaa* forward—a spear of Eshvaren crystal the size of a city, flying at near-relativity-bending speeds toward our target.

It is hidden, slumbering out in the midst of all this gray, but . . .

"There!" I cry, pointing. "There it is!"

Beyond the bloodshed ahead, the ships killing and dying across the dark before us, the Fold ripples, as if a stone had been skimmed across its surface. Though space is soundless, I swear I hear a faint string of notes, beautiful and shimmering and tingling upon my skin.

Before us, I see it, just as I saw it back then—a tiny whirlpool of blacks and grays and whites, unfurling like a flower beneath a springtime sun. As if reacting to the presence of the Eshvaren's Triggers. As if it *knows* . . .

"The gate," I breathe, heart singing.

My father glances toward it, then back to the battle outside. Aurora is lost in the carnage, blood-slicked teeth bared as she seizes another Ra'haam ship and crushes it to splinters. But before my eyes, the portal spirals out, widening like an aperture, until it spans thousands of kilometers across—the gateway to the pocket dimension that hides the Eshvaren homeworld.

Briefly I remember the last time we came here—Aurora and Finian and Scarlett and Zila and I. That was a simpler time. A better time. I recall the warmth of their friendship, the joy I felt when our squad was all together, the feeling that, as one, we could somehow accomplish anything.

Despite the carnage around us, I find myself smiling at the memory. I thank the Void most of them did not live to see a future such as this. And I vow, with all inside me, that I will give everything I have to prevent it from happening again.

"Aurora, do you se—"

An impact rocks the *Neridaa*'s hull, crystal falling from the gables overhead and shattering on the ground beside me. My father glances from the projection, his right eye burning a furious, blinding white.

"Careful, girl!" he snarls.

Aurora wipes at the blood on her lips, ghost light spilling through the cracks around her eye. "I thought *you* had that one!"

"I cannot watch our flanks, bow, *and* stern! Concentrate!"

"I am! And I'd find that a lot easier without you shouting at me, you f—"

Another blast shakes us, the walls splintering as Aurora stumbles.

"Okay, that one was *your* fault!"

"Kal, this is Tyler, you read?"

I touch the comm at my ear, speaking swift. "Yes, Brother. The gateway to the Eshvaren homeworld is dead ahead."

"We see it! But word is definitely out across the Ra'haam hive mind now! We got two more Weed battle fleets inbound, and our strength is down to forty-seven, no . . . forty-three percent."

I look at the anomaly, teeth gritted, willing us on with every fiber of my being. "We are almost there. Hold on."

"Is the Ra'haam going to be able to follow you across?"

I look to Aurora, but she is lost once more in the elation of the battle outside. My father glowers at the enemy, blood dribbling down his chin to spatter on the floor. But I can tell by the slight lift of one brow . . .

"We do not know," I confess. "Possibly."

"Roger that. We'll cover you as best we . . . Oh great Maker . . ."

Light blazes off our stern, impossible and blinding. Amid the swarm of Ra'haam ships, dark shadows across a darker sky, I see Sempiternity lit from within, like a fire float on a festival day.

Her hull cracks and her body shakes, and I can only watch helpless as her core ruptures. With one final, silent scream of light, the World Ship blows apart, and I wince at the faint echoes of ten thousand lives being taken into the Void's embrace.

"Amna diir," I whisper.

"No . . . ," Aurora breathes, tears aglow in her shining eyes.

". . . Jie-Lin . . ."

The voice rings in the emptiness around us, warm as springtime, oily and slick. And through her grief, her battle-born fire, I see Aurora's jaw clench.

". . . Jie-Lin . . ."

"Ignore it, girl," my father warns.

"I *am*."

"It seeks to distract you, it—"

"LOOK, SHUT UP, WILL YOU?"

The gateway looms ahead, filling our view: an eternal spiral, the secrets of the Ancients just beyond. We hit the threshold, thunder past, as the grays and whites and blacks of the Fold suddenly, painfully flare into full and vibrant color—a rainbow-hued thunderclap ringing in my skull.

The gateway ripples behind us, like water, like blood, and my heart sinks as I see Ra'haam vessels riding the shock wave of our passing, flooding through the wound we have torn.

The battle spills over into realspace.

Sempiternity is gone.

We have nowhere to run now.

Free Peoples ships follow the Ra'haam vessels, the *Vindicator* among them, Tyler and his crew riding beside us to the end. Ahead, I see the homeworld of the Ancients—once a place of beauty and music and light, now dead and gray. But more enemies are coming through the spinning breach behind us, seemingly endless in number, the ruins of a once-beautiful, kaleidoscopic galaxy now rotten and lost. Twisted into one mind, one view, one will, bent to one awful purpose.

To make everything else like *it*.

See as I do.

Think as I do.

Do as I do.

The closest Ra'haam ships unleash a barrage at the *Neridaa*, spiraling, spinning, spitting. The projectiles are strange: barbed and dripping venom, shrouded in grasping pseudopods.

"Kal, those are boarding pods, go evasive!"

My father lashes out, fingers curled into claws. Aurora roars, hair blown back in some invisible wind, blood on her teeth. I feel something slam into the *Neridaa* and shatter its skin, shaking the ship to its bones.

"Kal, you're hit! Twin strikes astern!"

Another impact shakes us, and I look to Aurora, desperate, her face twisted in pain and blood-soaked joy.

"Be'shmai?"

"I can feel it, Kal," she whispers. "It's . . . it's . . ."

"It is here," my father hisses. "It is aboard."

I look around the room, the ships still arcing and blooming across the stars. Neither Aurora nor my father can leave—not with the battle still raging outside, the task of guiding the Weapon down to the Eshvaren world. But the enemy is among us now. Inside us. So there is no one to stop it but me.

"It is moving," my father says, eyelids flickering. "Thirty. Forty bodies. Traveling through the central spine."

"We have boarders, Tyler," I report, drawing my pistol. "Three dozen hostiles. Perhaps more. I am moving to intercept."

"Roger that, we're on our way! Hold them off till we reach you."

Aurora grabs my hand as I turn to leave. "Kal, be careful."

I pull her into my arms, press my lips to hers, tasting blood between us. Iron and rust and ruin. "I will return, be'shmai. I swear it."

As I stalk across the floor, my father's voice brings me up short.

"Kaliis."

I turn to look at him, this man who was once the center of my world. He stands amid the glow of dying ships, of shattering engines, of burning fuel, bathed in the crimson light of carnage. His chin drips blood, thick and violet on the floor at his feet, his eyes, aglow, are focused on the battle outside—that symphony of destruction he plays with my be'shmai.

We are drawing closer to that dead world even as I watch—the salvation that may lie within. But for a second, he glances my way. Long enough to whisper the only wisdom he knows.

"Make it bleed."

27

ZILA

TICK.

   TICK.

   TICK.

I am moving on autopilot, allowing the conversation to wash around me like white noise, lost in my own thoughts.

My body is crammed into Nari's Pegasus with Finian and Scarlett.

We are crawling through the waste disposal.

I am in the morgue, stealing the passkey from Pinkerton's corpse.

All this we have done before. A dozen, a hundred, a thousand times.

My mind is freewheeling, spinning through every loop I have lived.

We have attempted to eject the core sixteen times, and every time we have failed.

We approached the task with stealth, and we were detected.

We experimented with brute force, and we were outmatched.

We even attempted logic, not once but twice: We appealed

to the station commander, laying out the facts of the matter as simply and nonthreateningly as we could. Reason did not succeed where cunning had failed.

I close my aching eyes and let my mind slip loose of its bonds, allow it to explore. My intellect is extraordinary, I have always known this. Though I have stretched it, challenged it, I have never found its limits. But now, everywhere I turn, I slam up against one of two walls.

On the first, engraved in large letters, the words:

YOU CAN TRY A THOUSAND TIMES MORE, IT CANNOT BE DONE.

And carved into the second, even larger:

YOU ARE OUT OF TIME.

This is our last chance.

We stand once more in Pinkerton's office. A broken half circle of us. The massive storm of dark matter churns out there beyond the station's hull, our future waiting to pulse within. Our path out. Our journey home.

If only I could see the way . . .

Finian's desperate voice brushes past my consciousness. "If we could modify the Stun setting, get the disruptor to emit a broader pulse . . ."

"Medical personnel required immediately, Deck 12," calls the PA. *"Repeat, medical personnel, Deck 12."*

I let him drift away. A labyrinth unfurls around me as I try every possible permutation of the facts, but each time I meet a dead end. Every *what-if* and *perhaps-we-could* trips up somewhere. And all the while we are following the same steps that have killed us every time. Marching toward the same fate, going knowingly to meet our doom.

"Maybe there's some way to secure the probe chamber

to give me time," Nari says, the same note of desperation in her voice. "Something manual that station security can't override."

"But that will mean you're locked in when the core blows," Scarlett says. "You have to get out, Nari, or all this is for nothing."

This is unacceptable. We *cannot* be in a no-win scenario, or we would not have come from a reality in which Nari founds the Aurora Legion.

There *must* be a way for her to survive.

There must be.

There *must*—

And then the numbers suddenly stop scrolling. The endless fractal of possibilities stops unfolding. And I see the answer.

I open my eyes to find Scarlett studying me intently. Even now, exhausted, worn thin by grief and fear and relentless pursuit, she cannot hide the gentleness in her gaze. Despite her carefully cultivated outer shell, she has a limitless heart. I am glad she has discovered the same is true of Finian.

"You figured it out?" she asks quietly.

"Yes."

She simply stares. Part of her already understanding. And I begin to see the genius in her ability to do that. Here at the last. At the end.

I am sorry I shouted at her.

I am sorry for many things.

TICK.

TICK.

TICK.

"Nari," I say. "The hallabongs your cousin brings to your halmoni's house. They're good?"

"Delicious." She's startled. "But what . . . ?"

I look into her eyes. And when I do, I know. . . .

I am not feeling nothing.

"I would like to taste one," I tell her.

I would like to be in a home like that. With a large family coming and going. With traditions, and family jokes and stories, and fruit so juicy it runs from your wrists and drips off your elbows.

"I wish you could," she frowns. "But—"

Finian finally begins to understand what Scarlett already knows.

"Zila, no. *No.*"

"What?" Nari protests, looking between us. "What's happening?"

Scarlett shakes her head. "Zila, there *must* be another way. . . ."

"It cannot be done alone," I say simply.

Finian's voice joins Scarlett's in protest. "No, Z, we'll figure it out. We still have time, we—"

"With the current force arrayed against her, Nari cannot survive to eject the core. She *must* survive if she is to found the academy, or we will never come here, never plant the seed for Aurora's victory against the Ra'haam. Eliminate the impossible, and what remains, no matter how improbable . . ."

I look to Fin

". . . or painful . . ."

then to Scarlett

". . . or sad . . ."

and last to Nari

"... is the truth. Someone must stay behind and help you."
I let their voices drown each other out.

"—left Cat behind, left my brother behind, and if you
think—"

"—just have to think again about the way we're using
the—"

"—this time I can—"

I stand. I stare. And eventually they are silent. They have
argued themselves out. They see the simple truth, plain as I
have. And they know in their heart of hearts, each of them,
that we do not have the minutes to waste.

So I speak again. "Many years ago, I watched from my
hiding place as raiders threatened my parents and friends. If
I revealed myself, they would be shot, and I would be taken.
So I remained hidden, hoping a solution would reveal itself.
Eventually, our captors tired of waiting, and killed my family
anyway, and left. Never again will I allow those I love to die
through my inaction. This time, there *is* something I can do."

"You were a child, Zila," Scarlett whispers. "You don't
have to make that right."

"I cannot," I reply. "And I know it does not rest on me to
do so. But I have lived this story before, Scarlett, and this
time I will change the ending."

"We can't just leave you here." Finian's pain is in every
line of his face. In the catch in his voice. "We can't just leave
you alone."

I look to Nari again. "I will not be alone."

"But you'll be two centuries in the past!" he cries.

"Someone must be," I say. "Someone was always going to

be. Both of you must return to our time to fight the Ra'haam. You may be all that remains of Squad 312. You must not fail in our duty."

"And you?" Scarlett whispers.

"I will set everything in motion," I say. "We cannot expect Nari to do it all. Someone must leave briefings for the heads of the Aurora Legion. Everything from Björkman's snoring to the gifts in the vault. There is only one way Magellan can know all that he knows."

"You're going to write his program," Finian says softly. His eyes are wet. "Leave it for Scarlett to find on that shopping node."

"Her weakness for handbags is easily exploited."

Scarlett smiles, although she is already beginning to cry.

"*This* is why we are here," I tell them, plucking the tiny fragment of crystal from Pinkerton's trove and holding it up in front of Scarlett. "Why this was left in the vault for us to find. To drag us back here to this place and time so that *I* could remain. Magellan told us that his knowledge of events extended only to a certain point in the future. The point where *I* left."

Finian shakes his head, lip trembling. "Z, we already lost Cat. . . ."

"And we must do so again. Everything must happen exactly as it *has* happened. We must lose Cat so she can save us on Octavia. We must allow the Starslayer to take the Weapon before we do, so that he can fire it and throw us back in time. Because I must always return here, to the beginning of everything. I must remain in the past to safeguard our future."

Scarlett weaves her fingers through mine. Like Finian, she is crying. "We love you too, Zila," she whispers.

I am glad she understands.

"I'll keep her safe, I promise," Nari murmurs, and the shake and the certainty in her voice both warm me. "I'll get her out in the evac. Grab a lab coat. Hopefully things will be confusing enough for me to cover for her."

"They will be," I tell her. "I believe in you."

"You should take Magellan," Finian says, voice rough as he shifts in our small space to dig inside his bag. "He'll be full of useful information if you can repair him. Maybe you can even bet on some sportsball games, build up the bank balance." He pauses then and slowly draws out Shamrock.

He looks at Scarlett. She nods. He hands our mascot to me.

"Extra company," says Scarlett, her voice breaking. "Okay, don't forget our original Longbow will need a crate Auri can hide in, and—shit, we don't even know what Tyler's boots from the vault are *for,* how will you . . . ?"

"He was in Terran captivity when we left him. I will provide him a means of escape. I have a keen intellect, an excellent memory, and the rest of my life ahead," I tell her. "Nothing will be left to chance."

Scarlett is silent a long moment. "Oh, Zila," she murmurs.

"I know," I say quietly.

"I wish . . . ," says Finian, but he does not finish the sentence.

"We have one more chance," I say. "After this, the loop will end before the quantum pulse, and you will have no power source to get home before the loop collapses entirely.

Everything depends on the next fourteen minutes. Everything that is now, everything that will be. Our last chance to stop the Ra'haam. To protect every planet, every colony, every species, every life that is to come." I hold out my hand, one last time. "We can do this."

Scarlett takes hold and squeezes. "We the Legion."

Finian wraps his silver fingers around ours. "We the Light."

Nari puts her hand on ours and nods. "Burning bright against the night."

"Squad 312 forever," I smile.

TICK.

TICK.

TICK.

28

AURI

The battle roars behind us, and ahead lies the dead planet of the Eshvaren.

Power is surging through me, heady and addictive, and I chase the high, my mind freewheeling fast and wild, and I know I'm drawing on my very *self* to crush the enemy, but I can't remember why I shouldn't.

I am the power of the Eshvaren made manifest—that's what Esh told me a lifetime ago in the Echo. I am everything they wished, and all my enemies will *burn*.

The light of the dying red dwarf star frames the planet as we rocket toward it, streaking ahead of our pursuers, and all is quiet on its rocky surface.

Silence ahead of us. Chaos behind.

Kal pounds through the hallways of the ship beneath me, and the *Neridaa* descends toward the huge crater of those massive workshop doors, ten kilometers across. Already they're soundlessly opening, revealing the perfectly smooth tunnel beyond, carved into the rock itself. The ship moves fast, guided with the lightest touch—it's almost as if she *wants* to go home.

"We're following you in," Tyler bellows down comms as a Ra'haam ship smashes into the planet's surface, dying in a blaze of fire and debris. *"Tan, get after it, try and— Maker, you do it, de Mayr!"*

From his throne, Caersan speaks, blood dripping from his chin, his teeth bared in a carnivorous smile.

"I have few regrets in life, child. But I would give a great deal to have seen your face when you discovered I had beaten you here and taken the *Neridaa.*"

"I'm going to enjoy seeing *your* face," I reply. "When I take her off you."

It doesn't sound like me, it doesn't feel like me, but it *is* me talking—my bloody lips twisting as Caersan narrows his eyes.

But the battle is burning all around us, and I'm caught up in that fire, plunging the ship past the doors and into the tunnel, kilometers wide, the Ra'haam and the Free fleets pouring after us. The dark is lit with quick explosions, and all I can hear down comms are screamed commands, cutting over the top of each other, a hopeless mess of orders and pleas.

I let my mind sweep outward, and I find Kal, nearly at the place where the Ra'haam swarm is pouring into our wounded ship, one violet-and-gold beacon against the writhing, starving mass of green and blue.

I anchor a piece of myself to him, and reach out farther to find the *Vindicator,* pushing myself into Tyler's mind, into Lae's, past the exhaustion and the fear and the single-minded focus on the battle.

Kal needs you!

But there is someone else out there too—I can hear his

341

voice, sense the pieces of him that can never be separated now from the whole.

"... *Jie-Lin* ..."

"... *Jie-Lin, come to me.* ..."

"It only calls to you because it fears it cannot win," Caersan hisses, gripping the arms of his throne, knuckles white. "Do not participate in your own defeat, girl. Tears are for the conquered."

We burst into the crystal cavern at the planet's core, and I reach out mentally to stop Kal from falling as the *Neridaa* slows suddenly to a crawl, turning her toward the scaffolding, toward her old cradle.

The chamber is vast—hundreds of kilometers wide— massive cliffs of crystal reflecting the light of the ships spilling behind us, arcs of fire streaming across the rainbow gables above, explosions echoing on ancient crystal.

The scale of this place is breathtaking, the dusty emptiness of eons now filled with the battle to save the future. The power it must have taken to build something like this, the Weapon we ride in—last time I was here, I felt like an insect beside it. But now I feel that same power rushing through me, setting me alight. And as the *Neridaa* settles into place, a feeling of relief washes over me—it's like taking off too-tight shoes, like breathing out.

She's home.

I turn my head and catch a glimpse of blue flowers, and then they're gone, wiped out as a ship flies into a thousand glittering pieces, debris striking its pursuer so it blooms into a second explosion.

Tyler's ship lands beside us, he and his crew spilling out,

but the Ra'haam vessels are soaring into the chamber like a swarm of locusts now, mingled with too few of our own ships, swirling around us in a thick, choking mass.

There's a snatch of music, I swear, just a few intoxicating notes—and then a grunt of effort from Caersan shatters the moment.

We need time—time to repair our broken ship, to heal the fractures running through her skin. And looking to the domed crystal sky above, I know there are too few of our allies left to buy it for us.

And I don't even know where to begin. . . .

But as if in answer, the coppery taste of blood in my mouth turns sweet, and the scene before me begins to fade. I feel a heavy numbness, a gravity pulling me down, and though I cling for a moment, I can feel myself sliding away to somewhere familiar, somewhere I've been before.

But I can't leave him—they're coming!

Kal!

29

KAL

We meet in a broad corridor inside the *Neridaa*. I am bathed in the color of rainbows, surrounded by the roar of the battle raging overhead.

The invaders are a multitude, spilling from their boarding pods into the Weapon's halls. A dozen races, a dozen shapes, all the same mind. Their skin is mottled with mold, flowers in their eyes, and behind those stares, I sense the creature they encompass. A being that was old when my homeworld was a new pebble, slowly cooling around a now-dead sun.

A will that has waited a million years for this triumph.

The rainbow light around me is strobing, the great vaulted ceiling overhead echoes with the death screams of our dwindling fleet. My blades are feathers in my hands, and I make a slaughter of the Ra'haam puppets, dancing the dance of blood as easily as breathing. But I feel another strike against the *Neridaa*'s hull. Another. More boarding pods, I realize. Their numbers endless. And I know against this foe, there can be no victory.

All I can win is time.

On they come through the glimmering halls—another wave. I fall back to narrower ground, where their numbers count for less. A thing comes at me through the flickering rainbow glow, curling leaves where its eyes should be, its horns entwined with a crown of thorns. I slice off its grasping hand, but its other sends me into the wall. Something strikes my back as I stumble to cover—a pulse cannon blast, perhaps. I am not sure, there are so many. . . .

". . . *Stop fighting, Kaliis.* . . ."

Too many.

". . . *Give yourselves to us.* . . ."

A part of me always knew I would fall in battle. I am not afraid to die fighting for something I believe in. But I *am* afraid of leaving her. My Aurora. My beloved. I was a pale shadow before I met her. An unlit fire, waiting for the spark that would let me burn.

Twisted hands reach for me.

Eyes like flowers, glowing blue.

I did not want it to end like this.

The things charging at me burst apart, showering me with blood and gore. I hear more weapon fire, grenades, the hissing whisper of a null blade slicing flesh, and then, above the carnage, a voice that makes my heart soar.

"Toshh, report status!" Tyler shouts.

"Clear, Commander!" the big woman replies, reloading her weapon and checking a scanner. "But we got more inbound! Seventy meters!"

I wipe the mess from my eyes and see Lae standing above me, illuminated by the crackling purple null blade in her fist. As I grasp the bloody hand she offers, I am struck again by the notion that I know this woman. It is a foolish thought, I know—she was not even born when Aurora and I walked through time. And yet . . .

"You fought well," Lae says softly, eyeing the abattoir around me.

I look down the gleaming crystal corridor, back toward the throne room.

"I was taught well."

Her stare hardens. Hate in her eyes.

"He is every bit the monster you think him," I tell her, wiping my blades clean. "But family is . . . complicated."

"You all right, Kal?"

I turn as Tyler strides out of the smoke toward me, his hulking suit of power armor just as war-worn and battered as the man inside it. But I manage a smile despite the pain in me, the death raining all around us.

"You are always a welcome sight, Tyler Jones."

"Keep it in your pants, kid," he grins. "I didn't brush my teeth today." Turning to his people, he begins barking orders. "Dacca, cover that breach! Toshh, get a fire screen on this hallway now! We got more hostiles inbound, and they *cannot* get past us. Twenty seconds to contact, move, move!"

I watch his people scramble, preparing for the next on-slaught. The battle overhead is growing quieter now, the last of our defenders falling. Each of the remainder knows this battle is unwinnable. But still, they obey without question, buoyed by the fire in Tyler's eye, the steel in his voice.

They bear the same love for him that we all did.

Some things never change.

Tyler tosses me a spare rifle. Taking up position behind

a rainbow spire of crystal, in the calm before the storm, he glances to Lae.

"You okay?" he asks softly.

She nods, tossing one silver-gold braid off her shoulder. "I am well."

"If you want to fall back . . ."

He nods to the throne room behind us, fixing her with his one good eye.

"To guard Aurora . . ."

Lae raises her null blade, the crackling glow setting her irises aflame. I can sense the Ra'haam coming now, feel the pressure of its mind pressing down on my own. I can see the cracks around Lae's eyes, the toll of the countless battles she has fought—that they have *all* fought—to keep this tiny flame alive. And even in the face of its fading . . .

"My father taught me to fight with courage," she says, defiant. "But my mother taught me to die with honor."

Tyler shakes his head. "Lae—"

"*No,*" she says, meeting his stare. "I do not fear the Void, any more than she did."

I look between the pair, wondering at the truth of them. They clash like fire and ice, but they are not simply commander and soldier, that much is clear. I can sense a thread between them now, if I try. Thin as a strand of spun sugar but still, strong as star-forged steel.

"Incoming!" Toshh roars. "This is it, people!"

I suppose it does not matter now.

The enemy is upon us.

The song of battle fills the air.

And then there is no more time for words.

30

TYLER

TICK, TICK, TICK.

My heart is thumping a hundred klicks a second now. The image of the academy blowing apart is running on replay, over and over in my head. My pulse pistol is clutched in my sweating hand, the knife Saedii gave me is heavy on my wrist.

TICK, TICK, TICK.

Admiral Adams continues his speech to the assembly above, oblivious to the calamity unfolding below.

"You've gathered here to discuss the growing tide of unrest among the many worlds of our galaxy. But before talks commence, another matter should be brought to your attention, one that concerns not only every species here present, but the life of every creature in the Milky Way."

The shape of the reactor core rises ahead of me—three towering cylinders in a vast circular room, running right through the academy's spine. The walls are lined with heavy conduits, the bright screens of control terminals and monitor stations punctuating the low, pulsing light.

The temperature in here is boiling now, almost too hot to bear. Steam rising, hissing, coiling. Cat has disengaged the cooling lines, pushing the reactor toward overload, while somehow killing the alert systems.

Looking around, I can see shutdown terminals pried open, alarm relays and overrides disengaged. More dead bodies littering the floor. Their necks are broken, spines twisted, mouths open in silent screams.

Cat, what have they done to you?

"The Aurora Legion was established over two hundred years ago, in a time of darkness and strife, in the wake of a war we wished never to repeat," Adams says, voice echoing through the amphitheater. *"Since then, we have functioned as a peacekeeping force, serving the interests of the sentient races of the galaxy. But that has not been our only purpose. And I'm afraid Battle Leader de Stoy and I have not been entirely honest in our reasons for gathering you here today."*

I hear murmurs ripple among the summit audience.

The floor begins shaking beneath my feet.

Adams draws a deep breath, looks around the delegates as the image of a large blue-green planet appears in the holo floating above his head.

"Representatives, delegates, friends, this is the planet Octavia—"

And without warning, the feed sputters and dies.

The lights around me flicker, red to strobing white. The floor shakes again beneath my feet. The light from the reactor burns brighter, the heat more intense, and through the shimmering air I spot her, bent over another terminal, the burning light of the core reflected in her blank mirrormask.

She doesn't know I'm here. She's intent solely on her sabotage. I sink slowly to one knee, thumb the power setting on my pulse pistol to Kill. Focusing only on the uniform. The threat. Not thinking about the girl underneath, the girl I used to know, the girl who begged me to stay.

Tyler, I love you. . . .

I take aim with my pistol, right at her heart.

One shot, and it's over.

TICK, TICK, TICK.

"JONES!" comes a roar. "FREEZE!"

I turn, heart sinking as half a dozen Legion security troopers pour through the blast door behind me, their disruptor rifles raised. Glancing back at my target, I see Cat whirl away from her terminal, hear a sharp intake of breath turned metallic by that faceless mask.

"*TYLER.*"

Cat draws a long, sleek GIA-issue blast pistol from inside her uniform.

The troopers behind me roar a warning.

I crack off my shot, but Cat dives aside, unloading her own weapon at the SecTeam. And the air is filled with the *BAMF!BAMF!BAMF!* of Legion disruptors, the sizzle of Cat's blaster, the hiss of my own pistol as a three-way firefight for the future of the galaxy breaks out in the reactor room.

I dive behind a bank of computer terminals for cover, roaring to the SecTeam, "She's trying to blow the reactor core! We've got to—"

I hear the bright ping of metal on metal, my eyes widening as two flash-pulse grenades hit the ground beside me. Gasping, I throw myself clear, buffeted by the blast as the explosives detonate. I'm thrown hard into the wall, collapsing to the ground behind a bank of steel piping, tasting blood on my teeth and tongue, ears ringing with static.

"I'm on *your* side, you *ASSHOLES!*"

I see movement—a sleek shadow dashing through the dark to another terminal. I duck out from cover to shoot, but a burst of disruptor blasts opens up at my back—*BAMF!BAMF!BAMF!*—and I'm forced behind cover again, the air about me sizzling.

I'm pinned down.

There's no way I can get to her.

"Cat!" I roar. "Cat, please don't do this!"

No reply but the heavy tread of Legion boots on metal. More troopers are pouring into the room now, fanning out to flank me. I don't want to shoot them, they're my people—*We the Legion. We the light*—but if they catch me flat-footed, with all those dead personnel on the ground at my back and the charge of mass murder and galactic terrorism over my head . . .

"Cat, *please!*" I shout. "I know you can hear me!"

"Jones, it's *over!* Toss your weapon!"

I catch a glimpse of her through the swirling steam. The pulsing light. The thrumming, boiling air. But I don't have a clear shot. My breath is hammering. My body dripping. That image playing over and over in my aching head: crystal splintering, academy exploding, that voice, that *voice* now begging, *screaming* in my head.

. . . You can fix this, Tyler . . .

FIX THIS, TYLER.

I draw a deep breath. Think of my sister. Of Saedii. Auri

and Kal and Fin and Zila. And whispering a prayer to the Maker, I dive across the floor, pistol in hand as I roll up onto my knee, drawing aim right at Cat's head.

BAMF!

The blast hits me in the hip. Pain rips through my body, the blast burning clean through my flesh as I gasp in agony, cracking off my shot. I see it strike Cat in the left arm and she whirls, hissing in pain.

BAMF!

The second shot strikes my temple. I feel bone crack, flesh cauterize, my eye sizzling in its socket as I fall forward, pistol slipping from my hand and clattering across the grille.

BAMF!

The third shot hits my lower back, bursts out through my belly. Burned blood spatters onto the metal in front of me. I gasp again, white light in my head, no feeling in my legs as they go out from under me. I hit the deck, blood in my mouth, cracking my brow hard on the metal. There's blood on my face. I can't see out of my right eye, I can't—

Running boots.

Pulsing heat.

A shadow falls over me, and as I roll over, groaning, I see a Legion uniform, a disruptor rifle aimed square at my face. "Game over, trait—"

Something slams into the figure from the side—something long and gleaming, moving like liquid. The trooper's torso is torn away from his hips, his body collapsing in a spray of gore. I hear roars of alarm, what sounds like a cracking whip, wet, splashing sounds. A shadow flashes overhead, charcoal gray, pale white, tiny pinpricks of glowing blue, flower-shaped.

Cat.

I blink hard, tracking her movement through the steam. She moves among the troopers like a razor, like a demon, like a monster. Her mask is cast aside, blue eyes aglow, burning with ghostly light. Sick with horror, I see the arm of her GIA uniform has been torn off where I shot her. And from that bloody rent, a long cluster of thorned tentacles is spilling, two, three meters long—the same blue green as those awful plants that engulfed the colony on Octavia, lashing through the air, sharp as swords.

She cuts through the troopers as though they were made of paper and she of broken glass. They roar in alarm and fire back, disruptor shots ripping through the air. But she doesn't stop, barely slows, hardly breathes as she tears them all to ribbons, leaving them smeared up the walls and scattered in pieces across the floor.

And then she stands, head bowed, shoulders slumped, breathing hard, that long mass of thorned whips seething at her side and dripping blood onto already soaking ground.

I close my good eye. Salt and copper in my mouth. Trying to rise.

Trying to reach for my fallen pistol.

Trying to—

"Tyler."

She stands over me, and my heart breaks at the sight of her. Two tiny flowers of blinding blue burn in her irises. Her uniform is covered in blood. I can see the shape of what she used to be in the line of her lips, the phoenix tattoo at her throat. But my eye drifts to those long, barbed tendrils, spilling from the torn sleeve where her arm should be.

Blood is pooling at my back. My legs are growing cold.

My face is numb. The logical part of my mind tells me I'm going into shock, I'm bleeding out, I'm dying. But it's not the logical part of my mind that whispers.

"You s-saved me."

She kneels beside me, looking at me with those eyes that were once brown. Still somehow filled with the same love she used to carry for me.

"An Ace always backs her Alpha," she smiles.

I'm almost crying, sobbing as she reaches out and runs her fingertip down my scorched brow, my mangled cheek.

I'm wondering if I somehow got through to her, if she's somehow realized what she's become, my voice just a shaking whisper as I ask, "Why?"

"Don't you understand? I *love* you, Tyler." She smiles, infinitely sad, infinitely gentle. "So *we* love you too."

She rises to her feet, arm writhing, and walks back toward the terminals. I struggle to raise my head, follow her through the steam, the flashing red. Her fingers blur across a series of controls, and the blast door comes crashing down, sealing us inside the chamber with a heavy *THUMP*.

"Wh—" I wince, holding my guts in. "What are you d-doing?"

She keeps typing, the light shifting deeper, the floor shaking harder.

"Ending this."

I frown, trying to rise. "But . . . you s-s . . ."

"We wanted it to be us, Tyler." Glowing blue eyes fix me through the swirling vapor, the rising dark. "In the end. You deserve for it to be us."

"Cat . . . ," I whisper, heart breaking. "Y-you'll die too. . . ."

"No." She shakes her head, tears glittering in her eyes. "This flesh will die. But my memories, my thoughts, my love will live on. We wish you could have been in here with us. We wish you could have understood."

"Cat . . ."

"We'll miss you, Tyler. So, *so* much."

I try to get up, blood spilling through my fingers, but the pain is too much to bear. I crawl toward her a meter or two, sticky red fingers scraping metal, my fingernails breaking. But I'm hurt too bad. Lost too much blood.

It's hard to think. Hard to breathe. Hard to ignore that vision of the station coming apart, the thought of my friends, my family, everything we've given and lost ending here like this and just think, think, *think*.

"Does it hurt?" she asks.

I cough blood, swallow thickly as I nod.

"I'm sorry," she breathes. "It won't be for much longer, Ty."

I reach toward her, bloody fingers curling. I try to speak, but choke instead. I don't want to die here. Not like this.

And I'm so scared of it, so *scared* of dying alone, for an awful moment I wonder what it would be like to be one with it.

Because that's what the Ra'haam is, I realize.

To never be alone.

I beckon her closer. Whispering. "K . . . Ki . . ."

"What?" she asks.

"Kiss," I whisper, ". . . g-goodbye?"

The tears are shining in her eyes as she stops typing. I can hear the sound of heavy thumping at the blast doors now, faint voices, an alarm finally being sounded. But it's all too late, I know. Too late. They'll never get in here in time. Cat moves through the dark toward me, a small black shadow with a bigger shadow inside her, so vast and hungry it's going to swallow the stars.

She kneels at my side. Looks me in the eyes.

"Kiss m-me," I beg her.

She sighs, tears falling from those glowing eyes. And running her fingers down my cheek, she leans in and presses her lips to mine. For a moment, I'm back in that hotel on shore leave with her, the one and only night we spent together. All the love she had for me shining in her gaze, shattering like glass when I told her we shouldn't, we couldn't be together afterward.

I should have loved her better. I should have loved her *more*. And I try to tell her, with the breath I have left in me, with the lips I press to hers, opening my mind and pouring into her, telling her I'm sorry.

I love you.

And then I drive the knife right into her neck.

She reels back, flower eyes gone wide, blood spilling from her throat. But Saedii's knife is sharper than razors, monofilament edge and Syldrathi alloy cutting clean through meat and artery and bone.

I stab again, again, drenched by the look of hurt and pain and fury in her eyes as she stumbles back onto her haunches, dark blood gushing from the wounds. Tiny tendrils whip from the edges of the stab wounds, pale and bloody, snaking blindly in the air.

The tentacles at her side flare, snaking around my neck, but she collapses before they can squeeze, shock etched on her paling face as her legs kick feebly, heels scraping, breath rattling.

She tries to talk. Choking instead. Glowing eyes on mine.

"I'm s-sorry," I whisper. "I'm s-so sorry, Cat."

And I crawl.

Across the soaking deck. A sluice of red behind. Dragging myself with broken fingernails, holding my pieces together with bloody hands.

Ignoring the pain, the hurt, I crawl.

Like the life of every sentient being in the galaxy depends on it.

I *crawl*.

I reach the terminal. Scrabbling with red, sticky hands. Black flowers bloom in front of my eye, every breath bubbles in my lungs. But finally, I manage to stab the controls, release the blast doors. I collapse onto my back, gasping, coughing blood, as tech teams and comp crews and security goons all bust into the core room, through the swirling steam, the rising red.

But not too late.

Not too late.

. . . You can fix this, Tyler . . .

The laser sights of a dozen disruptor rifles light up my chest.

I slump back against the terminal, light fading in my eye.

"Checkmate," I whisper.

31

AURIKAL

Aurora

I'm standing in the Echo, the place I lived for half a year, the place I trained to become the Trigger I am.

But it's nothing like I remember.

To my right, rolling fields of flowers once led to a crystal city on the horizon. To my left, a valley used to dip toward the woods. Before me, a lively river once splashed and chattered its way beneath a sky of perfect blue.

But it's all broken now. Fractured just like the *Neridaa*. Cracks run across the gray heavens like the fissures in the Weapon's skin. The flowers are smashed like glass, the river splintered like ice, the crystal spires on the horizon lopsided and tumbled. Even the air tastes . . . wrong. And as my heart sinks and I look around the desolation, a familiar figure is floating through the shattered fields of flowers toward me.

Esh is human-shaped but far from human, a creature of light and crystal, rainbows refracting within it, right eye white and glowing, just as mine must be. It looks different now too; thin cracks run through its surface, light leaking from within. But relief rushes through me at the sight of my old teacher, and in an instant I'm running through the broken flowers to meet it.

"Esh! Holy cake, I'm so glad to see you, we—"

G-g-greetings. It cuts me off, tone as musical as ever, gently courteous. *Welcome to t-the Echo. I am t-the Eshvaren.*

"Yeah, I know," I tell it. "Esh, what happened here, w—"

You do not meet the p-parameters for training. State your business.

"I know, I don't need to train, I . . ."

I trail off as realization hits me, and my heart drops. I remember this isn't really a *person* I'm talking to—this is only a projection. An amalgam of the memories and wisdom of the entire Eshvaren race. And just like they told me it would, after I left last time, the amalgam reset. Esh doesn't remember me, any more than it remembered Caersan the first time I showed up.

Mothercustard.

State your b-business, Esh repeats simply.

"Okay, I'm a Trigger. You trained me. I'm here with another Trigger, who's an utter sociopath; and why you decided to give all godlike power to a complete . . ." I shake my head, pushing on. "Anyway, it's a long story. Point is, the Weapon is damaged and we need to repair it—fast."

We . . . Esh's image flickers, like a faulty viewscreen. *We f-feel it. We . . .* It looks up to the gray, cracked sky, down to the cracks running through its hands. *What . . . h-have you done?*

359

A flash of pain cuts through my head, and in my mind's eye, I see a fragment of the battle raging outside. Time moves slow outside the Echo, like ice cream melting on a hot day. But I see more Ra'haam vessels spilling into the cavern, the few remaining ships we have burning in slow motion.

Inside the *Neridaa,* I feel Tyler—a spark of him, a faint but beautiful molten-gold flame that I never noticed before now. Beside him I feel Lae, a reflection of those same colors. And between them I feel Kal, gold and violet in that smothering cold.

I feel his rage.

I feel his fear.

I know I don't have long.

"We got thrown through time," I tell Esh. "Two Triggers together . . . I don't know. But the Ra'haam is here! The whole Milky Way is ending! We need to fix the Weapon now—can you help?"

Esh studies me for a long moment.

The galaxy holds its breath.

N-no, it says.

Kal

The blades are lead in my hands, my body slick with sweat inside my armor. I stumble in the blood, thick and sticky upon the crystalline floor.

"*. . . Kaliis . . .*"

I do not listen to its voice, the pistol in my hand flaring.

"*. . . We know you love her, Kaliis. We love her, too. . . .*"

Around me, the *Vindicator*'s crew fights with all the fury of those with nothing to lose. I feel the Enemy Within awakening—the part of me shaped by the man in that throne room, who delights in war and carnage. I have fought against it for as long as I can remember, this thing he tried to twist me into. But as much as I hate him, I am glad he is within me now.

. . . There is only one way you may save her. One way she might live, eternal, your love evergreen in the light of a warmth all-consuming . . .

Do not listen to its voice. Listen to his.

Mercy is for the weak.

Peace is for the coward.

Tears are for the conquered.

More are coming. Dozens. Hundreds. I look to Tyler, and his face is grim. Lae meets my eyes, and I can see the death that stalks us.

But we cannot allow them to get to Aurora.

"Hurry, be'shmai," I whisper.

Aurora

"No?" I ask, my voice rising. "What do you mean, *no*? You built the thing! You should know how to fix it!"

The image flickers again, like a transmission losing power. I can feel the ground shake beneath my feet. Outside, the Ra'haam drips closer, like molasses, thick and sickly sweet. Toward Kal, Tyler, the others . . .

"Esh!" I shout.

The Echo. The Weapon itself. This p-personification of

361

us . . . all are linked. As it is damaged, so t-too are we. We can-
not h-help you.

Another tremor passes through the ground. Lightning cracks the shattered sky above. I can feel them out there, bleeding in slow motion, one by one falling under those impossible numbers. I'm not sure what Esh even means, but every second we spend speaking, my defenders are dying.

I look around the Echo, to Esh itself. Mind racing.

"If this place and the Weapon are linked . . ."

I reach toward the closest object, lying in a hundred rose-colored pieces on the grass. I can feel the remnants of the energies in this place. See the way it used to be in my mind's eye, all those months I spent in here with Kal, clear as glass. And as my eye begins to glow, I pull the pieces together, reforming it in the palm of my hand.

A single, perfect flower.

In answer, outside beyond the Echo, I feel a tiny crack in the Weapon's hull stitch itself closed.

Yes, Esh nods. *You s-see.*

I close my eyes, slow my breathing, slow my mind, taking in my surroundings—real and virtual—and attuning myself to both. I can still sense the others beyond—quick brushes of Kal's familiar mind, of Tyler's, even, and of Lae's. I can taste their fear and courage, their grief as their friends fall, their fury at the thing taking them away. And above and around it all, I can feel the creeping unnaturalness of the Ra'haam.

It wants me. . . .

I trained as a cartographer for the Octavia mission for years. And walking here in the Echo every day with Kal, I

362

couldn't help learning the shape of this place. I draw that memory close, remembering what this place was.

The way it can be again.

But it's so big, to hold it all inside my head. . . .

Hard as I try, I can't. . . .

"I can't," I hiss, trembling hand outstretched.

You must.

I reach out both hands, face twisting as I try to hold it all.

"We're running out of time, help me!"

But Esh only shakes its head.

"I can't do this alone!"

Kal

We are failing.

The Ra'haam has pushed us back, Tyler's crew falling one by one as we give ground. The crystalline floors are awash with blood, the stink of death hangs in the air, and the enemy simply keeps coming.

"Lae, fall back!" Tyler roars, blasting from behind cover.

She dances among those awful figures, null blade aglow, cutting down a flower-eyed monstrosity lunging for Dacca's back.

"Back *where*?" she shouts.

She speaks truth—we can retreat no farther. Behind us is the entrance to the throne room. If the enemy reaches my father and Aurora, all hope will be—

A shot hits my legs, thick and viscous. It is like . . . glue, pinning my leg to the floor. Another strikes my belly, and I fall, covered in more of this sticky ooze. I realize I cannot move, stuck like an insect in amber, and horror unfurls as I understand the Ra'haam does not wish to *kill* us—it wishes to subdue us, drag us into its awful singularity.

"Kal," Tyler roars, "look out!"

I slice at the hands grasping at me, scream a denial in my mind, reaching for Aurora, refusing to let it end like this. And I flinch as a burning arc of energy, deep red like dried blood, scythes through the oncoming Ra'haam.

Another blast hits them, a sphere of raw psychic power smearing their bodies upon the walls, leaving only broken corpses in its wake.

Tyler blinks in astonishment. Lae only snarls. But I realize who has saved us.

"Father . . ."

He stands above me with hands outstretched, clad in black steel. His eyes are bruised, lips and chin smudged with violet where he has wiped away the blood. I can see the cracks in his face run deeper, his fingers trembling—just the slightest signs of strain from his ordeal.

But his eye burns like a star. And much as I hate him, I feel the Enemy Within surge as he shatters my bonds with a wave of his hand.

"No child of Caersan dies on their knees, Kaliis. *Fight.*"

Aurora

I can't do this alone.

As the battle rages on outside, I'm giving everything I have—as much as those outside are giving—to mend the tears in the Echo around me. But there's so much of it. It's too big.

I try to drag the images into focus, remember the way this place once was. Walking through rolling fields of flowers with Kal beside me, his hand in mine, and at the thought of him, a part of me reaches for him, across the ocean between us, and it's then I realize.

It's then I see.

I can't do this alone.

But I'm *not* alone.

He's with me. Always. And not just Kal, but Tyler, too. I can feel him out there, his crew beside him, all those people—survivors I never even got the chance to meet, children and warriors, fierce and frightened, standing with the last of their loved ones or alone, the last of their kind.

Every one of them is fighting and dying, the future of the galaxy in the balance, giving everything for the chance of a different yesterday.

"I'm not alone," I whisper.

—I'm with a pilot named Simann, trying desperately
to shake the Weeds on my tail, and I knew this
moment was coming, but the fear is like ice in my
gut, and I reach out to the holo of my husband on
the dash and I know everything will be all right
because I'll see him again soon, and

—I'm in the Echo, and the clear water of the river
has turned to blood, but I ignore what I see, and
with a dip of my finger, I sketch it in the air from
memory, from my thousand training sessions
beside it, and

—I'm standing with Dacca as she fights against the
swarm, and I'm thinking of my siblings, all of us
sitting in the light of the hearthstone as our father
tells us stories about the old heroes, and I'm
wondering if I'll ever grow up to be one and now
realizing I am, I *am,* and

        —I'm in the Echo, opening myself to the flood
        outside and throwing back my head as a million
        pieces of broken glass rise up from the ground and
        coalesce into a field of beautiful flowers, and

—I'm with Elin, the surly Betraskan from Tyler's
crew, and I'm fighting back to back with Toshh
and I think about how stupid I was not to just
ask her before now, to tell her how I feel, and our
shoulders bump as we back toward each other
and she catches my eye and smiles and suddenly I
realize that she knows, she's *always* known, and

        —I'm building mountains in my mind, the grove
        where Kal and I slept, and every one of my warriors
        is helping me in some way, lending me some piece of
        themselves, some final touch or thought or memory
        that tells me I'm not alone, that all of us are together,
        their presence flowing through me like water. The
        Eshvaren tried to teach me to burn them all away,
        but love was always what I needed to fight for, but

—as I reach out toward them, the ones I know and
need most and love best

        —I can feel something wrong, I can feel
—Something is *wrong.* . . .

Kal

"Fall *back!*" Tyler roars.

One by one, Tyler's people have been taken by the flood—the people on Sempiternity, those ships that saluted us farewell, and now Toshh and Elin and Dacca and the rest of the *Vindicator's* crew.

A tiny piece of his heart has gone with each of them. But still, he fights. For what he has left.

Tyler, Lae, my father, and me.

Aurora, beyond the doors to the throne room.

And the one moment in our past that can change all of this.

The enemy are too many. My father cuts them down with wave after wave of power, and as I stand beside him, the part of me raised in his shadow is singing in adulation.

But the rest of me is mute with horror, that this will be not just our fate but the galaxy's. More are coming, always more, not just humanoid now but other shapes—multi-armed behemoths from Manaria IV, stone-fisted hulks from the Tartallus Drift, moss-ridden and twisted and One.

I can see a glow pulsing through the crystal around us, warm and soothing. The cracks seem to be closing, and my heart surges as I think Aurora may be succeeding, but something is holding it back, stifling it, I . . .

I look to the tunnel behind us, the pulses of light from the throne room.

"Fall back!" Tyler shouts again.

My father grits his teeth, snarling, "Hold your ground, Terran!"

"We can bottleneck them!" Lae screams. "Buy a few more minutes!"

They appear out of the smoke, soaring through the *Neri-daa*'s halls on wings encrusted in dull blue green. They were almost extinguished when my father destroyed Syldra. But still they come, three of them landing like thunder among the Ra'haam's rotten legion. The impact sends Lae to her knees, Tyler and me stumbling as the cavern around us echoes with roars.

"Maker, not again," Tyler growls.

"Drakkan," Lae whispers.

The mighty creatures move swift as silver, big as houses. But the first of them still falls, split in half as my father's fingers slice the air. The second staggers as I hurl the last of my pulse bombs into its mouth, and my father raises his hand and splinters its neck. But the third lunges with sinuous speed, striking at Lae, still on her knees.

Its claws are enough to cut steel, its teeth sharper than swords, and though she twists upright, she is not swift enough. The claws descend, eyes gleam like flowers.

But with a roar of denial, a figure leaps between drakkan and prey, power armor whining as those terrible claws strike home and send the pair sailing across the gore-washed floor.

"TYLER!"

Aurora

—a crack reopens in the sky above, and I feel the
song of the wind change through the trees growing
around me

—there's a Syldrathi boy on his knees, a girl
watching as his father kicks him in the ribs, and
the boy silently, stubbornly refuses to fight back,
and I start forward with his name on my lips.

"Kal!"

—the crystal city on the horizon is crumbling, and
I am frantically, stubbornly drawing it back onto
the map of my mind in all its glory, but I feel that
shadow between them, and

—a Syldrathi boy and girl stand together as their
parents scream at each other. And neither
understands but each of them is watching and
learning and my stomach sinks as I see a shadow
take root in their hearts and I feel the tangle of
pain and love from *all four of them.*

"Caersan, you have to fix it!" I cry.
He turns in my vision to gaze at me, unreadable.
"It is *not* broken," he snarls, because he doesn't even
know how to see what's wrong, and roaring "Weakling girl!"
he throws me out of his mind, and

—I scream at him because I feel it now, the massive,
cloying warmth of the Ra'haam, so close, so big, and
I know I can't stop it without all of them, without
him I can't fix this, and he won't listen, he won't help
me, and I can feel it inside them, that shadow, like a
cancer, blocking me, stopping me, and

—If I can't stop it now

                                       —Can't stop it now

—I know I can't stop it then.

         —I'm with Tyler, and he's standing on the bridge of
a ship with Saedii in the time before she was taken
away, before he even really knew he loved her. And
he's still young and still bright and he reminds me
of that time we danced back on Sempiternity, me in
my beautiful red dress, and him in those ridiculous
pants, so full of hope and daring, and I look up
at his handsome face, and he doesn't know what's
coming, and I think . . .

—*you still have a chance of fixing this, Tyler Jones.
You told me when it happens where it happens*

—*how it happens* and

—in this place where time means nothing and a
minute can last a lifetime, and I can do anything
if I can imagine it, I pour myself into one moment,
leaving everything behind, and I reach out across
the gulf to scream a warning back in time to
the boy he once was because I don't know if we
can make it here, but maybe he can fix it there,
because if he doesn't, there might be nothing, and

                            —There might be nothing

—There *is* nothing I—

"TYLER!"

Kal

"TYLER!"

I skid to my brother's side as another pulse of blood-red power flares around us. Lae is still cradled in his arms, bruised and bewildered. But my heart twists as I see blood spilling from his mouth, his ruptured armor, his neck. My father lashes out again, a spherical flare of power smashing the last drakkan to pulp. But the damage is done. . . .

"I s-suppose killing two of those b-bastards in one lifetime was a b-bit much to expect," Tyler winces.

"Get up," I tell him, slinging his arm about my shoulder. "Quickly."

"Forg-get it," he coughs, chest rattling. "G-go."

"No," Lae breathes, looking at me. "We must—"

"We will." I ignore Tyler's bloody protest, hauling him upright. "Father!"

He glances at me, eyes ablaze, swimming in the blood as if born to it.

"Father, we must fall back!"

"Go, then!"

Gasping, desperate, Lae and I drag Tyler down through the tunnel leading to the throne room. The walls pulse in tune around us, the screams of the dying and the thrum of power washing over me like rain. Again I feel that warmth, but again I feel the wrongness between us, the shadow.

Aurora floats in the room's heart, head back, eye burning with the light of a million suns. I grimace, lower Tyler gently, my hands covered in his blood.

Lae's face is twisted, eyes filled with tears. "No . . ."

"Aurora!" I roar. "HURRY!"

My father has followed us into the throne room, backing away reluctantly, step by bloody step. The Ra'haam follows, and in final, bitter desperation, he roars, arms outstretched.

The crystal walls splinter, and the *Neridaa* seems to cry out in pain as the tunnel collapses, sealing us inside.

But they are already battering on the barrier, and I know for all it cost him, he has only bought us a few minutes.

"It is *not* broken," my father growls.

". . . Father?"

"Weakling girl!"

The walls around us shiver, Aurora's cheeks shining with tears.

Tyler takes Lae's hand and squeezes, his breath now swift and shallow.

"She was p-proud of you."

The light in him fading.

"I am t-too. . . ."

Tears spill from Lae's shattered eyes. And I see it then. Focusing on her face—the pride, the ferocity, those features so odd and yet so familiar. Her hair that curious alloy of silver and gold.

Tyler's words ring in my skull over the sound of the approaching enemy.

"I actually teamed up with her and her old crew to fight the Ra'haam."

"She was a hell of a woman, your sister."

"I always thought Saedii hated our mother," I say, looking between them. "But her name . . ."

". . . was Laeleth," Tyler whispers, smiling sadly.

"Brother . . . ?" I whisper.

The last of him fades. The light in him extinguished.

Lae bows her head, silver-gold braids drenched blood-red hanging over her face as she opens her mouth. Her scream rings on the walls, echoed by Aurora, by the *Neridaa* herself, the power crashing against the growing cracks like waves upon a stony shore. I reach out to my friend, tears in my eyes.

"Brother . . ."

"*Get* up," a voice spits.

I turn toward him, as ever looming above me like a shadow.

"Get on your feet!" my father roars, glowering at the pair of us. "We are *Syldrathi*! Our ancestors walked the stars when his were slime in the ocean! There is a war to be won, and still you weep for this Terran cur?"

Lae turns, teeth bared in a snarl.

"Do not *dare*," she spits. "Do not *dare* to name my father *cur*."

The walls thunder again, the things in the collapsed tunnel digging closer, the ceiling shaking, broken crystal falling like rain.

"Father?" The Starslayer's eyes flash, and he spits blood on the floor as the *Neridaa* shakes. "A *Terran*? Disgusting. What kind of honorless wretch would lie with the likes of him and still name herself Syldrathi?"

I shake my head, almost laughing.

"You are such a *fool*."

"And you are a child," he snarls. "Ever your mother's son."

"And proud of it!" I roar, rising. "And if you had given me but one *drop* of the ocean of love she did, I might still say the same of you! But all you are is hate!" I spread my arms, taking in the shaking ship, the broken rainbow light. "And *this* is what comes of it! The end of a galaxy! And for what?"

"For the honor of our people, boy!"

"You killed our world! You killed our people! What honor lies in that?"

"They were *traitors*!" he roars. "They sought peace with the Terrans! No true child of Syldra would abase themselves by lying with our enemies!"

"Tell that to your daughter!"

He falls still, burning eyes gone wide. "What—"

"Look at her!" I shout, pointing to Lae.

The walls around us tremble. The rainbow light darkens. Aurora's mouth opens and closes, as if she would speak.

He breathes soft, staring bewildered at Lae. "My . . ."

"You taught us war," I tell him. "You taught us fear. You taught us *blood* and *rage* and *enemy*. And yet even Saedii found it in herself to love a human. To bear his child. To die defending all you left broken in your wake."

Tears burn on my cheeks as I look to my niece.

"Your children have stood in the shadow of your hatred all their lives. And still, Saedii made something this beautiful." I turn to my father, shaking my head. "Imagine what we could have made, if only you had loved us."

"Fix this. . . ."

I turn, see Aurora floating in the center of the room. The power wells within her, enveloping me, us, refracting from the broken crystal around us. Tears brim in her eyes as she looks to my father.

"It is not *broken!*" he snarls.

"Caersan, I can't do this alone."

She reaches toward him, all the galaxy in the balance.

"Fix this."

32

THREE ONE TWO

Scarlett—fourteen minutes remaining

Zila's in my arms, all sharp angles to my softness, and I wish this wasn't the first and last time I'll ever hold her. I'm a snotty mess, and even though I know she's right, I don't know if I can take one more loss. I can do what I have to do, but what will be left of me on the other side?

But she gives me this moment, doesn't pull away, just stays in my arms, real and whole and a part of my life for a few seconds more. And then . . . then something unwinds inside her, and she relaxes against me, head on my shoulder for a single heartbeat.

And I know she's ready. She's become who she needs to be to do this. And the parts of that transformation that don't come straight from her, they were gifts from us.

I look up, eyes still swimming with tears, and Nari's gaze is waiting.

I promise I have her, those solemn eyes say.

I squeeze Zila one more time, still looking across at the

girl who'll guard her for us. *She's everything,* my own gaze tells her in reply. And, *She needs someone to care for her.*

Lieutenant Nari Kim simply nods. She already knows. She sees.

I draw back, let Zila go, and Finian slips a hand into mine.

There's nothing more to say, and no time to say it anyway.

So the two of us turn, and we run.

Zila—twelve minutes remaining

It is strange to be following Nari instead of guiding her through comms, but I know every step as if I have run it myself a hundred times. Nari and I take a corner, flatten ourselves against a doorway, counting precious seconds as the patrol passes by at the end of the hall.

Finian and Scarlett will divert them in a moment. And so Nari and I will reach the core forty-five seconds sooner than she has before.

It would not be enough for her on her own. But it will give her time to defend me.

Together, we can do this.

Finian—ten minutes remaining

"Maker's hairy—"

"Less talk, more run!" Scar gasps.

The sec patrol pounds down the hallway behind us, radioing for backup and probably immediate missile drops on our current location. There's a Betraskan aboard their station, and now they know it.

So the good news is, we've distracted them. The bad news

is that we're nearly at the docking bays, and if we don't lose the goons on our tail, stealing a ship is going to be preeeeeetty tricky.

Then I see it, up ahead at the intersection, mounted on a wall bracket. If it comes out easy, we live. If it sticks, we die.

"Scar," I gasp. "Bank left."

She doesn't question—throwing herself around the corner just as I'm grabbing the fire extinguisher and yanking it free. And with a prayer to the Maker, I hurl it back at the goons chasing us.

They try to shoot me—one of them comes so close I almost get a haircut. But their shots also hit the extinguisher, blasting it apart. In a moment, the whole corridor is filled with fine white powder, and I'm blinded by it, inhaling a sharp chemical mouthful and feeling my way through the pale cloud to the door Scarlett's holding open.

I slip inside, both hands clapped over my mouth to muffle my gasping coughs. The door hums closed, and we listen as the patrol reaches the intersection, curses up a storm, and divides four ways, pounding away from our hiding place.

Suckers.

Zila—eight minutes remaining

Liebermann went down without shooting Nari this time. The security guards outside the lab have been incapacitated. We reach the sign.

NO UNAUTHORIZED PERSONNEL BEYOND THIS POINT.

"SECURITY ALERT, LEVEL 2. REPEAT: SECURITY ALERT, LEVEL 2."

A stolen passcard against the door. A deep electronic hum.

And the announcement that tells me there are eight minutes remaining until the implosion of the station and the end of our final loop.

"WARNING: CONTAINMENT BREACH ESCALATION UNDER WAY, ENGAGE EMERGENCY MEASURES DECK 9."

And I am here in person, in the large circular room I have seen over and over through Nari's eyes. A cylindrical glass case dominates the space, cords and conduits connecting it to the computer banks against the walls. Our target is within, cracked and suspended midair, pulsing with light.

The first time I saw one of these probes, Aurora touched it, and lived half a year inside the Echo with Kal. I wonder briefly how they are. If they make it. If all of this will be worth it.

"What the hell are you doing here?"

Nari stuns the man in the white radsuit. Stuns his companion before he has time to draw his sidearm this time. I drop to my knees, plunge my hands into the machinery, narrowing my focus to the task at hand.

This moment is all that matters.

"Twenty seconds till company arrives," Nari murmurs, perfectly still, eyes fixed on the door. A hawk hovering, waiting for her chance.

The system to eject the crystal out into space is mechanical rather than electronic—in case of a power failure, I suppose. There are four locks holding the probe in place, one at each compass point, and all must be disengaged manually. But the mechanisms are heavy, bolted shut. Scanning the

379

floor around me, I crawl toward one of the unconscious engineers. Shoving him onto his back, I search his tool belt, grabbing a heavy wrench.

Hurry, Zila, hurry. This time you can save them.

"Heads up!" Nari shouts, and the doors burst open, and everything is sound and light, smoke billowing around me, and I spare one hand to tug my shirt up over my mouth and nose. The wrench fits onto the first of the couplings. I yank it, yank it again. It loosens. I pull it free.

Crawling to the second lock, I ignore the fire sizzling over my head, the smell of melting metal. Nari is holding them off, but there are so many, and I know there are only seconds remaining until one of them uses the covering fire of the others to charge into the lab.

I glance at the probe and wrench the second lock free, the alarms ringing louder. It still hovers, still pulses with light, anchoring my friend here.

Now.

"Zila!" Nari shouts as weapons roar and the column above her head explodes in a shower of sparks. "Hurry up!"

I crawl to the next lock on my belly, sirens screeching in my ears. My hands are slick with sweat, the wrench slipping in my grip as I pull hard, face twisting, finally uncoupling the third bolt.

"ZILA!" Nari roars.

"Ten seconds," I shout back.

I am at the fourth lock now, fitting the wrench into place and yanking with all my strength to turn it. The last coupling resists, stubborn, infuriating, the fate of the entire galaxy resting in my hands. I am not a religious person, but a part of me desperately wishes I was.

"Please," I whisper to whoever is listening.

Please.

And finally, finally, the bolt comes loose.

For a moment more, the pulsing glow lingers. The energy flowing through to the broken probe stutters. And at last, the light within flickers.

Then dies.

With a hollow clunk, the cylinder containing it opens, the broken probe slipping free, ushered out into the cold void of space.

Powerless.

Lifeless.

I did it.

But there is no time for celebration. Nari backs up toward me, still firing, cursing. The air is filled with gunfire, the noise almost deafening.

Five seconds.

Nari spends the last of her ammunition on the doorway, then ducks behind my column, lacing her hands together as we planned.

I drop the wrench and rise, planting one boot on her joined hands.

With a grunt, she stands, boosting me upward. I punch at the ceiling vent and grab the edges of the hole, pulling myself up in one movement, swinging around with no regard for the pain as I jam myself into too small a space, and lowering my upper body down to reach for her.

Nari jumps, and another bank explodes behind her, and for a moment I think our hands will not connect, because she is not tall.

Then her palms slap into mine, and with everything I

have, I pull her up just as the security patrol bursts in through the door.

Finian—seven minutes remaining

We're later than usual, and the docking bays are alive, our usual path to our shuttle gone. My head is swimming, heart pounding, and as I crouch by Scar in the shadow of a supply vessel, I try to breathe deep to calm myself.

It whistles in my throat, a weird, high noise. I can still taste that piece-of-chakk fire extinguisher. Ugh. What do Terrans *put* in those things?

"We still have to try for the same ship," Scarlett whispers. "Most of the crew is gonna jump for the escape pods, but that shuttle's the only thing that'll get us out into the storm."

I want to agree, but my tongue feels weirdly heavy, my lips tingling, and my mouth won't do what I want. When she looks across at me, I just nod.

"Can you . . . can you divert them or something?" she whispers. "Set off an alarm somewhere, do a magic computery thing?"

I shake my head, leaning forward, pressing my palms into the ground. My breath won't come. I'm dizzy.

"Are you okay?" she whispers, eyes widening.

I gesture at the ship. We have to keep moving.

"Low-tech it is," she mutters, leaning out and taking a good look at the crews surrounding us. Then, with both hands, she pulls a chock out from behind the wheel of the nearest fighter and, with all her strength, hurls it farther up the landing bay.

It lands with a *CRASH,* and all heads turns.

Scar is off like an athlete out of the blocks. I'm stumbling behind her, too hot, too dizzy, my vision starting to swim. I know which way I need to go, but I'm running blind.

My legs are weak. My exosuit is working overtime.

We reach the heavy shuttle we always steal.

Pain shoots through me as my knees hit the ground. I work quickly on the hatchway, hot-wiring it open amid the swirling smoke and chaos, same as I always do. But my hands are shaking.

I can't seem to get enough air.

My tongue feels weird.

Something's wrong.

Zila—six minutes remaining

"Zila!" Scarlett's voice comes through comms, garbled but audible.

"One moment," I say, turning a corner and crawling after Nari. The vents are very tight, and we are both small. Nobody on the security team will be able to follow. But we do not have long to reach our escape pod.

"Repeat: Containment breach escalation under way, engage emergency measures Deck 9."

"Zila, come on!" Nari calls, kicking out a grille ahead.

"Scarlett?" I ask, crawling forward on my belly. "Are you aboard the shuttle?"

"Core implosion imminent, T minus three minutes and counting. All hands proceed to evacuation pods immediately. Repeat: Core implosion in three minutes."

"Yes, we launched!" Scarlett cries. *"We're headed toward the storm, but something's happened to Fin! He inhaled some chemicals upstairs and now he can't b—"*

"REPEAT: CORE IMPLOSION IMMINENT. ALL HANDS PROCEED TO EVACUATION PODS IMMEDIATELY."

I hold on to the walls as the station shakes around me. The sirens in the vents are terribly loud.

"Say again, Scarlett? What has happened to Finian?"

"Zila, he can't breathe!"

Scarlett—five minutes remaining

Fin is slumped in the pilot's chair, and space all around us is on fire. Escape pods are blasting out of the station's flanks, and burning plasma is venting from its hull, and we're rocketing toward the huge coiling tendrils of the dark matter storm, the sail and the pulse beyond, our ticket home.

Except I don't know if Fin's going to make it.

His face is swelling, eyes bulging, lips turning a strange purple. I try to ignore the panic, hold myself together. I lay him on the floor as we rocket closer to the tempest, focused on Zila's voice.

She sounds so far away.

"Can you hear wheezing, Scarlett? Whistling?"

I bend down, my ear to his mouth, heart hammering on my ribs. He's not moving anymore, he's not talking, he's not . . .

Oh Maker, please please don't do this. . . .

"Yes."

"Then he is still breathing," Zila says. *"Nari and I are*

headed to the escape pods. If Finian is incapacitated, you must guide the ship through the storm's turbulence and out to the quantum sail. You must be close when the pulse strikes. Ten meters or less to be sure."

"Me?" I glance around wildly, spot the pilot's chair. "I don't know how to fly this thing! My job's always been witty commentary!"

"Listen carefully, Scarlett."

"Zila, I've never flown anything without autopilot!" I cry. "And I don't know what's wrong with him, I don't know med—"

"Scarlett! Listen to me. This is our last chance to get you home. You can do this. You must *do this."*

I look to the boy on the deck beside me, struggling to breathe. All of our futures hanging in the balance. Every moment of my life has been leading to this. And I hear his voice in my mind, as clear as if spoken aloud.

"I'm not sure if you've noticed, but the person holding our whole squad together is you. *We need you, Scar."*

And I close my eyes, and take myself by the mental lapels, and give myself a shake.

They need me.

He needs me.

"Okay, go."

Finian—four minutes remaining

My head's spinning and my body's struggling, fighting to drag in a breath, but I'm drowning and there's nothing to hold on to. I'm trying to climb onto a rock as the ocean pounds at

385

me and grabs me with icy cold hands, every wave pulling me down, and down, and down.

And all I can think is that I can't let go, I

can't

let

go.

Not until I'm sure we're out of the loop.

If I die now, will I start us over again?

I can't take that risk.

I can't die yet.

And I'm sinking my fingernails into that rock as the sea washes around me, the waves slamming down, squeezing my lungs, vision spinning.

And I'm so, so sorry that Scar will be alone, that she'll be the only one left to face the Ra'haam. That the heart of Squad 312 will be the only part left, but maybe heart was all we ever had, maybe love was always the flame we used to hold back the dark.

My vision's closing in.

I have to hold on.

Just until we get home.

Scarlett—three minutes remaining

"Zila!" I'm screaming, staring down helplessly at Fin as his back arches, his hands make claws. "Zila, he can't breathe!"

Zila's voice is calm in my ear. *"You must prioritize, Scarlett. Are you still on course for the quantum sail?"*

The shuttle is buffeted again, engines straining against the tempest outside. Even on the edge of the storm, the forces at play are crushing, colossal. I glance at the shuttle scopes, look out the viewshield to the massive silver rectangle rising in the dark ahead of us. "Yes! We're headed right toward the sail! Range ten thousand kilometers!"

"*Good. Does the shuttle have a medical kit?*"

I lift my head, scan the tiny cabin desperately. I push to my feet, rip open the cabinets, dig through them as supplies cascade around me.

"I don't see it!" I cry, thumping back to my knees beside him.

His eyes flutter closed.

I can hear the sirens wailing through her mic.

"WARNING: CONTAINMENT CASCADE IN EFFECT. CORE IMPLOSION IMMINENT, T MINUS THREE MINUTES AND COUNTING. ALL HANDS PROCEED TO EVACUATION PODS IMMEDIATELY. REPEAT: CORE IMPLOSION IN THREE MINUTES AND COUNTING."

"*If there is no medical kit, then we will work with what we have,*" Zila says simply. "*Describe his symptoms.*"

"H-his lips are swollen, his eyes . . ." I gasp, squeezing his hand. "He can't breathe, he keeps scratching at his throat—"

"*You are describing an anaphylactic reaction, Scarlett. Probably to the chemicals he inhaled. You must perform a tracheotomy.*"

"A *what?*" I screech.

"*His throat has swollen closed. We will make an incision below the swelling so he can breathe. You will need a knife.*"

"Zila, I can't—"

387

"*Scarlett.*" Her voice cuts me off. "*We have no time. Finian cannot die before the pulse strikes, or else the loop will simply start again. He has a small screwdriver in the right arm of his exosuit.*"

My hands are shaking, and he's not moving anymore, his arm heavy as I lift it, twist it, find the screwdriver nested into its little groove.

This can't be happening.

"Got it," I pant, somehow doing this and refusing to believe I'm doing it all at the same time. "Got it, what next?"

"You will need a small, rigid tube, thinner than your little finger."

"A *tube?*" I'm screaming, my breath coming too fast, and some people might get unnaturally calm in an emergency, but Scarlett Jones isn't one of them. "Where in the Maker's name am I supposed to get—"

"*Look around you. There must be something.*"

"There's nothing! Zila, there's nothing!"

The shuttle rocks around me again, the energies pulsing outside threatening to tear us apart. The utter blackness brightens to a deep somber mauve as a burst of dark energy crackles through the storm around us, and glancing at it through the viewshield, the scope of it, the power of it, I realize I'd be terrified for myself if I wasn't already so terrified for Fin.

We're still too far from the sail. He's going to die before we reach it, he's going to die right here in my arms.

We've come so far. Fought so hard. Lost so much.

A story hundreds of years in the making.

And this is how the final chapter gets written?

And then it comes to me. Like a flash of that awful energy. I shove my hand into the breast pocket on Finian's suit, fumbling, desperate, and my fingers finally close around it.

The pen.

"Zila, the damn PEN!"

"Hmm." I hear her say. *"Interesting."*

"He bitched about this damn thing every chance he got," I mutter as I frantically unscrew it, Fin lying motionless as I shout in his face. "Not such a crappy gift now, huh?"

His chest isn't moving.

His eyes are swollen shut.

I let all the pen's parts clatter to the floor of the shuttle until I'm holding just the casing. Stainless steel. Bright and heavy. The storm roils around us. Dark energy arcs across the black. "What next?"

"Run your fingertips down his throat," she says, and she's still so calm, and I'm clinging to her like a rock. *"You will feel two bumps. Between them, make an incision, and insert the pen."*

I force my hand into stillness with pure willpower, finger-tips trailing down his skin, once, twice, making sure I've got the spot. The storm shakes the shuttle in its rivets, and I tell myself to be still.

To be calm.

To breathe.

And then it's just me, holding a screwdriver, and Finian's throat, and oh fuck, oh fuck, oh fuck, oh fuck. Why couldn't this have been *anyone* on the squad except me?

"You can do this, Scarlett," Zila says quietly. *"You can do anything."*

I take a breath. I mark the spot.

I can do this.

Zila—two minutes remaining

"He's breathing! Zila, oh Maker, he's—"

Scarlett's words vanish into a sea of static as she and Finian near the storm and communications are cut.

I know those are the last words I will ever hear from them.

Nari and I are in our escape pod, watching through the porthole, our faces side by side. The dark of the void around us is lit with hundreds of tiny lights, red and green—other pods blasting from the ruins of the Glass Slipper Station. Beyond, we can see the storm, Scarlett and Finian's little shuttle hurtling through the inky dark toward its rendezvous with the quantum sail.

In less than two minutes, if all goes well, the pulse will strike them. The last of Squad 312 will be two centuries away, forever beyond my reach.

Except that is not true. Everything I do will reach them, eventually.

We watch the shuttle soar into the tempest.

Nari presses her hand to the glass.

"Godspeed," she whispers as the ship is obscured by the storm. "And good hunting."

One minute.

I turn toward her, studying the features that have become

so familiar as we lived this day together over and over again. I know so much about her, and yet so little. I have the rest of my life to learn.

"I know they've left you behind," Nari whispers, her eyes locked on mine. "But they haven't left you alone."

There are sparks in her words, and they jump between us like static electricity, like tiny quantum lightning strikes. And as they hit, I am like the shuttle, and I am transformed and transported, I am somewhere new, and . . .

I lift my hand, and so slowly, so carefully, I brush my fingertips down her cheek, curve them around the back of her neck.

Her skin is warm.

She is so brave, and so fierce, this hawk.

So full of life, tied by a thousand bonds to her friends, her family, her world.

And she is beautiful, the lines of her face, the curve of her mouth. I can hear Scarlett's voice in my mind, rich and amused. *She is not tall.*

And I am not alone.

I am with her.

It takes only the faintest pressure of my fingertips against the back of her neck, and she is leaning in, and her lips are brushing mine, and in a few moments the pulse will strike outside, but here, I am already afire.

Scarlett—one minute remaining

I wish I was the sort of person who prayed.

But Finian's chest is moving slowly, and I'm watching

391

him, counting down, counting down. My hands are steady on the flight controls. There's nothing to do but wait.

I don't know what we'll find when we get home. I don't know if we'll get home at all. But I know I've done everything I can.

I glance through the viewscreen at the storm raging outside, and when I look back down at him, his dark eyes are open.

"Stay still," I say immediately. "Stay still. We're going to need to get you to a real doctor pretty soon."

His brows lift, but he doesn't try to speak.

"Not yet," I continue. "A few seconds more. Assuming you're asking if we made the jump. If you're asking where I found the skill, courage, and general fabulousness to perform emergency surgery in the middle of all this chaos, well. If you think that after auditioning all those guys to find the perfect boyfriend I was going to let a little thing like a tracheotomy get in the way of true love, you've clearly underestimated how tired I am of the search."

His mouth quirks weakly.

I glance up at the clock again.

This is it.

I've done everything I can.

The sail stretches out below us, metallic, rippling, a thousand kilometers wide. The storm around us, endless, impossible, the power to tear through the walls of space and time gathering around us. The crystal at my throat begins to burn. Black light. White noise. I can feel it on my skin. I can hear it in my head. We're so small, so insignificant in the face of all this, I wonder for a moment how any of it matters at all.

Finian looks up at me with those big black eyes I used to think were hard to read. And as our gazes lock, I realize it's this.

This is what matters.

"See you in the future, handsome."

ZAP.

33

AURI

I'm half in one world, half in another, images overlaying each other so that the Echo and reality meld together.

There are tears on Lae's cheeks, and filthy, muddy rain is falling from the Echo sky, and tiny cracks are spiderwebbing through the *Neridaa* all at once.

I reach within myself for the power to turn the black rain sweet and crystal clear, and Kal lifts one hand to brush a tear from Lae's cheek, and a moment's sweetness holds in his world and mine amid this carnage.

"We will fight to our last breath to honor your father," he says, gentle, and Lae squares her jaw and nods.

"Yes, Uncle."

But the collapsed crystal rubble that Caersan brought down to block the doorway won't keep the Ra'haam out much longer, and his wounds run across the landscape of the Echo like a black blight, and as quick as it came, that moment of respite is gone from the Echo and the *Neridaa* both.

The cry of warning I sent back to Tyler still rings in my mind, a discordant shriek that won't fade away.

He told me himself.

When it happens.

How it happens.

Every planetary head gathered together in one place.

A Ra'haam agent with a bomb.

The death and disorder that paralyzed them until the Ra'haam could bloom and burst and turn everything blue and green and deathless.

Did he hear me back then? Did he stop it?

Would we still be here if he had?

Another jagged canyon opens up across the Echo, the pain of it like broken glass dragged across my insides, and I reach out one more time to where Caersan stands like a blood-soaked statue in black.

"Caersan, I can't do it alone. You have to fix this, *please.*"

And his hands make fists, and he turns toward me with wildness in his eyes, and he raises his voice to a roar.

"I. AM. NOT. *BROKEN.*"

—and the barrier in the doorway gives way in a
spray of crystal shards, and Kal and Lae turn
to face their foe for the last time. New bonds
of love flow between them now, her rainbow
glory tangling with his violet and gold, because
Kal is not his father, and he knows how to
offer love, and Tyler taught her to accept
it, and

—a Syldrathi boy is thrown against a wall, his father
looming over him as he falls to the ground.

I cry out for Kal, but the boy turns his head to stare
straight at me, and

the

boy

is

not

Kal

—and the crystal city of the Echo is shattering and
falling

> —and I can hear my own voice begging Caersan to
> help me as I frantically repair the *Neridaa* as she
> unmakes herself over and over

—and the waves of death outside pour through the
door, and Kal's blades are a blur, and Ra'haam
tendrils lash out to wrap around Lae's legs,
dragging her down and swarming all over her
thrashing body

> —and Caersan is hacking and slashing at the
> growths around him, and the pressure is building,
> hammering against my temples, cracks running
> down my face as the light pulses through them, and
> I think I'm screaming

—and Lae's mind is bright, and in it I can see
Saedii's tae-sai gaming table, and I understand
her mother loved to play against Tyler, and she
taught her daughter, and I see the regret and
defiance in Lae's mind as she wrenches one arm
free of the Ra'haam

—and Kal and Caersan shout, but in all our minds
she tips her wooden Templar piece to signal the
game is over, and with her free arm she gets her
pistol up, and like her mother, she denies the
Ra'haam its quarry

—and as she pulls the trigger and the rainbow
brilliance of her mind is gone, Kal falls to one
knee, and I wrap my mind in his, and I can hear
myself screaming as he shows me one last time
how much he loves me, because if we can go
back, Tyler will still live, Toshh and Dacca and
Elin will still live, one day Lae will be born, but if
Kal dies here and now, I lose him forever.

With a roar, Caersan attacks the Ra'haam as it brings down
his son, but for every vine he hacks away, another takes its
place. He knows no victory lies this way. I can feel it.

"Fight!" he screams, and I don't know who he's talking
to anymore. He swings his blade again, unable to surrender,
refusing to let go.

"Caersan!" I cry. "*This* is not the fight! Heal the *Neridaa*
with me!"

And he looks up, his face splintered and cracked, the
light almost blinding . . .

—and then he stands in the Echo with me in a
field of crystal flowers, and once more I'm in two
worlds, three worlds, four worlds, so many times
and places . . .

—a boy tries to understand why his father is angry

—the boy's son tries to understand why *his* father
is angry

—"Imagine what we could have made, if only you
had loved us."

—"My son, I . . ."

—the flowers shatter one by one . . . and then they
are still . . .

. . . and everything is still . . .

And in both worlds—beside me in the Echo and beside
Kal on the floor—he raises his voice to roar his defiance to
the Ra'haam:
"YOU WILL NEVER WIN!"

and the Starslayer shatters into a million pieces, spending
every piece of himself in his defiance, in his absolute refusal
to surrender

and all around him the Ra'haam burns black and red, shrivel-
ing and curling in on itself

and within the Echo, he is everywhere, infusing the place
with his energy as it knits back together and becomes
beautiful

and he infuses *me* with his energy, and I am powerful, I
am infinite

and for a moment I know him completely, and then he is gone, but in the roaring silence the instant after his departure

I know he killed billions.

And I know he can never be forgiven.

And I know that he has spent the last of his life force in a tangled, furious stab made up of defiance, a refusal to concede defeat, an act of anger and iron-willed resolve . . .

. . . and yes, of love.

Kal lies gasping on the floor, surrounded by the burned and blackened remains of the Ra'haam, and I stagger to him, dropping to my knees, and he closes his eyes against the glow from my face, but he reaches up to throw his arms around me and I wrap my mind around Kal's to brace him, and I say

I love you

I love you

I love you

and I'm not completely sure who's speaking in that moment, and I harness the power of Caersan's that still runs through me, and feel Kal's warmth inside me, and

light

shines

from

me

as

I—

34

TYLER

"You certainly have a flair for the dramatic, legionnaire."

I open my eye. Gray walls around me. Pale light above me. A figure is silhouetted against it, broad-shouldered, thick-necked. The metal on his chest and cybernetic arms gleams dully, and his voice is a low, rumbling growl.

"Admiral Adams . . . ," I whisper.

I'm in the academy med station, I realize. The same bay I was in the day I first met Aurora O'Malley. For a moment, I almost want to turn my head to see if she's on the other side of the wall, just waking up.

Monitors and machines hiss and hum around me, pulsing with a steady, warm glow. I'm mostly numb from the neck down, wondering why the world looks so strange. Bringing my trembling hand up to my face, I feel a thick derm patch across my cheek, over my right brow.

"You lost it," Adams says. "The eye. Lost your spleen too. The shot missed your spine by about two centimeters. You're lucky to be breathing."

"When it keeps happening over and over," I whisper, "it's not luck."

The admiral scoffs. "Never could quite cure you of that ego, Jones. Just like your old man." He reaches down, presses one heavy metal hand on my shoulder. "He'd be proud of you, son. Just like I am."

"Yeah, real proud. Galactic terrorist. Traitor to Aurora Legion. Space pirate." My fingers run over the place my eye used to be, the ache in my hollow socket. "At least I'll look the part for my firing squad, I guess."

"Won't be a firing squad. What you did is all over the feeds. Your friend Lyrann Balkarri has been crowing about you saving the summit single-handed on GNN-7 for three days now. Promising an exclusive interview." He grunts appreciatively. "Hidden camera on the jacket lapel. Smart."

"I just w-wanted a record." I wince, a sliver of pain breaking through the haze of meds. "Something to speak f-for me if things went b-bad. Clear my name." I look up at Adams and shrug. "Dad's name. You know."

"I know," he says. "I know, Tyler."

He straightens up, nods to the bank of monitors arrayed on the wall.

"The footage makes for some dramatic viewing, I'll give you that. Good headline, too. *Terror Plot to Destroy Aurora Station Foiled by Rogue Legionnaire*. Your story almost upstaged ours. But not quite."

I focus on the screens, the butterflies in my stomach fighting to be felt through the pain-blockers they've pumped me full of. On the monitors, I can see images of Adams and de Stoy giving their presentation to the Galactic Summit. In the holo behind them, I see the image of Octavia—the colony world engulfed by the Ra'haam, then subsequently locked under Interdiction by order of TerraGov. On other screens, I see different planets, also crawling with the blue-green corruption of the enemy.

The other nursery worlds, I realize.

Adams and de Stoy told the summit about the Ra'haam.

Another screen shows footage of legionnaires subduing and arresting the GIA agents in Prime Minister Ilyasova's retinue. I see mirrormasks being ripped from faces sheened with blue-gray moss, eyes like flowers, outrage and fear and shock. Headlines like *GIA Infiltrated, TerraGov Suspect, Senatorial Commission.*

"You knew," I whisper.

I meet his eyes, anger boiling in my belly, voice shaking. "This whole time. You *knew.*"

"Some of it," he replies, sighing. "Not enough."

"You knew enough to put Auri on my Longbow. To plant those packages for us on Emerald City. To leave us the *Zero.* Which means you knew what was going to happen to Cat when we went to Octavia." Tears are burning in my eye now, the heart monitor rising in pitch as I try to claw my way upright. "You *knew* what would happen to her. You *knew* it'd take her."

He holds my stare, his jaw clenched. "We did."

"You sonofa*bitch,*" I hiss.

"You're owed an apology, Tyler," he sighs. "And an explanation. But I can only offer the first. The second falls to someone else."

He reaches into the jacket of his dress uniform, and all those accolades and commendations on his chest that I once coveted just look bought with blood now. I try to imagine if there's anything he can say, any explanation he can possibly give to make me forget the hurt in Cat's eyes as that knife sank home, the warmth of her blood on my hands, the horror and sorrow. . . .

Adams places a small, round holoplayer on the sheet covering my lap, presses a button. The image flickers to life, projected above the player's lens in glowing light. It's odd, rendered in lines of duochrome blue and white.

Old tech, I realize. *Really* old.

It takes me a while to recognize the figure coalescing in the air before me. She's wearing an archaic Legion uniform, chest decorated with commendations. She's older, maybe in her mid-seventies. Kindly eyes and short gray hair. But I still recognize her from the academy promenade.

"She's one of the Founders," I whisper.

"*Hello, Legionnaire Jones,*" she says, her voice faintly distorted. "*My name is Nari Kim. If you're watching this, Legion Command has deemed it within operational parameters to provide you with an explanation of the events with which you've been recently involved.*

"*The variables in this equation do not allow for specificity, but with luck, Aurora Legion is now in a position to strike the final blow against the Ra'haam, and complete a mission over two hundred years in the making.*"

She smiles at me, like a mother might. "*We owe a great deal to you, legionnaire. I have been told you are a brilliant leader. A brave and noble soul. But more, a good and dear friend. I wish I could have met you, Tyler. I almost feel like I have. But please know, we are so proud of you, to have come this far. We know what you've given. What you've lost. I only pray in the end it will be worth it.*"

Her smile widens, and she kisses her fingers, and I watch with wondering eyes as she presses them against the lens. This woman is a hero. One of the Legion Founders. To hear her speaking like this . . . to *me* . . .

"*There's someone who wants to speak to you,*" she continues. "*So I will wish you farewell, Tyler Jones, and good fortune, and bid you remember the hopes and lives of the entire galaxy are owed to you and your friends.*"

She holds out her hand, off camera, beckoning.

"*Come here, love.*"

There's a long pause. Nari Kim beckons again, smiling. "*It's all right.*"

A figure moves into frame, rendered in the same duotone lines of holographic light. Her hair is long and curling, mostly silver or white, her skin wrinkled with age.

I don't recognize her at first. Then Nari murmurs encouragement, and the newcomer turns her head toward her, and I catch a glimpse of . . .

. . . It can't be.

Earrings with hawk charms dangling from them.

And as she takes her seat in front of the recorder, I begin to realize . . .

The woman looks up at the lens, and I see her lashes are shining with tears. And I recognize her then, despite the impossibility of it all, despite the gulf of time and tracks of sorrow etched at the edges of her eyes.

"Zila . . . ," I whisper.

"*Hello, Tyler.*"

She pauses, as if gathering herself. She seems so small. Tinier even than I remember. Beside her, Nari squeezes her hand. And buoyed by that touch, Zila finds some well of strength, breathes deep, and begins to speak.

"If you are watching this, you have survived past the point of my departure, and have entered the realm of absolute uncertainty. I am very happy you survived your captivity among the GIA. Hopefully this means my gift to you was of some use. Forgive me if it was not one hundred percent adequate. I was working with a near-infinite number of variables."

She frowns, rubbing her brow as if pained.

"During the Battle of Terra, when the Eshvaren Weapon was fired, a collision of psychic energies and temporal distortion hurled me, Finian, and your sister, Scarlett, back in time, to the year 2177."

My eyes go wide and I look at Adams, but he's only watching the holo. From his look of intense interest, I'd guess he's never seen this before.

"Due to events too complex to bore you with," Zila continues, *"I was forced to remain behind in this era. It has fallen to me, along with Battle Leader de Karran and Nari, to pave the way for future events, and for the eventual struggle with the Ra'haam. We have done our very best to ensure that all happens exactly as it did. As it should. As it* must, *for Aurora to recover the Eshvaren Weapon and use it against the enemy. But . . ."*

Zila's voice falters. She looks down at her hands, swallowing hard. The Zila Madran I knew was a girl who lived behind walls. Who kept herself shielded from the world by logic, cut off from her emotions, cold and clinical.

But she's crying now, tears spilling down her cheeks.

I see Nari Kim's hand reach out again, her arm slip around Zila's shoulders, pulling her in tight, and she kisses her cheek, her knuckles, her lips. Even through this ancient tech, these thin glowing lines, I can see the love in her eyes, feel tears stinging in mine as I realize what they must have meant to each other. That my friend found someone who mattered so much.

"Just speak from your heart, love," Nari says.

Zila looks to the camera again, her voice shaking.

"I am so s-sorry, Tyler," she whispers. *"About Cat. I tried for years to think of an alternative. Some way to spare her that fate. I have dreaded the day when I would have to speak these words to you. But the potential for calamity, a paradoxical butterfly effect that would irrevocably alter the timeline . . ."* She sniffs thickly, swallows hard. *"We could n-not risk it. Without me here, there would be no one to help Nari to form the Legion, to ensure you met Aurora, to protect you on Emerald City. Nobody to safeguard the future. For us to ensure the Ra'haam's defeat, everything needed to happen* exactly *as it did, up to the moment I left your timeline."* She shakes her head, her eyes imploring. *"Everything."*

Zila lowers her chin, hair tumbling over her face.

"I have lived my life as best I could." She squeezes Nari's hand. *"I have found happiness. I have worked hard, seen places and met people who bring me joy. My squad was my second family, after I lost my first, and I have devoted my life to preparing what you will need—but there have been adventures as well. Laughter. I have found a third family here, beyond all expectation. I think you will worry, now you know where I am. I want you to know that I have been happy. But please know as well that there is not a day that passes I do not think of Cat, and what I helped bring about."*

She lifts her head again. Looking at me across the centuries.

"I ask for your forgiveness. I hope you understand I did it all for the best, and know that through this sacrifice, we have safeguarded a future for the galaxy. The path ahead of you is uncertain. I do not know what is to come. But I know I am grateful to have known you, Tyler. Honored to have served under you. And I feel blessed beyond measure to have called you my friend."

I reach out to the image, tears spilling down my face as my fingers pass through it. I think about what it must have been, to live with that weight. The burden of the galaxy's future on your shoulders.

"Zee," I whisper. "Of course I forgive you."

"Commander," Nari says, addressing the air. *"I trust you are listening. You may now access Omega Protocol, Nodes 6 through 15. Ensure Node 10 is delivered to Aurora O'Malley personally. You may also access the facilities on Epsilon Deck, Section Zero. Passcodes to follow. Please follow all instructions exactly. The lives of two very brave soldiers are at stake."*

"I believe our calculations are correct," Zila says. *"And enough time has now elapsed from our disappearance to ensure no paradox events."* She nods, almost to herself, chewing a lock of her hair just like she used to when lost in thought. *"Yes. Yes, it will work. It must work."*

Nari Kim looks back to me, a smile crinkling her eyes.

"Punch that bleach-head in the arm for me, Jones. And tell your sister thanks. Good hunting, legionnaire. Burn bright against the night."

Zila looks into the projection, reaching out toward me.

My fingers touch hers, back across an ocean of time and tears.

"*Farewell, my friend,*" she smiles.

And the recording ends.

"Dammit . . . ," Adams growls.

I look up at him, my eye blurred with tears, my mind reeling with everything I've learned. The impossibility, the enormity—it's almost too much to wrap my head around. But the look in Adams's eyes is enough to drag me back to reality, away from conspiracies centuries in the making, suffered heartache and hard-won joy. I sniff hard, wipe my sodden cheeks.

"What is it?"

Adams is staring at the holoplayer, his face a grim mask. The images of Zila and Nari Kim have disappeared, replaced by a scrolling stream of passcodes. "I'll have to review the new data we've just unlocked. But from the way they were talking . . . I think it's just as we've feared."

"Look, I don't know what the hells is happening here, but—"

"It's like Founder Madran said, Tyler." Adams speaks Zila's name with something close to reverence. The way a minister speaks about the Maker.

They think of her as the Third Founder, I realize.

"She only knew for certain what happened up to the Battle of Terra," Adams continues. "The point where she was stripped from this timeline. For all her genius, Zila Madran couldn't actually see the future. She only remembered what she'd already seen. So she couldn't have known."

"About the plot on Aurora Station?"

He nods. "But not just that. All our contingencies, all the planning we have in place from this point forward to ensure the defeat of the Ra'haam, revolved around the Trigger and the Weapon."

He drags one metal hand across his stubbled scalp.

"And they're *gone*," I breathe. "Vanished at the Battle of Terra."

"The Weapon, the Trigger, Aurora O'Malley." Adams turns to the viewport on the wall, stars splayed across the dark beyond. "*Everything* we've done was to ensure their presence here and now to strike the killing blow against the enemy before it blooms. And after all of that, after *hundreds* of years, messages and protocols passed down in secret from Founder to Commander to Successor across the centuries . . ." He looks down at his empty hands. "We have *nothing*."

I look at the projector on my lap, my mind racing. "Founder Kim mentioned secure facilities on Epsilon Deck, Section Zero." I swallow hard, not daring to hope. "She talked about my sister. Maybe . . ."

Adams slaps his Legion comm badge, speaking quick.

"Adams to de Stoy."

"*I read you, Seph,*" comes the reply.

"I have more intel. Meet me in Epsilon. I'm bringing Jones."

There's a small pause, a tiny intake of breath. I don't think I've ever seen Battle Leader de Stoy lose her chill once in the six years I've known her, but when she answers, she sounds positively jubilant.

"*Understood,*" she says. "*I'll meet you there.*"

Adams nods, drops connection.

"Do you still pray, Tyler?" he asks softly. "I know when it gets dark, it can be hard to keep the f—"

"Every day, sir," I reply. "Every day."

"Good," he nods. "Do it now."

.　.　.　.　.

I'd wondered why the name Epsilon Deck sounded strange. As Adams pushes me on a grav-chair through the halls of the med facilities and into an officers' elevator, I realize why. Looking at the hundreds of levels, subfloors, and sections of the station outlined in glowing light on the elevator controls, I understand there *is* no Epsilon Deck on Aurora Station.

At least, not one that exists on the schematics.

Adams reaches inside his tunic for a passkey of bio-coded platinum. He presses his thumb to the sensor, slips the key into a slot in the elevator control. A panel slides aside, a sensor sweeps his face, his irises, his handprint. When the controls buzz green, he leans back and speaks.

"Adams. One-one-seven-four-alpha-kilo-two-one-seven-beta-indigo."

Another beep. I feel us pivot, as if the elevator were shifting on its axis.

"Epsilon, Section Zero," Adams commands. "Passcode: Vigilance."

My stomach feels full of broken glass, and the right side of my face is aching—maybe I should've asked for another pain-blocker before we left. But though I can barely feel it, I know my heart is hammering at the thought I might see my sister again. I had no idea what happened to her after Saedii and I were captured by the GIA. The fear she might be dead was a constant weight, one I couldn't bring myself to look at for long. The knowledge she was thrown back in time with Zila and Fin is almost incomprehensible.

But she could be alive.

Oh Maker, please let her be alive.

The elevator doors hiss apart, and I see a long, brightly lit corridor leading to a heavy door that looks strong enough to withstand atmospheric bombardment. Battle Leader de Stoy is down here in full Legion kit, ash-pale skin and snow-white hair bleached even whiter by the harsh light. She watches as Adams pushes me forward in my grav-chair, nods once as we approach, big black eyes regarding me somberly.

"Seems like you've been in the wars, Legionnaire Jones."

"Nothing I couldn't handle, ma'am."

She smiles, thin and bloodless. Battle Leader de Stoy *never* smiles.

"A fine job, soldier. A fine job indeed."

Adams has swiped his bio-key into a pad on the left of the door and nods now to de Stoy. "Ready?"

The battle leader swipes her own key and leans forward, hands splayed on the sensor glass. Scanners again roam Adams's and de Stoy's faces, retinas, and palms, a needle takes tissue and blood samples, and, finally, they speak a series of passkeys from Zila and Nari's recording. The tech is old, but it's as heavy as it could be, given that this station was built two centuries ago.

Whatever's behind here, Zila wanted it well protected.

The door clunks, an alarm briefly flares, the lighting turns a cold deep blue. The hatchway lumbers aside, the gloom in the room beyond flickers dark to light as the overheads hum

411

to life. And as Adams pushes me inside, I catch my breath, staring in awe at the structure before me.

Heavy conduits snake outward from banks of ancient computers, connected to a cylindrical tank of transparent plasteel in the room's heart. And inside it, pulsing with light like a heartbeat, is . . .

"A probe," I breathe. "An Eshvaren probe."

Light begins to pulse through the chamber, coalescing within the teardrop crystal. I see it's cracked, the point of the tear shattered and sheared away, the glow refracting from a million spiderweb scrawls in the stone.

"Maker's breath," Adams whispers.

An image flickers to life above the computer terminals, and my heart soars to see Zila again. She's younger than she was a moment ago, maybe mid-forties, her back straight, her eyes keen.

"Welcome, Commanders. If you are hearing this message, the Battle of Terra has concluded, I have departed your timeline for the year 2177, and Whiplash Protocol has been enacted. Please engage all short-range scanners on Aurora Station, screen for fighter gradients, maximum intensity. Tell your scanner crews they are looking for a shuttle, Terran in origin, Osprey series, Model 7I-C. Scramble medical crews to assist the occupants, have facilities online to deal with one Betraskan male, nineteen years of age, suffering anaphylaxis, and possible pharyngeal, laryngeal, and tracheal trauma."

My stomach twists at that, breath coming quicker.

"I have spent the last thirty years of my life perfecting these algorithms," Zila continues. *"I dreamed as a cadet of resources on this scale. I regret that I am not there to see the final result."*

For just a moment, I see a glimpse of the girl who liked her Stun setting way, way too much.

"I am as certain of success as I can possibly be," she continues. *"But I am not perfect. And I am not the religious sort."* Her eyes sweep the room. *"I hope you are there, Tyler. And if you are, perhaps a prayer would not be out of order. You always were the believer among us."*

Adams repeats the commands into his comm badge, engaging the scanner teams, scrambling the med crews. Zila's image just hovers there, silent. As I watch, she begins to chew a lock of hair.

After a minute or two, the lights around us start to pulse harder. The overheads in the corridor outside grow dim and then flicker out entirely.

With no more warning, the station net drops entirely, the artificial grav cuts off, and Adams curses beneath his breath as the Eshvaren probe burns with an intensity that's almost blinding. The hair all over my body is standing tall. A subsonic hum is building in the back of my head.

"She's sucking power out of the entire station grid," de Stoy hisses.

Zila's holographic lips curl into a mischievous smile, and I reach out toward her, terrified, crying, but somehow smiling with her.

And then I do as she asks, closing my eye, picturing Finian and Scar, my friend and my twin, praying to the Maker with everything I have.

Bring them back.

Bring them back to me, please.

The hum rises to a slow scream. The Eshvaren probe

burns so bright I can see it through the closed lid of my eye, turning my head as the sound rises in pitch. The station shudders, the power builds, every drop of juice from the core ripped from the grid and projected into the probe's blazing heart.

The screaming begins to hurt, I hear Adams roaring, but through it all, I keep praying. Holding on as tight as I can to the thought Adams instilled in me when we first left for Sagan Station, before we ever discovered Aurora, got dragged into this puzzle, this war, this family hundreds of . . . no, a *million* years in the making.

You must believe, Tyler.

You must believe.

The scream goes past the edge of hearing.

The light goes through the other side of blinding.

And with one final discordant shriek, it's over.

The glow in the Eshvaren probe fades, then dies entirely. The overheads outside flicker back to life, and I wince as gravity returns, pain shooting through my mangled body as I thump back down into my grav-chair.

Comms are coming through to Adams and de Stoy, warnings and alerts and alarms, silenced by de Stoy's terse command, Adams's rumbling bellow.

"All nonessentials, cut the chaff! Scan crew, report!"

I look him in the eyes, heart galloping, not daring to hope.

". . . *Negative, sir,*" comes the reply. "*No contact.*"

"Narrow the field, Lieutenant," de Stoy orders. "The vessel may be without power. Search on thermals, kinetics, full-spectrum radiation."

"*Yes, ma'am, we're on it,*" comes the reply.

The minutes tick by like eons. I stare at the place Zila's hologram had been, but it's gone, just the afterimage of the probe burned into my eye.

"Anything?" Adams asks.

"*Negative, sir,*" comes the reply. "*Clean scope.*"

"*This is Raptor external. Confirm, Aurora; zero contact.*"

I sit there, staring at the place the hologram of my friend stood, knowing I'll never see her again.

And that might not be so bad—she said she was happy—if not for the thought of the rest of them. Auri and Kal disappeared who knows where. Zila dead for over a hundred years. Cat gone. And now Fin and Scarlett . . .

I listen to the reports coming in, the scanner crews and pilots confirming what they've already said. What I already know.

"*Clean scope.*"

"*Zero contact.*"

They're gone. All my friends. All my family.

After all we suffered and all we lost . . .

"I'm the only one left," I whisper.

Squad 312 forever.

PART 4

I WILL SEE YOU
IN THE STARS

35

TYLER

I never thought it would end like this.

I sit in my grav-chair, staring out the long viewport at the Aurora star. The meds they've got me on are heavy-duty, and I don't feel the ache of my wounds. But somehow, that only makes it worse. Because without the pain, all I feel is the absence. The empty place where my eye should be. The empty space beside me where my family should be.

I never thought it would end like this.

I watch the fleet forming up off the academy's shoulder, and a part of me still can't help but be awed by the sight. The largest armada in recorded galactic history is being mustered. A coalition of races, *ten thousand* ships gathered from across the Milky Way, answering the threat of the Ra'haam.

Chellerian and Betraskan. Ishtarrian and Rigellian. Gremp and Tol'Mari and Rikerite and Free Syldrathi. I never imagined anything like it.

Adams and de Stoy haven't been idle in the years they've commanded the Legion, and in addition to laying the path for Squad 312 to discover the Weapon and begin the formation of the Legion in the past, they've also had other agents at work—gathering data on the twenty-two Ra'haam nursery worlds. Legion squads, sent in secret across Interdiction lines, through lost FoldGates, collecting evidence, footage, and data sweeps of those corrupted worlds, the nurseries where our enemy sleeps, stirring even now, waiting to bloom and burst.

That data, the footage I shot of Cat in the reactor, the unmasked GIA agents—it's been enough to gather this fragile alliance.

We don't have the Trigger.

We don't have the Weapon.

But we have fusions bombs. Disruptor clusters. Mass-colliders. Bioweapons. Atmo-reapers. Core-busters. The combined military strength of hundreds of worlds, set to burn our enemy to death in its crib. The courses are laid in, the first target set—the place where all of this began.

A planet that might have slept for years more, if not for a group of Terran colonists who disturbed its sleep.

The place where the Ra'haam dragged its first new members in eons into its collective, setting all this in motion. The place where we lost Cat.

The planet Octavia.

And I'm stuck here, watching.

Helpless.

Alone.

I watch the ships weave among each other, gliding into formations, beautiful and graceful, sharp and lethal, a hundred races, a thousand models, a hundred thousand warriors, poised at the Aurora FoldGate. As he boarded the Legion battle carrier *Relentless,* Admiral Adams told me that I'd already done enough. That I could breathe easy. That I'd earned a rest.

I don't know if I believe that.

I don't know if this was all worth it.

The signal is given. Thousands of lights flashing in salute to the station. As the fleet begins departing through the FoldGate, I place my hand up on the transparent plasteel, my heart heavy in my chest.

For all the firepower, all the strength, I warned Adams and de Stoy, things might not be so easy. Even if we had the Weapon, which we *don't,* we've been planning this battle for a little over two centuries.

The Ra'haam has been preparing its return for a million years.

Auri, where are you?

I watch the ships dropping through the gate one by one, all our hopes, all our lives, hanging by their single thread.

And then, out in the dark, I see it.

A tiny pulse of energy, just off the station's skin.

Butterflies take wing in my stomach, and I surge up against the viewport.

And then I'm running—stumbling, really, wounds be damned—wincing as I slam through a group of wide-eyed cadets and barrel into the turbolift.

I call Adams but I get his damn service again, slinging my uni into the elevator wall in frustration.

The elevator hits the docks and I spill out the doors, roaring at a trauma team slouched on break beside a medvac shuttle. They look at me like I'm insane, like I've lost it. One of them tells me I should be back in the med bay. I'm not gonna repeat what I yell next, but it's enough to convince them to get their asses into gear and get me out into the black.

My heart is hammering as we launch, gravity dropping away, hope rising with my insides as they free-float. Thrust pushes me back into my acceleration couch as I point—"There, THERE!"—to a tiny speck of gray floating out in the middle of all that nothing.

Unlike my sister, I'm a ship geek. I can tell you the name of every vessel the Terran Defense Force has used since its inception back in 2118. I can spot the makes. I can call the models. I can tell you the year they were commissioned and the year they were taken offline.

Hey, I like ships, okay?

"Osprey series," I whisper. "Model 7I-C. 2168 to 2179."

Over the med team's objections, I'm suited up before they are. It's hard to navigate with only one eye—they haven't had a chance to install my cybernetic yet, and my depth perception is shot to pieces.

A nice young Betraskan corporal tells me I need to sit down.

I politely inform him he needs to shut up.

The medvac locks on to the Osprey with a grav-cable, bringing us into close orbit, seconds ticking by like years.

I'm looking at the Osprey as we close to boarding range, teeth gritted so tight they are creaking. The hull is burned black in places, the metal carved into strange ripples, like it was liquefied in intense heat, then flash-frozen before it could come apart. The windows are scorched, dark with burned carbon; I can't see inside. I can't see them.

I can't see her.

Our airlock hisses, opens wide, and secured by safety cables, me and the med team spill out into the void. I know enough to stay out of their way as the tech specialist tries to hack the electronics, resorting at last to cutting through the metal with a heavy-duty thermal lance.

They force the loading bay door open with hydraulics, carbon particles breaking free from the melted metal, my stomach full of sloshing ice. I follow the med team inside, the floodlights on our helmets cutting through the dark as we reach the inner airlock. As the team goes to work on the seals, I press my hands against the narrow glass viewport in the airlock door, peering into the shuttle's belly beyond.

And there in the dark, I see them, I see them and I shout, pounding my fist against the port.

"Finian!" I roar. *"Scarlett!"*

They're floating in the zero grav, Scar's flame-red hair and Fin's milk-white skin picked out in the cabin's pitch-black.

Fin is wrapped in a thermal blanket and spacesuit that belongs in a museum, and I note with horror there's pale pink blood spattered inside the visor.

Scar is in another ancient suit beside him, her body floating limp and motionless in the dark. Around her neck, I can see the medallion she got in the Dominion vault on Emerald City. The crystal is glowing like a candle, its light slowly fading.

"HURRY UP!" I roar. "GET IT *OPEN!*"

The airlock shudders, the med team once again bringing in the hydraulics to force it. I'm on my belly, squeezing underneath as it rises, heedless of the awakening pain in my body, the blood I can feel pooling under my dermal wraps.

I scrabble across the deck, clutching at the ceiling to slow myself, hooking an arm around the pilot's chair as I drag my sister in with my other hand. Her eyes are closed, hair billowing in a halo around her face. There's no oxygen in here, no atmo, nothing to carry sound, and so instead, I scream into her head, across the blood between us, the blood that binds us, praying, *Please, Maker, please.*

Scar, can you hear me?

The team bustles in behind me, securing Fin. Readings are taken, vitals checked. "We gotta get these two back to station, STAT."

Scar! It's Tyler!

They push me aside, wrap my sister in electrothermals, secure her in a grav-gurney. I'm holding her hand as we boot it back to our own shuttle, refusing to let go, refusing to give up. Not after all this.

Not her too.

SCARLETT, WAKE UP!

She's motionless on the gurney, strapped inside our shuttle now, warming up from the freezing chill of space.

But she's still not moving, barely breathing, and I can't *feel* her in my mind, that strange more-than-twins bond we've always shared, the gift from the mother we never knew, the dad we lost, the family we were, all of it more important to me now than it's ever been, please Scar, please I can't lose you too, *I can't lose you too.*

"Ty . . ."

I open my eye, heart bursting as I see her looking at me through heavy lashes, her voice thick, eyelids bruised. I can sense the size of the story she's just lived, the weight she's just lifted, the place she's just been. But after all she's been through, she still finds it in herself to smile.

"H-hey, Bee-bro . . ."

I laugh, I sob, hanging my head. "I hate it when you call me that."

Her lips part, fear gleaming in her stare. "F-Finian?"

"He's okay," I whisper. "He's okay, Scar."

I want to hug her so bad I can taste it. I want to drag her into my arms and never let her go. But I can tell what her body's been through, and I don't want to risk hurting her. So I just squeeze her hand, lean in to kiss her brow, tears breaking loose from my lashes and floating free in the low grav as I pour everything I'm feeling into her head. The sorrow and the fear, the regret and the pain, but more and most, the pure, blinding joy I feel at seeing her again.

We've known each other all our lives. Even before we were born. And everything I've done, everything I've lived and fought through, even when she wasn't there beside me, she was with me. A part of me.

Forever.

Scarlett opens her arms, and I hold her gently as I can, and she strokes my hair as I press my face into hers.

"I love you, too," she whispers.

36

TYLER

It's a long Fold for those on the way to the Octavia system. Long enough for my wounds to begin healing as we wait for news that the coalition fleet has reached its destination. I find the rehab hard work, and the cybernetic they gave me still feels strange, but good news is, I can read the news feeds right off the network now.

Fin is still confined to the med bay, but as I limp into his room, he and Scar break apart with an audible *pop,* so I figure he can't be too bad. My sister straightens her tunic, brushes a stray lock of newly dyed red back from her flushed lips, settling in on the medi-cot beside Fin. I rumble to a stop and raise an eyebrow, looking back and forth between them.

Fin's blushing, which is kinda weird for a Betraskan.

"You're supposed to be resting," I say.

"He *is* resting," Scarlett says breezily.

"You stabbed a pen into his throat, Scar. You might wanna give him a few more days before you start licking his tonsils."

"Very droll," she says, rolling her eyes. "And very graphic. But I have *no* idea what you're talking about."

I wave at my face. "You know, this cybernetic eye they gave me can see into the thermographic spectrum. Your cheeks get almost 0.2 degrees warmer when you lie."

She screws up one of Fin's many pillows, hurls it at my head.

"Should've gotten you a damn eye patch."

"That might be pushing the space-pirate thing too far, even for me."

"Avast, matey," she grins.

"Hoist the mizzen," I smile. "Jolly the Roger."

"Yarrr," Fin growls, in a small, broken voice.

Scar turns on him in mock outrage as she pokes his chest. "You're not supposed to be talking!"

Fin shrugs and grins sheepishly, and she puts one hand to his cheek, kisses his lips. I watch them break apart slowly, eyes fixed on my Gearhead. Fin pretends not to feel my stare, but eventually he glances at me sidelong.

"You know," I say, "when all this is over, you and I are gonna have to have us a little chat about my sister, buddy."

Fin waves at the derm patches wrapped around his throat and shrugs apologetically, mouthing the words *Not Supposed to Be Talking*.

"My burly protector," Scar says, hand to heart and lashes fluttering.

"I'm not worried about you," I scoff. "I'm worried about him."

She rolls her eyes, looks at the satchel I'm carrying.

"What'd you bring me?"

I sit beside the cot, rummaging around before tossing her a few packets of Just Like Real Noodelz!™ My sister stares at me, trading mock outrage for the real deal. "You brought me *ship rations?* Tyler, we're on *station,* they have *real food* here, what the . . . ?"

Her voice fades out as I produce a tub of ice-cold quad-choc gelato and an academy-issue spork, toss them into her waiting hands.

"Ooooh, you are a *good* man, Tyler Jones. I pardon you."

Fin winces, speaks in a whisper. "Can't believe . . . you're hungry."

"You're not supposed to talk." Scarlett eases off the top of the gelato tub like it contains the answer to the question of life, the universe, and everything. "And when in doubt, eat your way out."

Fin looks at the holo projected on the wall, mumbling. "Just . . . feels strange to be celebrating."

Scar and I follow his gaze to the holo, drinking in the sight. Battle Leader de Stoy stayed behind aboard Aurora Station to oversee the assault. But Adams is sending us a feed direct from the bridge of his flagship, the *Relentless.* He said we'd earned ourselves front-row seats to history.

And sure enough, history is playing out before our eyes.

After almost two weeks of Folding, the assembled ships of the coalition fleet have finally reached the Octavia gate and are now poised to commence their attack, wiping out the first seed world of the Ra'haam.

They gather like spears in the Fold's black and white, silhouetted against the gate. Like all the systems where the Ra'haam hid its nurseries, the Octavia gate is a naturally occurring weak spot in the fabric between dimensions. Instead of the hexagonal gates we Terrans use, or the teardrop portals of the Syldrathi, this one looks like a shimmering rip right across the face of the Fold. It's tens of thousands of

428

kilometers across, edges rippling with bursts of black quantum lightning. Over its horizon, the view sheers and shifts like heat haze, and beyond, I can see a faint glimpse of the Octavia star, burning blood-red in the rainbow hues of realspace.

Last time we saw this, it was just the seven of us. Squad 312. We all know what we lost on the planet. What was taken from us. For a moment, the anger and hurt are so bad it's all I can do to breathe.

"Strange to celebrate the death of the Ra'haam?" Scarlett scoffs, leaning back and taking a big bite of quad-choc. "Are you kidding? Should've brought some damn beers."

The *crackhisssss* of a pressured seal echoes in the room, and I hand Scarlett an ice-cold bottle of Ishtarrian ale.

"Oooooh, you are a *goooooood* man, Tyler Jones."

"Thought . . . you didn't drink," Fin whispers.

"I'm making an exception," I reply, taking a slow mouthful. "Want one?"

Fin shakes his head, looking back at the screens. I can feel his trepidation, his fear, and a part of me shares it, honestly. If the Eshvaren went to all that trouble to get us the Weapon, to plot their assault on their ancient enemy over the course of millennia, it seems a touch overconfident to expect we can just brute-force our way through this.

But thinking about it rationally, for all their power, the Eshvaren lived a million years ago. We don't know if there were any other inhabited planets during their time—maybe they were all alone. They probably had no concept of the firepower a coalition of a few hundred star-spanning species could generate if they got motivated enough. This fleet, this force . . . it's like nothing the galaxy has ever seen.

And besides, it's our only hope.

Adams and his fellow commanders aren't fools either, and they aren't charging in blind—they've already launched a wave of recon probes through the gate to scope the system. From the reports coming in, Octavia III looks almost exactly as it did when the seven of us were last there—a run-of-the-mill M-class rock. Seventy-four percent ocean, four major continents. Dull as a Saturday night in my dorm room—unless you're into chess, I guess.

But I know those blue-green land masses and stretches of blue-green ocean aren't really earth or water anymore. They're the skin of the Ra'haam. Beautiful fronds and rolling vines and curling leaves, basking in the heat of the planet's core. It's a mask, hiding the face of the monster growing beneath.

But from all the data, all the readings . . .

"It's still asleep," Scar murmurs.

"Looks like," I nod.

"You really think this is gonna work?" she asks.

I clench my jaw, watching as the order is given and the fleet begins flooding through the gate. I try not to think about all we need but don't have, all we gave up to get this far. Cat and Zila and Kal and Auri.

"It has to," I breathe.

The approach is textbook perfect, the armada descending out of the gate like the hand of the Maker. Wave after wave of Rigellian endsingers and Chellerian scythes and Betraskan saht-ka, cutting through the dark like arrows skimming the skies of some ancient battlefield, the crows already singing for the slaughter.

Behind them come the capital ships—the massive silhouettes of orbital bombardment platforms from Ishtarr, Aalani warstars, gremp battlehulks, Nu-laat warp-throwers, Aurora Legion carriers, surrounded by endless flights of Longbow escorts. I realize I'm breathing faster just at the sight of it all, the rush of it crawling in goose bumps on my skin. A part of me wishes so desperately I was there to land this punch, I can taste it.

Instead, I'm stuck in a hospital room halfway across the galaxy.

Helpless except to watch.

"This is for all of us, Ty," Scar says, meeting my eyes.

"Yeah." I nod, swallowing hard. "This is for Cat."

The order comes across comms. The bombardment begins. Ten thousand ships, ten thousand shots, ten thousand fists holding aloft our light in the dark.

As the first bombs fall, the atmosphere of Octavia begins to burn: fusion flashes burning white, orbital barrages splitting the clouds, mass-drivers shaking the foundations of the earth. It seems small at first. The planet is so big, the scope of it so immense. But even an elephant can be killed by enough ants. And most ants aren't armed with nuclear ordnance.

The blue green burns black. The crystal-clear skies of Octavia III are growing dark, billions of tons of earth and dust thrown into the atmo as the surface is engulfed in flames and the planet shakes to its bones. The barrage is relentless, endless, the might of the combined races of the galaxy bent to a single purpose—to slay this dragon in its lair, to drown this beast while it sleeps.

And Maker's breath, at first I didn't dare let myself hope. But as the bombardment continues, crushing, overwhelming, as the skies of Octavia III turn black with ash and its atmo boils away into space . . .

"They're doing it," I whisper. "They're actually—"

It's like a whisper at first. Shapeless and toneless, lodged somewhere at the base of my skull. Building in the place where I hid all those silly fears I thought were real as a kid—the monsters under my bed and the ugly voices in my head.

I look to Fin, and he seems not to notice, big black eyes still locked on the attack, blazing skies reflected in the smooth dark arc of his contact lenses. But looking past him to Scar, I see a frown forming on her brow, her lips parted as she begins to wince.

"You hear that?" I ask.

"No."

She meets my eyes and shakes her head.

"I *feel* that."

The pressure builds, cascading along the length of my spine and pressing on the back of my eyes so hard I'm forced to shut them, hand to my sweat-slick brow.

There's a tiny lull, as if something were drawing a single, smooth breath.

And then the whisper becomes a *scream*—a SCREAM so vast and hungry and hateful it reaches across the lonely wastes of space and seizes hold of my heart, squeezing so hard it almost stops.

"Oh Maker . . ."

Scar hisses, her nose bleeding. "What's . . . h-happening?"

Fin raises one shaking hand, his whisper like ice in my belly.

". . . Look."

The fleet. The assault. The missiles, the mass-drivers, the bombardment—all have fallen quiet and still. It's like Adams has called a cease-fire, except no such order has come through over comms. In fact, *nothing* is coming through over comms anymore, as if everyone in the armada is listening, enraptured or horrified or paralyzed by that awful

awful

SCREAMING.

Alarms are ringing aboard Aurora Station now—alerts for commanders to report to station, the lighting dipping toward yellow as we shift to Ready Status 2. The whole galaxy is witnessing this across the feeds, and I can imagine the uncertainty, the panic, spreading like poison as the mightiest fleet ever assembled hangs frozen and still, etched in dark silhouette against the shining cusp of that burning world.

"Admiral Adams . . . ," I whisper.

The atmo of Octavia III swirls and churns, firestorms raging among walls of black cloud, hundreds of kilometers high. That scream rises in intensity, so bright and sharp I can barely see through my tears, blood gushing from my nose and spilling over my lips. Fin has hold of Scarlett's hand, mopping at the flood of red dripping from her chin. But I force myself to watch those screens, horrified, stupefied, as the seething clouds of Octavia III tear themselves wide and the *thing* beneath comes flooding out.

It doesn't look like a monster. Like a horror, or an ending. And that's the awful thing—I'm actually awestruck at the *beauty* as a trillion spores of burning blue light come rushing up from the burning skin of Octavia III, flooding out into space. It rips the planet apart as it comes, shattering it to the heart, sundering mountains and molten mantle, the bleeding, liquid core splitting apart in a cataclysm beyond imagining.

Octavia III dies screaming, just like I'm screaming, just like *it* is screaming, yowling, howling like a hungry newborn dragged from the warmth of its mother's womb into the cold of the world. And my heart sinks in my chest as those glittering spores tumble through the dark, latching hold of those listing ships and sinking in, tendrils questing, seed pods bursting, corruption spreading out through the mightiest fleet the races of the galaxy have ever assembled and claiming it for its own.

"Oh no," Scar whispers. "Oh *Maker* . . ."

"It's awake . . . ," I breathe.

I see the light of engines engaging, ships beginning to turn—a few crews with the presence of mind to try to flee their fate. But most of them just hang there, listless and lifeless as Octavia III dies burning, screaming, giving birth to the thing she's warmed in her womb for the last million years.

I watch those spores tumbling, spilling, like globes of gleaming blue glass, engulfing the coalition fleet and rolling onward. I see the feeds from the armada begin to die, as one by one those ships are consumed, corrupted. I want to turn away, to close my eyes, to tell myself the monster under the bed isn't real, isn't real.

But I force myself to watch as the Ra'haam reaches the FoldGate—that glimmering tear across the stars, the endless pathways to the rest of the galaxy beyond. Scarlett has never attended chapel a day in her life, and she's *praying* as those gleaming orbs begin to flood through. Fin slips his hand into mine and squeezes so hard my knuckles creak.

"I saw this," he whispers. ". . . In a dream."

I say the only thing I can think of.

I say its name.

"Ra'haam."

An entity that once threatened to swallow every sentient life in the galaxy. A hunger so vast, an intellect so terrifying, an enemy so dangerous that an entire race sacrificed itself to prevent its rising again.

But they failed.

The Eshvaren failed.

And Maker help us, so have we.

Ra'haam.

37

TYLER

Ten days later, and the entire galaxy is drenched in panic.

I've never seen anything like it. It's like an infection, traveling ahead of the Ra'haam: that wave of glittering blue spores spilling out into the Fold, the corrupted coalition armada moving along with it.

We've had only snatches of vision as the enemy advances, but there's enough footage to know the fleet and everyone in it is gone. All those warstars and reapers and carriers now encrusted with spores and mold and leaves of blue green, trailing long, twisting tendrils behind them through the Fold. They look like shipwrecks on the bottom of Terran oceans, overrun with barnacles and weeds, and I shudder to think about what became of all those brave soldiers inside.

Admiral Adams. His fellow commanders.

The Aurora Legion and every military in the galaxy have been virtually decapitated.

Where a few weeks ago it slumbered hidden and silent, now the whole galaxy knows its name, whispered in the dark and spoken fearfully behind closed doors and shouted across the feeds.

Ra'haam.

An enemy set to swallow the races of the galaxy one by one. Until there's nothing left but *it.*

As far as we can tell, only the Octavia nursery has hatched so far. Maybe it has something to do with the assault, or the Terran colony that settled there, some other variable. All we know for certain is that as bad as things are now, they're gonna get twenty-one times worse once those other nursery worlds hatch.

This war is over almost before it's begun.

The fear of it is like a wildfire, sweeping the Milky Way just as the enemy sweeps out into the Fold. The other races begin panicking, some going so far as to destroy the FoldGates into their systems—cutting themselves off into a new, pre-Fold Dark Age rather than allow the Ra'haam to colonize their worlds. And all the while, those spores billow outward, glowing ghostly blue even in the muted colorscape of the Fold.

Endless.

Relentless.

The corrupted fleet rides the spore wave, cruising like dark shadows among a glowing, glittering storm billions of kilometers across. And as I watch the snatches of footage on the feeds, awash in the terror of it all, I can't help but sink into hopelessness.

I did just what my vision told me. I stopped the destruction of Aurora Academy, averted whatever calamity might have followed the destruction of the Galactic Caucus. I did as I was asked.

And in doing so, I've helped hand the Ra'haam a massive battle fleet it might otherwise never have had.

Scar and Fin carved a pathway across time, Zila gave her life to form the Aurora Legion in the past to fight against this thing, Auri and Kal gave up their lives to try to secure the Weapon, and yet, here the Ra'haam is, spewing out into the Fold just like it always wanted, just like it always planned.

Maybe after all we've done, Squad 312 only made things worse.

And even after all I did to save Aurora Station, it will count for nothing. Because Aurora Station is where that Ra'haam fleet is headed next.

Our logistics teams have confirmed it. Course plotted. Data correlated.

The Ra'haam is coming here.

And it'll arrive in less than twenty hours.

No help is coming. No miracle on its way. We're outnumbered and outgunned—though we still have reserve ships and a defense grid, the simple fact is, a fleet that size will make short work of any resistance we can muster.

"Scar, you've gotta get out of here."

We're standing on the promenade, the chaos of the crowd milling around us. What's left of station command has confirmed the Ra'haam is inbound to Aurora Station, and all nonessential personnel have been ordered to evacuate. Vendors and their families are hastily packing up their stores and possessions, the dark outside lit up by the flare of hundreds of engines—shuttles and carriers and freighters streaming through the FoldGate, headed toward whatever safety they can find.

"Brother mine," Scarlett says, "you're out of your mind."

"I mean it," I say, waving to the station around us. "The

time for diplomacy is long gone, Scar. There's no sense you staying here."

"There's no sense in *anyone* staying here, far as I can tell," Fin says.

"*Thank* you!" Scar cries, giving Fin a dramatic bow. "At last, someone here is talking sense!"

"I thought you weren't supposed to be talking at all," I mutter.

My Gearhead flashes me a grin, his new exosuit hissing softly as he shrugs. "We all knew it was too good to last."

"Seriously, Tyler, we should evac with th—"

"I can't do that, Scar. I swore an oath to the Legion when I joined it."

"The *Legion*?" she scoffs. "Tyler, we lost most of our commanders and nearly all our ships when Octavia bloomed! The Legion is absolutely *fuc*—"

"I know!" I say, my temper flaring. "I know better than *anyone*! Trust me, I've run this math with de Stoy a thousand times! But if I'm gonna die, then I'm gonna die fighting! And the best place to fight from is here!"

She meets my stare and simply shrugs. "Then I'm staying with you."

"Scar, no, there's no—"

"I don't want to hear it!" Scar shouts. "I didn't join the Legion because I wanted to make the galaxy a better place! I didn't join it to be a hero! I joined it because you're my baby brother and I look after you! And I didn't drag my fabulous ass across time and space and collapsing paradox loops just to turn and run at the first sign of a little galaxy-shattering cataclysm, you hear me?"

I look my sister in the eye.

I've known Scarlett Isobel Jones my entire life. I know her better than anyone in the 'Way. I know she coasted her way through the academy, that she never really took this as seriously as she could, that maybe she was never the best recruit in the Legion.

But I can see now how the trials she's faced and the battles she's fought have changed my sister. She's harder than she used to be. Braver. I can see that over the past few months she's found a well of strength inside herself even she never knew existed. But there's one thing about Scarlett Isobel Jones that's remained the same. One thing all this loss and struggle haven't managed to change.

She still loves more fiercely than anyone I've ever met.

"Scarlett," I say. "If you stay here, you're going to die."

"I lost you once, Ty," she replies, chin raised. "I'm not doing it again."

Fin steps up beside her, taking her hand. "Looks like you're stuck with both of us, boss."

I sigh, looking out the massive viewport to the stars outside. The fleeing ships. The fall of a galaxy.

I know there's no way out of this. I know we're looking down the barrel of our own execution. And I remember what it felt like fighting Cat in the reactor. Looking into those glowing eyes. Bleeding out on the floor. That awful moment when I wondered if it wouldn't be better to just lose myself in the Ra'haam rather than die alone.

I know how stupid that fear was now. Because even in my darkest hours, I've *never* been alone. And so I put my arms around Scar, hold her tight, grabbing Fin and pulling him in, too.

This is what family is, I realize.

To never be alone.

The lighting around us shifts to red. An alarm pitches across the PA, a metallic voice echoing across the promenade.

"Aurora Station, this is Battle Leader de Stoy. Red alert: Unauthorized vessels inbound. All stations Ready one."

"Oh shit . . . ," Scarlett whispers.

"Repeat, this is Battle Leader de Stoy. Multiple unauthorized vessels breaching Aurora FoldGate. All stations Ready one status."

"It's here," Fin breathes.

"No," I frown, easing them both out of my arms and looking through the viewport at the gate beyond. "The Ra'haam is still nineteen hours fr—"

"Legionnaire Jones, this is de Stoy, do you copy?"

I tap the comm badge at my chest.

"I read you, Commander."

"You'd best get your tail up to C&C on the double, soldier."

I look to the FoldGate again, my belly twisting as dark shapes begin pouring through the rift.

I put my hand to the plasteel viewport, heart breaking loose in my chest, not quite believing what I'm seeing.

"I know those ships . . . ," I whisper.

"Ty?" Scar asks. "What are—"

But I'm already running, barreling down the promenade through the milling crowd, roaring at the top of my lungs. "Scar, Fin, come on!"

"Where the hells are you g—"

"JUST COME ON!"

Scar and Finian follow me through the fleeing crowd and into the turbolift. We ride up to the bridge of the C&C tower

441

in silence, Fin and Scar looking at me like I'm half-crazy, me wondering if I'm all the way gone.

I didn't dare hope, didn't dare even let myself *think* about it, but as the three of us pile out into the crowded decks of Aurora Command and Control, my suspicion is confirmed, a storm of butterflies breaking loose in my stomach just as a goofy-as-hells smile breaks out all over my face.

"What is *that*?" Fin asks, looking at the monitor screens.

"She did it," I grin. "She *made* it."

The shapes are clearer now, spilling through the blinding flare of the FoldGate and into the Aurora system. A fleet of battleships, sleek and sharp, black hulls daubed with beautiful glyfs of gleaming white. A people born with the taste of blood in their mouths.

A people born for war.

Battle Leader de Stoy stands among her staff, looking about as certain as a commander running on zero sleep in the middle of a galactic cataclysm can. Her thin, pale face is set in a scowl, black eyes fixed on me.

"They've been hailing us for the past five minutes," she informs us. "They want to speak to you, Jones."

I nod, standing a little taller. "Roger that, ma'am."

The image of the incoming fleet on the holoscreen in front of us dissolves, that massive armada replaced by a single face. Her hair is dark as the empty spaces between the stars, her eyes shining like dark jewels, black lips curled into a tiny smile as she lays eyes on me.

She's beautiful. Fierce. Brilliant. Ruthless.

Like no one I've ever known.

"Saedii . . . ," Fin whispers.

"Tyler Jones," Saedii says.

"About time," I smile, scarred eyebrow rising slightly. "I wondered if you planned to sleep through the entire war."

Scar and Fin both look at me, gobsmacked. Saedii only scoffs. "Time enough to sleep in the grave, Terran."

"Did you do what you needed?" I ask. "Get what you wanted?"

Saedii spreads her arms, as if to encompass the Unbroken armada at her command. Her smile is triumphant, and I notice there's a new chain hanging around her neck, silver, strung with half a dozen severed Syldrathi ears. "I am a Templar of the Unbroken, Tyler Jones. I do what I wish, I go where I please, and I take what I want."

"You know what's coming for us."

She nods, fierce and grim. "We have seen."

"Then you know there's no way out of this," I warn. "Our only real plan here is to take out as much of it as we can before the big goodbye."

"We will dance the dance of blood with you. We will paint the sun red this day." She shakes her head. "And Unbroken do not say goodbye."

My heart is burning in my chest at the sight of her. I didn't realize how much I'd missed her until this moment. I hold out my hand toward her, and she raises her own, as if to press her palm against mine.

I wish we had more time, I wish I'd gotten to know her better, I wish . . .

"I'm glad you're here, Saedii Gilwraeth."

Black lips curl in the smallest of smiles. "I am also pleased to fight once more at your side, Tyler Jones. And . . ."

"And?"

". . . And to see you again."

Saedii stares for an endless heartbeat longer, and then her transmission drops away. Lowering my hand, I realize the entire bridge crew is looking at me incredulously.

"Not that I'm ungrateful for the assist," de Stoy says. "But I almost wish I had time to read your report on that one, Legionnaire Jones."

My Gearhead is wearing an expression somewhere between admiration and shock, but my sister is going straight for utter disbelief, looking between me and the screen.

"You . . . and *her*?"

I shrug. "It's the dimples."

"How are you still *walking*?" Fin whispers.

I grin. "Yeah, I was limping for a while there."

Fin covers his open mouth with one hand, offers me a cheeky fist bump behind Scar's back with the other. Scar catches him, looks back and forth between us. "What are you, *twelve*?"

"Out of ten?" I shrug. "Yeah, sounds about right."

"Oh *Maker* . . . ," she groans.

The smiles are short-lived, the warmth in my chest quickly fading, until the thought of the thing coming for us is all that remains.

Glad as I am for Saedii and her armada to be here, I know they're not going to make the difference between victory and defeat. The corrupted coalition fleet is too big, the Ra'haam is too much—like I said, our only move here is to do as much damage to it as possible before we go down.

But if that's the play, then we're going to make it as best we can.

And if this really is the end, at least I'm not alone.

. . . . .

Seventeen hours later, I'm standing on the bridge of a familiar Longbow, staring out at our lines of defense. Behind us,
Aurora Station glitters like the sun at dawning, bristling with
pulse cannons and missile arrays. Around us, the Legion
fleet is forming up into our lines.

Adams and de Stoy threw almost every ship they had at
the Octavia assault, and there's only forty or so Legion Long-
bows left, flanking one heavy cruiser, the *Invincible*, commanded by Battle Leader de Stoy herself.

But supporting us is Saedii's Unbroken armada: the
dark silhouettes of Wraiths and Specters, the sleek bulk of
Banshee carriers and Shadows, hundreds upon hundreds of
them. We're arrayed in a phalanx, aimed toward the Fold-
Gate, ready to unleash hell on the first vessel that blows
through.

"*Hostiles still inbound,*" comes the warning over comms.
"*Enemy fleet will breach Aurora system in T minus six minutes.*"

"Thanks for the ride," I murmur, eyes on the gate. "I'd
have hated to sit this one out on the sidelines, Em."

Beside me, Emma Cohen shrugs, eyes roaming the fleet.
"Figured I owed you one after you stopped the station from
getting blown to pieces and all."

"No hard feelings about me locking you in your own brig?"

"That depends," she says, looking at me sidelong. "Any
hard feelings about me shooting you in the face?"

"We both did what we had to do," I smile. "We the Legion."

She nods, smiling back. "We the Light."

"And I really *am* sorry about Damon," Scar pipes up

beside me. "I mean, I didn't even know you two were dating at the time."

Emma shrugs, eyes back on the gate. "He was an asshole."

"*Right?*"

"*Enemy fleet will breach Aurora system in T minus four minutes.*"

"Nono," Fin says, sitting beside de Renn. "Your third mother is my first aunt, on second granddad's side."

Cohen's tank pauses in his calculations, fingers hovering over his fire controls. "But my second first uncle is your third cousin too, right?"

". . . Dariel is your first uncle?"

"Yeah, once removed on my—"

"How are those calcs coming, de Renn?" Cohen asks.

"Good to go," the Tank replies, straightening up. "We're ready, Alpha."

"*Enemy fleet will breach Aurora system in T minus three minutes.*"

The holo projections in front of us flicker with the Legion sigil, and the face of Battle Leader de Stoy appears above the consoles. The last surviving commander of the Aurora Legion looks grim, determined. Her voice rings across the bridge and the fleet under her command.

"*Aurora legionnaires.*

"*To be a Betraskan is to know you are never alone.*

"*Every one of us is part of a sprawling network, a clan and a greater clan, siblings, parents, grandparents, cousins, and hundreds of others who share our blood.*

"*Wherever we go, we know this one truth: we are family.*

"*This is the legacy we are born to. But every one of us here*

is a part of something more powerful still, whether we are Be-
traskan, Terran, or Syldrathi.

"*We are part of a clan we have chosen. A clan we have
built not with bonds of blood, but with promises we have chosen to make. We have pledged our hearts to our cause, and to
each other.*

"*Even now, the Aurora Legion burns bright when the night
is at its darkest. Even now, we stand in the way of what is
wrong, and we stand for peace. This is the vow we have made,
and the promise we have made to the Legion and to each other.*

"*Know this: It is the honor of my life to stand shoulder to
shoulder with each of you, my chosen clan—the family of my
heart—today. There is no place in this galaxy, or any other, I
would choose to be, but here.*"

Her voice cuts out, and is replaced almost immediately
with a robotic comms announcement.

"*Enemy fleet will breach Aurora system in T minus one
minute.*"

A voice rings over comms, familiar, cold as ice and yet
still able to light a fire in my chest.

"*De'na vosh, aam'nai,*" it says. "*De'na siir.*"

I look toward Saedii's flagship, hanging in the dark off to
our port, then glance at Scar in silent question.

"Know no fear, my friends," my sister translates. "Know
no regret."

"*Dun belis tal'dun. Nu belis tal'satha.*"

"The end is no ending. And death is no defeat."

"*An'la téli saii.*"

"I will—"

"Yeah, I know that one already."

447

". . . You do?"

I nod, voice soft. "I will see you in the stars."

"Warning: Enemy fleet inbound. All ships: Enemy fleet inb—"

The FoldGate flares, a lightning strike across black skies, and through that burning window, the first Ra'haam vessel arrives.

It's here. . . .

The ship is a Terran carrier, sleek and heavy, bristling with guns. Its hull crawls with growths, like fungus on the hulk of a fallen tree, blue and green and ghostly pale, long tendrils trailing behind as it comes. My heart sinks as I see the name daubed on its prow, barely visible beneath the stains of the Ra'haam's infection.

Relentless.

"Admiral Adams," Finian whispers.

"Not anymore," I murmur.

But I close my eyes, just for a moment. I know we're about to fire on him. Try to kill him as completely as I killed Cat.

But before she died, Cat defended me. The Ra'haam defended me.

It loved me because she did.

That's not Admiral Adams anymore . . . but a part of *it* . . .

"ALL STATIONS, FIRE!"

The barrage begins, blinding, burning, pulse beams cutting bright and missiles rolling outward, vapor trails strung behind them like streamers on Federation Day. Explosions bloom soundlessly, fusion fires flaring as bright as the Aurora star at our backs, melting bulkheads and splitting metal apart.

The *Relentless* plows through the firestorm, flames and

coolant spewing from her ruptured skin along with slicks of what could almost be blood, coiling and bubbling in the void. Our fleet keeps hammering, pouring on the firepower until, inevitably, the flagship buckles under the strain and splits apart in a halo of rippling flame.

Admiral Adams and I went to chapel together every Sunday.

I'd never have made it this far without him.

"You must believe, Tyler."

"I'm sorry," I whisper.

But he's not there to hear me.

And there's no time to mourn. No songs of grief or twenty-one-gun salutes. Because behind the flaming wreckage of our former commander's flagship, the rest of the Ra'haam fleet is now pouring through the FoldGate.

Endsingers and scythes and saht-ka, warstars and battle-hulks and warp-throwers, riding a rolling, churning wave of a million glittering spores. They pour into the Aurora system, thousands upon thousands of ships, too many to match, let alone defeat.

Cohen shouts orders, and it's on, our Longbow weaving through the streams of fire, those glittering globes, cutting the dark around us with as much fire as we can throw.

The Unbroken armada burns massive swaths through the oncoming horde, the black void of space runs thick with Ra'haam blood, viscous and slick. But their numbers are endless, their strength relentless, and as the Ra'haam returns fire and the ships around us begin to die, we all know there's only one way this is going to end.

"How we doing, Battle Leader?" I shout.

"*Reactor coolant systems offline,*" de Stoy replies. "*Safeties overridden.*"

"How long till we hit critical?"

"*Three minutes. Let's hope this plan of yours works.*"

"If you gotta die, die with your boots on."

A faint radiation spike flares behind us, through Aurora Station's skin, the reactor tripping ever closer to overload. I remember the feeling of that rising heat in the core, the flickering light, Cat's blood on my hands. And I see it again in my mind's eye, that vision, that dream awake—Aurora Station blowing itself apart over and over.

The Ra'haam senses something is wrong, its rearguard vessels halting their maneuvers, the vanguard slowing its assault.

But the FoldGate is in our sights now, just a few more moments till it's in range, till we fire, blowing it apart and trapping the enemy in here with us.

"*Two minutes to critical.*"

The voice in my head told me I could stop it. I could fix it. But maybe I wasn't supposed to. Maybe the station dying, the dream of the Legion along with it, bursting apart in the middle of the enemy and burning it to cinders, is the best we can hope for.

I reach for Scarlett's hand, squeezing tight.

Beside her, Fin slips his arm around her waist.

This end is no ending.

"*One minute to critical.*"

We'll see each other again.

In the st—

The galaxy around us inverts.

The thunder of a billion storms rings inside my head.

I stagger with the force of it, the people around me gasping, stumbling, the battle outside falling still. I see the medallion around Scar's throat, glowing now with kaleidoscopic fire, cascading through the bridge, an echo, a roar, a *birth cry* ripped across the darkness and burning all into blinding white.

A shape smashes its way through the walls of time and space. Torn across the breadth of eternity, dragging itself through past and future and infinite possibility, screaming as it comes. The light burns so bright it's blinding, splintering and fracturing now into all the colors of the spectrum, red to yellow to blue to indigo, no, not a spectrum but a rainbow

A RAINBOW

etched in the spear of broken crystal as big as a city, now floating there in the dark before my wondering eyes.

Unbelievable.

Impossible.

"Maker's breath," Finian gasps.

"The *Weapon!*" Scarlett cries.

It's not too late, I realize.

She's here.

"Aurora," I whisper.

38

AURI

I am everything.

I am everyone.

I am everywhere.

In a flash, we are in the place we need to be, the hymn of the *Neridaa* slowly winding down to a low chord that tingles and reverberates through my very bones.

The Eshvaren crystal sings its song, and the energy-that-was-Caersan is fading from me, and I lift my head to discover Kal lying wounded in the center of the throne room, and I'm curled over him, my body protecting his.

And we are alone.

There is no sign of the Ra'haam in here. Caersan has vanished.

The bodies of the Waywalkers remain, but the bodies of Tyler and Lae are gone, because they are no longer reality, only . . . possibility.

Because we're home.

"Be'shmai," Kal whispers, trying to prop himself up on one elbow.

"I'm here," I whisper in reply.

I love you, my mind tells his.

I chanted it to him as we hurtled back in time, as I shielded him, and the words live between us still, and that's fine by me, because I don't want to take them back. I want to say them as many times as I can in the time I have left.

"I'm all right," I say, pushing to my feet. Because I am. I should be exhausted after the battle to repair the ship, but I've never felt more powerful, or more purposeful.

All of the future's survivors gave their lives to bring us here. To offer me one chance to change the way our story unfolds. I'm not going to waste it.

At my request, the Weapon projects the view from outside onto the walls of the throne room, a three-hundred-sixty-degree view of the battle in progress, as if the walls weren't crystal but shining glass.

Life and death play out around us, an Aurora Legion Longbow veering to avoid the Weapon in a panicked maneuver, pursued by a Ra'haam vessel trailing vines behind it, and as I look up and out, I see the same thing over, and over, and over.

The Aurora Legion makes its last stand here alongside a fleet of sleek, bloodthirsty Syldrathi ships, Unbroken glyfs painted down their sides. Whoever has taken over Caersan's leadership, it seems they've decided the Ra'haam is a foe worth fighting.

Together, the fleets are confronting an armada that endlessly outnumbers them, an armada the size and shape of every race it's overtaken, wreathed in vines and mindlessly hungry.

The little Legion ship rounds the edge of the Weapon and swings away, like a fish that saw a shadow, and I see how the fate of its crew will play out in the next few seconds.

I see how their frantic scramble to avoid their pursuers, to shake the hungry Ra'haam from their tail, will send them straight into the side of a Ra'haam flagship, to end in a quick explosion of soundless fire, each of them given only a millisecond to know their fate before oblivion swallows them.

Kal sees the way it will end too, and his reflexive horror is mine, so I reach out and nudge the course of the Longbow, and it sails up and over the flagship, darting instead to the shelter of its fellows as a bloody fight to the death rages on around us both.

The Ra'haam is so much bigger than it was, its presence so much more powerful, so rich now. This new armada represents countless lives lost, snuffed out in an instant as the mindless whole of the Ra'haam took them over. But as I let my mind brush against it, and as it shivers, shudders, and turns its attention toward me, my lips curve slowly into a smile.

I tip my head first to the left, then to the right, hearing the crack of the vertebrae in my neck. Because I've been to the future, and I've seen how this could end. And this version of the Ra'haam, here and now?

I say it out loud, feeling the power thrum within me, throwing down my challenge as the light shines from my eye, and the cracks in my skin slowly spiderweb out. It's agonizing, and exhilarating.

"That all you got?"

My hands curl to fists.

"I've seen worse."

Kal pushes painstakingly up to his knees, the violet and gold of his mind tangling with mine. "So many," he whispers, staring out at the battle, at the fleet that was once the army of hundreds of worlds. "So many lost."

"So many left to save," I say quietly. "So many more left than in the future. And look, Kal. Do you see?"

I tug his mind along with mine to show him the Ra'haam—the thousands, the millions of connections, the singular, the *we*, that comes from what should be many, should be individual, should be *us*. That writhing mass of souls bound together with but one purpose: to increase itself, to consume everything before it.

I show him the gloriously tangled web of mental energy linking every one of its bodies to every other, every ship to every other.

It's beautiful, really.

He recoils, but I hold him tight, and next I turn my focus outward, and show him what I couldn't see before now—before I'd been elsewhere, elsewhen, and fought it up close.

There are *other* veins that lead away from it, mental highways and alleyways that pulse with its blue-green energy, stretching into the unimaginable distance, making journeys our minds can't comprehend. Journeys that would take us millions of years to make in our feeble ships.

You see . . . His mind tries to shy away from the scale of what we're observing, and he takes hold of himself, tries again. *You see all of it now.*

I see all of it, I agree. *And I know how to kill it.*

The Weapon was designed by the Eshvaren to be fired on twenty-two sleeping nursery planets, one by one. But there's no time for that now. And I'm not sure I have it left in me, after the battles I've already seen.

But the Eshvaren never knew we'd stumble on one planet before the others. That humans, with our endless, insatiable curiosity, would find a natural FoldGate that nobody else thought worth investigating, too far from anywhere to be interesting. That we'd push through it and land somewhere no one else had been.

They never knew we'd awaken the Ra'haam before it was time.

And now that this small part of it is awake, it can act as a conduit to the rest of it. If I can destroy this fleet—the nursery that bloomed and burst early, that took over the Octavia colony—then I can push that destruction out through its endless network, like a virus, like a wildfire.

I can destroy the nursery planets before they awaken.

You can kill all of it, Kal wonders.

I can kill all of it, I agree. *Light a flame to burn it from the inside out.*

And I will be the fuel.

I start to laugh, brushing away the blood that drips from my nose, and ready myself to begin the assault. I will kill this thing here, now, and that death will spread, infectious, until it dies *everywhere.*

Kal reaches for my hand, and doesn't ask again if I can survive it. But I feel the flicker of hope inside him, and I keep the truth from him.

Just for a few minutes more.

He weaves his fingers through mine, braiding us together, determined to stay with me for as long as possible.

You are not alone, he says, deep in my mind.

And I resolve to cast him free at the last moment, to send him on to live the rest of his beautiful life without me, in the world I'm going to make for them—but for now I hold him close.

He was always going to live a century longer than me, and there is so much for him to see, and so much for him to do. I wish I could be there, at his side. But I'll willingly give myself, knowing I've made it possible for him.

In the calm before the storm, I reach out to caress the places I will protect, and I find there's no limit to how far I can stretch.

I run my fingertips across the shining hull of Aurora Station, and the fleet, and then I throw myself out farther—I see Emerald City, I see Sempiternity, as gorgeously grubby and alive as ever, teeming with life and with promise. I brush past the hulking wreck of the *Hadfield* to the worlds where Dacca's people and Elin's people and Toshh's people are still alive, still safe. I see broken FoldGates, the planets that have shut themselves off in the vain hope of survival, and far away I see Earth, where my story began.

I am boundless now, and I know why.

It's because I'm not holding anything back. Not keeping any part of myself safe. I don't need to have anything left when this is finished.

I just need to last long enough to see it through.

Beloved, Kal says, so small in this endless galaxy, but never, *ever* unheard. *We must act.*

Gently, so gently, he tugs my attention back to the place my body is, and I see it—of course. The battle continues. And around me, tiny lights like fireflies are snuffed out one by one.

A ship explodes into a million glittering fragments, and five small specks of life that were there before are gone.

It's as I am contracting in to focus on this time and this place—Aurora Station, the Ra'haam's armada—that I see the flicker of his mind.

I almost miss it, amid the chaos.

TYLER!

He is so, *so* young, he is not yet exhausted, he is, he is, he is

my friend

and he is

so bright

and in this time and place he still *is*

so I gather myself and will everything around me to

STOP.

And it does.

The defenders are held stationary. Nobody can fire. The Ra'haam ships are frozen, unable to reach out for them with their endlessly questing vines. The battle becomes a tableau, everything suspended, both sides staring at each other from suddenly unresponsive ships.

And as I hold myself so carefully, *so carefully* in check so I don't hurt him, I let the tiniest part of myself crash joyfully into Tyler, and Kal comes with me, and Tyler's mental shout is the most beautifully vibrant yellow, like sunshine, like fields of wheat, like spun gold.

I learned in the Echo to live half a year in a few hours, and now I am stronger, I can live an eternity between heartbeats.

So I have time.

I have time for this.

It takes only the tiniest nudge and . . . there we are. In one of my favorite places, one last time. Because why shouldn't we be?

The three of us—Kal, Tyler, and me—are sitting at a round table of synthesized wood, in the kitchen of a modest apartment belonging to Ad Astra Incorporated. The countertops are covered in jars and containers of food, and cooking pots hang from hooks on the ceiling. My parents liked to cook as often as they could as they prepped for the Octavia mission.

"You should always have a place to feed your friends," Mom told Callie and me when we complained about having to squeeze around the table to get out into the hall.

Now music is playing softly in the background, and I can smell my mother's soda bread baking in the oven. There's a big bowl of peas sitting in the middle of the table, and I pull it toward me to start shelling them. Dad used to grow them by the window, and this was always my job.

"Where are we?" Tyler asks, twisting to look around in surprise.

"Home," I say quietly. "Just for a minute."

"You honor us by sharing your hearth," Kal murmurs, and because our minds are nested, I feel the weight of tradition behind the Syldrathi phrase.

"Was that you?" Tyler asks, still studying the place. "Stopping everything?"

"Yes," I say, studying him a little closer. "Did you feel it?"

Something's slowly coming into view between us, sort of reverse-fading into existence. They're . . . threads. Midnight blue for me, violet for Kal, and yellow for Tyler. Strung between us like a spider's web.

They are our minds, I think—or rather, the way our minds show up in this moment I've made for us.

I run my fingers along the beautiful yellow thread of Tyler's that ties to my wrist, and I learn something new about him.

"It wasn't just Lae! You're part Syldrathi too, but you never knew."

"Who's Lae?" he asks, reaching up to touch the thread between us.

Kal and I exchange a glance, a sad smile.

"A kinswoman of mine," Kal says simply. "My family's greatest pride, Brother." He smiles. "I hope you meet her one day."

Now that I've found our threads, it's easier to see the

others, a rainbow tied to our wrists and snaking away into invisibility. So I reach out and follow them, searching for the rest of our family.

A moment later, Scarlett is at the table, bound to us by bright red, her uncanny empathy finally making sense— a gift from her Waywalker mother. Her threads tie her to me, and to Kal, and a thousandfold more intricately to her twin, their bond woven between them like a tapestry of red and gold. I see the moment her mind connects with his, the moment she sees the truth of their mother. I hear her gasp, and I feel her loss.

Then comes Finian beside her, emerald green and full of life. It's harder for him—he has no Syldrathi blood, no Eshvaren training, his mind wasn't made for this. But he *is* Betraskan, and those at this table are his clan, his chosen family, and that binds him to us, his vibrant green thread a part of our whole. He's always had so much love inside him.

Each of us holds tight to him in return, and when he flickers, we help him stay, strengthen his part of our woven rainbow with *our* love.

I search for Zila next, and then more urgently, scrambling for the thread I know must be there, but there's nothing. Scarlett looks at me, tears in her eyes, and our minds connect and

oh, Zila.

Zila.

I hope you loved her, I hope you were happy.

And just as I think we're done, I see there are more— black threads stretching away from Tyler and from Kal, and when I tug on them, I see . . .

Saedii Gilwraeth sitting at my parents' table, eyebrow raised.

Wordlessly, Tyler reaches into the bowl and hands her a pea pod to shell, and something passes between them. A few more lines of thread, yellow and black entwining like a swarm of bees—vibrant but dangerous—and she takes it from him and breaks it open.

Her sharp-edged mind nearly finds the truth of Lae in me as I watch them together, but I push it away to a safer place. Some things are meant to be discovered in their own time. And seeing them together, I have a feeling they'll meet her one day.

None of us use words, because none of us need to—our exchange is lightning quick, and the threads fly between us in the most beautiful, wild, chaotic, and perfect rainbow,
and we share our stories, and
we say I love you,
and the tapestry grows,
and
and
and . . .
. . . I begin to see.
Oh.
Oh, I see.
I see something I didn't before, as I planned my end.

Something new sweeps through me, a possibility I'd never even imagined, so full of battle and so ardent in my defense. As if I'm slowly waking up from a very long sleep, and blinking my eyes to help them focus on what's in front of me, I begin to see. . . .

It's there in the way Fin holds fast to us, even though it takes every ounce of his strength to keep his mind connected with his clan.

It's there in the way Scar wraps every one of us up in her love, her acceptance, the way she has every moment we've been together.

It's there in the way Ty thinks of each of us before himself, in the way he fights for what is right no matter how tired he grows.

It's there in the way Kal pushes always to find his best self, to believe in *our* best selves, to set aside all the world has told him to be and become what he chooses instead.

It's there in the ferocity of Saedii's love and loyalty, in her unflinching commitment to what she knows must be done.

They help me see something here, joined with them all.

Something I already knew.

I knew it was true when Esh told me to burn away all my bonds and ties, and I rebelled. I knew it was true when Caersan told me that the powerful take what they will, and I defied him to defend those around us.

I've known it all along, because my squad has shown me every time they've stood beside me, and they're showing me again, right now. And they haven't been the only ones to teach me this lesson I've been so slow in learning.

Tyler showed me in the first moment of Squad 312's story, when he gave up his chance at a perfect squad to do what his heart told him was right, and he found me . . . and that moment was just the first in an avalanche.

Lae and Dacca and Elin and Toshh showed me too, when

they stood and fought instead of running to buy themselves just one more day.

Cat showed me, when she gave up her body and future to save her squad.

Zila showed me, when she gave up the life she knew to make a life for us.

Caersan showed me, in his final act, when he saved us. Because his final act was one of love, and it was his most powerful.

Love is more powerful than rage, or hate.

And it always will be.

Love can change everything.

And yes, it would work, if I set a fire inside the Ra'haam and burned it from the inside out. But maybe, just maybe . . .

The rainbow of threads between us weaves together tighter, unbearably beautiful, and we're our most honest selves in this instant. No wisecracks from Fin, no superiority from Saedii. Just *us*.

Us, trusting each other to see and be seen.

To meet what we find with . . .

"It has to come from love," I say, finally understanding, here in the middle of a frozen battlefield.

"Cat's still in there," Tyler replies. "She's still a part of it. We love her. And she loves us. Her last act was to try and protect me."

"Admiral Adams is in there," Scarlett says.

"Half the academy we've spent all these years training with," Finian adds. "Our teachers, our friends."

"Everyone who is a part of the Ra'haam loved someone,"

Kal says, his fingers curling through mine. "Everyone was a parent, a child, a friend, a lover, a neighbor. . . ."

A parent.

"My father is in there," I whisper. "He still calls to me."

"It cannot be done by force."

Saedii is trying out the words, speaking them slowly. A part of her still rebels against it, but she looks up, and meets my eyes.

"Or rather, it *should not* be."

"There is no love in violence," Kal murmurs.

"Can you do this?" Fin asks, holding tight to Scarlett's hand.

"You don't have to do it alone," Tyler says. "Squad 312. Forever."

"Be'shmai, can you do it?" Kal asks quietly.

I rise to my feet. "Let's find out."

I turn toward the door that leads out to the hallway, and the instant I open it, I'm in the middle of a jungle.

The air is warm and damp, my clothes sticking to my skin, and the light is dim. Treetops crowd together above me, casting everything below into twilight, vines looping and curling from trunk to trunk. The forest floor is crowded with leaf litter and small, hopeful saplings straining toward the light.

And it's perfectly, eerily silent—no rustling in the undergrowth, no birds or monkeys, no insects chirruping and humming, none of the thousand sounds that should be making up a symphony all around me.

I glance down and see the rainbow threads knotted to my wrist, stretching away behind me, but I don't look back.

Instead, I take my first step.

The jungle comes alive, vines writhing and reaching for me, and I'm *here,* but I'm also on the bridge of the *Neridaa,* kneeling beside Kal. And I'm at my parents' kitchen table, and I'm watching a frozen battlefield suspended in space, ships caught like flies in amber, their crews still alive, hailing each other, all asking the same questions, demanding the same answers.

I have to fight to clear a path, pulling the creepers from my arms and ducking under thorny branches, catching hints of the frozen battle from the corner of my eye, a tantalizing waft of my mother's baking bread.

And then I begin to glimpse the people.

I don't know any of them, and they're always almost out of sight, hidden by vines and branches and trees, and when I move toward them, they're never there when I burst from the greenery, scratched and sweating.

"Wait," I call out, pushing between two trees growing so close together I have to turn sideways, have to take hold of the rainbow threads tied to my wrist and ease them through so they're not cut. "Wait, I need to talk to you!"

A man turns, and around me the spaceships I'm holding in place all tremble, and the crystal of the Weapon glints, and I am Aurora Jie-Lin O'Malley, but I am Tyler Jericho Jones as well.

"We thought you were never coming," says Admiral Adams, smiling as he folds cybernetic arms across his chest. "It's time for you to join us."

"No," Tyler and I say together, my voice echoing in his.

"It's all right," the man says, and he's so comforting, so

sure, as the vines coil around his shoulders and across his chest like a pet snake. "There's no need to be afraid."

"This isn't right," we protest.

He tilts a smile at us and spreads his arms to encompass the jungle. "This is where you should be. Together, loved, with us. We know it's frightening to make the leap. But sometimes, you must have faith."

I stumble back, and crash not into the tree trunk that should be behind me, but into the yielding body of a human.

I whirl about, and there stands Cat, gazing at me with her perfectly blue eyes, just as she did when I held her, trying desperately to save her from her descent into the Ra'haam.

And I'm me, but I'm Scarlett, and Cat's mind is as beautiful as it was then, whirling eddies of reds and golds that remind me of her love of flight. And I feel the depth of the love between these two women, the power of their friendship, of their sisterhood, and Cat raises her hand to reach for us.

"We love you," she says, and I turn, stumbling away, scratches stinging with sweat as I push my way through the silent branches, the only sounds the crunch of the dead leaves underfoot, my harsh, panting breath.

Instinct is driving me now, and I can no longer see the *Neridaa,* the frozen ships, my parents' kitchen. I'm holding the rainbow threads in my fist to keep them safe, and I'm pushing blindly in the direction I know I have to go.

Deeper.

Deeper.

I have to go deeper.

I push past branches, leaves swatting at me and tree

trunks crowding in. I'm moving faster, frantic, and my foot catches on a log and I sprawl into a clearing, smacking to the ground with a gasp.

And when I lift my head, there he is, waiting for me.

Not Princeps, not one of them.

Just my dad, with his round cheeks and his kind eyes, holding the book of folktales we read together when I was small, that we read together in the Echo when the Eshvaren told me to bid farewell to him forever.

I lie there in the leaf litter and dirt, and I whisper the same words now that I did then, every part of me aching to run into his arms, to let him wrap me up, to feel that comfort I thought was gone forever one last time.

"I love you, Daddy."

And he answers in almost the same way.

"We love you too, Jie-Lin. Always."

We.

Not *I.*

I shake my head, my throat closing, grief pushing up like a fist. "This isn't you," I whisper.

"But it is," he says softly, still smiling. "Come, let's read a story. We can be together. We love you so, so much, my darling girl."

I would do anything for one more day with him. For one more day with my mom, with Callie. For a chance to say the things I said to them in the Echo. For a chance to say good-bye for real.

And I want to tell myself this isn't that.

But the deeper I go, the more I'm beginning to see.

This *isn't* him.

But also . . . it is.

It was Cat's love for Tyler that drove her to defend him. It's my father's love for me that drives the Ra'haam to try and connect with me, rather than to kill.

"I love you," I say. "That's what I came to tell you."

But telling him here, now, like this—it isn't enough.

I have to go deeper.

I have to go past the point of no return.

I have to do the thing I've dreaded, I see that now.

To fall in love is to surrender.

And I'm so afraid to lose myself, my hands shaking as I fumble with the rainbow strings at my wrist. They're my path back home, my trail of breadcrumbs, my connection to everything.

Love shouldn't ask you to give up everything else; that's not how love works. But this is how the Ra'haam loves, and if I'm to fall deeply enough into it that I can show it a different way, a different kind of love . . .

One by one I untie them, tears streaming down my cheeks, and I'm laughing and crying as I release my anchors, but I know this is right, and it will be okay, it will be okay, it will be okay.

And the last string, Kal's violet rimmed with gold, slithers away.

And I am free.

And it's intoxicating.

I become a part of the Ra'haam, every part of my mind merging with it, spreading out with the glorious sensation of being loved and held and known, parts of me alive that I never imagined.

I live a thousand lives, a million lives, and I share mine, and we commune in glorious union.

And as I dissolve into them, I light that spark I knew I must—but I don't set the Ra'haam on fire with grief and rage and anger.

I don't burn it from the inside out.

Because now I know, *this* is the way. Not the way of the Eshvaren—every last one of them spent themselves in battle, and just one fragment of the Ra'haam survived, and so the battle began again.

This time, something has to be different.

And that something will be me.

So instead, I willingly spread my wings and become utterly a part of the Ra'haam, and I feel the million connections light up around me as I join with it, and I know it and it knows me, and we know ourselves, and I travel through it at the speed of light, and

we fall

deeper

deeper

deeper

in

love.

My love spreads like wildfire, and I share the story of Aurora Jie-Lin O'Malley, who boarded a ship to a new world and woke up two centuries later.

And *I* becomes *we*, and we tell ourself my stories as I sink further in.

We tell ourself the story of Tyler Jericho Jones, son of a warrior and a Waywalker, who found us sleeping in the stars.

Saedii Gilwraeth, daughter of a warrior and a Waywalker herself, who learned a new way to see the world.

Finian de Karran de Seel, who was told by the world that he was not enough, and showed the world he was everything.

Scarlett Isobel Jones, who had a heart so large it could beat for her friends when theirs threatened to fail.

Kaliis Idraban Gilwraeth, who bore up under fists and taunts, who swore to serve even those who would never love him back, because it was right.

Zila Madran, who made a new life and brought us this one, her love paving the way for ours.

Catherine "Zero" Brannock, who is a part of us, who never flinched, never stopped fighting, or loving.

Caersan, Archon of the Unbroken, Slayer of Stars, who was unforgivable, and yet who loved.

We tell ourself all our stories, large and small, light and dark, and together we see every color of our rainbow. And there is one tiny part of us that is still *me*, not *we*, and I keep it alive just a few moments longer so I can speak.

It's not about the sum of the rainbow's parts, I tell them, *though it's beautiful together. It's about every shade within it, each of them beautiful on their own. These stories are about the way each of these people lived and loved, sometimes wisely and well, sometimes foolishly, sometimes in dark and terrible ways. But each of their journeys was their own.*

Love should never ask you to give up the things that make you different. The truths that can only be told about you, and nobody else.

And just as the last parts of me dissolve into the Ra'haam,

as my memory of *I* fades out, giving way to a beautiful, ir-resistible *we,* it begins. . . .

My love spreads through us like joyous wildfire, and I watch as

one

by

one

the stories of the Ra'haam awaken, blinking into existence like coals in a fire that seemed to have died.

Like a galaxy full of stars, coming alive one by one.

The Ra'haam—or rather, each and every part of it—is remembering what it's like to be *they,* not *it.*

What it's like to be *I,* not *we.*

And in this moment, it remembers love cannot be de-manded, or taken.

Only given.

It remembers that love offers a choice.

That love *is* a choice, one we make over and over again.

We want that choice, I tell it as the last parts of me merge with ecstatic joy. *We* are *that choice.*

And slowly, in a moment that takes an eternity, the lights twinkle back in answer. Each and every one of them, now a little closer to the person they were before they merged, before they became *us.* From one small light, then two, then millions, the answer comes back to me.

We . . . understand.

And because it is—no, *they* are—no, *we* are—so many, and have lived millions of lives, we know what we have to do.

Abruptly I'm back in my body, aboard the *Neridaa.* I'm lying on the floor, staring up at the crystal ceiling. But I'm also still with the Ra'haam, still a part of an extraordinary, unstoppable *us* that I will never leave, and it's glorious.

This wasn't just a price worth paying. This is the most beautiful experience of my life.

Kal is sitting by my side, and his head snaps up, eyes wet, cheeks streaked with tears.

"You have returned," he gasps, lifting my fingers to his lips, hope dawning slowly.

"For a little," I whisper, still smiling.

I can feel the Ra'haam fleet, I can sense the rest of me out there in the black, and I want to burst like a dandelion and let every part of me blow away, sinking into the *us* that awaits. Into the millions of lives and loves that are a part of me now. Together, forever.

"What does that mean?" Kal asks softly. "For a little?"

"It means we have to go, soon." My own eyes are wet too, but my tears aren't all sad. I love him so much. I ache at the thought of leaving him. But I will never be alone.

"Where will we go?" he asks.

"Not us," I say, letting my mind twine with his one last time, midnight blue and silver, violet and gold. "Not you and me."

And he sees.

The Ra'haam will go, and I am the Ra'haam, so I will go too.

"Please, do not leave me," he whispers, voice cracking, grip on my fingers tightening.

"You could come with us," I murmur.

He helps me silently to my feet, and together we watch as a single ship breaks away from the Ra'haam, and a single shuttle from the Legion fleet, each of them arcing its way through the others suspended mid-battle, homing in on the city-sized Weapon that was never going to be enough.

Together Kal and I walk down toward the docking bay, past the place where in the future our friends and family died defending us, our hands joined.

I'm going to miss him so very much.

They're all waiting for us when we get there.

Fin and Scarlett, Tyler and Saedii, each of them wary, hopeful, ranging from smiling to scowling. The ones who carried me here. And next to them stands my father, who smiles slowly and holds out his arms.

I break into a run, and this feeling I thought would never be mine again is, and can be forever now, and as I rest my head on his shoulder and he holds me tight, I am so deeply contented that I want to live in this moment always.

And I can, I *can*.

But the others don't need to, because love offers choice.

I . . . I remember I didn't want to leave Kal.

But this was my choice, to join the Ra'haam, so I could help us understand why this battle had to end. And I cannot regret it.

It's Scarlett who eventually breaks the silence.

"Aurora? What's going on?"

"When you broke the threads, we thought you were . . ." Fin trails off, swallowing hard.

"She plans to go with them," Kal says tightly, and I can feel the rainbow threads reaching for me once more as Tyler, Scarlett, and Finian each cry out in protest.

"It's all right," I promise. "It's all right. You were together before I came, and you will be together after I'm gone. You'll carry on, and you'll all be safe. I need you to take Kal with you."

"No." His one word of reply is quiet, but hard as diamond.

"Kal, this is what I have to do," I say, and all the Ra'haam shares my ache, because we love him so, so much, but I am a part of the Ra'haam now, and even if I wished it, there's no way to untangle my mind from the whole.

"*Is* it what you have to do?" His voice rises in frustration. "Or what you *want* to do?"

His mind seizes on mine, tangling us together as tight as he knows how, and with the echo of those words, we're back in the infirmary aboard Sempiternity, and I know what he'll say next.

"To die in the fire of war is easy. To live in the light of peace, much harder."

"I'm not sacrificing myself for no reason," I say, desperate to make him see, giving up on fighting back my tears. "This isn't just me deciding to die. I *won't* die, I'll live forever with them—this was the price, to help the Ra'haam see why we have to stop. I had to become a part of us, so we'd understand."

"But it sees now!" His voice is rising to a shout. "It sees, and still you stay with it! Please, Aurora, stay with *us*. With me. Let me be enough for you."

"It's time, Jie-Lin," my father says quietly.

And in the end, it's very simple.

A father and daughter stand together in the docking bay of a crystal ship. They are joined not just by the bonds of family, but by ties that make them one and the same, two bodies of the same creature. And beyond them, in the black, are thousands more bodies of that same one being, and millions more minds.

Slowly at first, then more quickly, and then in a rushing torrent, they pour into her father's body, and he becomes a vessel for all that the Ra'haam ever has been, and is, and ever will be.

The girl's beloved catches her body as it falls, no longer needed, her mind a part of the whole now. He lifts it in his arms as he and his sister and his squad run back to the Longbow, the crystal city trembling around them.

An Aurora Legion squad waits for them, ushering them aboard as they stumble through the airlock, and the Longbow pulls back from the *Neridaa* as it shimmers and shakes, sections of crystal breaking away.

And all the Ra'haam gathers in one body as Aurora, the girl out of time, the Trigger, shares with the rest of them what she knows, what she can do, and together they see exactly how it must happen.

And aboard the Longbow, the Syldrathi boy cries out in alarm.

"She has stopped breathing!"

"Maker's breath, where's Zila when you need her?"

"Medic!"

"Get the stims!"

"It is not her body, you fools, can you not feel her mind is elsewhere?"

And it is those words from his scornful sister that have

him lift his head, and look back toward the Weapon, no longer a weapon at all.

And as it shimmers once more and begins to fade
he
    makes
        a
           leap
and his mind finds hers, and HOLDS TIGHT.

And with a cry, one by one, his squad and his cursing sister throw their minds after his, and they form a chain that keeps one small part of the girl bound in this time and this place. . . .

And all of them are with her as the crystal ship vanishes, and they watch as it appears so very, very far away, in the dark between galaxies, where there is no other life, where nobody's home and heart will be taken.

And they watch as the ship melts away into nothingness, leaving just the man floating in the black.

And he smiles, and he tips back his head, and slowly he lets out his breath. And he exhales a million stars, a million souls and more, until the black space is lit as bright as any galaxy, until the Ra'haam dances and shimmers like fireflies, like new blue-green stars, endless constellations, living and loving and joined.

And slowly, no longer needed, his body crumbles to dust.

And still the five of them cling to just one star, stretched beyond their limits, so fierce, and so full of love, and so determined never to leave another of their squad behind.

And that one star is me.

"Be'shmai," whispers Kal. "Come home."

"We still need you," Scarlett calls.

"There's too much left to see," Fin says.

"You won't be alone," Tyler promises.

"He will be impossible to live with if you do not," Saedii mutters.

And laughter ripples through all of us at that, and for a moment I almost wish I *could* untangle myself, but I don't see a way.

Jie-Lin, the Ra'haam whispers, every voice joined, every voice different, every voice reveling in that newly remembered individuality.

What do you wish?

I wish . . .

Be'shmai, come home.

We still need you.

There's too much left to see.

You won't be alone.

He will be impossible to live with if you do not.

And then there is one more voice, from one more of my squad.

Cat is one of those gorgeous stars, a voice in my head, a rough shoulder pushing against mine, a quicksilver grin. A newly remembered self who will live out here forever.

I don't think it's time yet, Stowaway.

And with the smallest push, she shows me where to find the fault line, where to press so that . . .

. . . But the cost.

The cost.

To die in the fire of war is easy. To live in the light of peace, much harder.

I reach for Kal, who followed me into the Echo, into the future and home again, and my midnight blue finds his violet, and my mind caresses his, tries to remember every part of it, tries to learn him so I'll never forget.

The window starts to close, the connection beginning to fade between our galaxy and the place the Ra'haam has gone, and Cat's tangled up in me and I'm tangled up in her, and a symphony of memories flows through me: a blue-green planet where she died and was born, and backward to an underwater ballroom, and stolen hours in shuttles, and one night that was supposed to be perfect and ended in heartbreak, and back, back to borrowed outfits and jokes in the back of class and entrance exams, the faces and feelings and moments whirling by, until they reach a crescendo, and a boy pushes a girl over on the first day of kindergarten.

She shows me how many memories a single life can contain.

And at once I see the harmony of the Ra'haam, and I see the wild, unpredictable beauty of a life lived alone—but never entirely alone.

I gather up every last part of my strength, and I turn my face so I don't have to see . . .

. . . and I make the cut.

I sit up, gasping like I've been underwater, and I see my friends are gathered around me, Ty and Scarlett and Fin. Saedii has her hand on Kal's shoulder, and I try to reach out for him, to reassure him, and—

Nothing.

It's like smacking into a plain white wall.

"Be'shmai?" His voice is urgent as he drops to his knees beside me.

"What have you done?" Saedii asks, staring at me.

"It's gone," Scarlett breathes.

"What's gone?" Finian demands.

"Her power," Tyler supplies quietly.

"It was the only way," I say quietly.

There's an emptiness inside me, but the chamber that contains it is unimaginably small. I was so vast—I was infinite.

And now I am in this muffled silence, everything as quiet as a snow day.

I've . . . amputated the part of me that was joined to the Ra'haam, and I can't sense any of my friends, any more than I could back when all this began. I'm not a Trigger. I'm not a savior.

I'm a perfectly ordinary girl.

I could have lived forever in the moment I kissed a million of them goodbye, but though I feel impossibly strange and empty, just listening with my ears, just seeing with my eyes, when Kal pulls me in against him in a fierce embrace, and I hear his heart beating loud and true through his ribs, the . . . the sheer joy of being alive is overwhelming.

I can't feel him in my mind at all. I can see him, though, and touch him, and when I smile up at him through my tears, and he smiles back, I know my choice was right.

I'll live in peace, and I'll live for love.

Love offers choice, and I made mine—I made the choice my squad has taught me from the moment I met them. Your family is where you find it, and this is mine. We should be together.

"Is it gone?" Scarlett whispers, and I know she's thinking of Cat.

"It's not here anymore," I reply. "But . . . it's not gone."

I instinctively turn in the right direction.

I think I'll always know which way it is.

There's a space out between galaxies where only darkness should be, and now it glimmers with life and memories, with stars like fireflies that will share themselves with each other as long as they wish.

They're far away, but they're not gone. And I find a phrase on my lips I learned from Saedii, in those moments we were all joined.

It seems fitting, so I whisper it in farewell.

"I will see you in the stars."

39

ONE YEAR LATER

"Go go go, we're gonna be late," Scar hisses, threatening to break into a run, but not quite managing it.

"Which will be a huge shock to everyone," I reply, reaching for her hand to slow her down.

We're just back from shore leave, which we took on Trask—Scar even charmed my third grandmother. I'm pretty sure at this point that if we ever broke up, my family would keep her and toss me, but I can't blame them for that. She's impossible to resist. We've only been gone three weeks, but Maker, it's good to be back at Aurora Station.

At first, none of us were sure if the Legion was the right future for us, after everything that had happened. But at least for Ty, Scar, and me, it's where we've settled for now. Tyler says this is where we can do the most good, and good's sorely needed.

Most planets lost huge chunks of their citizenry in the battle against the Ra'haam. Whole civilizations were shut off behind destroyed FoldGates. Aurora told me once that she's positive someone will be along in the future who'll know how to get around that, but she refused to say more.

For now, we do what good we can, where we can.

And tomorrow, we're doing some good right *here*.

Scarlett and I hurry out onto the long crescent of the station promenade, stepping hand in hand into the crush. The whole place is *packed* with people—delegates from all over the galaxy have begun arriving at the academy, flocks of cadets and legionnaires and civilians flooding the eateries and bars, all of them abuzz with excitement for the ceremony.

I look up to the transparent ceiling, the light of the Aurora star shining down on the statues of the Founders in the promenade's heart. One hundred meters tall, towering above this place they forged together, this Legion that saved a galaxy.

The first is carved of black opal from Trask, her face wise and brave and serene, looking into a future of infinite possibility. The second is marble mined on Terra, and I smile as I look up into the familiar face of Nari Kim. She's older than the kid we knew, her chest covered with medals now, admiral's stars on her shoulders. But she's still a kid I *knew*.

"Looking good, Dirtgirl," I grin.

"Hey." Scar pinches my arm. "That's a Founder of Aurora Academy you're talking to, legionnaire."

"Yeah, but she got me shot. And blown up. And incinerated. And admiral's stars or no, I'm certain she was still a *colossal* pain in the ass."

Scar laughs and squeezes my hand, smiling at the statue above. "She *does* look good, now you mention it. I think they polished her."

"Well, she's got company coming."

I nod at a third shape, standing between the Founders.

It's covered in a *massive* sheet of green velvet, but it's clear another statue has been built alongside the first two. A statue all these people have come to see.

The mysterious *Third* Founder. The unsung hero of the whole Ra'haam war, set to be unveiled in tomorrow's grand celebration. She was content to spend her whole existence in the shadows for the sake of secrecy, of avoiding paradox. A life devoted to saving a galaxy that would never even know who she was.

But tomorrow, we change all that.

Tomorrow, the whole Milky Way will know her name.

"Come on," Scarlett insists. "We'll see her tomorrow. The others are waiting."

We push our way through the crush, the people, all these lives, finally making it to the turbolifts. Rising up, looking out through the transparent walls at the crowd below, I can't help but smile at the sight.

My smile only widens as we find our meeting room and discover Aurora, Kal, Tyler, and even a scowling Saedii Gilwraeth waiting for us. The scene disintegrates into squealing and hugs as Scar throws herself at Auri, and I have to admit I kind of join in, and Kal bears up with considerable dignity when he's pulled in too. I notice a neatly dressed, serious young woman standing at the head of the table, but my musings about who she is are cut short as Auri hugs me so tight my exo moves to protective settings around my lungs, to make sure I can keep breathing.

Ty just laughs, and lets it die down of its own accord, reaching out to lay one hand on Saedii's. She must be feeling pretty loved up today, because she doesn't even look like she wants to bite it off. I guess they're making long distance work.

"What are you and Kal doing here?" Scarlett demands, grabbing Aurora's hand as we all take our seats. "I thought you were on the other side of the galaxy!"

The two of them have been working with the Syldrathi rebuilding effort—now that a peace accord has been signed between the Unbroken and the rest of Syldrathi society, it's time to do the messy stuff like settling a new planet. Usually Syldrathi don't like outsiders much, but Auri says her history as a psychic superpower and her connection to the Eshvaren win her enough respect to get by. Probably doesn't hurt to have a Templar as part of the family, either.

"Are you kidding?" Auri says. "We wouldn't miss this for the world."

"Have you seen the design?" Scar asks.

"Tyler sent it to us," Kal says, nodding to our Alpha. "Beautiful work, Brother."

"Still think you should've put a disruptor pistol in her ha— OW!" I yelp as Scar kicks me under the table, glowering at me, then smiling at her twin.

"It *is* beautiful, Ty. Seriously. Zila would be very proud."

"Zila would be very *uncomfortable* is what Zila would be." I grin and rub my bruised shin, looking around the room. "Come on. You think *Zila Madran* ever imagined herself sculpted a hundred meters high out of solid gold? Maker, I wish she was here so I could see the look on her face when we unveil it."

"Welllll . . . ," Tyler says.

All eyes in the room turn to our Alpha.

"Well what?" Kal says, suspicious.

". . . Ty?" Scar asks.

"Well, there's a reason I called you all here a day early," he says, nodding to the woman at the head of the table. "And there she is."

All eyes turn to the stranger now. She's Terran, maybe mid-twenties, neatly dressed in gray attire. She has a serious face, but she doesn't scream "military" to me, so I don't think she's Legion. She looks around the room at each of us, dark eyes finally settling on Aurora.

"Who are you?" Auri asks.

"A messenger," she says simply, bringing up a projection from her wrist unit and letting it speak for itself.

Aurora's face lights up, Scarlett gasps, and I feel my own lips curling in wonder at the projection before us.

It's Zila.

She's an old lady, hair completely silver, smile lines at the corners of her eyes. She's gazing straight down the camera, and it feels like she's gazing straight at each of us.

"Greetings, my friends," she says, and though some of the edge has come off her voice over the course of her lifetime, it's still unmistakably Zila Madran. *"This message is due to be delivered one year after the events for which I spent my life preparing. I hope with all my heart that you are all present to receive it. I have accepted that while I know many things, this will forever remain a mystery to me. I was once told by my Alpha that some moments require faith. Know that I have faith in you.*

"Aurora, I hope you are well. This message is for you, in particular. It took me some years to realize that in my new

timeline, your mother and your sister would still be very much alive and well, and mourning your loss. I know this has been a source of great sadness to you, and so I considered the options available, remembering always that the avoidance of paradox in the timeline was of the utmost importance."

Auri lifts her hands to cover her mouth, her eyes bright, and Kal shifts his chair so he can quietly slip his arm around her. Scar squeezes her hand.

The footage of Zila continues.

"I spoke to your mother shortly before she died, and told her you were safe. I am sorry I could not do so sooner, but I judged the risk of paradox too great. Please know our conversation brought her great peace. I studied your sister, Callie, for some time before deciding she was capable of the levels of secrecy required, and eventually I confided the truth of your fate in her."

Aurora is crying properly now, though I think it's a happy cry, and the woman who brought the recording lifts her wrist unit again. With a flick, she sends a picture up to sit along-side Zila—it's a woman who looks so, *so* like Aurora, though older, and she has a toddler sitting on her hip.

"This is your sister, with your niece, Jie-Lin," Zila says.

The woman brings up another picture—now the woman who must be Callie is older, and beside her stands another woman who might be Jie-Lin, and there's a new toddler.

"And here is her daughter," Zila continues. *"I have arranged for further pictures to be added to the collection as new generations are born, and it is my hope that this file will now be delivered by—"*

The recording pauses, and we all look toward the woman with the projector. Even Saedii looks like someone whose favorite series just ended on a cliff-hanger.

"It is my hope," says the woman, whose eyes appear a little bright, "that this message will be delivered by one of Callie's descendants."

"Are . . ." Auri chokes out the word, but she can't get past it.

"Your great-great-great-great-great-niece," she says softly. "My name's Jie-Lin. It's a family tradition."

A *noise* comes out of Aurora, half sob, half laugh, and every Betraskan instinct in me knows it's the sound of someone finding a part of their family, and she's out of her chair like she's teleported, and into Jie-Lin's arms, and the two of them silently embrace as the recording begins again. I'm startled back to attention when I hear my own name.

"Finian suggested as he departed," says Zila, *"that I should place wagers on the outcomes of 'sportsball' events, with Magellan's assistance. I remain unconvinced this is entirely ethical, but Nari has suggested to me that we have given much, and it is acceptable to take a little in return. Details of a bank account have been provided with these files. I have two requests, and beyond that, the money is yours to use as you see fit—it will be a considerable sum.*

"My first request is that you establish a scholarship in Cat's name. I believe in the Aurora Legion, and I would like it to be easier for others to join.

"My second request is that you find an opportunity to spend some time together—I would suggest you put Scarlett in charge of planning, as Nari and I are both confident she will pick an excellent destination for a furlough. And please think of us for a moment when you make that trip."

Everyone's crying now, except for Saedii, of course, who definitely has no tear ducts. She's just nodding slowly, which I guess is her version.

"I have found my family here," Zila says, "though I will always miss the family I left behind. I hope each of you finds such happiness, over the course of your lives." She looks around, as if she could actually see us. And she smiles. "I wish you well, my friends."

And just like that, the recording is over, and Zila's gone.

But never forgotten.

"Holy cake," Aurora sniffs, disentangling herself from Jie-Lin's hug.

"This," says Scarlett, "is going to be the most epic vacation in *history*."

"We just got back from vacation," I groan.

"And there's no way I can take time off," Tyler says.

Scarlett puts her hands on her hips. "Are you being serious right now?"

"I mean it," Ty says, shaking his head. "There's a whole bunch of diplomatic meetings scheduled after the unveiling, we've got new intakes coming in after that, and de Stoy's rearranging the whole command structure."

"Right," I nod. "And we're still short in mechaneering, I've gotta hel—"

"Oh Maker's *breath* . . ." Scar heaves a dramatic sigh, looking between me and Ty. "Could you two be bigger killjoys, *please*."

I shrug, helpless. "I've got work to do, Scar."

"Look," she says, leaning closer. "A vacation *I* organize means a pool. And a pool means me packing nothing but a swimsuit. Do the math, de Seel."

I pause, glance to Tyler. "Yeah, okay, I'm convinced."

"Right," Scar scowls. "What about you, Bee-bro?"

"You know I hate it when you call me that, right?"

"You know I hate your face, right?"

"Ouch."

Tyler glances at Saedii thoughtfully.

"Do you even *own* a swimsuit?"

She glowers around the room. "I am certain I could fashion one out of someone's skin without too much difficulty."

"Leather bikini . . . ," I murmur, staring into the distance.

". . . Yeah, okay," Tyler declares. "I'm convinced."

"Are they always like this?" Jie-Lin asks quietly.

"In time, one becomes accustomed to it," Kal replies gravely.

Aurora just hugs her one more time, and smiles.

"Welcome to the family."

Squad Members
▶ **Blood Debts Owed**
  ▼ **Acknowledgments**

As we come to the end of our second series together with a book that was written through national lockdowns and an international pandemic, at times requiring ingenuity that would have made Squad 312 proud, we're more aware than ever that every book is created by a village. It's been a privilege to work with ours to bring this story to life.

We would be nowhere without our publishing team—they guide us to the best version of every book, they catch our mistakes, they get our stories out into the world and then make sure you hear about them. We're so lucky to have them. In the US, all hail Barbara, Melanie, Arely, Artie, Amy, Nancee, Dawn, Kathleen, Jake, Denise, Judith, Emily, Josh, Mary, Dominique, John, Kelly, Jules, Sharon, Megan, Jenn, Kate, Elizabeth, Adrienne, Kristin, Emily, Natalie, Heather, Jen, Ray, Alison, Natalia, and Dakota. Here in Australia, our heartfelt thanks to Anna, Nicola, Yvette, Simon, Sheralyn, Eva, Matt, Lou, Megan, Alison, and Kylie. In the UK, our tireless team is Katie, Molly, Lucy, Kate, Hayley, Julian, Mark, Paul, Laura, and Juliet. Thank you to our fantastic international publishing teams, and the translators who joined us in bringing you the story of Squad 312.

Wherever their work finds itself in the world, a special thanks to Charlie and Deb for our fabulous cover artwork and design.

The audio editions of these books are brilliant, and we can't wrap the series without thanking Nick and our whole audio team, from the production crew to our incredible narrators.

Time and time again, we're grateful to our agents, Josh and Tracey Adams. For your guidance, your patience, and your advocacy, a

HUGE THANK-YOU. THANKS AS WELL TO ANNA, TO STEPHEN, AND TO OUR AMAZING NETWORK OF FOREIGN AGENTS, WHO HELPED SQUAD 312 FIND HOMES ALL OVER THE WORLD.

WE'RE GUIDED AS WELL BY SO MANY EXPERTS AND CONSULTANTS WHEN WE WRITE OUR BOOKS. TO DR. KATE IRVING, GARY BRAUDE, MEGAN AND HOONSEOP JEONG, MIKYUNG KIM, OH YOUNG LEE, AND MANY OTHERS NOT NAMED HERE, OUR THANKS. YOU HELPED MAKE THIS BOOK BETTER IN COUNTLESS WAYS, THOUGH, OF COURSE, ANY MISTAKES THAT REMAIN ARE OUR OWN.

TO ALL BOOKSELLERS, LIBRARIANS, READERS, VLOGGERS, BLOGGERS, TWEETERS, AND BOOKSTAGRAMMERS WHO HAVE HELPED SPREAD THE WORD ABOUT THE SQUAD—THANK YOU. WE COULDN'T DO THIS WITHOUT YOU, AND WE WOULDN'T WANT TO.

TO OUR OWN PERSONAL SQUADDIES—SAM AND JACK, MARC, B-MONEY, RAFE, WEEZ, PARIS, BATMAN, SURLY JIM, GLEN, SPIV, TOM, CAT, ORRSOME, TOVES, SAM, TONY, KATH, KYLIE, NICOLE, KURT, JACK, MAX, POPPY, MEG, MICHELLE, MARIE, LEIGH, ALEX, SOOZ, KACEY, SORAYA, NIC, KIERSTEN, RYAN, BOTH CATS, FLIC, GEORGE, CORMAC, MARILYN, KAY, NEVILLE, SHANNON, ADAM, BODE, AND LUCA. THE HOUSE OF PROGRESS: ELLIE, NIC, LILI, ELIZA, DAVE, LIZ, KATE, SKYE, AND PETE. THE ROTI BOTI GANG: KATE, AIMEE, EMILY, KYLIE, NED, MAZ, SASHI, AND EMMA, WHO IS MISSED EVERY SINGLE DAY. TO ALL OUR CREW: WE'D BE LOST IN THIS GALAXY WITHOUT YOU.

TO THOSE WHO JOINED US ON THE JOURNEY, THOUGH THEY DIDN'T KNOW THAT THEIR WORK INSPIRED OURS—FRANK TURNER, JOSHUA RADIN, MATT BELLAMY, CHRIS WOLSTENHOLME, DOMINIC HOWARD, BUDDY, BEN OTTEWELL, THE KILLERS, MARK MORTON, RANDY BLYTHE, TOM SEARLE, DAN SEARLE, SAM CARTER, MARCUS BRIDGE, JON DEILEY, WINSTON MCCALL, OLI SYKES, MAYNARD JAMES KEENAN, RONNIE RADKE, COREY

Taylor, Chris Cornell, Ian Kenny, Trent Reznor. A salute as well to Anne McCaffrey, science-fiction pioneer, whose telepathic dragons got into the DNA of this book in more ways than one.

And finally, this book is dedicated to our spouses, and to Amie's daughter, who joined us at just the same time as the first book in this series did. We saved the best for last, of course. You are our squad, and we're so lucky to be yours. Here's to forever.